An Orphan's Courage

Cathy Sharp is happily married and lives with her husband in a small Cambridgeshire village. They like visiting Spain together and enjoy the benefits of sunshine and pleasant walks, while at home they love their garden and visiting the Norfolk seaside.

Cathy loves writing because it gives pleasure to others, she finds writing an extension of herself and it gives her great satisfaction. Cathy says, 'There is nothing like seeing your book in print, because so much loving care has been given to bringing that book into being.'

Also by Cathy Sharp

The Orphans of Halfpenny Street
The Little Runaways
Christmas for the Halfpenny Orphans
The Boy with the Latchkey

An Orphan's Courage

CATHY SHARP

HarperCollins*Publishers*

This novel is entirely a work of fiction.
The names, characters and incidents portrayed in it are the work of the author's imagination. Any resemblance to actual persons, living or dead, events or localities is entirely coincidental.

HarperCollins*Publishers*
The News Building,
1 London Bridge Street,
London SE1 9GF

A Paperback Original 2018
2

www.harpercollins.co.uk

A catalogue record for this book is available from the British Library

ISBN: 978-0-00-821163-9

Set in Sabon LT Std 11.5/14.5 pt by
Palimpsest Book Production Limited, Falkirk, Stirlingshire

Printed and bound by CPI Group (UK) Ltd, Croydon CR0 4YY

This book is produced from independently certified FSC™ paper to ensure responsible forest management.

For more information visit: www.harpercollins.co.uk/green

CHAPTER 1

'Want some pocket money?' the drunken voice asked, and a large hand waved a pound note at Jinny Hollis enticingly. He leered at her in a way that sent chills down Jinny's spine and she shook her head as he rose to his feet and stumbled across her mother's kitchen towards her. 'Come on, it isn't hard to be nice to me, is it?'

Jinny drew back, feeling the vomit rise in her throat as she saw the lascivious gleam in his eyes. She kept her gaze fixed on the face of the latest of her mother's punters, backing away, moving towards the door and freedom. He was good-looking in a dark, brutish way with black hair slicked back with hair oil and unshaven chin. Jake wasn't the first to offer her money in order to be allowed to fumble beneath her skirts, and his approach was the same as that of all the others. When her mother was in the room they played the nice uncle, but as soon as Jinny was alone with them, they tried to molest her. Some offered enticements, money, small gifts and food but others just made a grab for her. She'd been forced to endure rough hands up her skirt and under her blouse more times than she cared to remember, and once, one of them had got her down and tried to force himself on her. Her screams had brought Nellie from next door running in at the kitchen door and her irate neighbour had batted the unfortunate *uncle* with her rolling pin until he swore at her, got to his feet and bolted.

Jinny would have screamed for Nellie now but she knew it would be useless; her friend had gone shopping down the market and wouldn't be back for ages. Jinny's back was against the door now. She wrenched at it, pulled it open and tried to escape into the back yard, but Jake lunged at her, pinning her against the doorpost so that she could feel its sharp edges cutting into her flesh.

'Got you at last,' he muttered as he pressed his slack wet mouth against hers and the stink of his breath made the gorge rise in her throat. In desperation she brought her knee up and went for his groin with every ounce of her strength. He gave a yell of shock mixed with pain and staggered back, his eyes filled with a vicious rage that terrified her. Yet her action had saved her, because as he drew back, stunned and winded, she made her escape into the yard and ran for her life.

Tears stung Jinny's eyes as she ran, her chest heaving; she fought for breath and against the storm of emotion overtaking her now that she was – for the moment – out of danger. Forced at last to stop running because her chest hurt and she couldn't go any further, Jinny leaned against the wall of a derelict factory and closed her eyes, letting the tears flow.

Why did everything have to be so horrible at home?

Jinny's mother was almost always drunk when she came back from the pub where she worked behind the bar until late at night. There was usually a man in tow, sometimes known to Jinny and, at other times, a complete stranger. Mabel Hollis just didn't seem to be able to manage without a man about the place, even though several of them had treated her badly. Some of them beat her and she often had black eyes when she finally got up in the morning, others simply sponged off her, expecting her to provide food and lodgings, as well as the other comforts Mabel offered. Quite a few considered that Jinny should be a part of the bargain, and she'd been fighting them off since she was twelve and was always in trouble at school for turning up late, because if she didn't do a few chores in the house no one did, and the safest time to do them was in the morning before Jake and her mother got out of bed.

Jinny's mother seemed to have money for drink and for having her hair bleached and set in the deep waves that men seemed to find so sensual, but she seldom remembered to go shopping for food, and often ended up shoving a few pennies in Jinny's hand and telling her to get some chips. Mabel dressed and behaved like a tart, and Jinny was ashamed of her. Now that she was coming up to her fifteenth birthday and preparing to leave school Jinny thought desperately of getting away somewhere – anywhere she could live by herself or with friends, away from her mother's sluttish ways and her men. She couldn't really call them customers, because most of them didn't pay a penny towards their keep and some lived off Mabel for as long as she was willing to provide them with whatever they needed.

'What's up then, Jinny?'

Her eyes flew open as she heard the voice close by. Micky Smith was three years older and had left school at fifteen to work on the Docks. At school he'd never noticed her, except once when she'd been at the centre of a group of vindictive classmates who were jeering at her, pulling her dark hair and calling her mother a whore and a drunken tart. Even though Jinny knew the accusations were true, she'd tried to defend her mother against their insults and given one of her tormentors a black eye. Several of the others had charged at her, knocking her to the ground, and she'd been struggling to throw them off when suddenly she'd found herself free and a grinning Micky Smith had been looking down at her. He'd offered her his hand, pulled her to her feet and then turned to the gang of sullen girls watching.

'Jinny's my friend,' he'd claimed. 'If any of you harm her again, you'll answer to me.'

Jinny hadn't even thanked him, because she'd hardly spoken to him previously and didn't know what to say. For a moment their eyes met and then he'd walked off, leaving her standing alone.

'Micky's pet,' one of the girls chanted at her mockingly. 'Giving it 'im, are yer? Yer just a bleedin' little whore like yer ma . . .'

'Whore like yer ma . . .' the other girls hissed but none of them tried to touch her as she brushed past them.

Jinny might have gone after Micky and thanked him then, but he was with some other lads and they were laughing and looking her way. She'd had the feeling they were laughing at her, probably saying what they'd like to do to her or naming her a whore like the girls had.

Now she stared at him, wary and half-mistrusting as she noticed that he was no longer dressed in patched trousers and a jacket with holes at the elbows. He had on a pair of black drainpipe trousers, a blue cloth jacket with velvet on the collar and suede shoes with thick crepe soles. His white shirt sported a thin black tie, which was knotted and pinned with what looked like a diamond tiepin. Knowing that Micky's father hadn't worked in years, because of an accident on the Docks, and his mother went charring at several offices, Jinny wondered how he'd managed to become prosperous all of a sudden.

'I haven't seen you for a while,' Jinny said. 'Not since school . . .'

'I've been busy,' Micky said and grinned. He had black curly hair, swarthy skin and very dark eyes; his hair was long, nestling into his nape and he had dark sideburns, rather like those worn by Elvis Presley, the American singer. All Jinny's classmates swooned over Elvis Presley and talked about his records and the Rock 'n' Roll dances they attended on Saturday nights. Jinny couldn't afford to go to the dances and she didn't have many friends – she couldn't ever take them home so she was never asked to their birthday parties – but Nellie had an old-fashioned radiogram and she liked Rock 'n' Roll, too. Jinny had heard her playing Elvis over and over again through the thin walls that separated their terraced houses.

'I seen 'im at the flicks and 'e's a bit of all right,' she'd told Jinny when she went next door for a slice of bread and dripping and a rock cake, as she did most days after school. Nellie had a picture cut from a magazine, which she'd stuck up on her kitchen wall, much to her husband's disgust, but Nellie only laughed and said if she were twenty years younger she'd be off to America to join the girls who flocked about their new heartthrob. Of course she didn't mean it, because she and her husband got on well and had two grown-up sons with families of their own, but Nellie liked to tease her long-suffering husband. Both of Nellie's sons were in the Army and no longer lived in London, but she looked forward to their infrequent visits with her grandchildren, of whom she had three. Colin had two young boys and Brian had a girl of a few months. Jinny knew how much she missed them but she was a cheerful woman in her early fifties and never let on to them that she wished they'd come back home.

'They've got good lives where they are. I was worried to death when they had that trouble over the Suez Canal last year, but it seems it's all over now, and Brian's in Ireland now . . .' Nellie had told Jinny as they looked at photos the elder son Colin had sent from Cyprus where he was currently stationed with his regiment. 'Why should they want to come back 'ere then? I know Harold Macmillan says we've never 'ad it so good, but 'e ain't living 'ere in this courtyard, is 'e?'

'What were you cryin' for?' Micky asked; a sparkle in his dark eyes that made Jinny aware that lost in her thoughts she'd been staring for too long. 'Are you in trouble?'

Jinny nodded, hanging her head, tongue-tied and

ashamed. 'It's just one of Mum's blokes . . .' she said, because he expected an answer. 'He tried to grab me . . . so I gave him one where it hurts with my knee – and he'll half kill me when he gets the chance . . .'

Micky nodded his understanding. 'Jake Harding is a nasty piece of work. Your ma should send him packing. He's a troublemaker down the Docks – if you knew what I know . . .'

'Why don't you tell me?'

'Best you don't know, but he's in with a bad lot and one of these days . . .' Micky shook his head.

'He hits Mum,' Jinny said and shuffled her feet. 'He's one of the worst she's had – and . . . I'm frightened of him . . .'

'No need to be,' Micky said. 'I'll sort him for you if you want?'

Jinny looked at him and smiled. 'He's a big bloke,' she said. 'It's lovely of you to offer, but I don't want you to get hurt for my sake . . .'

Micky looked amused and touched his pocket as if it contained a secret only he knew. 'Don't you worry about me, Jinny girl. I can take care of myself – and I take care of my own too.'

'I never thanked you for what you did at school . . .'

'You didn't have to,' he said. 'I don't like bullies.'

'Jake is a bully,' she said. 'He offered me money for a start but when I said no he tried to force me . . . he's not the first to try. Those girls were right that day; Mum is a whore – but she doesn't even get paid half the time . . .' She raised her head defiantly. 'I'm not like her and I don't want to be.'

'I know that, Jinny.'

'How can you? Everyone thinks I'm like my mum and she's a slut.'

'Your mother was all right until your father went off and left her. I suppose she got lonely and desperate . . .' Micky said and looked grim. 'He was a bad 'un, your dad, Jinny. I don't mind a bit of thievin' if it comes to that, especially if something is just begging to be liberated – but your dad was a mean sort. He stole from his mates and he got punished for it, so in the end he didn't have much choice but to clear orf – otherwise he might've been lynched.'

Jinny felt the tears burn behind her eyes. She could recall only little things from the time when she'd had a father, but he'd been kind to her and her mother had been happier then, too.

'You're rotten to say that about my dad,' she said resentfully. 'I thought I could trust you, but now I see you're like all the rest . . .'

She turned and started to walk away, but Micky came after her and grabbed her arm, turning her to face him. 'I didn't mean to hurt you, but it's the truth. He stole from his works and he broke into houses, but he took from his friends too – and he took a reward for ratting on someone, letting him carry the can for what he'd been part of – and they don't forgive that around here.'

'Leave me alone,' Jinny said and shook his hand off. 'I don't believe you – you tell lies . . .'

'I do lots of stuff,' Micky called after her as she walked swiftly away. 'But I don't lie to you and I'm still your friend. I'll look after you, Jinny, and one day you'll understand that you can trust me . . .'

Jinny didn't bother to look round. She knew that it

was likely he was telling the truth about Sam Hollis, but she couldn't bear to hear it. The only bright memories she had was of her dad giving her a pretty doll one Christmas and tussling her hair whenever he came home from work. He'd bought her sweets and told her she was his princess and she'd thought he loved her. To a girl who hadn't had much love in her life that was precious and she wouldn't easily forgive Micky Smith for ruining her memory of her dad.

Jinny set out in search of Nellie. When she told her what Jake had done, her kind neighbour would offer her a chance of a bed with them, and this time she was going to take it. If her mother wanted Jake around she would have to take care of their home herself, because Jinny wasn't going back while he was staying there.

CHAPTER 2

'Well, I shall be sorry to lose you, Hannah.' Sister Beatrice frowned over the top of her glasses at the young woman sitting in the chair at the other side of her desk. She put down the newspaper she'd been reading, an article about the launch of a campaign to stop smoking, because of new research into cancer diseases thought related to the practice. As always she wore the dark grey habit of a nun with a white starched apron and simple headdress, a heavy silver cross and chain about her neck. 'I must admit I've come to rely on you as one of my most trusted staff – and it's so difficult to find girls who want to work here these days . . .'

'I've loved working with you at St Saviour's,' the carer said and looked genuinely sorry. 'But this is a wonderful chance for my husband to have his own business. We'll be moving across the river and he'll need help in the shop – so what with that and having another baby . . .' She placed her hands on her bump and smiled. 'I just shan't have the energy or the time . . .'

'Oh, I understand perfectly and I wish you well in your new life,' Beatrice agreed. 'Your husband and your family come first of course. It's just that I shall need to find someone to take your place when you leave.'

'Well, I do know of someone looking for her first job. She's just left school and her neighbour asked me if she thought Jinny might be taken on here as a kitchen help, but she's an honest girl and bright. I think you might like her – and Nancy was only fifteen when she started, wasn't she?'

'That was rather different,' Beatrice frowned at her, because Nancy was a special case. 'This girl is hardly old enough to be given the care of children, but I suppose she could be taken on as a girl of all work. If she is willing to do kitchen work, as well as anything else she's asked, that might solve a part of our problems. We've had a succession of girls coming for a few weeks and then leaving in the kitchens since Muriel retired last Christmas. Unfortunately, Mrs Davies can be a little difficult . . .'

'Yes,' Hannah replied ruefully. 'I've run afoul of her tongue a few times, but she's just finding her way and Sandra says her bark is worse than her bite.'

Thank goodness for Sandra, who had become a friend as well as a colleague since she joined their staff! Beatrice relaxed mentally as she thought of the young woman who had begun as a part-time secretary and occasional carer after her stint in prison almost two years previously. Sandra had been imprisoned after a farcical trial on trumped-up evidence and only the perseverance of her friends had got her free with her name cleared. In truth she owed her freedom mainly to Ikey, the man who was now her husband; Sandra owed him far more because he'd rescued her children – Archie Miller from an uncertain fate on the streets and June from the clutches of unsuitable foster parents. Beatrice had employed her without a reference and given her a temporary home here at St Saviour's in the nurses' home until she'd married, and Sandra had more than repaid her since with her friendship and her hard work.

As Ikey's wife – or Nathaniel Milvern as he was known in his professional life, as a police officer – Sandra had no need to work but she'd continued to come into St Saviour's every day. They'd married very quietly in the spring of 1956, because Ikey was still recovering from the brutal attack on him. However, he was now back at work and involved in several projects aimed at helping London's unfortunates who lived on the streets.

'Yes, I believe Sandra can manage her,' Beatrice nodded, and glanced through her diary. 'Very well, send this young woman to see me . . . the day after tomorrow in the morning at ten thirty. I shall ask Sandra to join me and we'll see. If this girl . . . what was her name again? . . . If she is suitable we'll give her a chance.'

'Jinny Hollis,' Hannah said and stood up. 'She's a pretty girl, sensible and pleasant, but she's had a terrible home life for years, Sister, but I know you won't hold that against her. She needs a job and somewhere to live, so her neighbour told me. Had she been brought in when she was younger I know you would've taken her in – as you do all the kids in trouble.'

'I take as many as I can,' Beatrice said and sighed. 'Unfortunately, we're only a halfway house now and many of our children are moved on to the new place after just a few weeks. I regret that we were forced to give up the one wing of St Saviour's, which means we only have room for sixty orphans at the most, but I suppose it is progress . . . or so they tell me . . .'

'You haven't thought of taking a position at Halfpenny House in Essex?' Hannah asked, on her feet now and lingering at the door.

'No, I think not,' Sister shook her head emphatically. 'I've spent the last twelve years or more here in Halfpenny Street at St Saviour's; it's where I belong and I have no desire to move.'

'It wouldn't be the same without you,' Hannah said, hesitated, and then offered shyly, 'I shall miss working with you and Wendy and Sister Rose and the others . . .'

Beatrice inclined her head but said no more as the carer left. She'd said all she had to say and since the parting was inevitable there was nothing to do but accept it. She'd lived too long and suffered too many partings, each of which left a little shadow on her heart, but God gave her strength to carry on with her work. Her fingers clasped the heavy silver cross she wore on a long thick chain and she winced as she felt stiffness and pain; it was arthritis, she imagined, and it was gradually working its way through her body: shoulders, back, neck and now her hands. She flexed her fingers trying to relieve the pain and felt it ease; exercise helped. Beatrice had learned that from watching her father, who had been a butcher and used to working in cold conditions and standing for long hours. He'd developed a severe form of the disease as he'd grown older but he'd been too stubborn to give in and had carried on working until he died . . . of a heart attack.

Beatrice shook her head, dismissing old memories, which could have no bearing on her life now. She'd taken her vows after tragedy drove her to despair but for years now she'd led a busy, interesting life here at St Saviour's, looking after the children given into her care. It was a demanding job sometimes, needing all her strength and patience to carry her through, but it was her life. Indeed, she did not know what she would do if the job were no longer hers. A return to the convent would be unfortunate; here in St Saviour's she'd become used to warmth and the comfort of her office and her room in the nurses' home, and she ate well – better than her fellow nuns did at the convent, she knew. Beatrice remembered how cold it had been in the small impersonal cell that had been hers when she first became a nun. Over the years her room at St Saviour's had acquired some small comforts, a few books, a picture or two – mostly of gardens. She did appreciate gardens, though it was years since she'd had one to tend, as well as the little things the children had made for her, all of which she treasured. At the convent such treasures, if not exactly forbidden, would not be understood; she was supposed to have given up all worldly pleasures, but she feared that her years in nursing had somehow made her fonder of her personal comforts than was right.

Perhaps fortunately for her turn of thoughts, the telephone shrilled and she picked it up, smiling as she heard the voice at the other end.

'Sergeant Sallis, how nice to hear from you again; I thought you'd forgotten us.'

'I'm pleased to say things have been quiet for a while, but we had two children brought in this morning – found wandering down by the Docks, both of them filthy and hungry, and the boy has been beaten quite recently . . .'

'Bring them in and we'll see what we can do,' Beatrice said and shook her head, because it was the same old story. Things were supposed to be getting better now. It was a brave new world and filled with clever inventions and hope for a bright and exciting future, but in some of London's meaner streets, of which there were still far too many, the old evils of poverty, dirt, cruelty and neglect still flourished. 'Are they related?'

'Brother and sister. His name is Andy and hers is Beth. If they have a second name they're not giving it, but we'll make some inquiries and discover who they are.'

'Very well – until then we'll look after them as always.'

'Thank God for St Saviour's. If ever you close your doors, Sister, I don't know what we'll do. Social Services don't know what to do with the kids – and they ship them off somewhere so they feel disorientated and miserable, and that's why half of them run away again. I'm sure they would rather be on the streets that are familiar to them than sent off to some cold clinical place where they can't even make themselves understood half the time . . .'

'Let's hope it doesn't happen for a few years,' Beatrice said and smiled. She liked the police sergeant who had been bringing her waifs and strays from the streets for as long as she could recall. St Saviour's was always the first place they thought of, though of course these days the Welfare people had to have their say and would no doubt make an appearance to check the details. However, they were normally kept busy with cases of abuse within the family and had little time to bother over a home proven to be more than adequate.

'I've heard rumours . . .' Sergeant Sallis said. 'They

have been talking about redeveloping that whole area again . . .'

'Oh, we had that some years ago,' Beatrice said blithely. 'There's a covenant on the building so I'm not too bothered about the threat of redevelopment – they can carry on around us as much as they like but our Board won't budge.'

'I'm relieved to hear it,' he said. 'I'll bring the children in myself – and we want to know if they tell you anything about the beating. It was nasty, I can tell you that, and I'd like to bring whoever did it to justice.'

'Naturally, we shall keep you informed.'

Beatrice replaced the receiver. Sometimes the children told the nurses things in confidence once they were settled and no longer terrified, but she could pass on such information only if the child gave permission. Much as she agreed with the police officer that the perpetrator should be punished, a child's confidence must be respected.

Rising to her feet with a suppressed groan, Beatrice decided it was time for her to visit the sick wards. Wendy had some cases of a particularly nasty tummy bug in the isolation ward at the moment, one of them a girl from the council home next door, but fortunately the room kept for lesser ailments was free and they would put the two new arrivals in there until they were sure they were ready to be assigned to their dormitories.

Once again, she regretted that the wing next door had been taken over by the council for their disturbed girls. She wished they could return to the past when St Saviour's had been able to house so many more children for as long as necessary. However, that had been taken out of her hands and, no matter much she disliked it, it was a fact of life that she could not escape and she must make the most of what she had . . .

Ruby Saunders read the letter again and frowned.

> *My dear Miss Saunders*, Miss Sampson had written. *I should like you to visit me this afternoon at about three if you can manage it. I have something important to discuss with you – something concerning St Saviour's that will be to your advantage . . . please be prompt. Ruth Sampson.*

Ruby folded the letter and frowned as she placed it in her top drawer. A request from Miss Sampson was tantamount to an order, so no matter what she'd planned for her afternoon she must attend her at her office.

Relations between them had been a bit strained for a while after that business with the Miller girl, because Ruby should never have been taken in by those people who'd applied to be foster parents – but what had happened subsequently hadn't been her fault. The Children's Department should have checked the Baileys' details more thoroughly. All she'd done was recommend them as possible foster parents.

Ruth Sampson had had her fingers rapped publicly when the papers got hold of the scandal. The department had tried to keep it private, but somehow one of those scandal rags had nosed out the story and made a meal of it, though the child hadn't been named. So Ruth had been reprimanded and Ruby had borne the brunt of her displeasure, but she'd weathered it and hung on, and now it seemed that she was being offered a reward.

Ruby had been made to eat humble pie after the truth came out about those awful people who had abused June Miller and for a while she'd felt regret, but then her natural sense of certainty had come back and she'd begun to resent the way Sister Beatrice seemed to have an almost free hand next door. St Saviour's was inspected about once a year or so, but it seemed Sister Beatrice always managed to get away with a glowing report. Ruby, on the other hand, had been questioned about her methods of discipline more than once and now had to suffer twice yearly intrusion into her regime.

She'd felt she was being criticised and, after the last interview was over, asked whether they were dissatisfied with her.

'We have been told that you threatened one of the girls you sent on to a remand home with violent punishment if she misbehaved there . . .' Mr Irvine, the Department's chief inspector, told her.

'You shouldn't believe a thing these girls say,' Ruby retorted furiously. 'Some of them become violent and have to be restrained. I worked in a remand home for some months before I applied for this job and I saw how necessary it is to use force at times . . .'

'We *are* aware that in extreme cases it is sometimes necessary to restrain a violent case, but always the minimum amount of force is to be used. Did you not tell a girl that if she caused more trouble she would be subdued by drugs and locked in a padded cell?'

'No, of course I did not!' Ruby retorted and then felt

the hot colour rush up her neck and into her face as she remembered she had said something of the sort to Betty Goodge. 'Well, I told her it might happen if she was violent . . . she attacked me and I had to subdue her . . .'

'Did you know that she tried to commit suicide the day after she was committed to the remand home?' Mr Irvine asked coldly.

Ruby felt sick and shaken. Her voice dropped to a whisper as she said, 'No, I was not aware of that . . . but I'm sure I had nothing to do with it . . .'

'You think your threat was not related to her act of desperation?' the inspector asked sarcastically. 'Did you not know the girl's history, Miss Saunders? As a child she was sexually abused and beaten systematically, and when she fought back she was locked in a cellar until she ceased screaming. We knew she was a thief and a little wild, but we sent her here rather than a remand home to give her a chance for a better life – your threats affected her mind powerfully and she went into a decline after her attempt at suicide and is now in the care of a psychiatrist in a secure hospital.'

'I didn't realise she'd been locked in a cellar . . .' Ruby felt hot and uncomfortable. 'I do not see that I can be held accountable for what happened to her at the remand home.'

'Neither did Miss Sampson,' the inspector told her. 'However, it has been decided that we shall visit more often in future and see how things are going here. For the moment I find that everything is in order – but I must tell you that the Department frowns on the use of threats . . .'

Ruby had fretted with frustration after that last visit. It wasn't her fault if a wild girl had tried to take her own life because she'd been sent to a place where the discipline was harsh. Besides, the attempt had failed and had probably been staged to gain attention. Betty was now in a hospital and most likely running rings round the staff there . . .

She glowered at the wall that divided her office from the orphanage next door. It had been Ruby's ambition to take over there when Sister Beatrice retired – and surely that couldn't be much longer.

She wondered what Miss Sampson had to say to her and hoped she wasn't in her bad books again . . .

'Well, that is the intention,' Ruth Sampson said, giving Ruby a triumphant look. 'It isn't confirmed yet, because we still have to come to terms with the Board of St Saviour's – but I'm fairly certain that it will go ahead by the end of the year. We shall take over the whole building and you will be in charge of both sides . . . if you wish to accept the position . . .'

'Yes, of course . . .' Ruby stared at her, unsure of what she was hearing. 'You're saying they're closing their doors and we'll be in complete control of the orphans as well as our girls . . .'

'Yes, that is the idea. St Saviour's cannot continue to support two homes, as I'm sure they realised, but they kept it on because Sister Beatrice fought the closure and local people supported her – but now they've realised it is untenable . . .'

'What will happen to her – to Sister Beatrice?' Ruby asked, feeling an odd pang of sympathy for the woman she'd resented at the start but now rather admired from afar.

'Her methods are outdated and since I am in overall charge I should not accept her continuing presence. You will run the kind of home we require with the proper standards. We shall continue to take in children from the streets for a short time, but other centres are being planned and eventually we shall be what we are now but much larger . . . It makes more sense for sick children to be dealt with in specialised centres these days before being moved out to the country. The nurses next door are an unnecessary luxury.'

'Yes, I suppose so . . .' Ruby was a little disappointed. She'd quite liked the idea of taking in the children in need. 'So it will happen by Christmas?'

'Possibly the following January . . . but it isn't settled yet. There could be complications so you must keep this to yourself. Were it to become known . . . I wouldn't put it past that woman to stir up the local population again . . .'

'Of course, you may rely on my discretion . . .'

'Naturally.' Miss Sampson smiled. 'I was sure I could . . . This will be a promotion for you, Ruby.'

Ruby agreed and left the office, feeling thoughtful as she walked back to her home. Once, she'd thought she felt more for Miss Sampson than she ought, but the gloating in her eyes as she'd spoken of Sister Beatrice's dismissal had left a nasty taste in Ruby's mouth. Ruby didn't like the old bat much, but she did respect her and felt oddly guilty that she was being sent packing just like that. It seemed unfair after all her years of service . . .

As she entered the building where her small flat was situated, Ruby saw a young woman burdened down with parcels and bags and realised she must be moving into the vacant apartment above. Seeing the girl drop some of her parcels, she darted forward as the lift opened.

'Here, I'll give you a hand with those,' she said and scooped them up. 'I'm Ruby and I live in the flat below you.'

'Hi, I'm Carla.' The girl's bright eyes made Ruby feel an odd tingle at her nape and she dropped her own. The flame of her hair as it curled about her face was striking and there was something about the girl that instantly appealed, her smile reaching out to Ruby's lonely heart. 'Come on up, I'll be glad of help with all this lot – and then perhaps we can get to know one another over a cup of coffee . . .'

'Well, I'll give you a hand in with all this stuff – but I've got some reports to write this evening.' Ruby saw Carla's smile dim and wished the words unsaid, but she couldn't go back on them and perhaps it was best she didn't. Ruby couldn't afford to get too close to a girl like this; she had to think about her career . . .

CHAPTER 3

'Keep yer mouth shut, Beth,' Andy Rutherford hissed at his sister as they trailed in the wake of the police sergeant. 'If they know where we came from they'll send us back, and I'd rather die than be made to do that.'

His younger sister Beth nodded, silent and instinctively obedient. Her large brown eyes were wide with distress as she held on to Andy's hand, her face pale with fear. The last thing she wanted was to be sent back to a life that terrified her. She was seven years old, pale and vulnerable, and all she'd known in her short life was abuse, hunger and fear. Love was something she felt for her elder brother, because he was her protector and her refuge, though she couldn't put a name to her feelings. She only knew she was safe with Andy: he'd taken a beating for her more than once, saving her from the Beast . . .

'It 'ull be all right,' he whispered with a reassuring smile, his eyes lighter in colour than hers and his sturdiness making him seem so much stronger and fitter than his sister. 'Not like before . . .'

Beth's hand trembled in his and nodded silently. She believed in Andy, who was six years her senior and seemed to the timid girl wise and brave and her only protection from those who wanted to hurt her.

Sergeant Sallis glanced back at them and smiled kindly. 'Don't be frightened, Beth,' he said. 'I told your brother they were good people here and they are. Sister Beatrice looks stern, but she's the kindest person I know – and Staff Nurse Wendy is lovely, as is Sister Rose.'

'Why are they called sisters?' Andy asked curiously. 'Is it a place for nuns?'

'Bless you no, it's a proper children's home, one of the best around,' the police officer said. 'Sister Beatrice is a nun but she's also a nursing sister – and Sister Rose used to work in the London hospital.'

'That's where they took Ma when she was bad,' Beth said and Andy squeezed her hand hard, making her look at him in protest. 'I wasn't going to say,' she whispered.

Sergeant Sallis looked from one to the other, but didn't press for more information, merely nodding to himself before moving off again. Beth was a little nervous of anyone in uniform, but Andy had told her they could trust him.

'You can tell by his eyes,' Andy had whispered to her when the police had taken them in and fed them. 'He's all right, Beth. I wouldn't trust him just because he's a copper, mind. It's the way he smiles with his eyes and means it – not like the Beast . . .'

Beth felt sick at the mention of the Beast. She'd clung to her brother, shielding behind him as the policeman told them he was taking them to a place where they would be safe and looked after. Once before, after their mother died, someone had told them that and it hadn't been true, because they'd been made to go and live with the Beast, but Andy was listening and agreeing to the policeman's suggestion.

'We've got to do what he says for now,' he'd whispered to Beth. 'It won't be for long, love. As soon as I can work I'll find us some rooms and I'll look after you. I won't let anyone hurt you ever again . . .'

Beth nodded, and held on tightly to her brother's hand. She'd been cold and hungry for days, because they'd slept rough in a little deserted shed down by the railway, living on the food Andy managed to beg or steal. He'd tried to get work, because he was strong, but the bosses kept turning him away – he wasn't old enough to work legally, they said, and they would be in trouble if they let him do a man's job. Once or twice since their escape, Andy had found work washing down lorries that had carted dirty loads and he'd come back to her stinking like drains, but the only place he could wash was in the men's toilets and he had to be careful. He'd taken his shirt off to wash once and a queer bloke had come after him, offering him money to do something that Andy thought was rude. So now he filled bottles of water and they washed their faces and hands as best they could in their little hut, but both of them were itching and Beth thought she'd seen something moving in her brother's hair. She shuddered at the thought and longed to be clean again, but she would remain dirty all her life rather than go back there . . . to the Beast's house.

She felt sick at the memory of the months since her mother's illness and sudden death in hospital. Left alone at the mercy of the Beast, they had lived in terror, never knowing whether he would return drunk or sober. Beth sometimes thought her step-father was worse sober than when he was drunk; drink mellowed him for a while and if she was careful and kept out of his way, she had little to worry about. However, when he was sober, he swore at them both, expected Beth to do the chores her mother had done and gave them very little to eat. They were, he vowed, nothing but a nuisance and he could not be bothered to bring up children who were not his.

'The silly bitch shouldn't have gone poking her nose in where there was sickness,' he muttered furiously as he landed a blow on Beth's arm when she reached for a piece of bread spread thinly with dripping. 'If she hadn't gone and caught scarlet fever, we should've been eating a decent dinner instead of this rubbish – and I'm havin' that last slice so keep your dirty fingers orf it!'

Andy was made to do all the chores Beth couldn't manage, like digging the allotment and cleaning the gutters out when the rain came pouring down the walls because they were choked with filth. He had to polish the Beast's boots and clean the bike he used to get to his work in the canning factory, fetch him fags and beer from the pub on the corner, and clean the stove out in the mornings, as well as putting the rubbish out in the bins. All the jobs the man of the house was supposed to do and the Beast had never bothered with, leaving them to his long-suffering wife and then her young son.

Beth wasn't good at ironing and sometimes she got a few blows because she'd creased the Beast's trousers wrongly or scorched his shirt. When he wasn't at work, and despite his slovenliness about the house, Beth's step-father liked to dress well if he was going out. He'd tried to thrash her when she'd accidentally scorched his best blue shirt and Andy had stepped in to stop him, but the Beast had turned on Andy, beating him until he fell to the ground and lay still.

The Beast had stared at the boy lying unconscious at his feet and shrugged, before snarling at Beth, 'Tell anyone about this and I'll kill the pair of you. I'm going out . . .'

He'd slammed off out of the house, leaving Beth to kneel by her brother's side and bathe his forehead with cool water as she wept. Andy had come round at last, feeling sick and woozy, but gradually the mist had cleared, and that was when he'd told her that they had to run away.

'But where shall we go?' Beth asked plaintively. She hated the Beast but she was even more terrified by the idea that they would run off somewhere, because at least in this house that had been their father's they had beds and there was sometimes food to eat.

'We've got to go, Beth,' her brother insisted. 'Next time he will kill us – besides, he'll probably have us put in a home somewhere if we stay. He doesn't want us around now that Ma is dead, and I hate him.'

'I hate him too,' Beth agreed, and allowed him to persuade her that they should escape while their step-father was out down the working men's club he liked to visit on Friday nights, playing darts for the local team.

They'd taken some of their clothes, the few that fitted and weren't falling apart with wear; they'd also taken an old flask that had once belonged to their father filled with water from the tap, what was left of the bread and dripping, Andy's pocket knife, two chipped mugs and two spoons from the drawer, two towels, their spare shoes, Beth's rag doll and a Biggles book that Andy's father had given him long ago.

There was no money in the house. The Beast had made sure of that, giving Beth's mother only a small amount for shopping each week. After her death he paid for everything himself, never sparing a copper for either of the kids, and giving them only enough food to survive and that grudgingly.

Perhaps it was because they'd been hungry for a long time that the hardships of life on the streets hadn't hit them immediately, but by the time the police picked them up after a tip-off from one of the railway workers, Beth was so hungry she cried most of the time, and Andy wasn't much better.

The promise of baths, food and clean clothes was tempting and Beth's feelings swayed between apprehension and hope when the policeman told her they were nearly there. When she looked up at the severe building with its grimy walls and small windows up in the attics, she pulled back and her fear made her want to run, but Andy pressed her hand and Sergeant Sallis smiled at her, as if he sensed her nervousness.

'It's all right, Beth,' he said. 'It doesn't look much, but it's warm and they look after you here. I promise you . . . cross my heart and hope to die if I tell a lie . . .'

A reluctant smile came to her face and she stepped forward, some of her fear evaporating as she saw a woman in a pale grey uniform and a white frilly cap standing in the hall.

'Ah, you must be Andy and this is Beth,' the nurse said and her smile lit up her face. 'My name is Staff Nurse Wendy, and I'm going to look after you. I think you both need a nice wash and then I'll tuck you up in bed and bring you something lovely to eat.'

'It's not time for bed,' Beth said solemnly and she saw a twinkle in Nurse Wendy's eyes.

'No, but I think you must be tired and hungry after all you've been through, and I want to make sure you're quite well before you go to the dorms – and perhaps start school . . .'

'School – can I go to school?' Beth's heart did a little skip, because it had been ages since she'd been allowed to go. The Beast said she had work to do for him and didn't need all that nonsense.

'Yes, you can and you should,' Nurse Wendy said and looked at Sergeant Sallis. 'Thank you for bringing them to us. I shall look after them now.'

'Yes, I'm sure of that,' he replied and hesitated, before offering his hand to Andy to shake. 'You've been a sensible lad. If you ever need my help, please come and tell me and I'll do my best to sort things for you.'

'Thank you, sir,' Andy said. 'When I can work I'll ask you for a character reference so I can get a good job.'

'You should study hard and do something worthwhile, lad. I think you've got it in you to do well . . .' Turning to Beth, he said solemnly, 'It has been nice to meet you, miss. I know you'll be safe here with these kind people.'

Beth thanked him shyly, and then she saw that Nurse Wendy was holding out her hand. She hesitated, looked at her brother, and when he gave her a little nudge, slid her hand into the nurse's. She had begun the long journey back to trust, but was still anxious enough to look over her shoulder and make sure that Andy was following close behind . . .

CHAPTER 4

'Are you certain she said I was to go for an interview today?' Jinny asked, looking at Nellie as she pushed a mug of hot strong tea in front of her together with a slab of bread and jam. 'Just like that, really? I asked at half a dozen places this week and they all said to come back when I had some experience of work . . .' She spread her hands wide. 'How can I get work experience if no one gives me a chance?'

The radio was playing behind them, the music of Bill Haley and His Comets blasting out, making Jinny want to dance the way her friends had shown her at last year's Christmas party at school, when they'd put records on the Dansette record player that a teacher had brought in.

'Well, yer've got your chance now thanks to my cousin's daughter,' Nellie said. 'I saw Hannah when I was down the market, a few days after you left school and told 'er you needed a job. I said you wanted to work for St Saviour's. It weren't quite the truth, but a little white lie does no harm now and then.' Nellie wagged her three chins and laughed as she saw Jinny's smile widen. 'That's it, love. You'd have somewhere to live as well as a job, see – and it's not that I don't love havin' you 'ere but you ain't safe while that devil is still livin' next door . . .'

'Oh, Nellie, why couldn't you've been my mother?' Jinny said and got up to hug her. The music on the radio had changed and the words of Elvis Presley's record 'All Shook Up' flooded the room. 'Listen, he's your favourite . . .'

'Yeah, I like Elvis,' Nellie chuckled and turned the wireless up until her neighbour banged on the thin wall. 'Miserable old meow she is . . .'

'Oh Nellie,' Jinny said and hugged her. 'I do love you. You're a good friend to me. I don't know what I would've done if it hadn't been for you . . .'

'Go on with yer, girl,' Nellie said and gave her a friendly push. 'Get that tea down yer and then go and 'ave a look what you're goin' ter wear fer the interview. I reckon that navy blue skirt yer made last week would be about right, but what about a blouse? I'd lend yer somethin' of mine, but they'd drown yer . . .' She went off into a peal of laughter and Jinny laughed with her at the idea.

'I've got my white school blouse,' Jinny said with a sigh. 'It's the last thing I had new for school. Ma grudged it to me but she had to give me the money, because the old one split at the seams. I'll pay you back for the material for my skirt, Nellie – I promise.'

'I told yer it don't matter,' Nellie said and took her purse down from the shelf. ''Ere, go and get yerself somethin' orf the market . . . and don't refuse. When yer earnin' yer can give me a treat . . . take me to the flicks or somethin'.'

'Yes, I shall,' Jinny promised. 'We'll go to see Elvis in his film if you like . . .'

Nellie's face lit up at the promise, even though she'd already seen her hero on the big screen twice. She pressed a ten-shilling note into Jinny's hand. 'Get a good one, girl. Somethin' smart, like, not second-hand rubbish. I saw some pretty new blouses for five bob on the market – that stall near the fishmonger. Well . . . not too near, 'cos then they'd smell like 'e does . . .' She went off into a cackle of laughter.

'Nellie, you do say awful things,' Jinny teased, but she took the money and slipped it into her pocket as she reached for her school coat. It was worn and threadbare on the sleeves, but better than the shapeless dress she was wearing. She would wear it to go shopping, even though it was so warm she didn't need a coat. As she aimed a kiss at Nellie's cheek and left, she made a mental vow to repay everything the good-hearted woman had done for her.

Jinny had done what she could by helping out about the house as much as she was allowed, but Nellie wanted no repayment, and she would have to find ingenious ways of giving back the kindness she'd received in this house, but once she was earning money she could bring her friend fruit, sweets and perhaps the latest records – and she would take her out, to the flicks and other places.

All she needed was a job, but that was easier said than done. She'd started by sending out polite letters, but when most of them had either gone unanswered or brought abrupt rejections, Jinny had started a tour of shops: Woolworths, Peacock's, and the Home and

Colonial, as well as the Co-op and a couple of dress shops, also factories, cafés and hotels. She'd been offered two hours scrubbing out offices in the mornings and had thought she might take it, but Nellie discouraged her.

'If you get stuck wiv something like that, you'll be in a rut and never get out of it,' she'd said and patted her hand. 'I'll ask about a bit, love. See if I can find out about something better . . .'

Jinny had agreed but it hadn't stopped her looking. Unfortunately, nothing had turned up and by the time she'd applied for the scrubbing job, it had gone. Nellie had said it was just as well, though Jinny had regretted it, but now she felt excited. She was being offered a proper interview at St Saviour's by some people named Sister Beatrice and Sandra Milvern, and that sounded important. She didn't know what sort of a job it was but she didn't really care. Anything decent and legal would do; she just wanted to earn some money and repay Nellie's kindness – and her friend was right, it would be better to get away from here so that she wouldn't have to put up with Jake's glaring eyes every time he saw her.

'Bitch,' he'd hissed at her the last time he'd blocked her path, his hand gripping her arm in a punishing hold. 'I'll get even with yer one of these days. Just wait and see . . .'

Jinny hadn't answered. She'd been frightened of pushing him into something violent, but with Nellie's husband standing at the door waiting for her, Jake had left it at veiled threats. He hadn't wanted one of Bert Strong's hammer fists in his face although Bert was quite a bit older than Jake, who couldn't be more than early thirties, he was a big tough man who worked as a Docker, an amateur champion boxer in his day.

The sun was warm and Jinny undid her threadbare coat, wishing she'd left it at home, but she felt like a scarecrow in her old dress, which was one of the few things her mother had brought round and shoved in Nellie's arms when Jinny was out one day.

'You've got the ungrateful little bitch, so you keep 'er,' Ma had hissed drunkenly. 'I don't want 'er back . . .'

Jinny wished that her mother had brought her extra shoes and more underwear, but she suspected that anything worth selling had gone down the second-hand stall for beer money. Jinny had been left with the school things she'd been wearing and a couple of old dresses; plus a nightgown, some knickers, a cardigan and a skirt that had seen better days. None of it was good enough to sell or Jinny would've sold it and bought material to make something new, but Ma hadn't given her anything worth having.

She bit her lip, feeling the sting of tears. Why did her mother blame her for what had happened? She'd come round to Nellie's screaming at the top of her voice that Jinny was a scheming bitch and sporting a black eye.

'It's your fault 'e give me this 'ere,' she'd yelled and gone for Jinny until Nellie had hauled her off and given her a push into the nearest chair. After Nellie had finished telling her off, she'd looked a bit ashamed and said, 'Well, she must 'ave flaunted 'erself to make 'im go fer 'er like that . . .'

''E's a pig and a brute,' Nellie said bluntly. 'You know that, Mabel Hollis, so don't come round 'ere blamin' that girl; 'e'd 'ave anythin' in a skirt and Jinny's a lovely young girl – in case you 'adn't noticed . . .'

'Too damned pretty,' her mother said and started crying tears of self-pity. 'What chance 'ave I got when she's around? They look at me an' then they look at 'er and I've 'ad it . . .'

'That ain't Jinny's fault. She don't encourage Jake and you know it – but she's stayin' wiv me now so that's it . . .'

Mabel glanced round the neat kitchen, taking in the painted dresser, which was fresh and bright and set with blue and white crockery, the scrubbed pine table, blue and white voile curtains at the windows, and mismatched chairs, and shining linoleum on the floor. Nellie didn't have a better home than she did, but it just looked better – and it smelled better – and perhaps in that moment Mabel was aware of her failings as a mother and housewife.

'Well, she's better orf wiv you any road,' she said and stopped crying. 'I'll bring 'er fings round then . . .'

She'd seemed ashamed of herself as she left, but when she'd brought the old clothes round later she'd been in a temper again, and had obviously decided that she would dispose of the better clothes that her daughter possessed.

Jinny was nearing the market in Petticoat Lane. The thought of the ten shillings in her purse was so exciting that she could hardly contain herself as she wandered from stall to stall, keeping her hand in her pocket to protect it from wandering fingers that might try to rob her. Pickpockets frequented the various lanes that housed the several markets in the area; all kinds of merchandise was sold in these lanes, second-hand clothes, shoes, and better clothes, as well as crockery; leather and cloth bags, straw hats, curios, and a variety of other goods in the lane itself, but in the next streets there were caged birds, food stalls, rags and pens containing rabbits and small livestock, like one-day-old chicks and ducks.

Jinny lingered by a stall selling new clothes. She looked through a rail of skirts, none of which were more than ten shillings, and found a tweed one she liked a lot, but what she really needed was a new blouse.

'Sell yer that fer seven bob if yer want it, luv,' the stallholder said and winked at Jinny. He had a nice smile and she didn't feel in the least threatened. She was tempted, but knew she needed a blouse more than another skirt.

'I like it, but I need a blouse,' she admitted. 'Perhaps another week – if I get my job . . .'

'Yer can 'ave it two bob down and half a crown a week,' the trader offered. 'Yer've got an 'onest face, luv.'

'Thanks,' Jinny said and smiled. 'I need to see how much I can get a blouse for first – and maybe I'll come back . . .'

'Maybe you'll win lots of money on Ernie's new Premium Bonds,' he said and grinned at her. 'I'm gonna buy one fer a quid next month and if I win the big prize I'll be rich – and then I'll give all me customers half price . . .'

He nodded and Jinny moved off, passing the stalls selling new blouses, most of which would take the whole of her ten shillings and more, to the second-hand stalls further down. In the previous street the goods shown were much worn and unwashed, but on one stall with a notice proclaiming the goods were nearly new, the clothes were hung on hangers and nicely presented.

Jinny saw some lace blouses and went to look. She immediately saw two pretty ones that she liked; one was yellow voile with little white spots and the other was cream silk and had a lace frill at the cuffs and tiny pearl buttons. Both looked as if they might have been new, and she looked at the price tags with some apprehension. They were priced at six shillings each – which meant she could afford one of them and still put a deposit on the skirt.

'Do you like 'em?' The young woman came round from the back of the stall with a friendly smile. 'They're a bargain they are – cost you two guineas each new they would.'

'They look as if they were expensive,' Jinny agreed. 'Is there anything wrong with them?'

'Nah, they're perfect, and I washed 'em meself,' the girl said proudly. She was wearing a full skirt, pretty blouse and white bobby socks with winkle-picker shoes. 'I'm good at things like that – you 'ave to be careful with real silk . . .'

'Are they both silk?' Jinny asked, feeling a flutter of excitement, because she'd thought they were lovely without knowing what they were. 'Why did the woman who owned them sell them?'

'She 'ad a baby and they wouldn't fit – 'sides, she's got loads of money . . . she was tellin' me she were at Wimbledon when Althea Gibson beat Angela Mortimer. I 'eard it on the radio, but I'd love to 'ave been there – wouldn't you?'

'Oh, I've never thought about it . . . I did play tennis

at school, but I wasn't very good.' Jinny touched the material of the silk blouses reverently. 'I'd like them both but I can only afford one,' she said hesitantly. 'I'm not sure which to choose . . .'

'How much 'ave yer got?'

'Eight shillings to spend on a blouse . . . I need two for something else,' Jinny said and took the money from the purse in her pocket. 'I think I'll 'ave the cream one . . .' she decided but before the stallholder could act someone snatched the money from Jinny's hand and started running. 'My money . . .' she cried and started after him. 'He's pinched my money . . .'

People stared but made no attempt to stop the rogue from fleeing through the crowded market. He was getting away from her and Jinny's heart sank as she saw him disappearing into the throng. The money Nellie had given her had gone and she wasn't likely to see it again, and that meant she couldn't buy anything. Tears pricked her eyes and she felt such a fool for holding the money out so eagerly to show the stallholder. What an idiot. She should've waited until the blouse was wrapped and kept a tight hold on it. Feeling miserable, Jinny turned away, knowing that she'd lost her money and there was nothing she could do.

Retracing her steps, she went back to the stall selling the blouses and almost in tears told the girl that she couldn't buy either of them.

'If you've got them next week, I'll buy one – if I get my new job . . .'

'Wanted it to make a good impression I expect?'

'Yes, but my school . . .' Jinny broke off as a hand clutched her arm and she turned to see a somewhat out-of-breath Micky Smith. He grinned as she stared at him and handed her the ten-shilling note he was holding. 'What . . . ?'

'Sorry it took me so long to get 'im,' Micky said, looking proud of his achievement. 'I didn't realise straight away what he'd done and then someone said you'd been robbed. I managed to get it off him but he got away . . . I'll find 'im though and I'll make 'im sorry . . .'

'You got my money back?' Jinny was disbelieving and then overwhelmed. 'That's so kind . . .' She choked as the tears became very real. 'Thanks. I can buy my blouse now . . .'

'You can have the two for nine bob,' the girl said. 'I reckon you deserve it after a nasty turn like that. I don't like thieves. They nick things off the stall if me and Dad don't keep an eye out.' She smiled at Micky. 'You was brave and clever to get that back, Mick.'

'Yeah,' he agreed, his grin widening as the purchase went ahead and Jinny parted with the note for her paper bag and a shilling change. 'Be seein' yer, Maisie. Tell yer father I've got a bit of business fer 'im later . . .'

'Righto,' Maisie said and looked pleased as Jinny took her purchases and moved off, Micky at her side. 'I'll see yer later then . . .'

Micky nodded but didn't look back at her. He walked with Jinny as she moved away. 'The bugger didn't hurt yer, did he? I wish I'd seen him sooner . . .'

'No, I'm all right,' Jinny said. 'I'm going for a job interview tomorrow at St Saviour's, and I needed a new blouse. I was just deciding which to buy and got my money out too quick – and he snatched it before I knew he was there.'

'Probably been followin' yer, waiting to get yer purse,' Micky said. 'They do that in the market when it's busy. Was there anything else you need now?'

'I was looking at a skirt but I bought two blouses so I can't afford the deposit now . . .'

'Let me buy it for you,' Micky offered immediately and Jinny sensed his eyes on her dress. 'You can't go like that . . .'

'I've got a decent skirt,' Jinny said, 'but the trader was kind – offered to let me pay so much a week. I'll just tell him I may come back next week if I get my new job.'

'Which stall is it?'

'This one,' Jinny said and blushed as the young stall-holder came out to her. 'I was just telling Micky I can't buy the skirt today but if you've got it next week I may buy it . . .'

'What yer, Mick,' the trader said and grinned. 'Nice bit of work. If this young lady is yer girl she can take the skirt and pay me later . . . no deposit needed . . .'

'I'm no one's girl,' Jinny said quickly. 'I've got a shilling – if you'll take that as a deposit I'll pay you as soon as I get my first wage . . .'

'If Jinny says she'll pay, she'll pay,' Micky assured him. 'Wrap it up, Dave, and take her shillin' . . .'

'Anythin' you say, mate,' Dave said and put the skirt in the bag, accepting Jinny's coin with a grin. 'If it ain't right you can bring it back – and pay me when yer like . . .'

'I'll pay next week if I get my job,' Jinny said, her cheeks warm. 'Thanks so much. I wanted to look smart for my interview and now I'm spoiled for choice.'

'A pretty girl like you deserves nice things,' Dave said. 'I'll see you right any time you want something new and can't afford it . . .' He grinned at her as she walked off with Micky.

When they were out of earshot, Jinny looked at Micky. 'I got a bargain with my blouses and it was nice of Dave to let me have this before I paid him – but you're not to give him the money, Micky. It wouldn't be right. I'm not that sort of girl . . .'

Micky laughed softly, but there was a faint look of hurt in his eyes. 'Did you think I would try to buy yer for the price of a skirt off the market? I wouldn't be so cheap, Jinny – and I know you ain't like that . . .'

'I didn't mean that . . .' She blushed hotly, because she had and now She was ashamed of thinking ill of him. 'I know you're generous but . . .'

'No, I ain't.' Micky shook his head. 'I like yer, Jinny. I always 'ave – but if I decide to make a play fer yer, you'll know – right? If yer my girl I'll treat yer proper . . .'

Jinny shook her head, embarrassed. She was too young to be anyone's girl and wasn't sure what she wanted from life yet. Once upon a time all girls ever thought about was getting married, but these days life could be more exciting and, having made the break from her home, Jinny wanted to enjoy it before she settled down.

'Who says I'll be your girl?' she asked crossly, more because she didn't know what to say than because she was angry or disliked him.

'Oh, you'll have me if I ask,' he said and smiled. 'I ain't the ignorant lout you think I am, Jinny. I can talk proper if I want but it suits me to be the way I am, especially with the market lads, right? Let me tell you now, Micky Smith is goin' to be someone one day – one day soon – and when I am I'll be lookin' for the right girl. It might just be you, if yer lucky . . .' He winked at her. 'I'll give yer a ride on me motorbike if yer good . . .'

'You've never got a motorbike . . .' Jinny stared in disbelief.

'Oh, ain't I?' Micky laughed. 'I'll be orf to the Isle of Man one of these days – you'll see . . .'

Jinny stopped in her tracks as he walked off laughing. Was he joking or had he really got a motorbike? He was such an odd mixture, the flashy wide boy at one moment, a dashing hero the next, chasing that thief to recover her money even though he was out of breath when he came back. His speech was as mixed up as he was and she believed that he could put on a posh voice when it suited him, just as he could be one of the lads in the market. She wondered again what he did to earn the kind of money he so obviously did; he wasn't going to tell her, but whatever it was both Maisie and Dave had respected him, almost as if they looked up to him – as if he had influence or importance in their lives . . .

Jinny frowned. She had reason to be grateful to Micky but she wasn't sure how she felt about him, or whether she wanted him to be important in her life or not. At the moment all she wanted was to be accepted for the job at St Saviour's . . .

CHAPTER 5

'Oh, damn,' Rose said on seeing her bus disappear round the corner just as she got to the stop. She'd been busy all morning, visiting Mary Ellen at her home and giving her a hand with some washing in return for being able to use her new electric washing tub for her own things. She'd been interested in hearing all about her sister's progress at teaching college and forgotten the time. 'Damn, I'm going to be late.'

'Sorry, I couldn't help overhearing that . . .' Rose turned to look at the man who had spoken. He must have been in his late twenties with fair hair worn a little too long and falling into his eyes; he was dressed in work overalls stained with paint, black boots, a short-sleeved shirt and a red spotted handkerchief knotted about his throat. 'I've got my van across the road. Can I give you a lift, nurse?'

Rose hesitated, because she'd never seen this man before, but he had a gentle smile and she was inclined to trust him. 'Well, I need to be at St Saviour's in Halfpenny Street – if you're going anywhere near there . . .'

A grin broke out, making him seem far more attractive

than he'd looked at first glance. 'You're one of those 'Alfpenny angels,' he said. 'As a matter of fact I've got an appointment with your Sister Beatrice this mornin'. Hop in and I'll take you there . . .'

'Did Sister Beatrice ask you to call and see her?' Rose said as he opened the passenger door for her to get in. The smell of paint and turpentine would have told her that he was a decorator by trade even if she hadn't already guessed it. His radio was playing something that sounded like skiffle but he switched it off. 'Are you from Thompsons?'

'Yeah, that's me,' he said and went round to the driving seat. 'I'm Rob and my brother Nick and me started up about two years ago. We'd both had enough of working for wages so we decided to give it a go on our own. I'm just thankful they took that petrol rationing off. I know they had to after that trouble with the Suez Canal last year, but I'm glad we're not still restricted. You need a vehicle in this job.'

'We had rationing for years during the war.'

'I know, but I wasn't driving then. I was seventeen when it ended.'

'And now you have your own business . . .' she said as he drew out into the traffic. 'I know it can be hard starting up on your own. You can't afford to employ many staff, but that means you have to work all hours yourself . . .'

'That's about us,' Rob replied without looking at her. 'It's easier for me, because I'm not married, but Nick is a widower with two young boys – and his house is mortgaged.'

'I know what it's like to worry where the next penny

is coming from. My father died when I was quite young and Ma could never quite manage. It took me years to earn enough to look after myself.'

'As long as the work keeps coming in, we'll manage,' Rob said. 'Nick has gone after a big contract on a new housing estate this morning, and if he gets it, it could make all the difference.'

Rose didn't say anything to that, but she could understand what it meant to a fledgling business. It was 1957 now and the country had just about shrugged off the hardships of the war; the prime minister said the country had never had it so good, but Rose had known what it was like to be really poor. After their mother became ill and died, Rose had been forced to put her younger sister in St Saviour's and train as a nurse for very low wages. She'd tried to help Mary Ellen along the way, to see that she had a few treats, but it had been difficult for a long time.

Rose had buried her grief as she trained hard to become a nurse and she'd done well at the hospital. Matron had wanted her to go on and rise to the top of her profession, but Rose had fallen out with one of the senior doctors and left before he had her sacked. She'd been lucky to get the job at St Saviour's and was enjoying her work. Love hadn't come her way, but she had friends and she got on well with Mary Ellen and her husband Billy these days, although just now and then she was very aware of the passing years and sometimes wondered if she would ever have a family of her own.

'Here we are.' Rob's voice brought Rose back from her own problems and she realised that she hadn't spoken to him for several minutes.

'Oh . . .' she said, feeling embarrassed. 'Thanks so much. I'm sorry; I was lost in my thoughts . . .'

'I expect I was rabbiting on too much.'

'No, of course not.' Rose smiled at him. 'It's just that you talking about what you want for the future made me wonder about my own . . .'

'Ah, thinking of getting married and settling down?'

'No, nothing like that . . . Just thinking about work and whether I should make a change . . .'

'I see . . . well, good luck whatever you decide,' he said and jumped out of his van, coming round to open the door for her.

Rose smiled; she liked being treated like a lady. 'Good luck to you, too,' she said. 'I hope you get that big contract.'

'My brother needs the luck,' Rob said and smiled too. 'I've just got to hope that Sister Beatrice has accepted our price for the work . . .'

Rose almost told him that his price would have gone to St Saviour's Board for the decision, but decided not to mention it. He was a pleasant man and she was grateful for the lift, but she didn't expect she would see much of him, even if he got the job. Pushing all other concerns from her mind, Rose hurried up to the sick ward to relieve Staff Nurse Wendy. It was Wendy's afternoon off and she was planning on a visit to the hairdresser and then she was going out for the evening with a friend. They had tickets for *The Mousetrap*, Agatha Christie's long-running play.

Wendy had surprised everyone by her continuing friendship with a man some years her senior. They'd all thought her a career nurse but Rose knew that Wendy was considering a proposal of marriage. If she were to marry and perhaps leave, that would leave Rose and Sister Beatrice – which meant that Sister Beatrice would be looking for new nursing staff again.

Rose couldn't leave her in the lurch at such a time.

'Oh, there you are.' Wendy turned with a smile as Rose entered. 'I'm glad we have a few minutes before I leave. I wanted to tell you about Beth . . . she seems to have a temperature this morning and I think we should keep an eye on her.'

'You haven't called the doctor? What does Sister Beatrice say?'

'She was in earlier, but Beth was all right then. I rang her office but she didn't answer . . . but I'm sure she'll be back soon – so if you're worried . . .'

'I know she has an appointment with someone just now,' Rose said. 'I'll pop in and look at Beth and I'll keep an eye on her. If she gets any worse I'll get the doctor to come and see her.'

'It's probably nothing. You know what children are, up one minute and down the next, but she was under-nourished when she came to us and I don't think she eats enough . . .'

'We'll have to see if we can tempt her,' Rose said and frowned. 'Muriel used to know exactly what to send for kids who didn't eat much. I don't think Mrs Davies is half as good a cook as Muriel was but I'll ask her to send some strawberry jelly and ice cream . . . if she has it, or perhaps rice pudding. Muriel always had some ice cream for the kids but Mrs Davies seems to think it's a waste of money.'

'Yes, jelly and ice cream might tempt the child. If we

haven't got any in the kitchen, I'll pop to the corner shop and buy a small block of strawberry and vanilla,' Wendy said and checked her files again. 'Otherwise, we're pretty quiet. I sometimes wonder how long we shall go on like this, Rose. We are busy when we have new children brought in, and now and then we have some of them falling sick – but it isn't like it was when I first came here. We were much busier then. It was so different . . .'

'Yes . . .' Rose sighed with regret. 'Everyone says it hasn't been the same since they opened the new home in Essex . . .' She hesitated, then, 'Would you go and work there if you were offered the chance?'

Wendy looked at her for a moment and then shook her head. 'I think if St Saviour's were to close I should go back to hospital nursing . . . perhaps try and specialise. I suppose they would make me retrain. Things have moved on since I came here and it would be hard work catching up . . . and I'm not sure what I want yet . . .' She shook her head. 'You're not thinking of leaving us?'

'I've thought about specialising in paediatrics,' Rose said. 'I thought when I left the London I would be settled here, but it isn't the same as it was even when I came here . . .'

'No, I agree,' Wendy said. 'I think I've only stayed this long because of Sister Beatrice. If she weren't here . . .'

'The whole thing would close down,' Rose said and laughed. 'I sometimes think we've outlived our usefulness. The Welfare people have their own centres to take in kids in trouble now, and they pass them on to the permanent homes within days, hours sometimes. Sister Beatrice believes in winning the trust of our kids before they move on, and I know she's right. It's too drastic to just ship them off to the country when they really don't know what's happening. I think that's why a lot of them run away and come back to London. They would rather be on the streets than in a home they hate.'

'The Children's Department is too clinical, too concerned with the law and not compassionate enough,' Wendy said. 'I've never forgotten the way they dealt with the May twins, Sarah and Samantha; giving them to their father's sister was so wrong – and there was June Miller . . . that was a disaster. She should never have been fostered with those awful people that abused her.'

'No, that was wicked,' Rose said. 'Perhaps we are still needed for a bit longer. I know Sister thinks so . . .'

'Yes, she does,' Wendy said, 'and the kids love her. Billy Baggins and Mary Ellen still come and see her, even though he's doing so well running that warehouse and all those market stalls – and, as you know, your sister is well on the way to becoming a teacher. She told me that she still thinks of St Saviour's as her family, and she's always doing things for the kids. She remembers when Angela Adderbury was here and used to give the children stars and encourage them to do lots of projects for stars.'

'Yes, Mary Ellen and Billy have done really well, but there are lots more kids that have got on because St Saviour's was here,' Rose agreed, but she couldn't help wondering how long it would continue just the same . . .

'We've been given a budget for the work,' Beatrice said to the young man who had presented himself in her office in his overalls, as if prepared to start immediately if given the go-ahead. She rather approved of that and it was part of the reason the Board had chosen his firm from amongst those that had tendered. 'You're a decorator, but you do realise there are some plumbing jobs included in the specification?'

'Yes, of course. My brother Nick is a builder. He does bricklaying, carpentry and plumbing. I'm lazy; I just make it all look good at the end . . .'

Beatrice saw the twinkle in his eye and smiled inwardly. He reminded her of someone but she couldn't think who at the moment. 'Well, your figures seem to be satisfactory, Mr Thompson. When can you start?'

'I'd like to do some preliminary work today, Sister,' Rob said. 'Just make a few notes and then I'll order the materials we need. Did you have any preference for the colour schemes in the kids' dorms?'

'We've always stuck to the same basic colours – doesn't it cost more if we change?'

'No, because we use three coats,' he said. 'We don't just splash on one watered coat and then a top coat. We could make this place look brighter and more modern, if that was what you wanted? Or we can stick to the basic cream but use a lighter, newer colour . . . I could even do a feature wall with stencils, pink and flowery for the girls and blue and sporty for the boys . . . perhaps a racing car . . .'

'Good gracious.' Beatrice removed her spectacles and rubbed the bridge of her nose where they'd pinched. 'For now I think perhaps a lighter cream for the communal areas. I'll speak to my staff about the feature walls. You don't need a decision on that right now?'

'No, I'll get started on the utility rooms; kitchen,

bathrooms. Nick will put in the new sinks and toilets where we agreed and then I'll paint the reception areas, finish up with the dorms and fit the nurses' home in a bit at a time – I'll be here at seven thirty in the morning, if that isn't too early?'

'I am always here by seven – unless we have an emergency in the night, but there will be someone on duty.'

'Then I'll just have a look round and make some notes – and we'll see you in the morning.'

Beatrice nodded and sighed as the young man left her office. She was certain she'd seen Robert Thompson before but she just couldn't recall it. He was in his late twenties so he couldn't have been one of her children at St Saviour's and yet there was something about his eyes . . . and the smile that lit up his face that touched a chord in her memory . . . and then it came to her: he was a little like someone she'd once loved. For a moment she felt a suffocating pain in her chest, but the next second it had gone.

She shook her head and straightened her cap, smoothing the plain grey habit she wore. She'd noticed that one of the children Sergeant Sallis had brought in was looking a bit flushed earlier that morning. It would be a good idea to just pop in and see if she had developed a fever . . .

Something was nagging at the back of her mind as she walked to the isolation ward where the two children were still housed. Neither of them was ready for school or to join the dorms yet, although Andy seemed to be coming on in leaps and bounds. Beth was a quiet, nervous child who clung to her brother and seemed frightened of speaking lest she did something wrong. Beatrice suspected that she'd been badly treated for some time and she wished Andy felt able to tell her, because whoever had done this to them needed to be punished . . . but without confirmation it would be difficult for the police to do very much.

Rose was standing by the girl's bed, taking her temperature when Beatrice entered. She turned and smiled and the satisfied expression in her eyes told Beatrice that the child was fine.

'Beth was feeling a little poorly when Nurse Wendy gave her a wash this morning, but she's better now and I'm going to ask for some more jelly and ice cream for her.'

'Temperature normal now?' Beatrice asked, her practised eyes going over the little girl. Beth still looked a little flushed but her forehead wasn't sweaty and she felt cool to the touch.

'A little higher than normal but not enough to call the doctor for,' Rose said. 'Did you want to see Wendy's report while you're here?'

'How are you feeling, Beth?' Beatrice asked the child.

She glanced nervously at her brother and then said, 'I'm all right, Sister . . .' She hesitated, then, 'When can we get up and go outside please?'

'Do you feel you're ready to go to school, Beth?'

Again the slight hesitation, and then Andy got out of bed wearing his St Saviour's pyjamas and came to sit on the edge of her bed. 'We want to go to school, Sister, but . . . if we tell you where they'll tell him . . . and we can't go back there or he'll kill us . . .'

'The Beast . . .' Beth said, her voice trembling and

her eyes filling with tears. 'Tell her, Andy – tell her how he beat us and didn't give us enough to eat after Mum died . . .'

'Is this man your step-father?' Beatrice asked, her voice sterner than she intended. 'Let me promise you that if he was the one that beat Andy before you came here, he will not be allowed to have the care of you again.'

'If the school tells him we're there he'll get us on the way back here,' Andy said and Beatrice saw a flicker of fear in his eyes. Beth's hand reached for his and he held it tightly. 'I can stand up to him, Sister – but I don't want him to hurt Beth again . . .'

'Well, you don't have to go to school just yet. Nancy is our head carer and she will give you a few lessons to do in the mornings until you feel able to return to normal school – but if you can trust me and tell me the name of this man I may be able to have him punished. He should be in prison for what he has done to you.'

'He would come after us and take us back,' Andy said. 'I want to go to school but I can't protect Beth, because she goes to . . . the juniors . . .'

'Yes, I understand your concerns,' Beatrice said, treating his opinions with the respect they deserved. 'Perhaps, if you wished to return to school, I could have a word with your headmaster? I have already spoken to Miss Sampson from the Welfare people about you, Andy, and for the moment she is content to leave you in my care – but the Department would like to investigate your case and punish the man that hurt you . . .'

Andy shook his head stubbornly, and Beatrice nodded, because she knew that he needed time before he could really trust her. 'Yes, I do understand. Do you wish to let Beth have her lessons with us for the moment and try to attend school yourself?'

'Can I think about it, Sister?'

'Certainly . . . ah, here is Nurse Rose with your meal. I shall leave you to enjoy it and let you decide what is best. If you felt it was just too dangerous to stay in London, I could send you to Halfpenny House in Essex. It is more modern than we are and the people there are good people. It might be better for you if you fear your step-father's retribution . . .'

Andy gave her a long considering look and then inclined his head. 'I'll try goin' to school tomorrow,' he conceded. 'It depends on what them people do . . . but he was given custody of us when Mum died and he lies all the time. He'd say I was making trouble for him out of spite . . . but he's a bully and a beast, and we're never goin' back there.'

'Will you believe me when I say I shall do all I can to make sure you stay with us?'

Andy hesitated for some moments and then inclined his head. 'I trust you – but the Welfare people sent us back to him after we run away when Mum died. He said he would look after us, but he made us do everything; he wouldn't let Beth go to school and told them she had a cold when they came askin' why – and he hit me whenever he felt like it, especially when he was drunk.'

Beatrice had heard the story so many times before. It happened time after time, when the children were left to an uncaring relative who drank. She also knew that Andy was speaking the truth when he said that the Welfare people had given them back to their step-father's care when they'd tried to escape after their mother died.

It was their policy to leave children with a relative unless they had reason to believe that person was unfit – and that wasn't always easy to judge. People were very good at putting on a show when they had a visit from the Children's Welfare Department.

'I shall make sure certain people know what this man has done to you – but it would be so much easier if I knew his name.'

'He'll just smile and deny it all and they'll believe him,' Andy said, 'and then he'll know where we are and come after us . . .'

The fear of the man they called 'the Beast' had gone too deep to be erased with vague promises. Beatrice knew she had to talk to someone at the Children's Department . . .

Suddenly remembering that she had an appointment with a young woman, Beatrice turned hurried steps towards her office. She was late and she could only hope that Sandra had remembered Jinny Hollis was coming for an interview . . .

Luckily, Sandra was already there and had given the young woman a cup of tea. She'd been sitting down when Beatrice entered but got to her feet, a faint flush in her cheeks as she said hello. It was obvious that she had nice manners and Beatrice approved. She thought that perhaps they'd been lucky Hannah had recommended the girl and she smiled, inviting her to sit once more.

'Drink your tea, Miss Hollis. I'll have one too, Sandra – and then we'll hear what this young woman has to say . . .'

*

Beatrice had just entered her office that afternoon when the telephone rang. Picking it up, she discovered it was Angela Adderbury, the woman who had helped her run St Saviour's for years and was now helping to run Halfpenny House in Essex.

'Angela, how nice to hear your voice . . .'

'Sister Beatrice, I'm glad I caught you. I wanted to tell you something; it isn't set in stone yet, but there's a definite chance that St Saviour's will be closing next year . . .'

'Oh no! This can't be true . . . surely they wouldn't . . . ?' Beatrice felt the shock hit her like an icy wave. Her heart raced and for a moment she felt a little light-headed.

'Rest assured that both Mark and I will fight it – but I'll keep you in touch. For the moment this is confidential but I wanted you to be aware – of course you know there is always a place for you here . . .'

'You're very kind, Angela, but the Board might not agree . . . besides, my life is here. There are still children in dire need, Angela . . .'

'I know and I promise I'll do everything I can to stop the closure – but I wanted you to reassure you of my support in case the worst happens . . .'

Beatrice was recovering her composure and decided to change the subject. 'Thank you for letting me know; now tell me, Angela – how are you and the twins? I see Mark when he's in London, but it's ages since I've seen you.'

'Oh, the twins are fine. We took them to Scotland in the Easter holidays and they loved it. Mark is talking of teaching them to ski this winter; he'll take them to Switzerland I imagine.'

'That sounds wonderful. Is everything going well at Halfpenny House now? I know you had a few problems . . .'

'Some of the older boys took a long time to settle down. One of the carers was too harsh and I think he upset them, but since he was asked to resign things have run smoother. I found a new cook too and the food is better. I've introduced a new regime of fresh salads and vegetables . . . the kids were getting too many suet puddings, chips and fried stuff . . .'

'I dare say fresh vegetables are easier to get there than in town?'

'Yes, and I've formed a relationship with some local farmers. It's much cheaper to buy direct from the farm and fresher too. You must come and stay with us soon, please say you will.'

'Well, perhaps – just for a day,' Beatrice said. 'Oh, I can hear voices at the door . . . I must go. Please keep me in touch . . .'

Beatrice replaced the receiver and sat very still staring into space as her heart raced. It was ridiculous, but the news had made her feel quite ill . . . as if she couldn't breathe for a moment. How foolish. She'd always known this could happen; it made perfect financial sense for the Board to close St Saviour's now that they had their modern country home. Still, it had upset her for a moment, but she was fine now, perfectly fine . . .

CHAPTER 6

Jinny felt as if she were walking on air when she finally left St Saviour's an hour and a half after she'd entered it, having been given a job and shown a nice airy room in the nurses' home that would be hers for as long as she worked for the orphanage.

The orphanage didn't look much of a place outside, a bit austere with tiny windows in the attics and scarred grey walls. It had come through the war without suffering a direct hit, but there were cracks in the brick walls and the roof had patches of thick moss, though inside it was much better. You could see several alterations had been done over the years to modernise it, and it was kept lovely and clean. Sister Beatrice had told her it was due for a paint-up and the builders were going to do several much needed repairs.

'It shouldn't trouble us too much,' she'd told Jinny. 'I'm sure they will keep out of our way as much as possible . . .'

'Oh, I'm sure it won't bother me, Sister,' she'd said and the nun had smiled a little.

Jinny was now officially one of the 'Alfpenny girls,

or angels as a lot of people called the nurses and carers. St Saviour's of Halfpenny Street was well known to East Enders, and the people who ran it were generally praised in glowing terms. Jinny had been nervous of meeting Sister Beatrice, who was often described as a bit of a dragon, but she'd been a little subdued when she finally arrived late for the interview, after Sandra had already made Jinny feel comfortable and given her a cup of tea in her office. Sister had apologised and the interview had begun somewhat later than expected, but both Sandra and Sister Beatrice had seemed genuine and kind people to Jinny; she'd expected to be put through a lot of difficult questions, but they asked mainly about her family life, and then, only after a few minutes' pleasant chat, what she wanted to do in the future.

'I don't mind cooking and cleaning, and I like sewing,' Jinny had answered truthfully. 'I liked reading at school, and writing compositions – but I'm not good at maths, though I can add up and divide, but I can't work out logarithms and equations and that sort of stuff . . .'

'Nor can I,' Sandra admitted and she'd laughed softly, her blue eyes full of mirth. 'A part of this job will be helping in the kitchens, the preparation of food, washing up and that sort of thing – also cleaning the children's dorms, collecting dirty laundry and dealing with it. We have a woman who comes in early to scrub the floors, but bathrooms, changing beds and that sort of chore is what we'd expect from you before you start work in the kitchen, Jinny. In time you may be asked to help with children when they are admitted – and if you have the right sort of patience, reading and playing with the little ones . . .'

'Oh . . .' Jinny hardly knew what to say, because it all sounded like a dream to her. She was going to get paid for doing things she liked?

'Does the idea not appeal?' Sister Beatrice asked and frowned. 'You're a little too young to go straight into the job of carer . . .'

'Oh no! I mean yes, it does appeal,' Jinny said and blushed violently. 'I didn't think it would be so nice . . . I mean, do I get paid as well as my room and food just for . . . doing what you said?'

'The wage is two pounds fifteen shillings a week, plus your uniforms, your food and your room. You're expected to keep it clean, but the sheets are done at the laundry with St Saviour's . . .'

'Are you offering me the job?' Jinny was breathless, hardly daring to believe that she could be so lucky.

'Yes – if you want it,' Sister Beatrice said, looking a little stern.

'Oh yes, please,' Jinny said. 'When can I start – tomorrow? Can I move in this evening?'

Sister Beatrice smiled. 'I think that is an excellent idea, Jinny. You will be here nice and early in the morning so that you don't keep Mrs Davies waiting . . . and now I think Sandra should take you to meet Mrs Davies, and Nancy, and then show you where you will sleep and the other rooms . . .'

Jinny thanked her, still not quite believing her good fortune as Sandra led her off to meet various members of staff and then to see the lovely neat, clean room that would be hers. It was larger than the one she had at Nellie's, not huge but big enough to have an elbow chair and a desk, as well as the bed, chest of drawers and single wardrobe. Jinny didn't have many possessions other than her clothes, but she realised that she could gradually make this room into her home and it was such a lovely feeling that she turned anxiously to Sandra.

'Do I have to pay rent?'

Sandra smiled and shook her head. 'No, Jinny, it is part of your wage. Sister Beatrice doesn't force girls to live at the nurses' home but she thinks it is a good idea, especially for the younger ones. You're asked to be in by ten thirty at night, because then we can lock the gates and know that our staff and children are safe from intruders.'

'Oh yes, I'll be in by then. I don't go out much in the evenings – but I promised Nellie I'd take her to see Elvis Presley at the Odeon when I get my wages. She's been that good to me, but we can go first house . . .'

Sandra nodded, looking at her steadily for a moment. 'Sister Beatrice may seem stern to you, Jinny, but she cares about the children, and she cares about her staff. Be honest, do your job well, and you should be very happy here. I know I have been.'

'Thank you . . .' Jinny blushed, because she hadn't told them all the details of her unhappy home life, but she thought they probably knew most of it because of Hannah. 'I shan't let you down.'

'I am sure you won't,' Sandra said. 'Well, get off and pack your things – we have supper at half-past eight so if you're here by then you'll meet some of the children, because we all sit together for meals . . .'

'What yer!' Micky's voice hailed her as she approached the corner of Lilac Lane just before she turned down into the ancient courtyard where Nellie's and her mother's house stood at the middle of the terrace. He'd just come out of the grocer's shop and was clutching a racing paper, a packet of cigarettes and a large paper bag filled with what looked like biscuits, cakes and crisps. 'How yer doin'?'

'I'm all right,' Jinny beamed at him, unable to control her excitement. 'I got my job at St Saviour's. They've given me a nice room to myself and I start tomorrow. I'll be able to pay for that skirt when I get my wage and take Nellie to the flicks . . .'

'That's great.' Micky grinned all over his face. 'You can come to the flicks with me any time you say, Jinny. There's a film comin' soon I want to see – *Bridge on the River Kwai* . . .'

'Thanks . . .' She hesitated, not wanting to cut him off and yet knowing that she wasn't ready to become involved too much with someone like Micky. 'I'll probably be working most of the time for a start. I'm not sure how much time I get off . . .' She glanced at the paper bag and, perhaps because she felt awkward, teased, 'If you eat all that lot you'll get fat and then you won't be able to run fast enough to catch any more thieves . . .'

'They ain't fer me,' Micky said. 'Just fetched 'em fer a friend. He's got two little kids and he's bin orf work for weeks. The Social don't pay enough to keep a flea alive, let alone a few treats for the kids. I'm as fit as a fiddle, don't you worry.'

Jinny nodded and moved from foot to foot uneasily. 'I'll see you around then, Micky.'

'Yeah, I pop up all over the place,' he said. 'Go

and tell Nellie yer good news; she'll be sorry ter lose yer . . .'

'Nellie is a good friend, but she couldn't keep me there forever,' Jinny said. 'She took me in when I needed help, but I'll be all right now. It's a nice place to work and Jake won't come after me there . . .'

'If he bothers you just let me know and I'll put him right,' Micky said but Jinny shook her head. She didn't want them fighting over her, especially as she thought Micky might come off worse. Jinny liked Micky as a friend and she was grateful for his help over her stolen money, but she wasn't ready to be anyone's girlfriend just yet. She wanted to work and get some money saved so that she could stand on her own two feet and she thought Micky was the sort who would expect her to be his once he put his mark on her.

Jinny was too young and she wanted some fun before she became romantically involved. Her mother had been pregnant with her at fifteen and married the day she became sixteen – and that was enough to make Jinny vow she wouldn't get caught in the same trap. There was a big exciting world out there and she wanted to have some fun before she got wed . . . if she ever did.

'Run on home and behave yerself,' Micky said and turned away, whistling cheerfully as he set off up the road.

She couldn't help being curious about what Micky did for a living. He always seemed to have money in his pocket, and he was wearing a smart suit that morning, and yet she saw him about quite a lot and he didn't seem to have a regular job. Unless he worked at night . . .

*

Nellie hugged her and told her she'd known she would get the job all along. There was a suspicion of tears as she helped Jinny pack her things into a big old shopping bag that she'd had for years.

'I'll bring it back when I get time off,' Jinny promised and Nellie gave a little shake of her head.

'Yer can always come back ter me if they don't feed yer enough or treat yer bad,' she said. 'I shall miss yer, love, and that's the truth – but I know it's best fer yer to go. Jake were sniffin' round 'ere earlier and I think 'e were lookin' fer you, Jinny. I went out in the yard and started shaking mats over 'im. 'E give me such a look and went orf quick then! I don't trust that bugger and that's the truth.'

Jinny nodded, knowing that there was no real privacy in the communal yard that all four houses in the terrace shared. They were Victorian houses and due to be pulled down as part of the general clearance and rebuilding that was going on all over London. One of these days the tenants would all get notices to quit their homes and the bulldozers would move in, but it had been threatened for as long as Jinny could recall and most people had given up expecting it to happen. If the renovations did go ahead the council were due to rehouse them in one of the more modern estates built in the suburbs. Jinny's mother had said she wouldn't let the 'bloody council' stick her in 'one of them soddin' flats stuck up in the sky', but Nellie was quite looking forward to it.

'I wouldn't mind living somewhere the rats didn't invade every time it turns cooler,' she'd once told Jinny after chasing one almost the size of a cat out of her kitchen with a broom. 'I'd like a nice modern flat with proper electrics and all the rest, better for us as we get older – but I'm not sure the old man will go fer it. 'E'll probably look for somewhere cheap down near the Docks. They ain't goin' ter pull the lot down in one go, are they?'

Jinny had agreed that they would probably find another terraced house going cheap somewhere if they tried. She thought a nice modern house or flat would be much better, but most of the residents were against the demolition of their homes, and some of them talked of barricading the entrance to the court so the bulldozers couldn't get in. Since none of them had yet received notice it seemed a long way off to Jinny, though you couldn't go far these days without seeing buildings that were either being knocked down to make way for big stores or new office blocks, or renovations to bring buildings up to standard. Old London was fast disappearing and being replaced by new buildings, though here and there you could still come across a bomb site that was grown over with weeds and littered with rubbish and posters stuck up on billboards, and kids playing in the debris, despite the notices to keep clear.

Jinny couldn't wait to get away and start her new life. St Saviour's and Halfpenny Street weren't much better than these sadly dilapidated houses from outside, but inside it was very different. Even though it was due for a paint-up and some of the basins and toilets were to be renewed, it was far superior to anywhere she'd lived before, the bathroom and tiny kitchen at the nurses' home modern and sparkling clean.

Sandra had told her she could take a bath when she

liked, but it was best to check with the others when they wanted to use it and fit in to a rota so there were no arguments.

'Sometimes it's easier to have a wash in your room,' Sandra told her. 'When I stayed here I found the later in the evening you try the better. Most of the girls use it as soon as they finish work, before they go out. Mind you, it's only Sister Beatrice, Mrs Davies, Rose and Nancy who live here at the moment, but we're looking for another carer so you may have more soon. The others sometimes use the facilities if they have to work late but that doesn't happen often.' Sandra looked round thoughtfully. 'It is rather a luxury for so few these days. I suppose . . . at one time all of the rooms were occupied.'

'Why don't we have as many kids as we used to?' Jinny asked curiously.

'The Board of St Saviour's built a new home on the outskirts of Harlow,' Sandra said. 'I haven't seen it, but Wendy says it's marvellous, lots of fields round it for the children to play . . . sports hall, dormitories and a good bus service to the school, youth clubs . . .'

'That sounds great for them, but surely . . .' Jinny stopped and flushed. 'I mean it's here the kids live and get abandoned or sick . . . isn't it? So it's here they need help first . . .'

Having settled into her room, Jinny found her way to the dining room just as the children came pouring down the stairs and started to rush in, pushing and shoving until Nancy appeared and asked them to form an orderly line. They did so but still continued to push and argue amongst themselves as they queued up to select what they wanted to eat and drink.

'They'll quieten down in a moment,' Nancy said as she saw Jinny lingering on the sidelines, not quite sure what to do. 'You can help Mrs Davies to dispense the cocoa and Ovaltine or hot milk. After that, you can find a place to sit down and eat yourself. Anywhere there's an empty seat. Now is your chance to introduce yourself to the children . . .'

Nancy wandered away to sort out an argument between two boys that looked as if it might develop into a fight, leaving Jinny to join Mrs Davies behind the long counter where supper was set out. It consisted mostly of thin slices of sponge cake, jam tarts and plain biscuits.

Two lads were lingering by the biscuits and Jinny overheard them moaning. 'It used to be homemade biscuits and steamed puddings for supper,' one of them said. 'They're old shop-bought things and they don't taste half as good.'

'The jam tarts are homemade,' Jinny said and offered him the plate. He glared at her for a minute and then took one. 'What sort of biscuits did you use to like?'

'Coconut – and almond ones and ginger ones an' all,' he said and eyed her with more interest. 'Tom likes hot chocolate pudding best and I like the plums wiv custard, but we don't get none of that, nah. You the new kitchen girl, then?'

'Yes, I've come to help in the kitchen and with lots of jobs,' Jinny said and offered him a mug of cocoa. 'I'll ask why we don't have our own biscuits and steam puddings if you like.'

'She'll chop yer ear orf,' the second boy said, glancing

at Mrs Davies with dislike. 'Nancy's the best; she makes all sorts when she's on duty . . .'

Jinny nodded but made up her mind to ask the cook why they didn't make their own biscuits when they were so much better.

'Thank goodness for that,' Mrs Davies said when the line of boys and girls had worked its way through. 'I don't know why they want so much supper when it's only a few hours since they had their tea . . .'

'Growing lads are always hungry, leastwise, that's what Nellie says; her sons used to eat her out of house and home before they went off to the Army,' Jinny replied, eyeing Mrs Davies curiously. She was a woman in her late forties and seemed disgruntled with her lot. 'They like homemade stuff better than shop-bought biscuits . . .'

'I don't always have the time,' Mrs Davies grumbled. 'Nancy gives me a hand sometimes and so does Hannah, but she's leaving – and that Elsa Janes is a lazy good-for-nothing. She went home after tea, because her stomach ached . . .'

'You had a lot to do by yourself,' Jinny sympathised, guessing that the best way to get on with her was to choose her words with care. 'I'll be here now and I'll be able to help you a lot more. I can make a start on the washing-up now if you like. I'll take all the empty plates into the kitchen and wash them . . .'

'You're not due to start until the morning . . .' Mrs Davies seemed uncertain but Jinny just smiled at her. 'Well, if you're sure, it will save me a job.'

Jinny nodded, loaded up the plates and carried the first lot through to the scullery so that she could make a start. There was far too much for one person to do here, and even though Nancy came to give a hand with the wiping up, it took ages to get through all the plates, mugs and dishes.

'Muriel used to have a couple of helpers when we had more children, but Mrs Davies has managed with just the one until now and unfortunately Elsa isn't always reliable . . .'

'I shall be,' Jinny said and felt good inside as she saw Nancy's look of approval. 'I think I'm going to like it here . . .'

'You should ask Staff Nurse Wendy for some cream for your hands,' Nancy told her. 'We usually have some in the kitchen but it keeps disappearing – get some for your room. You don't want to have sore hands.'

'Thanks, I'll ask her,' Jinny said, hesitated, then, 'Do you think Mrs Davies will teach me to cook? I can cook a bit but I'd like to make the steamed puddings and biscuits and cakes the kids enjoy . . .'

'Well, we'll see how things work out,' Nancy said, 'but I was taught by Muriel, our previous cook, and I'll give you a few lessons in your spare time if you like.'

'Thanks ever so. I should like that.' Jinny looked at her a little shyly. She liked the attractive young woman who looked to be in her early twenties. 'I'm so glad Sister Beatrice took me on. I want to make her proud of me . . .'

'Just do the best you can and always act honestly,' Nancy said and sighed as she looked round the kitchens. 'We really need a paint-up in here, but I dread the thought of workmen all over the place.'

'Oh, Mr Thompson seemed pleasant,' Jinny said. 'I saw him just as he was leaving this evening. He said hello and told me who he was and what he was doing . . .'

'Yes, I suppose he's all right,' Nancy said. 'It just upsets the rhythm of our life here . . .'

Jinny wondered at the tone of Nancy's voice. She'd been lovely to her, but it seemed she'd taken the young decorator in dislike . . .

Nancy made sure all the children were settled in their dormitories and that Mavis – one of their part-time carers – had arrived for the night shift before she left via the back entrance and crossed the garden at the rear. She was feeling a little unsettled that evening, and it was all the fault of that decorator. She'd just come from the bathroom in the nurses' home that morning and was still wearing her old dressing robe pulled loosely about her and tied with a soft belt when Mr Thompson had walked up the stairs, surprising her.

Her gasp of dismay on seeing him had been involuntary. She knew he was called Rob and was one of the brothers working on the renovating for both St Saviour's and the nurses' accommodation, and he had every right to be there, but she'd felt his eyes on her and his slow smile had embarrassed her, the appreciation in his eyes as they settled on her long hair hanging down over her shoulders. Nancy's hair was thick and shone like pale silk and she hadn't had it cut for years, twisting it up on top of her head so that it was held neatly in a sort of top knot for work.

'Sorry if I startled you, miss . . .'

'I'm the head carer Nancy Johnson,' she'd replied primly. 'I wasn't aware that you were starting here this morning . . .'

'Actually, it was you I wanted to speak to about the decoration up here,' he'd said, a note of apology in his eyes. 'I saw the kids going into breakfast and I thought I'd just nip in, have a check to see what needed doing most and then ask if you had a preference for the colour scheme?'

'I can't talk to you like this,' Nancy frowned at him. 'Excuse me while I dress. I was up late last night with some new arrivals. Make sure you knock before you enter any of the rooms, some of which may be locked – and then come and see me in the main building. My office is next door to Sister's . . .'

'Yes, Miss Johnson,' he'd answered meekly, but there had been a spark of interest in his eyes that made her shiver inside. Nancy knew Sister Beatrice wouldn't have given this man and his brother the run of the place unless she trusted them, and he had a pleasant friendly look about him – but there was something inside Nancy that wouldn't let her trust any man.

Their interview later had been formal and she'd given him a list of colours that the individual members of staff had asked to have in their own rooms, stressing that it had been decided on a pale cream colour everywhere else.

'We asked the children and no one could agree on a colour scheme, but we suggested that one wall could be done in a medium blue in the boys' dorms and notice boards fixed so that they can pin their pictures up. The girls don't want pink but suggested a pale greenish blue with somewhere to display their treasures. Do you think you could manage that, Mr Thompson?'

'Yes, Miss Johnson,' he'd answered, a twinkle lurking deep in his own bluish green eyes. 'And your own room – do you have a preference?'

Nancy hesitated, then, 'Pale green please,' she said and stood up. 'If there's nothing else, Mr Thompson, I am rather busy . . .'

'Yes, of course you are, and we need to get on,' he'd said, then, 'Most people call me Rob – and I do apologise for upsetting you this morning. I should've checked it was all right for me to go upstairs . . .'

Nancy had felt herself blushing and knew she was making too much of the incident. Decorators had to go everywhere they needed, to move about without hindrance, and any other morning she would already have been at work.

'I was just surprised,' she said. 'You have nothing to apologise for Mr – Rob . . .'

He gave her a breathtaking smile that made her heart jerk suddenly and beat faster than normal. 'Thank you, Miss Johnson. I shall ask everyone when it is convenient to do their rooms . . . I should like to make a start on the boys' landing today, if that suits you?'

'Of course,' Nancy said relaxing, because it was ridiculous to sulk. 'You have your work to do. I'll let Hannah know you'll be about. She's in charge of the boys' dorms this week . . .'

She got up to leave, but as she passed him, he touched her arm. His touch was light and she knew she could break from it with the slightest movement but it sent a frisson of something like fear down her spine, which she knew was stupid. After all these years she ought to have been able to put the past behind her, and she had, but it came back in moments like these.

'Please do not touch me,' she said frostily and saw the disbelief and puzzlement in his eyes, because after all it had been meant only as a delaying tactic, not an intention of force. 'Forgive me, that was rude – did you wish to say something more?'

'Just . . .' He shook his head. 'No, it would have no point. Forgive me . . .'

He'd given her another puzzled look, as if asking what he'd done to make her dislike him so much, and Nancy had felt foolish, because of course he'd done nothing that any normal woman could object to. The trouble was that she wasn't normal where physical contact was concerned; she just didn't like to be touched by a man – any man – and that Nancy knew was a very sad thing, because it meant she could never be married and have children of her own . . .

CHAPTER 7

Ruby's head ached as she looked at herself with dislike in the mirror on the wall of the cloakroom. By no stretch of the imagination did she look herself that morning – she felt like a dead rat the cat had dragged in off the streets – and it was her own fault.

She had no idea what had made her call in at an off-licence and pick up that bottle of white wine on her way home the previous night. It had been a bad day, of course, with two of her girls caught trying to steal sweets from the shop on the corner of Commercial Road, and Sergeant Sallis warning her that if this kind of thing continued, he would be forced to charge the thieves.

'I'm sorry, Miss Saunders,' he'd told her sternly. 'I know you have a difficult job with these kids, but unless you can keep control of them I'll be making a formal complaint to my chief constable and that could result in serious trouble for them – and you.'

'I'm sorry you've had this bother,' Ruby replied stiffly. 'I'll do my best to make sure it doesn't happen again – but I think some of these girls do not deserve a second chance. They would have been better placed in a house of correction in the first place.'

He'd given her an odd look and then left her to it. Ruby had had the girls into her office – a sullen girl of fourteen named Doris and a younger girl with a frightened air who was nicknamed Mouse but whose real name was Emmeline.

'Well, I hope you're properly ashamed of yourselves?' she asked and saw a flicker of fear in Emmeline's eyes but sheer defiance in the older girl's face. 'You're here because you're being punished for making nuisances of yourselves at the home you were placed in, and because the court decided to be lenient with you – but there are other places you could go, unpleasant places that I should be loath to send you to – either of you. Now what have you to say to me?'

'I'm sorry, miss,' Emmeline whispered. 'I didn't mean to do it – but I'm partial to sweets and me dad alus bought me sixpence worth on a Saturday till the day he died . . .'

Ruby felt a flicker of sympathy. It was rotten having no parents and both these girls had come to her from council-run orphanages. They'd been classed as rebellious and ungovernable, and had caused several pounds' worth of damage to their school. Because of that the courts had removed them from the home and placed them here in her care.

'It ain't fair,' Doris muttered. 'Why can't we 'ave a few pence for sweets once a week? Anybody would think we was bloody murderers . . . even the orphans next door 'ave that much . . .'

Looking from one to the other, Ruby knew instantly

that Doris was the ringleader and had no doubt led the younger Emmeline into trouble, both at their previous orphanage and here. If the courts had taken the trouble to examine the case more thoroughly, they would have been split up – and it was clearly what needed to happen.

'You're here to learn discipline and no sweets is one of our rules,' Ruby told them severely. She knew that most of the girls broke that rule whenever they could manage to get hold of a few pennies to buy them, and probably quite a few of them stole when they got the chance, but these two had been found out. Since the rules were already tight, she wasn't sure what she could do to punish them, short of sending them – or one of them – to the remand home. 'Well, this time I'm merely going to send you both to your dorms with no tea or supper – but if it happens again, you will both be sent away somewhere you do not have the freedom to roam the streets and steal from people . . .'

Something in the eyes of both girls made Ruby think of Betty Goodge and what had happened to her. She'd vowed after she was told of the girl's unhappy fate that she would never threaten another girl as she had Betty.

'I'll be good, miss,' Emmeline promised. 'Please don't send me to prison . . .'

Doris stared at her with huge miserable eyes, her whole body rigid with defiance and suppressed anger.

'Do you not realise how fortunate you were to be sent here?' Ruby asked them. 'You could have been sent to a place of correction – and I assure you their rules are much harsher than mine . . .'

'What 'ave we got ter look forward to?' Doris demanded. 'In the last place it was all bloody rules, nuthin' decent to eat, only watery stew and bread and people naggin' at yer all the time . . .'

Ruby stared at her for several seconds and then inclined her head. 'As it happens I agree with you,' she said, 'so I'll tell you what I'm going to do – in future every girl who behaves herself and gets no black marks during the week will have sixpence to spend as she pleases on a Saturday – any transgression of the rules and that privilege will be suspended, not only for the girl who broke the rule, but for everyone . . .'

She dismissed them both, wrote out a notice to that effect and put it on the notice board where all the girls could see it. Her decision was rather clever, Ruby thought, pleased, because the majority of the girls would soon put any defiant girls in their place who were careless enough to break the new code, if they too were made to suffer for the misdemeanour. Still in a mood of good will, she telephoned Miss Sampson's office and asked to speak to her. There was a pregnant pause and then the secretary said in a rather flustered tone, 'I'm sorry, Miss Saunders. Miss Sampson is too busy to speak to you at the moment. Please send her a memo if it's important . . .'

Anger had roared through Ruby as she jammed the receiver back on its stand. Ruth Sampson had always come straight on whenever she'd telephoned before and her rejection was like a slap in the face. She brooded over her wrongs for an hour or more and then, after some soul-searching, went next door to visit Sister Beatrice.

Ruby hated having to ask a favour of the nun. They had never really got on, and after the mistake she'd made over June Miller's foster parents, she always felt uncomfortable when talking to her – but if Miss Sampson wouldn't speak to her, she had no alternative.

Sister Beatrice looked at her impatiently as she entered. She hesitated, and then asked if she could spare a few minutes and reluctantly the nun agreed and Ruby moved nearer to the desk.

'I wondered if you would consider a suggestion I have,' she said tentatively. 'One of my girls . . . I want to move her from the influence of one of the older girls. She came to me because she caused trouble at her previous school and has recently been caught stealing sweets . . .'

'She doesn't sound as if she can be trusted . . .'

'I think if she was moved somewhere she would receive a different kind of care . . .' Ruby floundered, feeling about two inches high. 'Oh, forget it. I shouldn't have asked . . .' She would have left immediately but Sister's voice stopped her.

'Please sit down and tell me how I can help?'

Ruby sat, feeling as if she were back at school instead of the confident young woman well able to hold down a responsible job she actually was. 'Her name is Emmeline but the others call her Mouse – and I think that's the trouble, she's nervous and easily corrupted, but given a proper chance I believe she could do better. The home she came from doesn't have much of a reputation and I thought perhaps if you could take her at that place in Essex . . . away from Doris and the temptations of too many shops . . .'

'Do you have the authority to place her in our care?'

'Yes – well, I normally clear any transfers with Ruth

Sampson,' Ruby admitted, 'but I'm sending her a memo and I don't think she will object . . . I just think Emmeline would have a chance if she gets right away, but if she stays here I may have to send Doris to a remand home instead and I'm reluctant to do it . . .'

'So you do have a heart after all . . .' Ruby stared at the nun, shocked and annoyed but managing to control her temper. 'Forgive me, Miss Saunders, that was rude – but I must admit I had not thought you capable of acting with compassion.' Sister stared at her and Ruby felt uncomfortable under that intent gaze, as if the other woman could see right into her soul. 'Yes, I believe we could arrange that for you. I will telephone Angela Adderbury and see if they will accept her but I feel sure that, like you, Angela will believe the girl deserves a chance of a better life, and she can usually sway the Board to her way of thinking. When she was here she had all the market traders and businessmen falling over themselves to offer us help.'

'Thank you . . .'

'Before you go . . . I was wondering if we might allow some of your more reliable girls to mingle with ours. They could help with the little ones at mealtimes, and perhaps reading stories to them at bedtime – if you thought it might help some of your girls prepare for the future . . .'

'Well, yes, I had wondered if you would allow me to bring my girls here for tea sometimes. I think it might be a little treat for them – and really help to encourage good behaviour . . .'

'An excellent idea, Miss Saunders. Helping vulnerable children may perhaps make them realise that their lot is not so very terrible.' Sister Beatrice was actually smiling. Ruby swallowed her annoyance, because she felt peeved even though she was getting what she wanted. She thanked the nun, made her excuses and left, her pulses racing as she struggled to control her aggrieved feelings. She almost wished she hadn't bothered to approach the nun, but her conscience told her she owed it to the girls. Emmeline, because she'd have a chance of a good life in Halfpenny House, and Doris, because she needn't go to a remand home – and somehow Ruby was wary of sending any of her girls on there.

If Miss Sampson got her way it was the direction the home was going in the future. Ruby had wondered if Sister Beatrice knew anything about what was going on behind her back, but she'd given no sign of it. For some reason that made Ruby feel a bit guilty; although she'd rubbed up against Sister Beatrice a few times, she was beginning to see that she was actually a caring woman.

In a spirit of defiance, she sent a memo to Ruth Sampson to the effect that she'd arranged for Emmeline to be transferred to the Essex home and didn't bother with asking permission. If Ruth Sampson was going to ignore her, two could play at the same game!

So, maybe that was the reason she'd stopped off to buy the wine to eat with the pie and mash she'd bought from the corner chippie. Ruby rarely bothered to cook for herself, because there was always some kind of hot food she could take home from one of London's many shops selling everything from fish and chips to eel pie and curry hot enough to burn your tongue off.

Ruby had been smarting from the humiliation of the

day, miserable because a woman she admired – and let's face it, loved in a way that wasn't returned – had snubbed her. Sister Beatrice's kindness had made her squirm inside, because she felt guilty over being part of a plot to oust her from a job she loved and did so well.

Ruby had thought about going upstairs to Carla's flat and inviting herself for that cup of coffee the girl had offered when she moved in, but something – an inner unease – held her back. Supposing she'd misread the look in Carla's eyes . . . and even if she hadn't, the world frowned on the kind of relationship that Carla seemed to invite. Ruby knew that if she began such an affair its discovery could quite easily lead to the loss of her job. She would probably be considered unfit to have charge of the girls in her care, just because she wanted to be held and kissed by a woman rather than a man. The thought made her frustrated and angry, because for Ruby the love of another woman was as natural as breathing . . . In fact, Ruby felt at odds with the world and fed up with her life – and so she'd drunk the whole bottle of wine. And this morning she felt like death warmed up!

Never again, she groaned as she swallowed two Aspro and drank a glass of water. She was never going to touch wine again as long as she lived . . .

'Well, that is rather splendid of you, to come up and take her down yourself,' Beatrice said to Angela on the telephone. 'And thank you for responding so quickly to my request.'

'You know we all trust your judgement,' Angela said. 'Besides, I think we've had similar cases in the past. It sounds to me as if Emmeline needs some loving care, which is what we always try to give our children – and Mark agrees with me.'

'Yes, well, we all have him to thank for a great deal,' Beatrice said. 'It was his drive and concern for the children that got St Saviour's up and running.'

'So are you getting on better with Miss Saunders?'

'Well, I wouldn't quite say that,' Beatrice replied. 'At least it shows she has a heart . . . I'm afraid I offended her by saying that to her face, but it surprised me and the words were out without my realising . . .'

'That isn't like you.'

'No, but I had been used to thinking her rather a monster, and I suppose it shocked me that she came to me for help. I thought she was just one of those smart modern young women who care for nothing but getting on, but now . . . I think she is very unhappy. She normally doesn't let anyone see it, but it surfaced as she spoke of Emmeline. Her guard went up immediately, of course – but I think perhaps we can begin to understand one another better, and work together for the good of the children. I know her children are difficult . . . but we've had some difficult ones ourselves and with love and trust . . .' Beatrice sighed. 'I can only hope . . .'

'Yes, well, I'll see you next week then. I do need to talk to you face to face because we have important decisions to make,' Angela said. 'Give Miss Saunders the good news and I'll look forward to seeing you and bringing Emmeline back with me.'

Beatrice smiled as she replaced the receiver carefully. It was good that she had some happy news to pass on, she thought as she went down the stairs and out into the street. Children were just starting to come home for their tea, and she saw that some of the girls from the probationary centre were talking to her children. Some of them had actually entered the hall of St Saviour's and she could hear the sound of laughter, though one or two looked at her apprehensively, as if they feared she would be angry because they'd dared to step inside her domain. She nodded as she passed them and entered what had once been her new wing, feeling a pang at its loss – but perhaps it was being put to good use. If her influence could help Miss Saunders to make the right decisions for these girls, perhaps a lot of unhappiness could be saved in the future, especially if Angela's fears came to pass – and that was surely worth the loss of a few beds for her . . .

CHAPTER 8

Andy saw the man he most wanted to avoid hanging round the school gates and hung back, feeling panic as his eyes moved from side to side, wondering how he could avoid passing his step-father.

'You three . . .' Mr Barton, the sports teacher, appeared from nowhere, blocking their path. 'I want volunteers for sorting out the cricket and rounders stuff for Saturday morning. If you all give a hand it won't take more than twenty minutes.'

'I've got to meet my mum,' Sandy Jones said. 'We're goin' ter get some new boots and this is the only time she can go after work.'

'Off you go then,' Mr Barton said. 'What about the rest of you? I'll run you back to St Saviour's afterwards so you're not late.'

'Yes, sir,' both Andy and Keith Roberts, the other lad the master had cornered, agreed with alacrity. The promise of a ride in his old but beautiful sports car would have made them agree to almost anything.

For Andy it was a reprieve. His step-father would give up and go home long before he was finished helping the sports master and since they would be leaving by the back entrance, the Beast wouldn't know he was here. He just hoped he hadn't spotted him amongst the crowd of boys and girls in the school playground.

'Come on then,' Mr Barton said and smiled in his genial way. 'It's a chore but we have to pack the gear up ready to take on the coach with us. You're in the rounders team, aren't you, Roberts'

'Yes, sir,' Keith said and looked pleased. 'Andy is real good at catching balls, sir. You ought to put him in the team too . . .'

The master's dark intelligent eyes centred on Andy's face. 'Would you like to join either the cricket or the rounders team?'

'Yes, sir. Keith is a mate of mine and I'd like to play with him.'

'In that case we'll take you with us on Saturday,' the master said, leading the way into the gym where piles of equipment were waiting to be sorted and packed into canvas bags to make it easier to carry and stow on the bus that was to take them to the fixture with a rival school that weekend.

Keith grinned at him and gave him a little poke in the ribs as they followed Mr Barton's instructions. They soon had all the sports gear stacked and ready to be loaded the next morning. Mr Barton was in good form, cracking jokes and getting stuck into the task himself, looking pleased when they had it done in double quick time.

'Thanks, lads,' he said. 'I'm grateful for the help. I'll run you both home now and don't forget to be bright and early on Saturday morning.'

They thanked him, following eagerly to the red Morgan that was parked at the rear of the school, scrambling into the passenger seat, squeezing up together. Their teacher gave them a nod of approval and shot off at speed, making them both crow with delight as the car gave a throaty roar and its wheels crunched on gravel.

'Wow! I want a car like this when I'm old enough to drive,' Keith cried excitedly.

Andy didn't say anything, but he felt as if he'd reached the gates of heaven and suddenly the world was a golden place. He'd been glad to stay behind because he hadn't wanted his step-father to see him, but now he felt on fire with a new longing. He knew that it wasn't likely a boy like him would ever own a car like this, but he wanted to drive it – and other cars like it. He decided that he would learn to drive as soon as he was old enough and he would find some kind of work that involved cars for a living.

They stopped outside the home and Mr Barton turned to look at them as both boys thanked him for the ride. He grinned and nodded, lifting a hand as he drove away.

'That was fantastic,' Keith said. 'I've always wanted a ride in his car.'

'I hadn't thought it about it much,' Andy replied, 'but it was great. I'd like to drive cars like that for a living . . .'

'Who wouldn't,' Keith said and punched him lightly on the arm. 'You'd need to be good to be a racing driver. Come on, I'll beat you in to tea . . .'

Jinny stood behind the counter as the children walked in for their meal. She saw the group of three, two of whom who had criticised the selection at supper on her first evening and waited for some comment as she saw their faces and the look of surprise. Nancy had spent two hours that afternoon showing Jinny how to make almond biscuits and a Victoria sponge cake. They'd also made gooseberry crumble with custard and there were some squeals of excitement as the kids grabbed for the fresh crispy biscuits and a crumble that looked and smelled gorgeous. Jinny was proud of what they'd managed to produce on Mrs Davies' afternoon off, even though she'd only helped and Nancy was the one responsible for all the lovely food.

'Cor, this is better,' the lad Jinny knew was named Tom said and grinned at her. 'This is Nancy's cooking. She always makes lovely things . . .'

Jinny smiled and agreed, forbearing to tell him that she'd suggested the biscuits and the crumble. It had been just a suggestion; Nancy was the one who had created the little miracle, but Jinny had made some rock cakes herself and she was gratified to see they didn't last long as eager hands reached out for them. Tom ignored them in favour of the crumble and some biscuits as well as the tomato sandwiches Nancy had asked her to make.

'We have to give them some fresh fruit and vegetables, and tomatoes are the one thing most of them like, as long as it's in a sandwich with a little salt, pepper and vinegar. I slice them and season them on a plate first. Don't make the mistake of sprinkling vinegar on the tomatoes once they're on bread . . .' Nancy warned.

Tom took a bite of his sandwich as he moved away, stopped, turned back and took another quickly before they all went. 'Not bad,' he said. 'Did you make them?'

'Nancy showed me how.'

'Thought so,' he mumbled, his mouth full of sandwich. 'You're all right, new girl . . .'

Jinny smiled, because Tom wasn't easy to please. Nancy came up to her as the tables filled and children and staff took their places.

'Doesn't look as if we'll have much waste tonight,' she said, her glance passing along the table. 'I'll have the last of those sandwiches if no one else wants it – and one of those rock cakes. They look good . . . yes, lovely.' She smiled as she bit into it. 'Nan used to make these when I was about your age. She was the head carer here nine years ago and she helped me so much . . .'

Jinny felt pleased because one or two children were coming back for seconds and there wasn't much left. She was just about to take the last rock cake for herself when Tom came up and snatched it from under her nose.

'Jax says these are great,' he said. 'Just like my mum used to make before she died . . .'

'Oh, Tom, I'm so sorry,' Jinny said, feeling a wave of sympathy for the lad she'd thought was always complaining. 'I miss my dad too . . .'

He glared at her and walked off, seeming angry that she'd dared to offer him sympathy. She bit her lip, because she'd wanted to please and believed she had – and now he'd gone cold on her.

Jinny started collecting empty plates and taking them through to the kitchen. She was determined to wash everything before she left that evening, even though she wanted to pop over and see Nellie, who would want to know how she was getting on with her new job . . .

'Do we 'ave ter do this tonight?'

Elsa's sulky tones broke into Jinny's thoughts and she turned to look at the young woman who had spoken. Elsa was nineteen, older than Jinny, but sometimes she acted like a spoiled brat, making faces behind Mrs Davies' back when she asked them to do something difficult or time-consuming. In fact, Jinny thought the other woman spent most of her time watching the clock until it was time to go home.

'You know it can't be left overnight. Besides, we can get this lot done easily if we put our minds to it,' Jinny said. 'I'll wash and you can wipe. Put everything on the table and I'll stack it later.'

'They won't appreciate yer any more if yer stay late every night,' Elsa said but picked up a tea towel and began to wipe the dishes with obvious reluctance. 'You're just a skivvy to them upstairs and don't yer forget it . . .'

Jinny looked at her in amazement, because she'd met with nothing but kindness from everyone who had employed her. 'I'm glad to have a job and somewhere to live,' she said. 'It isn't too much to ask that I do my work properly, is it?'

Elsa sniffed but said no more. Aware that sulking wasn't going to do her any good, she started talking about her current boyfriend who was taking her to the dance at the social hall that weekend.

'Why don't yer come?' she said suddenly. 'It's a bit of fun and we get little enough workin' 'ere . . .'

'I can't dance,' Jinny replied, but felt sad that she had no one to take her. 'Besides, I don't have a partner.'

'Yer can soon pick up a chap,' Elsa said. 'Yer look all right and we all muck in tergevver anyway . . .'

'No, I don't think so, thanks anyway,' Jinny said. She didn't want to play gooseberry with Elsa and her boyfriend, and the thought of picking up a stranger sent chills down her spine. She might end up with someone like Jake walking her home!

Nellie gave her a beaming smile as she told her how the kids had enjoyed the rock cakes she'd taught Jinny to make. 'Well, fancy that,' she said. 'They ain't special, just plain home cooking. I should've thought that fancy cook of theirs could produce better stuff than my rock cakes . . .'

'She's all right cooking dinners and making scrambled eggs and toast for breakfast, but she doesn't like making cakes and biscuits or puddings for the kids' tea and supper. She says they only need a biscuit at supper and thinks out of a packet is good enough . . .'

'It's more'n a lot of kids get,' Nellie said with a sniff. 'I reckon them kids wot complained were 'avin' yer on, love.'

Jinny considered for a moment, then shook her head. 'No, Nancy told me the last cook used to make everything herself. She thought it was cheaper and better for them – you can get them to eat fruit if you put it in pies and crumbles . . .'

'We 'ad to make do with bread and scrape in my young days,' Nellie said, 'and durin' the war we 'ad wot we could get . . .'

'I remember everythin' bein' short,' Jinny agreed. 'But because we had to make do with less then doesn't mean kids should go short now, does it?'

'No, it don't,' Nellie agreed with a laugh. 'I reckon

them kids of yourn will be spoiled rotten if you 'ave anythin' ter do wiv it . . .'

'Oh, Nellie, you know you don't mean that,' Jinny said and laughed delightedly, because she could see the twinkle in her friend's eye. 'They've been through so much some of them. Sandra – she's Sister Beatrice's secretary and helps her with lots of things – well, she was telling me about children who've been brought to us . . . from parents who abuse them and beat them, orphans who've been on the streets until they were found and brought to us . . . and kids who've run away from other homes. Sandra told me that some places they treat the kids somethin' awful . . .'

'I've heard about places like that,' Nellie agreed with a dark look. 'It's disgusting if yer ask me – the councils that run 'em should take more care when they pick their workers. And they ought to inspect 'em an' all . . .'

'St Saviour's is run by a charity and they've got another home in Essex – on the outskirts of Harlow – so Sandra said. Her son was sent there when she was in trouble and he ran away. Archie says it isn't anywhere near as nice as St Saviour's. He doesn't live at the home now but he works on the market and visits his mum sometimes and comes to the kitchen afterwards for a chat . . .'

'You'd think folks would know better . . .' Nellie said. 'St Saviour's has always been known as a place of hope – leastwise, since that Sister Beatrice took over. It was the fever hospital once and people only went there to die . . . that's what the old folk used to say.'

'I like Sister Beatrice,' Jinny said. 'She can be stern. I saw her tellin' one lad off for running in the corridors, but she's been real good to me and Nancy says her bark is worse than her bite.'

'She 'elped many a poor family out after the war when things were bad,' Nellie replied and nodded. 'It looks as if yer've landed on yer feet there, love.'

'Yes, I think so,' Jinny smiled happily. 'I miss you, Nellie – shall we go to see Elvis next week? I've got Monday night off.'

'I'd like that,' Nellie said. 'It was lovely to see yer, lass, but be careful if yer go next door to yer ma. Jake don't get any sweeter. Yer ma was sportin' a black eye again this mornin'.'

'He's a brute. Ma should throw him out . . .' Jinny glanced in the direction of her mother's house. 'I thought he might have gone . . .'

'Not likely. 'E's got 'is feet under the table and knows where 'is bread's buttered. While she lets 'im come and go and don't ask for nuthin' 'e'll treat her like dirt – but that's 'er choice. If 'e lays a finger on you, 'e'll 'ave me ter deal wiv. And Bert would give 'im a clout an' all . . .'

'Oh, Nellie, I do love you,' Jinny said and threw her arms about her. 'I'd better go. They like us to be in before ten thirty and it will take me a while to get a bus . . .'

'Yeah, well, I'm walkin' yer to the bus stop. The mood that Jake is in, 'e might do anythin' if 'e sees yer. 'E's been scowling at me ever since yer left . . .'

'Why should you have to come out?' Jinny said. 'I'll be all right, Nellie. I've got a whistle in my pocket and I'll blow it if he comes near. It's a police whistle Sandra gave me and she says it will put the wind up anyone who tries to come after me.'

Nellie looked sceptical, but Jinny wasn't going to let her walk her to her bus stop. If she showed Jake she was frightened of him, he would grow bolder and she'd never be free of him.

'Well, if yer set on it,' Nellie said and Jinny bent to kiss her cheek.

Nellie stood at her door watching until Jinny was out of the little courtyard. Jinny hadn't seen any sign of Jake and was feeling confident as she approached her bus stop. A billboard was advertising a film called *The Curse of Frankenstein* which had been released earlier that summer and she smiled at the lurid pictures until her bus arrived. She saw it coming just at the same moment as she spotted Jake reeling drunkenly from side to side of the pavement and knew that he'd spotted her. Jumping on the bus as it slowed to a halt, she made her way to the front and saw that Jake was watching it draw away, a look of angry frustration on his face. He raised his fist and shook it at her and a shiver went down her spine, because she knew that he was still vengeful and if he'd caught her he might well have tried to drag her into the dark alley . . .

Jinny wasn't sure why Jake still hated her. She'd caused him some pain but that surely wasn't enough to make him so vengeful . . .

'Been to see Nellie then?' A voice she knew well spoke as the man sat down next to her. 'I asked her when you were comin' but she said she didn't know.'

'She didn't,' Jinny confirmed, getting out sixpence for the fare. 'I told her I would go when I could and I wanted to tell her how I was getting on at work.'

'Is it all right?' Micky asked, looking at her seriously.

'You were keen to get the job – are you pleased now it's yours?'

'I love it,' Jinny answered honestly and told him that Nancy had spent the afternoon teaching her to cook.

Micky nodded, a smile lurking at the corners of his mouth as she described the kids' reaction to their tea. 'Yeah, lucky devils,' Micky said. 'I never got nuthin' as good as that when I was a kid – nor did you, did yer?'

'Not after Dad died,' Jinny agreed. 'When he was alive Mum used to cook nice food when she could get it . . . but we couldn't buy lots of stuff in the war.'

'Not unless you knew where to get it,' Micky said and grinned. 'My old man used to bring stuff home sometimes – extra sugar and butter, meat . . . fell off a back of a lorry, that's what he said . . .'

'It was pinched.' Jinny pulled a wry face. 'Pinching stuff is wrong, Micky. I know loads of people did it then . . . or at least bought from the black market when they knew it had to be pinched, but things were hard then. We can buy stuff in the shops now – and wages are better too.'

'Yeah, my old man knew they were pinched and 'e paid for it when they caught 'im,' Micky said with a wry look. 'And so did Ma . . . and us kids. Wiv 'im in prison we never 'ad a penny in the house. Thievin' is a mug's game. There's other ways to make money without pinching what belongs to others . . .'

'What do you do?' Jinny asked, gazing up at him with interest. 'I've always wondered.'

'Oh, a bit of this and a bit of that,' he said with a grin. 'I'm not sayin' I'm a saint, but I ain't a thief . . .

I deal in stuff, see – and I help a few folk out when they need it, deliverin' and runnin' errands . . .'

'Good, I'm glad of that.' Jinny drew a breath of relief. She liked Micky and she would have hated to think he was a petty thief. 'You seem to earn a decent living anyway.'

Micky chuckled and nodded. 'Yeah, I do all right. I'm goin' ter be a rich man one day, Jinny Hollis – you just wait and see . . .'

He got up as the bus drew to its stop one halt before hers and sent her a wicked look as he jumped off. Jinny lifted her hand to wave goodbye, but he was already turning away, walking into a dark alley, his mind clearly elsewhere. He still hadn't told her what he was doing to earn the money for decent clothes and the motorbike he'd told her of but never seemed to ride, but it wasn't really her business to ask. A faint unease hung over her as she thought that he was keeping his secrets for a reason. He might not be a thief but perhaps what he was doing wasn't quite legal . . .

Jinny sighed and got up as her bus slowed up just down the road from St Saviour's. She got down and ran the last few steps towards the home, wanting to get in before the gates were locked, because otherwise she would have to ring for admittance. Some of the nurses had a key but she hadn't been trusted with one yet . . .

CHAPTER 9

Rose stopped to smile as she saw Rob painting the walls in the downstairs hall. His brother Nick was with him and they were both wearing paint-spattered overalls. Rob paused as he saw her.

'How are you today, Sister Rose?'

'Very well, thanks, Rob,' she said. 'How are you getting on – nearly finished here by the looks of it?'

'We've got a few doors and some skirting to paint here and then this bit is finished,' Rob said nodding at his brother. 'Nick just has a couple windows to fix and a few jobs in the kitchen then he'll be off to the next job . . .'

'I've repaired your cloakrooms and the bathroom taps and I've mended the leak in the roof,' Nick said. 'I've just got to fix the sink in the kitchen – but your Mrs Davies won't let me in there until she's finished her work so I've been giving Rob a hand . . .'

'Mrs Davies ought to let you get on with your work. It isn't fair to keep you hanging around . . .' Rose said. Nick was a few years older than his brother and his hair was much darker, but she thought he looked more distinguished and extremely attractive, his grey eyes seeming to hold hers.

'It's all right. I've been doing a bit of rubbing down for Rob,' Nick said. 'I'm in no hurry because I'll be finished here tonight and I couldn't start a new job today. Rob is the one with the big job to finish . . .'

'I'd better get on then . . .' Rose started to go on by but Nick made an urgent sound in his throat and his brother grinned.

'Nick is having a little party next Friday,' Rob called after her and she looked back. 'We were wondering if you and some of the other girls would like to come?'

'It's for Maudie,' Nick explained, an oddly shy expression in his eyes now. 'She's been coming in most days to do the housework since my wife died. She's getting married in September and I wanted to do something nice for her . . . but I'm not sure who to invite . . . I've got out of the habit of making friends . . .'

'Nick has got a nice garden . . . so we'll probably be out there most of the time . . .' Rob said. 'Say you'll come, Rose – and perhaps some of your friends will come too?'

'Have you asked anyone else yet?'

'Just Nurse Wendy,' Nick said. 'She wasn't sure but said she would let Rob know . . .'

'Well, I'll come,' Rose said and smiled at them. 'And I'll ask some of the others, but some will be on duty.'

'That's great,' Nick replied. 'Thanks, Rose.'

Rose nodded and went on up the stairs. Wendy was getting ready to leave and picked up her jacket and bag, pausing when Rose asked if she was going to the party.

'Are you going?' Rose said she was and Wendy nodded, 'I wasn't sure we could both go, but Paula says she'll stand in for me that evening. It would be nice to share an evening out with you, Rose.'

With just three nurses and Sister Beatrice, Rose and Wendy generally took the night shifts between them, because Paula normally preferred to work just a few hours in the mornings.

'I think it will be a pleasant evening . . .' Rose agreed.

However, she was surprised when Jinny came bouncing up to her at teatime and told her that she too had been invited and asked to bring a friend.

'I think I'm supposed to take a boyfriend,' Jinny said. 'I don't have one so I asked Nancy but she says she'll be working . . . but there is someone. I'm not sure if he would want to come. We're just casual friends.'

'I hardly know Nick or Rob,' Rose said. 'I'm not romantically involved with anyone. Ask your friend and see what he says. If he says yes you'll know he wants to see you more often.'

Jinny looked hesitant, then nodded. 'Yes, I could or I could ask my friend Nellie . . .'

'Well, I'm sure Rob and his brother won't mind,' Rose said, hesitated, then, 'I thought we might go to the pictures one evening – if you'd like to, and perhaps you'd like to come to my home one Sunday for lunch?'

'Oh yes, I should,' Jinny said, flushed with pleasure, because it was nice to make friends and all the staff had been lovely to her. 'I'm taking Nellie to see Elvis at the pictures this week, but I'd love to come to the flicks with you another day.'

'We'll arrange it,' Rose said and moved off. It was the custom for the staff to sit with the children for meals: Rose chose to sit next to Andy and his sister

Beth, because she was a little worried about the girl who had seemed pale and listless earlier. She hoped the child wasn't coming down with a nasty illness, and suspected it was more a case of her feeling nervous. Andy was perfectly happy, but Beth hadn't settled yet, and as Rose joined them she heard him telling his sister that he was going to play rounders with his school team the next day.

'Mr Barton said he would give me a trial,' he said and grinned at Rose as she joined them. 'He's got a great sports car and he gave me and Keith a ride in it 'cos we helped get the rackets and stuff packed for him. It goes really fast and I want to drive cars like that one day . . . like Stirling Moss. He's a real good driver so Mr Barton says . . .'

Rose smiled encouragingly, letting Andy tell them how he wanted to work with cars and eventually drive them.

'I asked Mr Barton about becoming a racing driver,' he said earnestly. 'He said if I learned to become a mechanic I could get a job with a racing team like Ferrari or Lotus, and perhaps try out for them – but first I have to learn to drive. 'Course I'm not old enough yet, but when I am I'm going to take lessons. Mr Barton says that he has a friend who teaches people to drive and he doesn't charge much – at least, he wouldn't charge me much, because I'm a St Saviour's kid . . .'

'Well, you need to be seventeen first,' Rose said with a smile, 'but if you work hard at school and try for an apprenticeship as a mechanic I'm sure you will manage it. Sister Beatrice might arrange that for you when you're fifteen . . .'

Andy looked at her and then at his sister, who was making a choking sound. 'What's the matter, Beth – are you going to be sick again?'

She nodded, jumped to her feet and ran from the dining room. Rose got up immediately. Andy rose too but she told him to carry on with his tea.

'I'll look after her, it's my job.'

'She's been sick twice but didn't want to tell anyone . . .'

Rose followed Beth to the cloakroom and heard her being sick. When Rose entered, she was kneeling and retching, hanging her head over the toilet, but nothing more came up.

Rose pulled the chain, took her through to the basins and washed her face. Beth looked at her woefully and gave a little wail.

'My tummy aches,' she said 'and I feel really, really bad all over . . .'

'How long have you felt this way?' Rose asked, placing a hand against her hot forehead, because Wendy had thought the girl was getting over the period of hunger and deprivation she'd endured, but now it seemed that wasn't so. 'Yes, you do have a temperature. We'd better put you to bed in the isolation ward. Don't worry, you have it all to yourself and I'll be there to look after you until Wendy comes on later . . .'

They left the cloakroom together just as Nick was walking towards them.

'Feeling sick again, is she?' he asked. 'I saw her retching in the garden just now when I was fixing the pantry window . . . I asked if she was all right but she ran away.'

'Yes, she's poorly . . .' Rose said and nodded to him, noting that Beth shrank to her side, as if she needed protection. Nick had smiled at her in a kind way so perhaps it was men in general that frightened the little girl?

Rose walked her to the ward, by which time she was truly concerned for the child who was looking very unwell.

She put her in a nightdress and tucked her up in bed, then gave her a few sips of cool water and left her to rest while she rang for the doctor. Doctor Morgan's receptionist said he was busy delivering a baby but the new doctor, Doctor Henderson, would be along in a few minutes.

'Thank you,' Rose said and replaced the receiver. She went back to Beth, who was burning up and obviously had a nasty fever. The poor little child had clearly been suffering but hadn't wanted to make a fuss. Rose suspected that Beth had learned not to ask for attention or cry at home, though Andy still wouldn't tell them the name of their brutal step-father, because he was afraid of reprisals if he reported the way they'd been treated to the Welfare.

Filling a small bowl with cool water, Rose began to bathe the little girl's forehead with her cloth, then down her neck and arms, hoping to reduce the temperature. She looked for a rash but could find none and was anxious because she couldn't see any reason for the vomiting and fever.

'Doctor will be here soon,' she told Beth. 'We'll soon have you better then, Beth dear.'

Beth looked at her pitifully and clung to her hand

and Rose's heart caught. She cared for the children she nursed and this little girl had touched her heart, because she was so brave and yet so damaged and hurt. Rage boiled in her at the man who had treated both Beth and her brother so badly and she thought of what she would do to him if she ever did confront him – but of course she couldn't stick knives into him or boil him in oil.

'Sister Rose?' A man's voice made her turn with a start, because she'd been lost in her thoughts. 'Is this the young lady with a nasty fever?'

'Doctor Henderson? Yes, this is Beth. She has been sick more than once and she has a fever . . .'

'Then we'd better have a look at her. Can you lift her nightdress, nurse? I want to examine her tummy please . . .'

Rose did so and saw Beth's eyes widen in fear. She squeezed her hand reassuringly. 'Doctor just wants to make sure you have no lumps in your tummy, Beth. He won't hurt you, I promise.'

Beth nodded, but her hand trembled and she flinched as the doctor began to press gently round her tummy. He looked concerned, his eyes meeting Rose's in inquiry, and she nodded slightly.

'Your tummy is fine, Beth,' he said very gently. 'May I please have a look at your chest? I promise to warm my stethoscope and be gentle.'

She nodded slowly, still wary but clearly understanding that he did not intend to hurt her. He listened to her chest and then pressed her ribs slightly, frowning as he felt her wince and flinch.

'That hurts you, doesn't it, Beth? Did you fall – or did someone hurt you?'

Beth stared at him in silence, a tear slipping down her cheek.

'He kicked her in the ribs after knocking her down the other week, before we ran away,' Andy's voice said from the doorway. 'She hasn't been right since but she wouldn't tell me what was wrong . . . she's afraid to tell. I said we mustn't tell anyone about the Beast. He's our step-father and he made Beth do all the housework, half-starved us and beat us if we disobeyed him . . . that's why we ran away.'

'Have the police been informed?' Doctor Henderson asked and Rose shook her head.

'Andy was afraid he might come after them if the police didn't lock him up. He thought they might not believe his story.'

'They will believe me, Andy,' Doctor Henderson said, looking stern and yet managing to sound encouraging. 'If you tell me I shall give them my report on your sister who has obviously been beaten and ill-treated – and if you'll let me examine you I may be able to see where you've been beaten in the past. If I put my report in they will lock this beast up, believe me.'

Andy hesitated, then lifted his head to look into the doctor's eyes. 'All right, I'll tell you, because he was hanging about outside my school the other night and I know if he sees me he'll follow me here and then he'll grab us.'

Doctor Henderson turned to Rose. 'Beth has bruising on her ribs and she is also bruised inside, which is causing the nausea. These injuries do not always present themselves immediately but this must have been building up for a while. I'm going to prescribe some medicine for her and I'm going to admit her to hospital, because I think one of her ribs is damaged and may have caused an infection.' He smiled down at Beth. 'You'll be quite safe in hospital, Beth. One of your carers can come with us and I'll visit you a little later to see how long you need to stay in hospital – but don't worry about your step-father. He'll never hurt you again, I promise . . .'

'His name is Arthur Phillips,' Andy said suddenly. 'Dad's name was Harris and Mum's name was Mary Harris until she married the Beast . . . He were horrible to her and made her ill and when she died he turned on us.'

'And where did you live?' Doctor Henderson asked, writing everything down on his pad. He nodded and made a note of the address. 'I'm going to call an ambulance to take Beth in – is there someone who could go with her, nurse?'

'Yes, I think Nancy will,' Rose said and smiled at him. 'I'll go and ask her, she's just next door giving the children drinks . . .'

'Good.' Doctor Henderson turned to Andy. 'You've taken good care of your sister, Andy, but now I'm going to make sure she gets better – and I want to thank you for trusting me.'

'You're all right,' Andy said and grinned. 'Mr Barton told me you had to trust people a little if you want to get things done – he's our sports master at school. I told him about the Beast today and he said it would be best to go to the police. I was thinking about it, but they might not have believed me . . .'

'They will listen to me, I promise . . .' Doctor Henderson turned as Rose and Nancy entered the ward together. 'Ah – I believe you must be Nancy. Will you accompany this young lady in the ambulance please?'

'Yes, of course,' Nancy said and smiled. 'I shall be pleased to go with Beth – and I'll wait to hear what they have to say.'

'Good.' He looked down at Beth and smiled in his gentle, yet strong way. 'You're not frightened now, Beth?' She shook her head. 'The hospital will soon find out why you're feeling so ill and we'll make it better.'

'Thank you . . .' Beth whispered and looked at Andy. 'Are you coming too?'

'I need to examine your brother first,' Doctor Henderson told her. 'Be a brave girl and go with Nancy and I'll bring Andy to see you later this evening – all right?'

She nodded and Rose helped her out of bed, slipping her feet into her shoes and popping a robe on over her nightdress. She put an arm about her and sat her in a chair to wait for the ambulance men to come while Doctor Henderson took Andy to the other end of the room and asked him to remove his shirt. He examined him and was just telling him to dress when the ambulance men arrived with a stretcher to take Beth. She gave her brother a pathetic wave but then Nancy held her hand as they went out and she lay back trustingly.

'She will be fine now, Andy,' Doctor Henderson said. 'I wanted her to go in by herself because I need to talk to you about her and I would rather she didn't hear what I have to say . . .'

Andy nodded, looking grave. 'You want to know if the Beast assaulted her – in a dirty way . . .'

'Yes,' Doctor Henderson said. 'I didn't do an internal

examination because she was too upset, but if she was assaulted we shall have to do it to present the evidence. I do not want to upset her unless it is necessary . . .'

'I don't think he did that to her,' Andy said. 'He hit her and made her do all the work but he didn't rape her, because she would've told me. Beth tells me everything – and she doesn't know what that is . . .'

'You're sure she would've told you?'

'Yes, I am.' Andy's voice was strong. 'I don't think he can . . . Mum told me he wasn't like a normal man, because of an accident he'd had when he was in the war. She didn't know why he married her but I do . . . he wanted the house and the money Dad left her . . .'

'Your father left her a house and money?'

'The house isn't much, but there was an insurance policy. Dad took it out two years before he died . . . said it would keep us safe if anything happened to him but it didn't . . .'

'Worked the opposite by attracting the wrong sort,' Doctor Henderson nodded. 'So that's why he treated you the way he did . . . didn't want you claiming anything from your father's estate. Of course it depends how it was left . . .'

'Don't know what you mean; it was Mum's . . .'

'Yes, but did your father leave her a life interest and then pass it on to his children?'

'You mean when Mum died it should've come to us . . .' Andy nodded slowly. 'I wondered why he took us. He never liked us . . . but it would've been the only way he could get what Dad left . . . if he left it that way . . .'

'It is a possibility and might explain why he treated you like slaves.'

''Cos he wanted us to die and then he'd have it all to himself . . .'

'Perhaps. I've no proof of that, and neither have you, so confine yourself to what you know when the police come to interview you – and they will after I tell them about Beth's injuries. In the meantime I'll look into things . . . if you will trust me to do it?'

'Yeah, thanks – and thanks for being nice with Beth . . .'

'I don't understand how anyone could be other than nice with your sister,' Doctor Henderson said. He turned to Rose. 'This young man has some old bruising, but it doesn't seem to have gone inward on him. I shall leave him in your care – and be in touch quite soon. Good evening, Sister Rose . . . and Andy.'

'Thank you,' Rose and Andy answered together.

'He's all right,' Andy said as the door closed behind the doctor. 'I'm glad I told him. When I saw my stepfather outside the school I knew he wouldn't give up – and I told Mr Barton this morning. He said to tell the police and I was going to ask Sister Beatrice, but now . . .'

'She will be very pleased,' Rose said. 'You don't feel sick or anything?'

'Just hungry. I left my tea to come and see what was happening . . .'

'Then I'll ask Jinny to get you something,' Rose said. 'Come down to the kitchen now and we'll see what's going . . . I could do with a sandwich myself . . .'

CHAPTER 10

Rose noticed they were out of tea in the staff room and went to the cash box they kept for supplying their own drinks and biscuits. Once the kitchen had supplied them with the basics and they'd only had to pay for extras like better coffee or a nice cake, but since Mrs Davies arrived she'd told them they would have to buy their own tea and biscuits.

Opening the cash box, Rose frowned, because she was sure there had been three ten-shilling notes and several half-crowns as well as some shillings and sixpences. Now there were only two ten-shilling notes and the change. She took two half-crowns and made a note in the book in the drawer to say it was for a packet of tea. Closing the drawer, she decided that she must have been mistaken. No one would take a penny of the money, because all the staff contributed and they'd agreed that if they had enough later in the year it would be used to buy treats for Christmas and little gifts for the kids.

She shook her head, forcing back the suspicion that pilfering had been going on for a while. Rose had wondered a couple of times whether a few bob was missing, but sometimes one of the staff brought in a packet of biscuits and forgot to make a note that they'd taken a shilling or two for them – although ten shillings was rather a lot.

She wondered if one of the girls from the probationary centre next door had nipped in and taken it. They weren't supposed to visit St Saviour's, except on a weekend for a special tea , but it was always possible . . . but no, Rose was letting her suspicious nature get the better of her.

It wouldn't do to say anything about it, because she couldn't be sure what ought to be in the cash box. Everyone was supposed to put in two bob a week but it was a voluntary thing and some of the staff couldn't always afford it – and Rose sometimes put in extra, as did Wendy and Sandra.

It would be more efficient if every penny was recorded in and out, but everyone was so busy and they'd always been able to trust each other. Rose thought it was awful if they couldn't do that and was reluctant to be the one to raise suspicions.

No, she wouldn't say anything for the moment, but she'd have a word with Sandra and suggest that they sort it out a bit. For the moment things would go on as they were, because no one wanted to be stuck with the responsibility of keeping accounts . . .

Jinny visited the market on Saturday hoping to see Micky and ask him to the party but first she went to the stall where she'd bought her tweed skirt and handed over her ten-shilling note, to pay what she owed for her skirt.

'Yer don't 'ave ter pay it all in one go,' Dave said and grinned at her. 'If Micky says yer all right that's good enough fer me.'

'I'd rather pay,' Jinny said and smiled shyly because he was looking at her as if he liked what he saw. 'I'm going to save up because I shall want a new coat in the autumn . . . and I'll come to you first.'

'You trust Dave to find you somethin' decent,' he said. 'I'll treat you right, luv.'

'Thanks,' she said. 'Have you seen Micky this morning?'

''E were about earlier. Can I give 'im a message?'

'I was going to ask him to a party for Friday next week,' Jinny said and felt herself blush. 'I've been asked to take a friend and I don't know anyone else . . .'

'Yer know me,' Dave said cheekily. 'I'll come wiv yer if Micky won't – but yer can ask 'im yerself, 'cos he's comin' now.'

Jinny turned as Micky sauntered up to her, dressed in a striped navy suit, blue shirt and the inevitable crepe-soled shoes. He looked like a Teddy Boy but wasn't rude like many of them who had been labelled by the press as louts for tearing up cinema seats and generally making trouble on the streets. He grinned at her as he came to join them.

'Buyin' more clothes?' he asked and glanced at Dave who nodded.

'Just paying what I owe,' she corrected. 'I'm going to save for a good coat for the winter and I need some more shoes. I took my best ones for work, because they're comfortable.'

Micky nodded as Dave smiled slyly. 'She was lookin' fer yer, Micky lad – lucky you!'

'Lookin' fer me?' Micky regarded her with new interest.

'I've been invited to a party in a garden, I think. They said I could bring someone so I thought of you . . . do you want to come on Friday? It's at half-past seven . . .'

Micky hesitated, then inclined his head. 'Yeah, I don't mind – what sort of folk are they?'

'I was asked by Rob Thompson,' Jinny said. 'His brother Nick is a builder and he's having a party for the woman that cleans his house.'

'Yeah, I know Rob and Nick,' Micky said and grinned. 'I've done a bit of business with him. Yeah, I don't mind goin' to that sort of party . . . We'll take 'em a bottle of plonk . . . I can't be doin' with posh folks.'

'They wouldn't ask me if it was posh,' Jinny said and giggled, because she suddenly felt excited. 'I didn't know who to ask . . .'

'I said she could ask me if yer didn't want to go,' Dave said and then went quiet as Micky shot a look at him. 'Only joking, mate. I know she's yours . . .'

'Yeah and don't yer forget it,' Micky hissed. 'Come on, Jinny. I'll take yer for a coffee or some fish and chips if yer like . . .'

She hesitated, because she didn't want him taking for granted that she was his girl, but then she gave in because she wanted him to take her to the party – and she did like him.

'All right,' she said. 'I'm not on duty until four this afternoon so we'll have fish and chips if you like – as long as you let me pay half . . .'

'Please yerself,' he said and winked at Dave. 'See yer later, mate. Tell yer father I'll be over same time as usual . . .'

Dave nodded, watching as they walked off in the direction of the fish and chip café. Glancing back, Jinny thought she caught a flash of disappointment in his face, but he turned to serve a customer with a smile and she couldn't be sure she hadn't imagined it . . .

Inside the café there was a queue for the takeaway meals, but further in there were several tables empty. Micky told her which one to get for them and stopped to put a coin in the jukebox, grinning as Elvis started singing his hit song.

'We'll have fish and chips and peas,' he told her as he sat down, 'and I'm havin' a Coke, what about you?'

'I'd like a dandelion and burdock if they've got any,' Jinny said. 'If not, I'll have a Vimto.'

'OK – and I'm payin',' Micky said firmly. 'Just so you know – when Micky Smith takes a girl out he pays . . .'

Jinny nodded, because she couldn't make a fuss now, but she would have to be careful about letting him take her out too often, or he would think she was his . . .

Jinny screamed as Elvis sang to the girl he loved on screen, hearing the screams, sighs and gasps from rows of adoring fans behind them. Nellie had wanted to see *Love Me Tender* again, and she had tears slipping down her cheeks as the romantic story came to its inevitable end.

'Oh, that was so lovely,' Nellie said as the lights went up and everyone started hunting for shoes, jackets and anything else they'd let slip from their grasp as they lost themselves in the story. 'It was real good of you to bring me, Jinny. A proper treat that was . . .'

'You deserve it,' Jinny told her. 'I don't know what I

should've done if you hadn't been there for me, Nellie. Besides, I liked seeing the film myself and you're my friend.'

They left the warmth of the Gaumont cinema and went out into the street; it was cooler now because there was a hint of rain in the air and they hurried to the nearest bus shelter and stood under it as the skies opened and it started to pour.

'You're goin' ter get soaked,' Nellie said, looking at Jinny in her skirt and short jacket. 'At least I've got me mac . . .' They saw a bus coming but it wasn't the one Nellie needed. 'You get on this, Jinny, no point in coming back wiv me. It will take yer back to St Saviour's – and I'll wait for mine . . .'

'I'll come back with you . . .' Jinny started to argue but Nellie pushed her forward and she got on, waving to her friend before going to sit down. Craning to look back at Nellie she felt uncomfortable at leaving her there waiting for a bus in the rain, though she knew it made sense on a night like this, but she would rather have seen her friend inside her home.

It was still raining hard when Jinny got off the bus just a few yards from St Saviour's. She ran towards it, not noticing the figure that had descended from the bus a few seconds after her, and went through the gate at the same time as Nurse Wendy who had just arrived for her shift and obligingly unlocked it.

'Awful night, isn't it?' Jinny said. 'It started to pour as we waited for the bus.'

'I shall be glad to get in,' Wendy said. 'I missed my usual bus and had to walk part of the way and I'm soaked . . .'

'I got wet too . . .'

Jinny made a dash across the garden and Wendy entered St Saviour's through the back door, the gate shutting with a clang behind them, locking itself.

From outside in the darkness a man stood looking at the forbidding front of the children's home. So that was where the little bitch had disappeared to; it was his lucky night and he'd hardly believed his luck when she'd jumped on the bus like that, walking past him without even seeing him. An unpleasant smile touched his mouth. He'd been trying to make that old hag Nellie tell him where she'd disappeared to but she was stubborn. Now he didn't need her help. She'd bad-mouthed him a few times and shook dust over him, the cow, but he didn't need her any more and he might teach her a little lesson . . . but nothing like the one he was going to teach that bitch who had dared to think she could escape him.

He was smiling as he turned to walk away. He might have grabbed her then if that nurse hadn't come up so quickly out of the murky night, but there was no hurry. Now that he knew where she was he could think about what he was going to do . . . think about how to make her suffer the most . . .

'Are you looking forward to the party?' Kelly asked before she left at six that Friday evening. Kelly was one of the carers and Jinny thought she seemed a friendly girl, popping into the kitchen for a chat when she had a little free time.

'Yes, very much,' Jinny answered the friendly carer with a smile. 'I'm off in half an hour and Micky is going to meet me on the corner at seven and then we'll go together. It's the second time I've been out this week . . .'

'Wendy told me she met you coming in late on Monday night.'

'I took Nellie to see Elvis at the Gaumont; it was lovely,' Jinny said. 'Have you seen it?'

'Yes, we went when it came out last year, but I'm looking forward to the new one now. I read about it somewhere and it's called *Jailhouse Rock* I think . . .'

Jinny nodded and got on with her task of washing the tea things. Elsa and Mrs Davies were doing the supper this evening and the other girl wasn't very happy about it, even though she'd finished early three nights that week.

'Some people have all the luck,' she'd grumbled when Jinny told her she was going to a garden party. 'I never get invited anywhere nice – all my bloke wants to do is drink down the pub and play darts with a load of his mates. They never stop talking about football. I hardly get a look in once they've bought me a lemonade shandy . . .'

'Why not go out with someone else then?' Jinny suggested, but all she'd got in return was a sour look.

Forgetting her, Jinny finished her work and glanced at the time. She would just have time to wash and change into her best skirt and blouse and meet Micky at the street corner.

Emerging from the side entrance at three minutes to seven, Jinny turned in the direction she'd arranged to meet Micky, but she hadn't gone more than three steps when someone grabbed her arm and she turned to find herself staring into Jake's cold eyes. His eyes were bloodshot and the stubble on his face told her he hadn't shaved for days.

'You!' she cried, shocked and stunned, because she'd thought herself safe here. 'Why can't you leave me alone?'

'I've come to see you, Jinny,' he muttered, leaning towards her so that she could smell his stale breath. 'Ain't yer pleased to see me?'

'No, I don't want to see you or talk to you,' Jinny said. 'Let go of my arm. I'm in a hurry. I'm meeting someone . . .'

'Too bad,' Jake muttered. 'Yer ma's sick and she wants yer. She threatened to throw me out if I didn't get yer to come back . . . so that's where yer comin' . . .'

Jinny was sure he was lying and yet she halted uncertainly. 'Why? What's wrong with her?'

'Yer'll know that when yer come, won't yer?' He gripped her arm tightly, trying to pull her with him, but Jinny resisted. She didn't trust him and she wasn't going to let him drag her away.

'Let me go or I'll scream. I know things about you, Jake, and if you hurt me I'll go to the police,' she threatened and saw his face tighten with anger. Her threat had been an impulse because she really knew very little, but Jake thought she did and he was furious. Jinny saw Micky standing at the corner of the street and breathed a sigh of relief. The sight of him gave her courage and she kicked out at Jake's shin, causing him to let go of her as he gave a howl, of rage more than pain. In that instant she ran towards Micky as fast as she could and he, seeing she was in trouble, came forward to meet her, putting his arm about her protectively. He looked at her face and then back at Jake.

'I'll kill the bastard . . .'

'No, Micky,' Jinny said. 'I'm not hurt. He wanted me to go with him – said Ma wasn't well, but I didn't believe him. I know what he wants . . .'

'Dirty bugger,' Micky said and looked hard at Jake who was staring at them in obvious frustration. 'Come on, love. I'll look after yer. If he comes near yer again he'll be sorry. I've got a few mates who'll let him know where he stands . . .'

'I don't want you to get into trouble because of him,' Jinny said. She'd been shaken by the suddenness of Jake's appearance, because she'd thought she was safe, but now she would be on her guard and she'd be more careful. 'I hate him but I'm not afraid of him, Micky.'

'He needs teaching a lesson,' Micky said and his eyes smouldered with anger but then, as Jake slouched off, it was gone in a moment and he was smiling at her. 'Come on, Jinny. Let's go to this party. You look lovely . . .'

Jinny tucked her arm through his and hugged it. Seeing Jake like that had upset her, but she wasn't going to let him spoil her night with her friends. He was a nasty piece of work but she would be careful to stay out of his way when she visited Nellie. She was sure he was lying about her mother being sick, but she would ask Nellie on Sunday . . . and for the moment she was going to have a good time . . .

CHAPTER 11

Rose hadn't enjoyed herself so much in ages. The food was delicious and set out in the square dining room; little pastry cases filled with prawns in pink sauce or some kind of meat pâté, mini sausage rolls, and cheese and pineapple on sticks, bowls of green salads, fresh crusty bread cut into chunks, butter, pickles and cold chicken, crisps and nibbles were offered in generous quantities. For those with a sweet tooth there was a large creamy torte, decorated with tinned fruit. The room had long French windows and opened out into a large garden so that people could wander in and out. A long table in the garden was covered with a red cloth and set with plates, knives, forks, paper napkins

Little fairy lights were strung from trees and bushes and several small tables and chairs were scattered about the large garden. Another table was crowded with bottles of beer, lemonade, orange juice and glasses with tall stems or thick tumblers. There was already a buzz of excitement as the party got underway to soft background music of The Platters crooning about being the great pretender.

'This is lovely,' Rose said glancing about her. 'Thanks for inviting me, Rob. I haven't been to anything like this before . . .'

'I'm glad you could come,' Rob said and smiled at her. 'Nick particularly wanted to ask you, but he didn't know how . . . Ah, here he is . . .'

Rob's brother emerged from the kitchen carrying a large tray of cold beers, icy trickles gathering on the thick glasses as he set it down. He turned to face them and smiled as he saw Rose. He was older than Rob and now that he wasn't wearing a cap, as he did for work, she noticed there were silver streaks at his temples but they only made him look even more distinguished and handsome. His smile lit up his face and reached his eyes, she noticed as he welcomed her.

'I'm so glad you could come, Sister Rose . . . I wondered if St Saviour's could spare you. Rob says you're the mainstay there . . .'

'No, that's not right,' Rose exclaimed with a laugh. 'Sister Beatrice keeps us all on our toes. I just look after my patients and help out where I can . . .'

'All the kids say they like Nurse Rose because she's always willing to help,' Rob said, refusing to back down. 'And she doesn't mind gettin' a parched man a cup of tea when he's been workin' for hours and forgot his flask . . .'

'Oh, that,' Rose said, feeling her cheeks warm as Nick's gaze rested on her with thoughtful interest. 'I'm always making a cup of tea for someone these days – Sister Beatrice or Wendy or the carers. We don't have as many staff as we used to, so I help out where I can . . .'

'See, what did I tell you,' Rob grinned. 'Get the girl

a drink, Nick. I've just seen Wendy arrive and I'd better make her welcome, because she's on her own.'

'And thus he deserts you,' Nick said, flashing her a smile that made her insides flutter. 'However, that's my good luck – what may I get for you, Rose?'

'Perhaps a glass of white wine,' Rose said. 'I prefer medium to dry – if you have any?'

'We've got all sorts here,' Nick assured her. He found a bottle of Graves and showed it to her. Rose nodded, because she'd chosen that wine more than once when friends had taken her out. Nick smiled as he handed her the glass of nicely chilled wine. 'I asked Rob to invite as many friends as he liked. He always seems to make new friends easily, and I find it more difficult . . . It really is nice to have you here, Rose. Is it all right if I call you that?'

'Everyone does,' Rose said, glancing back at the red-brick house with its French windows and slanted roof. 'You're a builder – did you build this house?'

'Yes – I was lucky to get the land cheap. Helen's father sold it to me. He didn't think I would get planning permission but I did . . .'

Rose hesitated, then, 'Helen was your wife?'

'I see Rob has told you I lost her some years ago,' Nick said and a shadow passed over his face. 'That was when my luck ran out. Did Rob tell you I was in business before but it folded after Helen became ill and then died? I neglected things, drank a bit too much, got into debt and had to go back on the tools for other builders – but now I'm on my feet again and Rob and I have joined forces . . . Hence the reason for this party – and of course my charlady's coming nuptials.'

'You'll miss her coming in all the time . . .'

'Actually, she fusses over me like a mother hen so it will be a relief to have the house to myself sometimes.' He flashed another of those special smiles at Rose. 'I think she believed I might top myself just after Helen died – and I came close to it for a short time, but I had the kids to think of . . .'

'I know how it feels to lose someone.' She shook her head as his brows went up. 'Not a husband – my mother died of TB and I had to watch out for my younger sister. I had to put her in St Saviour's while I trained as a nurse. She didn't like it, but I didn't have much choice . . .'

'It must have been rotten for both of you. Everything sort of goes grey at those times or it did for me . . .' Nick's eyes darkened to slate. 'I'm sorry for being so morbid, but you give off those kinds of vibes, as if you're willing to listen – perhaps it is because you're a nurse.'

'Yes, perhaps,' Rose agreed. 'This is lovely wine.'

'I like it, but Rob is more of a beer man,' he said. 'Let me help you find some food before it all disappears.'

It was a lovely summer night and being in the garden made everything seem so much nicer. They moved towards the table where the food and plates were waiting. Nick picked up two plates and began to select meat from the dishes of ready cooked food, salad and some crusty chunks of bread. When he'd consulted Rose about her choice they finally had plates loaded with enough food to last a week, and he led the way to an empty table at the far end of the patio, placing the plates down and pulling out a wrought-iron chair with a cushion on the seat for her.

'I'll fetch some more wine,' Nick murmured and went off in the direction of the bar, where he was waylaid by Rob and some other friends.

Rose decided to start eating the chicken wings, which smelled absolutely delicious and tasted wonderful.

'Hello, I never expected to see you here this evening,' a voice said, making her look up in surprise. 'It is Sister Rose . . . ?'

'Doctor Henderson,' Rose said and stood up automatically. He motioned her to sit down. 'I've never been to a garden party before – have you?'

'Occasionally abroad,' he said and hesitated, before sitting in one of the other chairs. 'You're on your own, but it looks like someone intends to join you?' He glanced at the loaded plate Nick had chosen for himself.

'Nick went to get some wine . . .' Rose said with a glance at her host who was still talking even though clearly trying to get back to her.

Then they both spoke at once, 'Have you known Nick long?'

Rose laughed and Doctor Henderson grinned, saying, 'I'll sit here until he gets back. I treated Nick's wife Helen when she was dying of her injuries. I'm not sure how much you know, but Helen was in a terrible car accident and she broke her back. There were internal injuries too and she died of them after some months of pain . . . but perhaps you knew all that?'

'No, I didn't,' Rose said, feeling tears sting her eyes. 'How awful that must have been for her – and for her family.'

'It was wretched, but at that time I was dealing with a lot of that kind of trauma at the London . . . we were getting several severe injuries from car accidents every week, mainly caused by drivers who were drunk, though I don't think that was the cause in Helen's case.'

'You worked at the London before you went into general practice?' Rose looked at him again and something stirred in her memory – something about him being asked to leave soon after she'd arrived there, because a patient had died and his administration of a certain drug was questioned until it was discovered that the fault was that of a careless nurse . . . She saw him looking at her oddly, as if he'd guessed that she'd just recalled the old gossip, but before she could speak, Nick walked up to them. He deposited the wine and three fresh glasses, then extended his hand. 'Stephen, it's good to see you. I see you've introduced yourselves – or perhaps you've met before?'

'Doctor Henderson attended one of our children the other day,' Rose said, then glanced at him. 'By the way, I visited Beth and she seems a lot better . . .'

'Yes, the infection is almost gone and you'll be able to have her back soon.' He rose from the table, accepting a glass of wine from Nick. 'I must let you two eat your food before it's spoiled. I'll wander over and see what I fancy.'

Nick nodded and then sat down in the chair he'd vacated. 'It's a small world, isn't it?' He lifted his wineglass in salute and smiled at Rose. 'I'd like to know all about you, Rose – why you wanted to train as a nurse and how you came to be working at St Saviour's . . .'

'I've heard from Miss Sampson,' Sister Beatrice told Rose when she visited the sick room on Saturday afternoon.

'She has been given Doctor Henderson's report and says that she will be applying to make the Harris children wards of court and giving us the official custody of them while investigations are made about other relatives who might be willing to give them a home. However, it does mean that we could move them to Harlow if we wished now that it is official . . .'

'I think it would be a pity,' Rose said thoughtfully. 'Andy is getting on well with the sports master at his school and talking about learning to drive as soon as he's old enough to get a provisional licence. Surely they should be safe enough now? The police will be investigating their step-father and he will in any case be forbidden to approach them . . .'

'Do you think that would stop a man like that if he was determined to harm them?'

'Once the court order is in place he couldn't snatch them back because he could go to prison just for that,' Rose said. 'I suppose in some ways it would be safer to pass them on, and yet I still think it a pity to move Andy.'

'Perhaps I should talk to him about it,' Sister Beatrice said. 'I know Beth trusts you and we're expecting her back here this week. She believes in you so perhaps you should ask them what they would like to do. I do not approve of forcing children to move out of London if they're against it – but some of them want to go. I'm taking a party of them down this weekend. There are three girls and one boy, and they're all exceptionally bright and could have a chance of going on to college.'

'You're talking of Becky and Susan Martin, and Jean Grant – but I'm not sure which of the boys?'

'Tom Allsop,' Sister Beatrice said. 'He came to us about six months ago. I think he has been in at least three care homes and he ran away from them all. His mother died when he was five and he's had a hard time of it since. When he was brought in off the streets he'd been caught stealing from a market stall. He was warned it was his last chance but he seems better here . . .'

Rose frowned, because she was remembering that he was the ringleader of the boys that had cheeked Jinny when she started work. Jinny hadn't complained and she'd seemed to handle them well, but Rose had noticed that she looked a bit anxious whenever Tom and his friends trooped in for their meal.

'Do you think it's a good idea to move him if he's settling well?'

Sister Beatrice frowned. 'You think I should give him a bit longer? We are a temporary refuge these days. I have to move them on eventually but perhaps . . .' she inclined her head. 'Perhaps I'll rethink Tom's move and just take the girls down this weekend.'

'Shall you see Angela when you're there?' Rose asked.

'Yes, I certainly shall. She has asked me to stay overnight with them and I am looking forward to it.' A little sigh escaped her. 'You are on duty over the whole of next weekend I think, as is Wendy, so you shouldn't miss me for a couple of days . . .'

'I'm sure we can manage, though it is always comforting to know you're here,' Rose said and smiled.

'Yes, well, as long as you can manage . . .' Sister nodded. 'I think you're right. I shall keep Tom here for a while longer – keep my eye on him. We don't want him slipping back into his old ways, do we?'

'No, though he said he only stole food because he was hungry. It may be best to keep him here until you're sure he's getting on well . . . after all he went through at his last place.'

'You're quite right,' Sister Beatrice said. 'Now, I understand you have two cases of a vomiting bug today. How are your patients coming along?'

Rose showed her the records of temperatures, pulse and regularity of vomiting, which appeared to be on the wane now that they were being cared for by the nurses. Sister Beatrice visited the two youngsters who were in the isolation ward and feeling sorry for themselves and then went off on a tour of the dining room and the dorms to make sure that everything was as she liked it.

Rose was left alone to care for her patients; she had a tonsillitis case recovering in the sick ward and her two rather less well children in the isolation ward, but her duties were not arduous that morning and left her time to think.

Nick had invited her to the theatre and supper on Wednesday, which she'd told him was her evening off this week. She'd thanked him and accepted, because it was time she went out more and she'd felt sympathy towards him for the terrible loss of his wife. They hadn't talked about Helen again, and Rose hadn't told him that she was aware of how his wife had suffered, but she felt a kinship with him because she understood the pain that came from losing a loved one.

'Nick seems really taken with you,' Rob had told her when they left the party late that evening with Wendy, Jinny and Micky. 'I haven't seen him so animated in ages . . . not since . . .'

'Since Helen's accident,' Rose said as he lapsed into silence.

'Did he tell you about that?'

'Yes, he mentioned something . . .'

'Nick doesn't often talk about it,' Rob said. 'He just refuses to talk about her months of pain. He seemed to shut it out of his mind . . . almost as if she'd just gone off and left him. It might do him good if he could talk to someone about her . . .'

'He needs to see Mark Adderbury . . .' Rose realised he didn't understand. 'He's a psychiatrist and gives up his time to help our kids free of charge. We don't see as much of him as when Angela worked at St Saviour's, because he's often at Halfpenny House in Essex, but he comes if Sister Beatrice asks to see him.'

She'd lapsed into her thoughts again until Rob said, 'Penny for them?'

'Oh . . . nothing,' Rose said. 'I didn't realise until this evening that Doctor Henderson used to work at the London . . . He left suddenly after there was some gossip; there were all sorts of stories at the time, but in the end he was cleared of any wrongdoing.'

'Ah, I see.' Rob nodded. 'I saw you looking a bit odd when he was talking to you. I would've come over but then Nick joined you.'

'It seems they know each other well.'

'Yes . . .' Rob hesitated, then, 'I hope you don't mind me asking – about Nancy. I was going to ask her to the party as well, but she seemed to cut me off, as if I might contaminate her. I just touched her arm and she pulled away as if I'd burned her . . .'

'I can't tell you Nancy's private affairs,' Rose said,

'but she was hurt when she was very young. I'm sorry; that's all I'm at liberty to tell you.'

'I was angry at first, bewildered as to what I'd done but then I started thinking and I wondered . . .'

'Nancy has made a new life for herself with us, but I'm not sure how she feels about what happened. I've never known her to have a boyfriend . . . if that makes you feel better?'

'It doesn't matter about me,' Rob said. 'I don't want to hurt her. I liked her but her feelings are what count . . .'

Rose smiled and touched his arm just as they all reached the gates of St Saviour's. 'You're a nice man, Rob. Nancy would go a long way to find someone more understanding . . . but she has to realise that for herself. I can only say . . . be patient but don't give up on her if you really care.'

'Thanks, Rose. I hope you find happiness – and I'll see if I can find ways to get Nancy to trust me . . .'

They all said goodnight and Rose followed Wendy and Jinny into the garden. As they walked across to the nurses' home the other two were talking animatedly about the party, but Rose's thoughts had been elsewhere. She was really looking forward to going out with Nick . . .

CHAPTER 12

Ruby saw the girls congregating outside St Saviour's when she returned from fetching her evening paper. They were talking naturally to some of the orphans and they all looked to be getting on well enough, until one of her girls struck a St Saviour's boy on the nose and he, not unnaturally, slapped her back across the ear. Ruby arrived just in time to pull the girl off her victim before a vicious fight could develop.

'What do you think you're doing, Susan?' she asked harshly. 'I saw what happened – and I suggest you apologise to this boy.'

'It wasn't my fault . . . he threatened me.'

'She's been bullyin' my friend at school,' the boy said and glared at both of them. 'I told her if she pulls Jean's hair again and upsets her I'll give her a good hidin' . . .'

'That is not the way to behave – either of you,' Ruby said. 'What is your name, young man?'

'Tom . . .' he said sullenly. 'Go on, report me to Sister then, I don't care. I shall still belt 'er if she upsets Jean again.'

'Have you been upsetting one of the St Saviour's

children, Susan?' Ruby demanded. She frowned as the girl nodded. 'Very well, you know the punishment – neither you nor any of the others will receive their sweet ration for two weeks – and you will apologise to Tom now.'

'I'm sorry I 'it yer,' the girl said, looking furious. 'But Jean is a sissy and if I don't pull 'er 'air someone else will . . .'

'Not if I'm around,' Tom said. 'And I ain't sorry I hit you because you're mean . . .' He glared at Ruby once more and then ran off into the home.

Ruby looked at the sulky girl standing in front of her. 'I don't enjoy punishing you, Susan – and your friends will be angry with you – but you must learn that you cannot hit others as you please. If you recall, it was your violent behaviour towards others that brought you here. Much as I should dislike it I might have to punish you further if you behave in such a way again – but you have apologised and so we shall say no more about it . . .'

'Sorry, miss,' Susan said, hanging her head. 'It's me temper – I just can't seem to stop meself . . .'

'Well, perhaps we should investigate that . . .' Ruby said and sent the girl in to get her tea.

She was thoughtful as she went up to her office. Punishing girls didn't always work and perhaps there was an underlying cause for Susan's anger. Ruby seemed to recall that Sister Beatrice had spoken of a psychiatrist who had helped their children several times – perhaps if she spoke to her about the problem he might have a look at Susan and see what was wrong.

After all, the last thing Ruby wanted was another of

her girls to try harming herself. Yes, she would speak to Sister Beatrice that evening before she went home. Susan needed help not punishment, although she would have to stand by the punishment she'd already given . . .

'Everyone got everything they should have?' Beatrice asked of the three girls she was accompanying to their new home on the outskirts of Harlow. She looked at their faces as they stood in the hallway of St Saviour's for perhaps the last time. 'You'll be issued with new uniforms when you get there so you only need your personal stuff.'

'Yes, Sister,' the two sisters said in chorus, looking excited at the thought of moving to the country. Jean Grant was silent, her eyes large and dark with anxiety.

'Are you all right, Jean?' Beatrice asked, feeling a prickle of anxiety. She knew from experience that moving a child who didn't want to go would result in unhappiness and in some cases a runaway. 'We talked about this and you said you would like to go . . . you haven't changed your mind?'

'No, Sister. I – I'm just nervous . . .' Jean glanced at the two sisters who were obviously not in the least afraid of going to the new home. 'But I do want to go to the country. I like trees and animals . . .'

Beatrice nodded. Sometimes, she wished that she would be there to oversee the transition of the children, because she knew that some of them felt bereft when they left the grimy streets they'd known all their lives, but she was needed here in London, even though she sometimes felt that age was catching up with her. There were times when she longed for a garden now – a garden of her own where she could grow flowers and fresh vegetables, and sometimes just sit and rest, but she didn't want to give up her work completely. No, she hoped she would be able to help care for these damaged children for the rest of her life.

Taking them outside to the bus stop, she discovered that Jean Grant had gravitated to her side and, as they waited for their transport, her hand crept into Beatrice's own. Feeling the child's hand tremble a little, Beatrice held it tightly until the bus came and she was forced to let go to usher them all into their seats. However, she made sure that Jean sat by the window and she sat next to her, shielding her from whatever made her nervous of the world. Perhaps she would ask Mark Adderbury to have a word with her, see if he could discover what made her so timid.

Opening her paper, Beatrice read an article about Oliver Hardy, who had died earlier that month, and his partner Stan Laurel. She noticed a small column about something called a 'drunkometer' that measured the amount of alcohol in the blood and which might be used to test drivers who had taken too much strong drink – and what a good thing that would be, she thought, finding that her thoughts strayed back to the young girl by the window.

Jean was one of the brightest girls in her class at school, and her teacher had written to Beatrice asking if she could be supported to attend a better school, one where she would stand a greater chance of gaining a university place one day.

It was something that had not occurred before at St Saviour's. Jean's family had been ordinary enough, her father a Docker and her mother a factory worker. Jean's mother had died when she was ten and her father had started to drink and neglect his daughter, but his drinking had led to his rapid decline and he'd died of a liver complaint, leaving his only child alone in the world. She had no relatives and was near to starving when the police found her hiding on the Docks and brought her in.

She'd been with them for over a year, because Beatrice had known she would need enough time before she could be moved, but after that letter it seemed her duty was clear. Beatrice had asked Jean what she would like to do, explaining that her teacher thought she could do better at a different school and might gain a university place if she worked hard. Jean had seemed to welcome the change, but now she was plainly nervous.

'Is anything troubling you, Jean?' Beatrice asked when they were settled on the train. The sisters had gone off to the toilets and they were briefly alone. 'Tell me what is making you anxious?'

Jean hesitated, then, 'I was bullied when I started school as a St Saviour's girl,' she said. 'Tom stopped them and it was all right . . . I thought he was coming with us . . .'

'Ah, I see.' Beatrice understood her fear. Bullying at school was not pleasant and it was always good to have a friend who could stop it. Ruby had come to see her about one of her girls who had taken to hitting other children, but she hadn't been specific so Beatrice wasn't sure if Jean was involved. 'Tom may be coming down later, but I thought he needed a little extra time with us – but what makes you think you may be bullied at your new school?'

'I don't know . . .'

Jean shook her head and looked down at her feet as Becky and Susie returned to their seats. Had she known Tom had been protecting Jean, Beatrice would definitely have brought him, and regretted taking Rose's advice to leave him behind, although it was a new start and perhaps Jean was just nervous and would be perfectly happy once she'd settled to her new life.

The only thing she could do was to ask Angela to warn Mrs Mellors to keep an eye out for bullying . . .

'I'm so glad you came down yourself,' Angela said as she welcomed Beatrice to her home. 'I've wanted to show you all the improvements we've made and to let you see some of the children's work. We're having a special tea at Halfpenny House today and I know the kids are looking forward to taking you round . . .'

'I should've come sooner,' Beatrice admitted. 'What a lovely garden you have, Angela. The countryside does have its benefits I see . . .'

'Yes, I love my garden and I enjoy working in it, at least in the summer.' Angela laughed. 'Mark refuses to have anything to do with it, other than to sit in and have a quiet drink on summer evenings, and we have a young man to do the heavy work, but I like weeding and planting.'

'Didn't I see one of our old boys with a wheelbarrow down at the bottom, in amongst the fruit bushes?'

'Yes, that's Joe Blake, do you remember him? He was one of the first to come here from St Saviour's. He started off with helping with the lawns and flowerbeds at Halfpenny House, and just carried on finding work in people's gardens after he left Halfpenny House. He rents a room at the local pub and I think he does quite well. For a lad who had known only the East End of London, he's taken to gardening like a duck to the proverbial water. We paid for him to have a short course at a horticultural college and he's repaid us a hundred times with his devotion to our garden. He told me just this morning that the council have offered him a contract to help look after their parks and green spaces. Joe says that even if he takes it, he won't let his regulars down, so he'll be working all hours . . .'

'I always like to hear of our children doing well. Oh, you might like to know that Mary Ellen has passed her recent exams and will be starting her first job as a teacher soon, just two days a week to begin with, I understand. And Billy Baggins is getting on marvellously. I think he's almost running that clothing factory now. Mary Ellen told me she still has more exams to take but is allowed to take classes as a teaching assistant in needlework and art, and other subjects will follow once she has the rest of her qualifications.'

'I knew she was doing well,' Angela said, leading the way into a pleasant conservatory that was shaded against the fierce heat of the sun. 'Do come and have some tea. The twins are with friends so I've been baking cakes all afternoon. You'll see them later, but they've gone to a birthday party. We bought a set of Dinky cars for them to take as a gift. I understand there will be a magician at the party so be prepared to be shown magic tricks all evening . . .'

Beatrice smiled. 'You seemed to have settled well here, Angela?'

'Yes, I have everything I could want,' Angela said, 'but I do still miss being at St Saviour's. Oh, by the way, I've been fundraising down here and I've been told you will be getting some extra money for taking the children out . . .'

'Extra money is always welcome. I'm afraid the children do not get as many trips out as they did when you were with us, Angela. Hannah and Kelly and their husbands organised a day at Southend for them recently, and Wendy went along with Nancy. Sandra, Rose and I held the fort, though most of the kids went on the trip. Hannah has now left us and we have a pleasant woman named Mavis on our team of carers. I believe she will fit in with us, but I'm not sure how long she will stay. We do not seem to have as many girls eager to work for us as we once had, though we have an excellent girl in the kitchens. Her name is Jinny and Nancy likes her a lot, but in general it is more difficult to find girls willing to do menial jobs.'

'I suppose it is a sign of the times,' Angela said thoughtfully. 'Things have changed a great deal since the war, Sister. There is far more choice for girls looking for work now and so fewer of them want the cleaning and caring jobs.'

'I suppose it is only natural, and I think there are more glamorous jobs today, in fashion and beauty – and even factory work pays more than we do I expect, though what could be more rewarding than helping to protect vulnerable children I cannot say.'

Angela nodded her agreement. 'I did tell you that we've managed to get another cottage in Norfolk so that we can take our kids on holidays in the summer terms? We have two now and let them out for spring and autumn to cover the maintenance, but we fill them each summer with our children; they look forward to it – but of course it is an added expense, which is why I've been organising fetes, bring-and-buy sales and a big dance . . .'

'You were always good at that,' Beatrice said, sitting on a chair with elbows and a hard back. She was afraid that if she sank into those soft armchairs of Angela's she would never get out again – and she didn't want to look as if she suffered joint pain. Despite all her years of service, and the reassurance from Angela and Mark Adderbury that she would always be needed, she still feared that one day she would be told she was no longer wanted as warden of St Saviour's.

'Oh, I enjoyed doing it, and I still do,' Angela said. 'It isn't the same as working with you, of course, but I'm very happy.'

'I wanted to have a word with you about the children I brought down today . . .' Beatrice ate a small piece of lemon drizzle cake. 'This is delicious, Angela. I may have made a small mistake . . .' She told Angela of her conversation with Jean on the train and her fear that the child might have been bullied at school. 'Perhaps Mark would keep an eye on her – and Mrs Mellors could look out for signs of bullying?'

'Mark will certainly do that, but unfortunately, Mrs Mellors is leaving us in a few months. She has decided to go and live with her sister in the South of France. We shall be sorry to lose her, because she has been reliable – not as good with the children as you, Sister Beatrice, but I don't suppose we could ever tempt you to come here?' Angela spoke in a light-hearted way, but Beatrice hesitated and Angela's gaze was suddenly alert. 'Or would you?'

'I'm not sure it would be possible,' Beatrice said thoughtfully. 'Halfpenny House is larger than St Saviour's ever was – and of course, I do not see how I could leave the children there while they need me . . .'

'I'm not sure how long that will be . . .' Angela took a deep breath, then, 'You will recall that I telephoned you to let you know that plans to close St Saviour's were being considered – and to build on an extra wing here if need be. I'm afraid the signs are not good, because the council wants to take it over for the Children's Department. Mark was against it at the start, but the terms are favourable and it would make us so much more secure here. I told you what I had in mind then . . . have you considered it at all?'

'You suggested that I might take over as the Superintendent here and you would be my assistant, much as you were at St Saviour's . . .' Beatrice nodded. 'I remember the conversation very well, Angela . . . and of course I have given it a great deal of thought . . .' She gave Angela a very direct look. 'Is it confirmed then?'

'Not confirmed but Mark says he thinks it will be at the next Board meeting . . .'

'And when shall I be required to leave St Saviour's?' Beatrice's voice was firm though her hand trembled a little on the arm of her chair.

'The takeover would not happen until after Christmas – a new beginning for the new year . . .'

'Ah, I see . . . may I take it that you expect it to happen?'

'I intended to come up and speak to you about it when a decision had been made finally, but we are waiting for several reports. I was asked to investigate the finances of the various options; I've been trying to work out which is best for all of us. Personally, I don't want them to give up St Saviour's altogether and I've made my feelings plain, but I'm only one voice. As you know, I've always agreed with you that we're needed in London to take the kids in off the streets, but the feeling is that the need is less acute there than it used to be . . .'

'I'm not sure I agree with that,' Beatrice said thoughtfully. 'Yes, conditions have improved since after the war. We've got new housing for some, but not all, and the free health treatment has made things much better for many families – but you would be surprised at how much need there still is. Quite a few of the children brought in recently have actually run away from their homes, because of family problems. Also, some of the older damp houses still exist and the tenants don't want to move out to the new flats; they want to stay where their friends and families are, and we occasionally get outbreaks of typhoid and other nasty infections. Not in the devastating way we did years ago, but there are still fatalities and broken homes, and children still need shelter and loving care and always will.' What Beatrice didn't add was that it was a matter of education, of people learning better hygiene and health practices, which was ongoing but slow.

'Yes, that is my point exactly,' Angela smiled her agreement. 'It's why I've put the case that St Saviour's must stay open in some form for the time being – but it might be under the direction of the Children's Department, not ours.'

'This, I am certain, would completely change the way things are done. Miss Sampson would most certainly turn off my staff, install her own and run things in . . . shall we say, a less hands-on way. It may be the modern way but it is not mine . . .'

'Unfortunately, I believe you are right . . .' Angela hesitated, then, 'It is for that reason that I would like you to come to us here, Sister Beatrice. I want to bring all the children we have at St Saviour's at the changeover down here – and I want you here at the helm, to help us improve our standards . . . and Mark agrees with me.'

'I thought you'd ironed out the few problems you had at the start?'

'We have most of them, but there are always new ones. Mrs Mellors is a decent woman but she isn't you, nowhere near as efficient and intuitive – and I know we can do so much better if you will consent to join us.'

'What do you feel is lacking?'

'Your compassion and good sense,' Angela said promptly. 'At first I thought you too strict but I soon learned that you temper your rules with kindness and love and I grew to appreciate your qualities . . .'

'Thank you, I am glad to have your good opinion,' Beatrice said and smiled oddly, because their relationship had been stormy for some time. 'If the takeover goes ahead and I should decide to accept the position – what happens to my staff?'

'We need good staff here and it's possible that those

that wished could find a job with us, though of course some would undoubtedly prefer to remain in London.'

'Yes, I see . . .' Beatrice was thoughtful, the back of her neck tingling. Most of her staff were East End born and would consider a move to the country too much of a wrench. 'I'm not sure if she would come but Nancy has been with us a long time . . . and Wendy . . . However, I doubt the carers would consider it. They all have their own lives in town.'

'Well, if Nancy and Wendy wanted to apply when the time comes . . .' Angela stared at her eagerly. 'Is there a chance that you might consider making the move?'

Beatrice hesitated, tempted to confess that at times she longed for a peaceful garden to spend time in at the end of her day's work – to tell this woman she'd learned to trust that perhaps only a few more years remained to her and she might need a more peaceful environment if the pain in her limbs grew worse. And yet still she couldn't bring herself to say the words.

'May I give you my answer when the decision is finally made about the future of St Saviour's?'

'Yes, of course,' Angela said. 'I'll show you the room I've prepared for you and then we'll go over to Halfpenny House and meet the children as they come back from school . . .'

Beatrice had visited Halfpenny House when it was very new and thought it rather soulless, but now the edges seemed to have softened, or perhaps she was seeing it with less hostile eyes. However, she noticed that the children's dorms now had cork boards on the walls so that they could pin up their treasures, and one of the rooms had been turned into an art department, and it was here that the children had taken her first. It had a relaxed atmosphere, with paint jars, brushes, piles of thick paper, also pots of clay in various stages. The kiln was outside in a small shed out of harm's way and they could only use it under supervision of Miss Savage, who was a qualified potter and art mistress as well as being a housemistress at Halfpenny House. She'd taken the place of a retired headmaster who had been dismissed for punishing the boys too harshly.

'We have some very talented children here,' Jill Savage told Beatrice when she greeted her. 'I find it a pleasure to encourage them to go on with their studies.'

'You must be dedicated, to work with the children after you finish at school?' Beatrice observed.

'Oh, I work at the college just three days a week, and the rest of my time is devoted to my own art, but I love encouraging children to find their inner selves and I feel that one of the best ways is through letting them paint or make what they want at the wheel. Hand modelling is also very satisfying, working the clay with your fingers.'

'Yes, I imagine the children would think so. Halfpenny House is lucky to have you,' Beatrice said. 'At St Saviour's, Angela encouraged the children to do their own projects, but to have a qualified arts teacher here as one of our staff is tremendous luck for them.'

'Thank you, I feel as if I'm the privileged one,' Jill replied. 'It's lovely to meet you. I've heard lots about you, from Angela and from the children. They often speak of you. I think when they came to you it was the first time they'd known kindness and the safety of a loving home. A lot of them wish you could be here to see their work.'

'My nurses and I do all we can to make them feel safe and happy at St Saviour's, but some have suffered too much in their young lives and I worry about them when they move on.'

'I think most of them are happy here,' Jill replied. 'We've had one or two run away, back to London and what they know – but the majority are willing to embrace a new way of life. However, after some adjustments to the staff and the new art department, I believe things are better here than they were at the start . . .' She lowered her voice so that only Beatrice could hear. 'I believe it is because Angela has had more time to oversee things here. I've noticed changes since I first came . . . projects for the children, the introduction of stars to earn treats. All these things help the kids to feel they have something to look forward to.'

Beatrice nodded. She'd met Mrs Mellors since coming to the home and wasn't impressed, because although well-meaning, the woman seemed vague about her hopes for the children. Angela would do much better and there was a part of Beatrice that very much wanted to be a part of it with her.

'Archie ran away two years ago, because I wasn't able to send his sister down with him. I've tried to make sure that the children who transfer now are ready and willing for a new way of life . . . but I've been glad to see them settled here this afternoon.'

Beatrice enjoyed meeting the staff, talking to Mrs Mellors about the new life she'd planned, which seemed of far more interest to her than her work at the home, and having tea with the children. Mark Adderbury didn't come to the little party at the school, but that evening he took them all out for a pleasant meal. When Beatrice retired for the night she was feeling tired, but surprisingly free of pain. Perhaps it was the fresh air or the holiday feel the day had held amongst old friends.

She thought for a while about Angela's offer, wondering whether she was too old to make such a move; if she was forced to leave St Saviour's, it would otherwise be a choice between returning to the convent where she'd taken her vows or looking for another nursing post – which she was unlikely to find at her age. Yet was she strong enough to take on the charge of such a large home? Perhaps she needed to visit the convent, spend some time in prayer and speak with the Mother Superior.

'I can't believe Sister Beatrice is actually considering making the move here,' Mark said when Angela told him in the privacy of their bedroom later that night. He gave her a quizzical look, his brows raised. 'The post of Superintendent was offered to you, Angela – are you sure you wouldn't prefer to be in charge?'

'Perhaps, if I didn't have the twins and you,' Angela said and looked at him lovingly. 'Yet I think even then I should feel better sharing the job with Sister Beatrice. I know we've agreed the twins are off to boarding school in the autumn, and at seven years of age they're looking forward to it – but I shall want to be free to go down for special days – and to take them away for holidays when they are at home. If I were in sole charge it might be too much – and besides, I always thought it was a two-woman job.'

'Yes, perhaps it is . . .' He released his tie and threw it over a chair. 'I've been told that most of the Board are ready to sign the agreement for the takeover. Apparently, they've agreed to keep St Saviour's as a reception centre for kids off the street until the new centres for street kids are up and running . . .'

'What about the disturbed girls? Will they be allowed to mix with the orphans? Sister Beatrice told me that she and Ruby had come to some sort of an arrangement and they've been having their tea at St Saviour's on Saturdays and Sundays for a couple of weeks now and they're thinking of extending it to every day . . . I think she hoped to see some relaxing of their strict rules. Are they going to integrate the girls and the orphans completely when they take over, do you think?'

'We haven't been informed of their plans,' Mark said. 'It may even be that they move their girls elsewhere in time and sell to the developers.'

'We mustn't tell Sister Beatrice. She'd hoped that would never happen.'

'As we did, Angela . . .' Mark sighed and eased his shoulders. 'Did you think Sister Beatrice looked older? I have an idea she had some difficulty getting out of the back of the car when we returned from the restaurant . . .'

'I hadn't noticed.' Angela looked thoughtful. 'I've never known for sure how old she is, but I think she must be sixtyish . . .'

'I imagine she's not far off,' Mark agreed. 'A move

to the country might be a good change for her, darling – if you could convince her of it.'

'Well, I've put the idea to her,' Angela said and smiled. 'She will decide in her own way and her own time. Now, do you want to tell me what sort of a day you've had . . . ?'

CHAPTER 13

Rose was smiling as she replaced the receiver that morning. Nick had telephoned and asked her to go for a drink that evening.

'We could have a drink – and something to eat in the bar if you like,' he'd said. 'I've been wanting to see you again, Rose – and I could pick you up whenever you're off duty . . .'

'I don't get off until nine this evening,' she'd told him, 'but I'd like to go just for a drink. It's a bit too late for a meal, but it will be nice just to have a chat and a drink. I really enjoyed myself the other night . . .'

'Good. I'll look forward to it,' Nick said. 'We had a lovely evening at that restaurant, didn't we?' She could hear the pleasure in his voice. 'I might be able to get tickets for a West End show one night – if you can tell me when you're free . . .'

'That would be a treat,' Rose said. 'I'll see you this evening then – and thanks for asking . . .'

'I'm looking forward to it,' Nick said.

Rose felt as if she'd got a spring in her step as she left the nurses' home and crossed the small back garden to the orphanage. As she approached, a boy came running out of the back door and cannoned into her, accidentally kicking her shin.

'What's all this about then, Tom?' she asked and gave him a severe look. 'You know what Sister says about running . . .'

'Don't care. I 'ate yer all . . .' he said and brushed past her, going back into the home and tearing off through the hall.

Rose stared after him in exasperation. What was the matter with him now? She recalled that Sister had intended to send him down to Halfpenny House, but they'd decided he needed a little longer here. He could certainly do with a bit more discipline. His shoe had scraped her ankle and if she'd been wearing nylons he would have laddered them.

She debated whether to tell Sister Beatrice, but decided against it. Rose wasn't one to tell tales, but she would certainly discipline him herself if she caught him behaving so recklessly again . . . Glancing at the little watch pinned to her uniform, she saw that it was late. Wendy would be ready to leave and Rose needed a cup of tea before she started work.

As she reached the staff room Rose saw that Sandra had the cash box out on the table and there was a small notebook beside it.

'I've counted the money and made a note of the total,' she told Rose. 'If everyone gives me their two shillings a week I'll keep a check on it for you and make sure it's right – we just have to be certain we leave a note to say if we take money to buy supplies.'

'Ah good,' Rose nodded. 'I didn't like asking, Sandra,

because I know you have enough work to do but I think we've been a bit careless in the past.'

'Yes . . .' Sandra hesitated, then, 'I'm guilty of that myself. Sister put me in charge of the children's treat money and I keep it in my desk – well, just between you and me, Rose, I think someone took two pounds from it yesterday. I put five pounds in, I know I did, but when I checked just now there was only four . . . and I'd got twenty-five shillings in for a start . . .'

'Oh, Sandra, that's awful.' Rose was shocked. 'It means we have a thief at St Saviour's . . .'

'Well, I suppose . . . but how can I be certain I put all the five pounds in? I've made the difference up myself, because I can't let the children go without their trip to the zoo next Saturday . . .'

'Yes, but it isn't right that you should have to do it . . .' Rose frowned. 'You must keep your drawer locked, Sandra, because you sometimes have a lot more money than we ever have in the petty cash box.'

'Yes, I do and I shall in future,' Sandra said and put the cash box away. 'Now we know exactly what we've got . . . and perhaps it will turn out to be just a mistake . . .'

'Let's hope so,' Rose said. 'Otherwise we shall have to start looking for the thief . . .'

'There's someone here to see you,' Mrs Davies said that morning, frowning at Jinny as she emerged from the scullery, still wiping her hands. 'Please don't be long, because we have a lot of work to do today.'

'Yes, Mrs Davies.' Jinny looked towards the door of the kitchen, where Micky was hovering and looking uncomfortable. Clearly Mrs Davies had shown her disapproval over him coming here. 'Micky? Was there something wrong?' She couldn't imagine he would make a social visit at this hour of the morning.

'It's Nellie,' he said, looking grim. 'She's been beaten and I took her to the doctor. She's had an X-ray on her arm but it isn't broken, just badly bruised – and she has bruises on her face, probably elsewhere but she wouldn't tell me it all . . .'

'Nellie is injured? How did it happen – did she have a fall or what?'

Micky glanced towards Mrs Davies and lowered his voice. 'She won't say but I've been told it was Jake. He went for her as she walked back from the market and left her lying on the ground, her face battered . . .'

'No!' Jinny felt sick and for a moment the room seemed to whirl. 'He's evil, Micky. Have Nellie or Bert been to the police?'

'She refused to go, says he'll only deny it and then he'll come after you . . . and she doesn't want Bert to know. He's got a right temper, as you probably know, though he never uses his fists on Nellie or his kids, and if he guessed what Jake had done I think he might kill him. Nellie is frightened he would get into trouble and lose his job at the Docks, because he was warned when he went for one of the blokes he was working with – Bert was angry because Sam Bullock had been bullying one of the younger lads, but of course he didn't say anything, because Sam could have been sacked. So he took the fine and kept his mouth shut – but if he got into trouble with the cops he'd be out of a job sharpish.'

'That's so unfair! Bert is a decent man. Nellie should tell someone, because Jake is a devil and he'll hurt her again if she doesn't report him,' Jinny said. 'He followed me home one night and knows where I live so he could come after me at any time. I'll go and see her this evening, Micky. I would go now, but Elsa phoned in sick so we're busy all day.'

'What time do you get off?'

'About half-past seven – why do you ask?'

'I'll be fetchin' yer,' he said gruffly. 'If Jake is on the rampage that's all he's waiting for. If he's done that to Nellie, can you imagine what he'd do to you? He's a bad-tempered brute, especially when he's had a few drinks . . .'

Jinny hesitated, then, hearing an audible sniff from Mrs Davies, she nodded her agreement. 'All right, we'll talk tonight. I've got to get on . . .'

They'd been working flat out all morning, but lunch was over and the dishes washed and put away. Mrs Davies said she was going to her room to put her feet up for an hour.

'I'll be back in time to help with preparing the tea and supper menu,' she told Jinny. 'Finish tidying up and then put your feet up for a few minutes, we've done plenty today . . .'

'I need to fetch the dirty cups from the staff room,' Jinny said. 'I'll check they've got tea and coffee and sugar supplies while I'm there . . . and take them some biscuits up.'

'They are supposed to supply their own biscuits,' Mrs Davies sniffed. 'They've got a petty cash box there, but

I'll bet it's full of money. All they seem to do these days is cadge biscuits and cakes from us.'

'Can you blame them when your biscuits and cakes are so much nicer?' Jinny said and smiled but Mrs Davies only frowned and went off for a rest, her shoulders stiff with disapproval. Perhaps she knew that Rose and Wendy had both told Jinny that they loved the biscuits that Nancy had shown her how to make. Mrs Davies normally left her to get on with the steamed puddings and cakes, saying that she didn't approve of spoiling the children with treats all the time.

After Jinny had drunk the tea she'd made for herself, she picked up a large wooden tray and went up in the lift to the staff rest room. As she approached, she saw one of the boys running down the corridor in the opposite direction. The door of the staff room was partially open. Entering, she put down her tray and started to collect the dirty cups, which had been left on side ledges and tables, and one on the arm of a chair. She was frowning as she set the tray down to check the sugar tin and the caddy where the fragrant tea was stored, and then the biscuit tin . . . and then her eye fell on the drawer in the table and she noticed that it was slightly open. Inside, she could see a black tin cash box and knew it must contain the petty cash for buying biscuits. All the staff paid a small amount in, because Mrs Davies had complained that her budget for the kitchen was not enough to cover supplying fancy biscuits and cakes for the staff's morning and afternoon break. Although Kelly had told Jinny that when Muriel was their cook biscuits and cakes had been supplied, as well as sandwiches for anyone who asked, it seemed that

Mrs Davies had her own rules. She was mean with the food for the kids too, grumbling about the amount of food they got through in a week.

Jinny knew that some of the staff had complained about the change; they'd never paid for things like that before and considered meals and drinks as a part of their wages, but Wendy had put in two shillings to start it and Rose followed so the others decided to add their mite, but since Jinny arrived, she'd been filling their biscuit tin for them whenever she made a batch of something nice for the kids. No one had mentioned it to Mrs Davies and the kitchen budget was still bearing up. The truth of it was that their cook was a bit of a misery and in Jinny's opinion she simply didn't want the extra work. Now that Jinny had taken over so much of the cooking, as well as the cleaning, she didn't seem as bothered.

Jinny left the drawer as she found it. An unpleasant suspicion lingered at the back of her mind as she took her heavy tray and carried it back to the kitchen to wash, dry and replace the cups in the staff room. When she returned with fresh crockery, she noticed that the drawer was now closed. Wondering who had been in since her departure and if they'd checked the cash tin, Jinny set out the clean cups and filled the tin with some biscuits she'd made that morning. She would make more and some of Nellie's rock cakes when she'd finished here and also rhubarb crumble for the kids to have with custard for supper.

Jinny washed everything after she'd finished, because it was time to start on the sandwiches and the bread and butter with homemade jam that was a perennial favourite with kids. Nancy had told her that she learned how to make it from Muriel, their previous cook, and Jinny wished that she was still around so that she could show her how to cook some of the kids' favourites. Nancy gave her cooking lessons whenever she had time, but she was very busy with her other work and Jinny wanted to know so much more.

'Oh, you've started,' Mrs Davies said when she arrived at just after four. 'I fell asleep and didn't wake until a few minutes ago. I see you've made cake and biscuits – and what's that you have in the oven?'

'I'm making rhubarb crumble,' Jinny said. 'I can just put it under the grill to warm it through again for supper and the custard won't take long to make at all . . .'

'I've told you before, it isn't necessary to go to that trouble,' Mrs Davies grumbled. 'Biscuits are plenty for supper with a hot drink. They will all get fat and lazy if you overfeed them . . .'

'They enjoy something warm,' Jinny defended herself. 'I don't mind making it – and the rhubarb wouldn't last until tomorrow. It needed using up or we should've had to throw it out.'

'Oh well, in that case . . .' Mrs Davies sniffed. 'I suppose there's no harm in it – but they won't get it on your nights off, I can tell you. If you go off to a better job like most of the girls I shan't put myself to all this bother . . .'

Jinny didn't answer, simply arranging the last of the food on to the plates and starting to carry it through into the dining room. Mrs Davies was clearly in an awkward mood and she wasn't sure how to answer her.

She'd told her she didn't mind the work, but that didn't help. Something more than usual wasn't quite right in their cook's world, but Jinny couldn't get close enough to her to find out why she was so tetchy. She considered whether she dare ask Nancy or Wendy to talk to her . . . but they would probably think she was complaining, and she wasn't – she just wanted the atmosphere in the kitchen to be comfortable.

Mrs Davies went through to her little office and sat down at her desk. Jinny glanced at her as she walked by carrying plates of food into the dining room. She appeared to be poring over a little black notebook and frowning, totting up figures of some kind. It must be her housekeeping records. Jinny didn't know how much Mrs Davies was allowed to purchase food and cook for everyone, but she did know that she often had to remind the cook that various supplies were running out and she invariably grumbled that everything they bought was too expensive.

Jinny left St Saviour's at half-past seven having finished all her work. Micky was waiting for her at the end of the road. He grinned as he saw her coming and walked to meet her.

'We've just missed one bus,' he told her. 'Do yer want to wait for the next or shall we walk to the next stop and catch it there?'

'Let's walk part of the way,' Jinny suggested. 'It was hot in the kitchen this afternoon and we've been without Elsa all day . . . I can do with some fresh air.'

She tucked her arm through Micky's and smiled up at him as he squeezed it against him. 'You look a bit hot,' he said. 'Are yer still enjoying your job or is it hard going?'

'Sometimes it's hard work but I like most of it . . .'

'What don't yer like?'

'Mrs Davies moans a lot, and she's got worse the past couple of days. I think she's had bad news . . .' Jinny said. 'I saw her reading a letter last Monday morning but she pushed it in her pocket when she saw me watching her and told me to get on with my work. Ever since then she's been grumpy and nothing pleases her, but I can put up with that; it's no worse than Mum used to be. I like the kids and the other members of staff are lovely – and everyone is so appreciative of what I do . . .'

'Well, yer can't 'ave it all – ain't that what they say?'

Jinny laughed as she looked up at him. 'Yes, that's what they say and I'm happier at Halfpenny Street than I ever was at home . . .'

'Good,' he said and something in his eyes at that moment made her nape tingle. 'What about comin' to the flicks with me one night?'

Jinny hesitated, and then inclined her head. 'I'd like that, Micky. I can't do it often, because I'm on duty until this time or later most nights – and I have to be back by half-past ten at the latest. I suppose the best time would be on a Saturday. I get one Saturday afternoon and evening off a fortnight – and Tuesday nights I have free most weeks, but we might not get to see the whole of the main picture . . .'

'Let's go to the Pally instead then,' Micky said. 'We can leave at ten and walk home and you'll be in plenty of time . . .' He suddenly leapt out into the road and flagged down their bus, grinning as it stopped for them.

'Come on, we'll be there in half the time and then I can walk you back later . . .'

Nellie's face was black and blue and Jinny's eyes filled with tears. Her friend was behaving as if it were nothing, but she knew she must be hurting badly, and her anger against Jake increased.

'Oh, Nellie, I'm so sorry,' she said and went to kiss her very gently on the cheek. 'You should tell Bert. He would give him a good hiding.'

'Can't say for sure it was Jake, 'sides, I don't want my old man in trouble with the police. 'E would go fer 'im if I said it were Jake,' Nellie said warily. 'Whoever it were jumped out at me as I walked through the alley where there's no lights, didn't 'e? I couldn't see nothin' but a dark shape . . .'

'Everyone knows it was Jake,' Jinny said. 'I wish we could go to the police and get him locked up.'

'Jake's a menace. Your mother told him to go, but 'e just gave 'er a hiding. She's scared of him, Jinny, but 'e's the boss of her and she's trapped now. 'Er only solace is the beer 'e gives 'er.'

'I hate him,' Jinny said fiercely. 'If I could, I'd beat him until he couldn't stand up. I'd break every bone in his body . . .'

'You leave 'im alone, girl,' Nellie said. ''E'll have it in for yer if yer say one word out of place. I thought 'e'd forget yer once yer weren't around, but 'e's one to bear a grudge. 'Sides, you used to keep the place decent and it's filthy now, never a clean shirt or a cup fer 'im; 'e wants yer back so you can wait on 'im . . . and warm 'is bed an' all if 'e got the chance.'

'He's already threatened me a couple of times,' Jinny said. 'He told me Mum was ill – is it true?'

'She were in a bad way after 'e thrashed her, but I don't think she's ill. I told 'er to come round when Jake had gone to the pub, but she said she was goin' wiv 'im. I told 'er yer might be 'ere but it didn't make no difference.'

Jinny sighed, knowing that her mother was lost to her. She lived for the drink she got from Jake and he was in control of her life; there was nothing Jinny could do to help her until she got rid of him.

'I wish he was dead or crippled in some way so he couldn't hurt any of us ever again,' she said vehemently. 'He's evil, Nellie, and he deserves to be punished – but if no one will tell the police he'll keep gettin' away with it.'

'That's the way of things round 'ere,' Nellie said. 'The lucky ones get a good man, like me, but yer ma was always one for the lookers and she always picked bad 'uns . . .'

Jinny nodded, tears pricking her eyes. 'I don't like to think of him at large, free to attack you or Mum whenever he's in a temper . . .'

'I doubt 'e'll bother with me again,' Nellie said. 'If I told my old man it were 'im fer sure, 'e'd get some of his mates and give Jake a thrashin' . . .'

'Why don't yer?' Micky asked, looking at her intently.

'You know my old man 'as history wiv the local police,' Nellie said. 'Got in a fight down the Docks and was warned that if 'e did it again 'e'd lose his job and probably end up goin' ter prison . . . Bert's the best 'usband ever but 'e's got a temper when 'e thinks somethin' ain't right . . .'

Micky nodded and there was an odd expression in his eyes. 'Tell him to keep 'is nose clean then, Nellie love. Some of us will see to it fer yer . . .'

'Micky!' Jinny said, rounding on him. 'You mustn't do anythin' that would get you into trouble with the law. We need evidence against Jake that we can give the police and stop him hurting folk. Surely someone will stand up in court and tell them what a bully he is? Perhaps if I talk to Mum she'll see sense . . .'

'You be careful,' Nellie warned. 'If 'e catches you round 'ere . . .' She shook her head. 'I'm all right and 'e won't touch me no more – you're the one 'e hates, and if you give 'im the chance 'e'll 'ave yer . . .' She hesitated, then, 'I'll talk to yer ma, Jinny love. If she'll go to the police I'll take 'er in until they've got 'im under lock and key . . .'

'Promise me you'll be careful,' Jinny said. 'I care about you, Nellie – you've been like a mum to me and I don't want Jake to hurt you again.'

'I know when 'e's gone out,' Nellie said and chuckled. 'I'll see if I can make 'er see sense, love – and then we'll talk again. In the meantime, you take care of yerself.'

'She'll be with me,' Micky said. 'We're goin' out now and I'll take care of her.' He looked Nellie in the eyes and she half nodded. 'Jinny will be fine with me . . .'

'Yeah, I reckon she will,' Nellie said. 'Just make sure 'e can't get to 'er, Micky. The bugger's mad and if 'e started hurtin' 'er 'e might not know when to stop . . .'

Jinny sensed something pass between them, some unspoken message that she wasn't supposed to know about. 'I'll be all right,' she said. 'I shan't go out alone at night and he daren't do anything in broad daylight . . .'

'Don't you worry, Nellie,' Micky said and winked at her. 'Jinny's my girl and I'll see that devil don't get near her . . .'

Jinny looked at Micky as they walked home, trying to read his face, but his expression was thoughtful and not easy to fathom.

'You won't do anythin' silly, will you?' she said as they stopped a short distance from St Saviour's in the entrance to a narrow alley. 'Please, Micky. I do like you and I don't want you to be in trouble because of Jake . . .'

Micky bent his head and gave her a quick kiss on the lips. 'You're too young to think about gettin' married yet, Jinny, and I'm not ready to settle – but I care about yer – and one day I'm goin' ter marry yer . . .' He smothered her protest with another kiss. 'I ain't gonna force yer, love, but you'll see how good I can be and one day you'll know . . .'

'Micky, I like you loads but I'm not sure . . .' He grinned at her and she felt suddenly shy. 'Perhaps one day many years ahead – but I want to do something with my life before I get married . . . I might train to be a cook . . .'

'I ain't ready yet either, but don't forget I look after my own.' He gave her a little push forward. 'Go on, get in and be safe. I'll watch until you're inside . . .'

Jinny did as he said, pausing at the door of the nurses' home to turn and wave before using her key to go inside. She was thoughtful as she went upstairs to her room. She did like Micky a lot but she hadn't intended to get into a permanent relationship just yet – but then, he'd admitted he wasn't ready to settle down either. If they went out for a while and one of them got fed up it would all blow over anyway. She should accept her good luck and not worry over things that didn't matter.

The thought that Jake was lingering in the shadows waiting for his revenge was like a dark cloud at the back of her mind. Jinny knew she'd made an enemy of him by threatening to go to the police, but she wasn't going to let it worry her. She was angry that he'd hurt Nellie and wondered what she'd done to anger him. Perhaps he thought Bert knew what he was doing down the Docks and that Nellie had told her Jake was in with a bad lot, but of course it had been Micky that had told Jinny. If he'd taken his fury out on Nellie because of her, Jinny wouldn't forgive herself. Jake hadn't actually hurt her the day he'd tried to grab her so there wasn't much she could report to the police, but if he ever did give her a beating Jinny decided that she wouldn't be intimidated; the moment she had proof of his wrongdoing she would report him and hope they sent him down for a long time. If she'd seen him actually beating her mother or Nellie she wouldn't have hesitated, but at the moment she could only wait and pray that he would be punished one day. If Micky was right and he was mixing with the wrong sort, perhaps they would sort him out . . .

CHAPTER 14

Nancy was coming down the main staircase, her arms filled with dirty linen that she was taking to the scullery to parcel up for the laundry. One of the sheets was hanging down and just as she reached the last two stairs her foot caught and she went forward sharply . . . into the arms of someone she couldn't see, because of all the laundry she was carrying, but knew because of the smell of paint.

'Whoa, steady there,' Rob's voice said kindly. 'Are you all right, Miss Johnson?'

'Yes, thank you,' Nancy said, looking up at him and feeling a little flustered. 'I just missed my step. It was lucky for me that you were there . . .'

'Well, as long as you're not harmed,' Rob said and his gentle smile made Nancy respond with a smile of her own. 'I was planning on finishing the landing upstairs this afternoon so I'll get on out of your way.'

'You're not in my way.' Nancy blushed as he looked at her. 'How are you getting on, Mr Thompson? It is all looking very fresh and bright.'

'There's still a fair bit to do yet,' Rob told her. 'This is a big place for me on my own and Nick has taken on other work now he's finished the plumbing – but I'm getting there.'

'Good.' Nancy lingered for a moment, then, 'Well, I'd better get this parcelled up ready for the laundry van to call . . .'

'You should get a basket or something,' Rob advised. 'If you'd fallen from the top you could've really hurt yourself . . .'

Nancy nodded but didn't reply. He'd sounded as if he really cared and that was a little unsettling, because she didn't know how to respond, and she hurried away feeling oddly uncertain. He had such a lovely smile and a nice manner – and a part of her still regretted the way she'd been sharp with him on that first day. Perhaps, she thought wistfully, if she'd been friendly he would have invited her to the party Jinny had never stopped talking about since that night . . .

Oh well, she probably couldn't have gone anyway, because she'd been on duty that night . . . although she knew Mavis would have swapped with her if she'd asked. Nancy dismissed the regrets as foolishness as she got down to work. She would be a fool to let herself go soft over Rob – because she knew she could never have a proper relationship with a man. How could she – after what Pa did to her when she was a child?

He'd ruined her, scarred her for life, leaving her with bitter memories and for many years disturbing dreams, though at last those had stopped coming. Nancy was luckier than her brother, because Terry's mind had been warped and twisted forever after what their father had done to them both.

Brushing away the moisture from her eyes, Nancy

got on with her job. This was silly, letting a few kind words get to her. She didn't need Rob Thompson to ask her out; she didn't need anyone but her friends at St Saviour's . . .

'Got yer at last, you little runt!' The voice of the Beast in Andy's ear made him start and he darted forward as he felt the hand grab his shoulder. 'You're comin' wiv me and we'll get that sister of yours an' all . . .'

'No! You can't make me,' Andy cried and wriggled free of his step-father's hold. 'I won't come back and Beth won't either. You've hit us for the last time and now you're goin' to pay . . .'

'I know you've set the cops on me,' Arthur Phillips growled. 'They came round the house lookin' fer me – Mabel next door told me – but I was out. You've been tellin' lies about me and you can just take 'em back . . . or I'll skin you alive . . .'

'I didn't tell lies; it's all true,' Andy defended himself. 'I know you want us out of the way so you can 'ave Dad's house but we ain't comin' back. I don't want the house or anythin' to do with you and I don't care what you say . . .'

'You little sod . . .' Arthur muttered and made another grab for him, but Andy kicked out sharply and ran back into the playground, his breath coming sharply in gasps of fear. He'd been lost in happy thoughts of playing for the school team and just hadn't seen the Beast hanging around. His head down and angry tears on his cheeks, he ran straight into someone's bulk and steady hands held him firmly.

'What is wrong, lad?' Mr Barton asked, looking down

at him and then beyond. 'Was that man trying to force you to go with him?'

'He's my step-father,' Andy said. 'The doctor said he would be arrested fer hurtin' me and Beth, but he's come after me and if he makes us go with him, he'll kill us . . .'

'Slow down, lad,' his teacher said and let go of his arms. 'I'll have a word with Mr Phillips . . .'

As the schoolmaster walked towards Andy's step-father he turned and walked off quickly, but not before he'd thrown him a look of menace. Andy shuddered, because he knew that one of these days there would be no one around to protect him.

'Hey you – Phillips! I want a word . . .' Mr Barton called but there was no answer. Arthur didn't even turn his head to look. After a moment he returned to Andy and stood looking down at him. 'He frightened you, Andy. I'll see you home – but first we'll go to the police station and talk to Sergeant Sallis. That rogue wants locking up before he does more damage.'

'Thanks, sir,' Andy said. 'I can stand up to him, but if he tries to grab Beth . . . she's terrified of him. He used to swear at her and beat her all the time. I told the truth because the doctor said the police would believe him, but now he's after us and I'm afraid of what he'll do . . .'

'The police need proof before they can pull him in for questioning. Your doctor knew you'd been beaten, but he only had your word it was your step-father. I'm going to bear witness to what I saw, which isn't enough but may help to convince the police that Mr Phillips is violent,' the teacher said. 'Come on, lad. We'll go in my car – your friend Keith can come with us if you like . . .' He smiled at him. 'I'll ask Sister Beatrice if it's all right – and if she agrees my wife and I will take the pair of you into the country and give you some driving tuition on a private airfield this Sunday. Now how would you like that?'

'Would you really?' Andy's smile lit his face. 'Could Beth come too – if she gets back from the hospital?'

'Is your sister poorly then?'

'Yeah, I ain't sure when she'll be back . . .'

'Well, if she is you can bring her or another friend. I'll hire a station wagon and take one of your carers too – make it a proper outing with a picnic basket and lemonade.'

Andy flushed. 'It's very good of you, sir.'

'I've got to look after my best runner on the rounders team,' Mr Barton said and laughed. 'Now, let's get Keith and then we'll get off down the police station.'

Andy sought out Sister Rose after tea that evening. He knocked at the door of the sick ward and was invited to enter. Rose smiled encouragingly as he went in.

'Are you feeling unwell, Andy?'

'I'm all right thank you, but it's only because Mr Barton stopped him . . .' He told her what had happened outside the school and how the teacher had taken him and Keith to see the police.

'That was unpleasant for you, Andy. What did the police have to say?'

'They said they were taking the complaint seriously and had asked Arthur in for an interview, but when Mr Barton told them what he'd seen Sergeant Sallis said he would have him arrested and questioned. It seems that although the doctor told them that both Beth and me had been beaten, they can't prosecute him without more evidence. At the moment it is only my word against his . . . no one has witnessed anything . . .'

'Yes, I see . . .' Rose frowned, because Doctor Henderson had been so certain his report would result in Arthur Phillips being arrested for assault immediately. The delay was putting Andy and his sister at risk. 'It was fortunate that Mr Barton was there.'

Andy agreed and explained the teacher had offered to take Keith and him with his own family into the country for a picnic and a driving lesson on private land.

'We can drive there even though we're not old enough to hold a licence,' Andy said. 'He's great – and he says one of our carers can come too.'

'I'll ask Nancy if she has time,' Rose promised. 'If not perhaps Jinny could spare the time . . . it depends who is on duty . . .' She hesitated, then, 'Unless you would like me to come?'

'Beth trusts you,' Andy said. 'If you've got time?'

'Well, I'll see if Nancy would like to go – if not, it is my day off. I would need to be back by six at the latest . . .'

'Mr Barton said we'd be back in time for tea . . .'

'Then in that case I'll come,' Rose promised. 'If it's what you'd like?'

'It's why I came,' Andy said and grinned. 'Everyone likes you, Nurse Rose. You're always so thoughtful and kind to us . . .'

'Then I shall certainly come,' Rose agreed. 'Go and tell your friends and I'll see you on Sunday . . .'

*

'So is it tonight you're going out with Nick Trent?' Wendy asked when they met as Rose came on duty the following morning. She smiled as Rose nodded a little apprehensively. 'It's the third time, isn't it?' She arched her brows teasingly as Rose nodded.

'It's dinner again tonight . . . last time it was a drink . . .' Rose smiled. 'We went to a lovely hotel that time and the food was wonderful . . . It's ages since I went anywhere like that . . . and Nick was really considerate. He opened doors for me and everything . . .'

'Careful, you'll be getting serious soon . . .'

'It's just friends . . . that's all I want for now anyway.'

'Maybe for you – but I think he might want more – a lot more . . .'

'Do you think so?' Rose asked. Wendy had lost two men she'd loved, both as a result of the war, and yet she'd rebuilt her life and was now going steady with a man she spoke of as a friend, but who took her out regularly and bought her flowers and chocolates; he wanted to marry her but Wendy wasn't sure she wanted marriage. Rose shouldn't let one unpleasant incident with Mike Bonner put her off men for life. He'd been a careless, selfish man, but she was over him now. 'I hope Nick isn't too serious just yet. I'm being silly but . . .' She broke off as Kelly entered the sick ward and started to speak heatedly.

'It's happened again. Two pounds is missing from the petty cash. I counted it yesterday after I put my two bob in – and now it's short. I know we said last time it happened it was probably a mistake and we wouldn't bother Sister Beatrice, but I think she ought to know we have a thief at St Saviour's . .

'Oh, that is a nuisance,' Rose said. 'I thought we could save up for the Christmas party, buy some presents for the kids, but if this is going to keep happening we shall have to put the box somewhere else.'

'Why not put it in a drawer in the nurses' office up in the attic?' Wendy suggested. 'We can lock that file and stop whoever it is from pilfering.'

'Good idea,' Rose agreed. 'It's a shame though, because it's not pleasant to know that someone would steal from us . . .'

'I noticed we were short a couple of weeks back,' Kelly said. 'I wasn't certain enough to say anything, but this time I know, because Sandra made it so easy to see after you suspected some money might have gone. We've had that box there for years and it was always safe . . . Who do you think would take money from our savings?'

'We've still got the builders in . . . but I'm sure Rob wouldn't,' Wendy said and sighed. 'I hate to think it's one of the children. We've never had this sort of trouble before. I suppose it might be one of the girls from next door . . . some of them were caught stealing from shops . . . and they do come in sometimes after school . . .'

'Muriel used to say the kids sometimes sneaked into her pantry to steal food, but money is different,' Kelly said. 'I know you didn't want to upset her, but I think Sister Beatrice should know.'

'Well, I suppose we ought to tell her,' Rose agreed. 'I know it's not nice, but unless something is said it will continue. Sister Beatrice should be the one to say something about it – perhaps before supper . . .'

'I'll tell her then,' Wendy agreed. 'I'll pop into her office before I leave – but she won't like it, because she's always thought we were like a family here and who would steal from their family?'

The three women looked at each other uneasily. None of them were under suspicion, because they'd all been paying in so that they could provide treats for the staff and kids at Christmas.

'But who would do something like that?' Wendy looked upset.

'I don't suppose . . .' Rose began and the others looked at her. 'I thought it was just a coincidence . . . No, I'm sure it was nothing.'

'What?' Kelly demanded. 'Have you noticed anything?'

Rose hesitated and then shook her head. It wouldn't be fair to mention the fact that she'd seen Jinny leaving the staff room with a tray and when she'd entered a few minutes later she'd seen the drawer where the cash box was kept was slightly open. Rose hadn't mentioned it then and she hadn't investigated the contents at the time, because it hadn't crossed her mind that the young helper she liked could have been stealing their money – but since then she'd been sure money was missing on more than one occasion. Two pounds was a lot and it wasn't fair on the girls who'd been saving for their Christmas do.

'I'll take the box up to our office in the attics and lock it up,' Wendy said. 'And then I'll tell Sister Beatrice what I've done and why . . .'

Kelly watched her leave and then turned to Rose. 'You've seen somethin', haven't you?'

'Yes, but I don't want to point the finger of blame without proof. I can't be sure what I saw had anything to do with her . . . and it wouldn't be fair to cast suspicion on her without some proof.'

Kelly screwed up her forehead, her gaze narrowed. 'Are you thinkin' it might have been Jinny? Or Mavis – she's new here too . . . or one of us?'

'Of course not,' Rose said, but avoided her eyes. 'I'm not going to say unless I know for sure – and I don't.'

'Jinny wouldn't steal from us,' Kelly said and looked annoyed. 'No, I know I was angry because the money had gone, but I like Jinny. She needs this chance and she's grateful. I know she wouldn't touch a penny.'

'It's just . . .' Rose sighed. 'This is between us and only because you guessed – I saw Jinny leaving the staff room with a tray the other afternoon and when I went in, the drawer was slightly open . . .'

'You didn't check the money?'

'No, it didn't occur to me then,' Rose said. 'I knew we were a few bob short a couple of times, but I thought it was mislaid or miscounted – and someone might have bought biscuits or tea or something . . . It was only when I noticed the ten-shilling note was missing that I started to wonder and I spoke to Sandra . . . and she told me in confidence that money had gone from her desk too.'

Wendy looked thoughtful. 'Jinny fills our tin with stuff she's made and she refills our sugar pot – and the food Mrs Davies has been serving up recently hasn't been very nice. I only eat a sandwich here now or a bit of cake if Jinny made it . . . She can't be the thief or she wouldn't do nice things for us.'

'Yes, I've noticed some of the children turning up their noses at lunchtime recently,' Rose said. 'I'm the same, I hardly ever ask for more than a sandwich or a piece of toast these days . . . and twice I've been told there's no ham, only cheese or corned beef . . .'

'The kitchen always supplied everything before Mrs Davies took over. She insisted that we should buy our own tea and coffee, because her budget wasn't big enough to supply the staff room as well.' Wendy sighed. 'When Angela was here she brought in proper coffee, tea and sometimes biscuits – but Muriel baked fresh every day, and then Nancy took over . . .'

'Angela was always getting fruit and stuff free for the kitchen,' Rose said. 'I suppose that's why Muriel never complained about her budget, but Mrs Davies doesn't seem to be so capable at buying – and her food certainly isn't as good either. That beef pie the other day had gristle in it . . . I couldn't eat it.'

'Did you tell her about it?' Wendy asked.

'I wouldn't dare,' Rose grimaced. 'She would probably walk out on us . . . I think the kids eat most of it . . .'

'They like what Jinny makes for tea best . . .'

'Yes, well, kids always like sweet stuff, don't they?'

'Thank goodness for Nancy and Jinny,' Kelly said and gave Rose a straight look. 'Jinny isn't the thief. I'd swear to that on my life.'

'I'm sure you're right,' Rose agreed. 'Someone is though. I expect one of the kids found the box and thought it was fair game. I'm really sorry for even doubting Jinny for an instant – but you must admit it is a nasty business . . .'

Jinny brought a tray up for Rose mid-morning. Besides a plate of sandwiches and little cakes for her patients, and a bowl of jelly and evaporated milk for the recovering tonsillitis case, there was a jug of barley water and a pot of tea. She knocked at the door and waited until Rose invited her to enter and then set the tray down carefully on the desk before asking if there was anything else Rose or the children needed.

'No, this is lovely,' Rose said. 'You've gone to a lot of trouble for us, Jinny. Thank you.' She looked at the jug of evaporated milk. 'I did ask for some ice cream with the jelly . . .'

'Mrs Davies says she can't manage ice cream out of her budget . . . You bought the last block we had and that's all gone.'

'I'll get another block and bring it in tomorrow,' Rose said and frowned. 'I don't understand it. Muriel always had ice cream in the fridge, especially after Angela got us that lovely big one with an icebox . . .'

'It's a shame, because it's something all the kids love,' Jinny answered cheerfully. 'I love working here and it's a pleasure to get things ready for you nurses and the children . . . and I wish I could write the menus . . .'

After Jinny departed, taking with her some used mugs to wash, Rose felt really guilty for even thinking that the young girl would help herself to money they were saving for little celebrations. She'd even put in her two bob since she joined them so she knew how important it was and it was ridiculous even to consider it. No, it had to be one of the kids – even though Sister Beatrice wouldn't like that suggestion very much . . .

Rose had more or less put the unpleasant thoughts from her mind when she left that evening to change and get ready for her dinner with Nick Trent. Washed and dressed in a pretty voile blue and white dress with a tight bodice and a floaty skirt, Rose was outside St

Saviour's by five minutes to eight. She was a little surprised when he drew up at the kerb in a smart black Morris car. He got out and opened the passenger door for her to get in, smiling at her.

'You look lovely, Rose. That dress suits you . . .'

'Thank you.' She blushed slightly as he tucked her dress in and closed the door carefully so as not to catch the skirt and spoil it. It was a long time since any man had been so attentive. Besides, Nick looked as though he really meant it. 'Where are we going?'

'It's a small Italian restaurant I know well,' he said. 'I did the renovations for Signor Cantonelli and they always give me a decent table and the food is very good.' His gaze seemed to caress her. 'I think you'll like their cooking, Rose – but you don't have to choose Italian-style food; they do plenty of meat and fish dishes that are very simple but just beautifully presented.'

'It sounds delicious,' Rose replied, feeling the vague shadows that had seemed to hang over her most of the day fade away. She was looking forward to the evening, because she enjoyed this man's company. 'I'm hungry . . .'

'Good.' He looked so pleased that she laughed, any lingering restraint melting away.

Rose stretched in the warmth of her bed and smiled as she remembered she wasn't due in until later that afternoon. She'd been late in last night, using her key and walking softly upstairs so as not to disturb anyone. It was seldom that Rose broke the rules and came back later than ten thirty, but it had been so pleasant sitting drinking wine and then coffee in what was rather like a garden room. Because the night was warm, Signor Cantonelli had opened the big glass windows that overlooked his courtyard garden and allowed the guests to feel they were dining outside. The smell of roses, honeysuckle and English lavender had floated to them and the tinkling of water as it cascaded into a small fountain was enchanting.

They'd sat on for ages after their meal, talking, sipping wine and then the delicious coffee their genial host had provided.

'It's so quiet you'd hardly think we're in the heart of London,' Rose said, because although she'd known places like this did exist, she hadn't been to any. 'And I do like Italian food, Nick. Thank you for bringing me here.'

'It's one of my favourite places,' he said and reached across the table to touch her hand. 'I thought you might like it, Rose.'

'I do,' she assured him and sipped her coffee. 'I think this is one of the nicest restaurants I've been to . . .'

'I'm so glad. I'd like to show you more of my London,' Nick told her. 'Perhaps we could go somewhere again soon?'

'I'd love to,' Rose said. 'But perhaps I could cook a meal for you at your house one day?'

'Thank you, I'd like that,' Nick said, 'but I've got two tickets for a musical next week . . . I thought we could go there and then have supper somewhere?'

'When is it?' Rose asked and nodded when he told her. 'Yes, I'm not on duty that evening. I should like to come . . .'

Shrugging off the bedcovers, Rose put her pleasant

thoughts to one side. She gathered her things and made for the bathroom, which was unoccupied. She wanted to do a little shopping before she went on duty that afternoon . . .

'The money was missing from my bag,' Kelly was saying as Rose walked into the staff room that morning. 'I left it with my coat in here yesterday – and I know I had three pounds, because I wanted to buy some shoes I'd seen and do my food shopping for the weekend. When I got to the till to pay for the shoes there were only two pounds in my purse, so I had to pay a deposit on the shoes and leave them until next week. My father will be furious, because he gave me two pounds to buy them for my birthday . . .'

'Oh, Kelly no,' Wendy said. 'This is awful – it's even worse than money going missing from the petty cash. We've got that in a locked drawer in our office now, but I don't know who would steal from you.' She looked really upset and Rose felt a bit sick.

'You're quite sure you didn't spend a pound anywhere – or put it somewhere else in your bag?'

Kelly shook her head. 'It was all in my purse. I never bring so much out with me unless I have special shopping to do and I'm really annoyed. Dad saved hard to give me the money for those shoes and he will be upset.'

'Whoever took it must have looked for the cash box and then decided to go for your bag, Kelly. It's bad luck. I think we shall have to put all money and valuables in the nurses' office and lock them up in future.'

'I told Sister Beatrice about the petty cash last evening and she was most put out,' Wendy said. 'I don't know what she will say to this – two thefts within two days are just too much . . .'

'Yes, it is too much,' Rose agreed. 'What did Sister suggest?'

'She asked me if I had any idea who might have taken the money, but I said no because I just can't believe it has happened . . .'

'Nor can I,' Kelly said. 'I never dreamed anyone would touch my bag. The cash box is one thing but . . . a bag is personal . . .'

'It's very unpleasant,' Rose said. 'Until we catch the thief it casts a cloud over us all, because it could be anyone . . . Oh, I don't mean us, but the children and Rob and . . . Jinny . . .'

'Why Jinny?' Wendy asked and frowned. 'She put her two bob in same as the rest of us and told me she thought it was a lovely idea. I'm sure she wouldn't touch it, Rose – and she would never go in Kelly's bag. I'm sure she wouldn't . . . and what about Elsa or Mavis – but Mavis hasn't been in today so you can rule her out.'

Kelly was frowning. 'Rose is right though,' she said. 'If we told the police we'd all be under suspicion. Nothin' like this has ever happened before and we trust one another, but no one else would . . . it just makes everythin' uncomfortable for us all.'

'What is Sister going to do?' Rose asked.

'She said she would speak to the children and staff this evening before supper. I know she didn't like the idea, but she can't stand by and do nothin' – but some of the kids are goin' to feel bad about this,' Wendy told them. 'A lot of them have come from homes where the father has a record for thieving and brutality. They're bound to think she's pointing the finger at them.'

'Well, she has to do something,' Kelly said. 'We've never had to lock things up before and I don't like it.'

'No, I don't blame you,' Rose said. 'Look, I'll lend you a pound so that you can get your shoes before you go home, Kelly. I don't need it so you can give it back when you like . . .'

Kelly hesitated, and then shook her head. 'I don't believe in borrowing off friends, Rose, though it's lovely of you and I'm grateful – but I shan't take it, even though I know you mean well.'

Rose understood her pride and nodded. She'd wanted to make Kelly feel better, but this petty thieving was troublesome for them all and wouldn't get better until they discovered the thief and stopped it.

Nick hadn't been working at St Saviour's for a couple of weeks. Besides, Rose couldn't believe that Rob or his brother would take money that didn't belong to them; they worked hard and were generous, bringing in a box of chocolates to say thank you for the cups of tea and biscuits they'd been given while working at St Saviour's. None of the carers or nurses would take money from each other, because they were all friends, and anyway it had only started happening recently – that only left Jinny, as the newcomer, and the kids, and Rose found that the thought of Jinny or the children stealing left a bad taste in her mouth. She wished it would all go away, but theft was theft and they couldn't just brush it under the carpet. Sister Beatrice was going to have to use her authority to stamp it out before it went too far . . .

CHAPTER 15

The kids had started to file into the dining room for supper when Sister Beatrice entered. They'd been told she was coming to talk to them and a hush fell as she walked to the little dais at the end of the room. Her eyes seemed to move over the children and staff, a hint of disapproval in her manner as she began to speak.

'It pains me to have to speak to you all on such a subject,' she said. 'Indeed, it has never happened at St Saviour's before and I find it upsetting that it should happen now. If anyone has a grudge against us or feels they have been treated badly please come and see me in my office later – but I am afraid that what I have to say is not pleasant. It has been brought to my attention that money has been taken from the cash box in the staff room and from a member of staff's bag, also from Sandra's office. This is a serious matter and one I should like to resolve without resource to the law. I would very much dislike having to speak to Sergeant Sallis about this – but if it continues I shall have no alternative. At the moment we have no particular suspects, and if anyone wishes to tell me anything I shall give them a fair hearing – but this must stop.' She looked round the room and her eyes seemed to linger on Elsa and then on Jinny. 'That is all I have to say and I hope that will be an end to this unfortunate incident.'

''Ere, I 'ope she don't think it were me,' Elsa hissed at Jinny as she moved to her side. 'She were lookin' at us the longest . . .'

'I'm sure she doesn't,' Jinny said but her throat felt tight and she was prickling all over because she'd sensed that Sister was looking at her and so was Sister Rose, and she didn't like the look in Rose's eyes. Surely, she couldn't imagine that Jinny had taken the money?

She had no time to think about it because the kids were queuing up for their supper and she was kept busy serving drinks and pouring custard over the apple pie she'd made that afternoon, but something was making the back of her neck prickle as she tried to remember. It wasn't until the rather subdued children had eaten their supper and gone and she was washing up in the kitchen that it came back to her. Suddenly, Jinny remembered that she'd seen Tom – the boy who had complained about the lack of good food on her first day – coming from the staff room on one occasion. And when she'd gone in to collect the dirty dishes, she'd seen the drawer containing the cash box slightly open.

Jinny hadn't told anyone. She hadn't looked in the box and she didn't know whether any money had been taken that afternoon – it was the afternoon that Mrs Davies had been late back after taking a nap in her room and Jinny had been on her own in the kitchen as she prepared tea and supper . . .

Jinny had forgotten it because she was too busy and

caught up in her own life, but now she wondered. Had Tom taken the missing money? And had someone seen Jinny leaving with her tray and was now thinking it might have been her?

Sister Rose had looked at her so oddly. Perhaps she'd seen Jinny walking away with the tray and then found the drawer still open. She felt hot all over and tears pricked behind her eyes. She liked the nurse a lot and had thought Rose liked her – but if she thought Jinny could do anything like that . . . it made her want to shout and punch something, because it was so unfair. Yet it would be just as unfair of her to blame Tom without proof. If she tried talking to Rose about what she'd seen she would probably think she was covering her own tracks. No, she couldn't do that, but it made her feel uncomfortable to know that she was under suspicion. No one had said anything to her, but Rose had looked so strange – and Sister Beatrice had definitely looked at her and Elsa longer than anyone else. Naturally, Sister wouldn't want to blame her nurses or the staff who had been with her for years. Mavis, Jinny and Elsa had been there the shortest time and so people were wondering if one of them was to blame.

Jinny felt hollow inside as she dried her hands and put the tea towels into soapy water to soak for the morning. She would wash them and put them out in the garden to dry if it was fine first thing. The laundry wasn't back yet this week and tea towels needed changing every day.

After saying goodnight to Elsa, Jinny went to the office to ask Mrs Davies if everything was all right. She saw the cook busily counting the money in her cash box and turned away feeling as if she'd been struck. It seemed as if Mrs Davies couldn't wait to count her money in case she too had lost some of her allowance for the kitchen . . .

The cook turned to look at her and scowled. 'What are you doing spying on me?'

'I wasn't,' Jinny said, clenching her fists. 'I just came to ask if there was anything else you needed me to do before I leave.'

'Nothing. I'm going to lock this money away. If there's a thief about I can't risk losing my monthly budget. It's hard enough to manage as it is . . .'

'Perhaps we could get some free stuff from the market like Mrs Adderbury used to when she was here . . .'

'What nonsense are you talking?' Mrs Davies snapped. 'I don't know what went on here in the past, but I don't buy low standard fruit and veg from the market. I trust proper grocers to provide me with quality food.'

Jinny didn't bother to argue. She'd seen the bills for food provided on a couple of occasions and they looked unreasonably high to her, especially as she often had to cut bits out of potatoes and carrots, but there was no point in getting her head bitten off again by suggesting that she could do much better by shopping with her friends on the market. Nellie had often trusted Jinny with her weekly shop, telling her that she got things fresher and cheaper than she could from the shops.

'I sometimes shop nearer home, 'cos it's a long way to trudge with a heavy basket,' Nellie had told her, 'but they don't 'alf charge if yer don't watch 'em.'

Judging by the bills she'd seen lying around after Mrs Davies had shown them to Sandra, St Saviour's was being overcharged for lots of things – but Jinny was only the kitchen help and no one would listen to her opinion. Besides, if they suspected her of stealing, she might not be here for long . . .

'I feel very distressed that anyone should steal from my staff,' Beatrice said to Sandra later in her office as they sat over their morning coffee. 'I can hardly believe it has happened – we've never had stealing at St Saviour's before. The money you lost was for the children's visit to the zoo . . . now who would be mean enough to take that?'

'I couldn't believe it until all the other thefts happened,' Sandra said. 'I kept thinking I'd mislaid it – and then Kelly lost money from her bag. Someone is a thief . . .'

'We've never had anything like that here before . . .'

'Has anyone given you any clue as to who it might be?' Sandra asked. 'I mean we do have the builders in, but I think they're honest. They certainly seem hard workers and nothing has disappeared from your office – or the nurses' home, has it?'

'Not as yet – or not that I've been told. The Thompson brothers have had the run of the place, but they've been so punctilious in asking permission to work in various rooms that I just cannot believe they would steal anything.'

'Well, it doesn't seem likely . . .'

'Most of my staff has been with me for years,' Beatrice said. 'I know they wouldn't steal their own money or Kelly's – but that leaves just the kitchen girls or one of the children . . . or the girls next door. They are supervised when they come to tea, but one or two of them have been sneaking inside at odd times, in the hope of being given something nice to eat. Mrs Davies told one of the older girls to clear off yesterday. She came up to tell me, because she's most concerned about her money. She says she can't afford to lose money or food from the pantry . . .'

'Jinny seems honest to me. Elsa is a little workshy but I can't see her stealing money myself. It might be one of the children, of course, but I would think they would just take a shilling or two, something that might not be noticed. Two pounds from the petty cash, my money, and then a pound from Kelly's purse is rather a lot. None of them has been buying lots of sweets, I suppose?'

'I hate to think of our children as thieves . . . but if not the kitchen girls or the girls from next door . . . who else?'

'You haven't mentioned me . . .'

'Sandra! As if I would ever think such a wicked thing after what you suffered. I know it isn't you.'

'I suppose . . . what do you know about Mrs Davies?' Sandra frowned as Beatrice looked at her oddly. 'I hate to cast doubt but . . .' she shook her head. 'No, that is unforgivable but we should all consider all angles . . . perhaps someone came in from outside and stole it . . . ?'

'There's something you're not telling me, isn't there?' Beatrice asked, looking at Sandra's pink cheeks. She was the last one to accuse an innocent person because of what had happened to her when she was arrested for a theft she hadn't committed. 'Please, tell me what is in your mind, Sandra.'

'Well, I've been meaning to mention it, but I know

you had difficulty in replacing Muriel . . . but I've questioned some of the items in Mrs Davies' accounts once or twice. She always has an answer I can't refute, but I've felt she was lying . . . I suspect that she is overcharging us and . . . I suspect she must be pocketing the difference, but I've never been sure.'

'What makes you think she's benefiting from the accounts? Some of the shops do charge a great deal, which is why Angela was so good at getting low prices from people she charmed . . .'

'Haven't you noticed that some of the food isn't as good as it ought to be? I've noticed that children leave meat on their plates sometimes and I asked one boy why. He said it was gristly and too fatty and made him feel sick . . .'

'If we're being cheated Mrs Davies should change her suppliers. Did you speak to her about it?'

'I did ask her if she was satisfied with her butcher and she told me it was all in hand so I didn't say anything more.'

Beatrice stared at her, feeling a little sick. Mrs Davies wouldn't be the first woman to steal small amounts of money from her employers in this manner – it often happened in the kitchens of rich ladies and was considered the cook's perks – but this wasn't a rich woman's kitchen. It was a charity-run home for disadvantaged children and the thought that someone could cheat those children of the good food they were entitled to turned her stomach.

'Why didn't you tell me before?'

'Because I don't have proof of anything,' Sandra said, 'and I hate to cast doubts on another woman's character.

Perhaps Mrs Davies is just paying too much without knowing it.'

'I should like to look over the accounts myself, and I will walk round at lunchtime sometimes,' Beatrice said. 'I do have Muriel's old books here and it would be interesting to compare, but I think if you've noticed discrepancies they are there . . . However, that doesn't mean that she has stolen from the cash box or from Kelly's bag . . .'

'No, of course not . . .' Sandra said but still seemed doubtful.

'If I discover discrepancies I shall speak to her quite severely . . .'

'I'll bring the accounts to you. I'm sorry if you feel I've let you down . . .'

'Not at all,' Beatrice said. 'You help me a great deal, Sandra, and I understand your reluctance to point the finger of blame. I should feel much the same myself. Mrs Davies is a widow and of good character. I find it difficult to believe that she would syphon off money for herself, though I do know that she had some money worries before she came to us – something to do with her son I believe.'

'Yes, but that doesn't make her a thief,' Sandra said. 'I know what it is like to be short of money to care for your children – and what it is to be accused of theft for no good reason . . .' She frowned. 'Does Mrs Davies have more than one child?'

'Just one son I think,' Beatrice replied. 'She told me he no longer lived at home and that's why I gave her a room here, because she could not afford the rent for a house.'

'Perhaps I was wrong even to suggest . . .' Sandra looked distressed and uncomfortable.

'I am glad you mentioned it. If St Saviour's is being overcharged we must change our suppliers,' Beatrice said. 'Angela was so good at getting us donations, of fresh fruit and vegetables as well as money . . .' She sighed. 'The trouble is, we've never had quite enough funds to pay for everything. I could not ease my conscience if I allowed our children to be cheated of what they are entitled to.'

'No.' Sandra rose to her feet. 'I'll ask for the accounts book. It covers the past six months so you can easily see any changes.'

'Yes, please do. I have to make my rounds now, but I shall be in my office again in an hour . . .'

Beatrice was thoughtful as her secretary and helper left. Sandra was efficient but Angela would have picked up any overcharging immediately and sorted it. A sigh escaped her. Perhaps life would be easier if she were to take up the offer to join Angela at Halfpenny House.

Yet she'd always felt her vocation was here in the poorest part of London, caring for the children when they were most in need. By the time they moved out to the country they had healed in body and spirit and she had helped that healing. Warmth filled her as sunlight filtered through the glass of the old windows, sending a shower of light across the room to the newly painted pale walls of her office. Only if she was forced to leave would she feel able to let go of the reins and move on . . . and in the meantime there was the unpleasant task of examining the books and perhaps an awkward interview with their cook . . .

*

'Oh, Jinny,' Sandra said as she went into the kitchen and found the young girl hard at work peeling vegetables and in the middle of making a large Yorkshire pudding. She'd left the mixture to stand in the yellow pudding basin while she peeled carrots and she washed her hands. 'Are we having roast beef then?'

'No, that's much too expensive,' Jinny said and laughed. 'We're having sausages done in the oven in a Yorkshire pudding . . . toad in the hole, Nellie calls it. She makes it a lot for her family and it tastes smashing with mashed potatoes, gravy and carrots and greens . . .'

'Where is Mrs Davies? I need the account books. Sister wants to check them . . .'

'She went off quick half an hour ago. Someone brought her a message . . .' Jinny frowned. 'She looked upset – said she was sorry but she'd have to leave the dinner to me . . .'

'Does this often happen?'

'No – well, she goes shopping in the afternoon sometimes but it's easy to manage tea and supper. Elsa's in the scullery peeling potatoes for the mash so we'll manage all right. I made the apple crumble early this mornin' . . .'

'It's rather awkward . . .' Sandra shook her head, because she couldn't discuss her thoughts with Jinny; it wouldn't be right. 'Do you know where the accounts are?'

'Well, Mrs Davies locked her money in a drawer of her desk last night, because of the thefts . . .' Jinny went painfully red. 'She accused me of spying on her but I was only going to ask if she wanted anything more before I went off . . . but I think the book is in the top drawer of her desk.'

'Well, I'll see if I can find it . . .' Sandra started towards the cook's office and then stopped. 'I'd like you to come with me, Jinny. I'd like a witness that I took only the book . . .'

Jinny stared at her in surprise. 'No one could think you would take anythin' . . .'

Sandra looked sad. 'When money starts to disappear, anyone and everyone is under suspicion, Jinny. I was once branded a thief and I do not intend it should happen again, therefore I need a witness . . .'

'Oh Sandra, that's awful . . .' Jinny said and shivered as if she'd turned suddenly cold. 'Elsa and me thought they was lookin' at us last night, but neither of us took that money. I swear I didn't – and Elsa was savage that anyone would think it . . .'

'It is uncomfortable for all of us,' Sandra said. 'We'll fetch the book together and then no one can blame either of us if something unpleasant happens . . .'

Jinny nodded, wiped her hands and followed Sandra into the cook's office. The top of the desk was littered with papers, recipes, some unpaid bills, old menus, pens, pencils and a ruler. Jinny pointed to the long top drawer and Sandra opened it, taking out the notebook that lay there. She opened it, read a few columns and then frowned. Seeing a pile of menu cards on the desk, she picked them up and took them with her.

'If Mrs Davies asks where her accounts are you may tell her I took them to Sister Beatrice, Jinny – and now I shan't keep you from your work any longer . . .'

Sandra went out, shutting the door behind her. She

frowned as she took the book up to her own office and sat down to check. There didn't seem to be anything wrong with her figures, other than they seemed rather high for the kind of food she'd been buying. But the only crime she could be accused of was culpability in letting the suppliers overcharge her for substandard food.

Mrs Davies was being overcharged by unscrupulous shopkeepers who thought that because she'd come from the country she didn't know the correct prices. It was a failing but not dishonesty, and the only way to stop it was for someone else to have charge of the buying.

Sandra didn't often eat at St Saviour's – perhaps one of Nancy's biscuits and a cup of tea or coffee mid-afternoon or morning, and a sandwich at lunch was all she bothered with – but she seemed to recall that Sister Beatrice had told her the children had been given a roast dinner every week once meat was off ration and readily available. Jinny had spoken as if that was too expensive to be thought of and looked surprised when Sandra asked the question.

She opened the book again and checked what kinds of meat were being purchased, frowning as she realised that only the very cheapest cuts had been recorded recently. Neck and breast of lamb, scrag end of beef, belly pork and offal and occasionally sausages. Eggs, streaky bacon and liver but rarely fish of any kind. It was the kind of fare that would have been generally acceptable during the war when the shortages were at their height, but surely a roast once a week or chicken would make a nice change for the children, and fish was good for them, also more fruit.

All Sandra could do was to draw Sister Beatrice's attention to this and leave her to deal with the cook. Sister would give Mrs Davies fair warning. If she wanted to keep her job she would provide the children with the good food they were entitled to . . .

'Have you been in my office?' Mrs Davies demanded of Jinny and Elsa some minutes after she returned from her sudden outing. 'Where have they gone – my accounts and the menu cards?'

'I ain't touched them,' Elsa sniffed. 'I ain't a bloody thief and if anyone accuses me of anythin' I'm leavin'!'

'Sandra came to fetch them for Sister Beatrice,' Jinny spoke up, though her knees felt weak because she could see that Mrs Davies was in a temper. 'I went into the office with her when she took them – she didn't touch the money you locked in that drawer.'

'I wasn't talking about the cash box,' Mrs Davies snapped. 'I'm talking about someone taking my accounts and menu cards – and I want to know why she came and got them when my back was turned.'

'Sister Beatrice asked for them,' Jinny said, seeing the cook's eyes snap with temper. 'She thought you would be here . . .'

'And of course you told her I'd gone off suddenly.' Mrs Davies advanced on her and suddenly lashed out, catching Jinny a blow on the side of the head. 'You sneaking telltale! How dare you get me into trouble. You'll be sorry for this, my girl. Get in that scullery and clean it from floor to ceiling; it's filthy . . .'

'I done it this mornin',' Elsa said indignantly. 'It ain't a bit dirty . . .'

‘Get out of my way unless you want the same as her,’ Mrs Davies said furiously. ‘I’ll be in my office and I want tea and biscuits – and knock before you come in, Elsa . . .’

Jinny felt the sting of tears but she blinked them back, refusing to let the woman’s spiteful temper make her cry. ‘We’d better do as she says,’ she said and Elsa stared after the cook angrily.

‘I’ve a good mind to leave,’ Elsa said and tugged at her apron strings. ‘There’s better jobs than this goin’. Why should we put up wiv it?’

‘Please don’t go,’ Jinny begged. ‘I know she’s awful but the others are lovely, and I want to stay, but if you leave I’ll have to look for another job. I couldn’t do everything alone . . .’

‘I’ll stay a bit longer for you,’ Elsa said. ‘You want to put some cold water on yer face, love. The bitch hit you hard . . .’

Jinny nodded, feeling the soreness where Mrs Davies’ ring had caught her lip. She’d tasted blood and knew it had bled. It would probably swell a bit and Micky would want to know who had done it when she met him that evening. He was taking her to a youth club where they had a jukebox and could dance to Rock ’n’ Roll music, drink coffee and play darts, and Jinny was looking forward to it. She only hoped he would believe her if she said she’d walked into a cupboard door . . .

CHAPTER 16

Rose entered the kitchen to find it empty that evening. She'd been hoping for a cup of tea before she started her shift, but no one was around and she hesitated to make it for herself. She knew Muriel had disliked anyone helping themselves, but rationing had made sugar and tea short and things were different these days. However, Mrs Davies was also pretty touchy and she didn't want to upset her. Jinny always made her tea and gave her biscuits when she was around, but it was her night off, of course.

Becoming aware of a light in the cook's office, Rose wandered towards it and knocked. A few moments passed before Mrs Davies opened it and glared at her.

'What do you want? I'm busy preparing menus for this weekend . . .'

'Sorry . . . I was wondering if I could make myself a cup of tea. We're out of milk in the staff room . . .'

'You know where the kettle is I suppose?'

'Yes – I just thought I should ask . . .'

'There's plenty of tea, milk and sugar . . . Now, you'll have to excuse me, I'm busy.' Looking beyond her shoulder, Rose saw a black cash box open on the desk and several banknotes lying beside it. All the drawers of her desk were open, papers pulled out and left lying on the desk; some had fallen on the floor as if she'd searched frantically.

'Have you lost something?' Rose asked.

'Did you take my book?'

'I've no idea what you're talking about?'

'I bet it was that nosy Sandra . . . or that bloody girl . . .'

'Do you mean Jinny? Why don't you ask her in the morning?'

'Don't you worry, I shall . . .' Mrs Davies slammed the office door in her face.

Rose was puzzled. Mrs Davies was clearly in a bad mood and she'd lied when she'd said she was preparing menus – she'd obviously been counting the money in her box. Was she keeping a sharp eye on it because of the thefts? Coldness settled at Rose's nape. It was uncomfortable for everyone with these thefts happening, because they all felt the shadow of suspicion – even Rose, who knew that she hadn't taken money from the staff's petty cash and she hadn't even been on duty when Kelly's money was taken. Yet she still felt uncomfortable, and she was sure Jinny felt the same, probably Elsa did as well. It was unpleasant.

Rose made a pot of tea and carried it up to the sick room, where she found Wendy just finishing her report for the day.

'Ah, tea, how nice, is there enough for me?' Wendy asked as Rose set the tray down. 'I think Elsa has gone on strike. She usually brings me one mid-afternoon, but she didn't today – perhaps it's all this fuss . . .' Wendy smiled as Rose poured milk into two mugs and then tea just the way they all liked it. 'You made this, I think?'

'Yes, I did,' Rose agreed. 'No one was in the kitchen and Mrs Davies was in the office counting her money – and in a foul mood.'

'Oh dear, I wonder what that's all about,' Wendy said and sipped her tea. 'Lovely, now why don't you tell me how you got on the other night – did you have a good time?'

'Yes, very nice. I enjoyed the meal and Nick was the perfect gentleman, opening the doors for me, asking me what I liked . . . Yes, it was lovely – and I do like him. He asked if we could go to the theatre to see a musical show sometime and I said yes . . . so he's going to ring me when he gets tickets.'

'Now that's what I wanted to hear. You deserve a bit of fun, Rose.' Wendy looked pleased for her. She finished her tea, put her cup down and frowned over her notes. 'I've got three patients in the isolation ward I think you should keep an eye on during the night. They all seem to be suffering from sickness and high temperatures. I feel it is an infection that they all have, but I haven't had a doctor yet. I thought it might be just something simple so I've been checking them every twenty minutes or so – but if they get any worse you can either ring yourself or speak to Sister . . .'

'Has she been in yet?'

'No, she popped in earlier this afternoon and said she might be late this evening, because she had an unpleasant duty – but I'm sure she will be here soon enough . . .'

'Yes, well, I'll check them again when you leave. What

about Beth? She came back from hospital today – how is she?'

'Much better. She didn't want to stay in bed, but I told her the doctor would come in the morning, and if he says she can go back to the dorms and school she can get up then . . .'

'Good . . .' Rose glanced through the report. 'Tom had cuts and bruises again – that lad is always in a fight at school.'

'Kelly made him come to me, because his leg was bleeding and he had a nasty gash, but I patched him up and the bleeding has stopped. He didn't want to stay in the ward so I let him go . . . but you're right. Something is upsetting that lad, but he won't talk about it . . .'

Rose nodded. Tom was sometimes a troublemaker but she too thought that his anger was caused by some emotional distress that he was unwilling to share.

She finished reading the report, then, 'You had two cases of nits I see . . . let's hope we don't have any more catching them.'

'They were in the early stages so I think it's all right,' Wendy said and reached for her bag. 'The district nurses don't visit the schools as often as they did so I make sure to check our kids regularly. I'll leave you to it then. I'm going to visit Nan and Eddie this evening. They've invited me to supper. It's Eddie's birthday and I'm taking him a present . . .'

'Oh, I didn't know . . .' Rose fished in her bag and took out a pound note, slipping it into an envelope and wishing Nan's husband 'Happy Birthday' in clear writing on the outside. 'Give him this and say I would've sent a card if I'd remembered. I like Eddie . . .'

'Me too,' Wendy said and waved to her as she left.

Rose went to Beth's bed in the far corner of the ward. The girl was fast asleep and looked peaceful. She left her sleeping and went through to the isolation ward, her bag lying open on the desk where she'd left it after giving Wendy the money for Eddie . . .

Rose saw Tom leaving the sick ward as she returned after visiting Sister Beatrice's office. She'd been concerned by the condition of one of her fever patients and Sister had said she would telephone for a doctor.

'You did right to tell me,' Sister said. 'Never take risks with the children's health, Rose. If you are ever in charge here for whatever reason, I want you to remember my rule – any deterioration, any slight change that you feel is wrong, get the doctor immediately. We are nurses and we care for the sick, but doctors are here to guide us.'

'Yes, Sister, I agree with you,' Rose said and was thoughtful as she left the office to return to the sick ward. Seeing Tom leave, she called out to him. 'Did you need me?'

Tom glanced back at her and she thought he looked startled for a moment, and then he shook his head. 'I wanted Nurse Wendy . . .'

'I can help you, Tom.'

'Nah, it's all right,' he said. 'Just somethin' I wanted to tell her . . .'

Rose watched him walk to the staircase leading to the boys' dormitories and frowned. 'If your leg is bleeding I can dress it . . .' she called as he disappeared from view but he continued to ignore her.

Entering the ward, Rose looked about her. What had

Tom been in here for? Had he been looking for Wendy as he'd said or was he lying – or was she just too suspicious because of all that had been going on recently? It wouldn't be fair to label a boy a thief just because he'd been where he shouldn't be – besides there was little for him to steal here. Pushing an open desk drawer shut, Rose shook her head, because she had other things on her mind of more concern.

Her patient, a boy of twelve, was burning up when she returned to him and Rose knew she'd been right in asking for a doctor. Ken was very unwell and she thought he might have a rash coming. She thought it might be a case of measles and wondered if the other two were suffering from the same; both had complained of feeling hot when she first came on duty, but only Ken had seemed to be suffering both high fever and pain . . .

Rose fetched a bowl of cool water and started to bathe the young lad's arms and face, because he was thrashing and moaning, hardly aware of her now – whatever was causing his discomfort was serious, because he was feeling really ill.

She'd just gently dried his skin when the door opened and Doctor Henderson entered.

'I think it may be measles,' she said to greet him. 'Wendy admitted three of the children with fevers today and he seems much worse than the others . . .'

'He's covered in spots,' Doctor Henderson agreed, 'and he's very hot. Poor lad feels dreadful I've no doubt . . .' He made a brief examination of Ken and then went to wash his hands at the basin before returning to Rose. 'Yes, I think measles is probably right. He has a rash over his arms, back, chest and legs and there are white spots in his mouth – has he coughed at all?'

'Yes, a few times,' Rose replied. 'What do you recommend?'

'Plenty of warm drinks and perhaps a Vitamin A supplement . . .' He frowned. 'This child looks a little underweight. Does he have an eating disorder?'

'Not as far as I know,' Rose frowned. 'Only the new arrivals generally need vitamins . . .'

'Yes, I know they get a good diet here, but I think in this lad's case it might help.' He looked down at him. 'Are you eating properly, Ken?'

'Yes, sir – 'cept I don't like fatty things much; they make me sick . . .'

'I see . . . and what sort of thing don't you like?'

'Fatty stews and gristly meat, sir, and I don't like liver . . .' He gave a little moan. 'Sorry, sir. My ma would say I shouldn't moan and I'm too finicky – but I couldn't eat the casserole yesterday or lots of times recently. It makes me sick . . .'

'I see.' Stephen Henderson raised his brows at Rose. 'Plenty of good warm drinks and that vitamin I think, nurse. Perhaps some nice soup and toast when he starts to eat again or a ham sandwich – feed him up a little and make sure he gets the right food. I'll just take a look at the others . . .'

Rose bent over Ken who was frowning. 'It used to be good when the other cook was 'ere . . .' he said and looked uncomfortable. 'Sorry I said, but I've always had a funny tummy . . .'

'I'm glad you did tell Doctor,' Rose said. 'You're entitled to say what you feel, Ken.'

'Ma would say I was lucky to have three meals a day. She never when she was little and that's why she died of consumption . . .'

'Yes, I know about your mother, Ken, but no one would blame you if you can't eat the food,' Rose said and frowned as she waited for the doctor's verdict.

'I'm pleased to tell you that Ken is the worst of them,' he said. 'We've had an outbreak of measles at the school so quite a few boys have gone down with it, but none of them is as covered in spots as Ken. However, I'm concerned that he hasn't been eating properly for a while. He looks undernourished and that isn't like a St Saviour's child. The others are in better condition, but a bit on the thin side. Are you having trouble feeding the children properly? I'm a little surprised, because I've been told this is an excellent home – but both of them told me they don't always get enough food to eat . . .'

'I'll speak to Sister Beatrice,' Rose promised, feeling concerned. Muriel had always prided herself on the food she'd given the children and Rose knew that Jinny liked cooking for them – so what was going wrong?

'Yes, I shall have a word myself I think,' Doctor Henderson said. 'Something isn't quite right here, Rose . . .'

'I don't eat here much these days. I used to but now I tend just to ask for a tomato sandwich when I'm on duty and eat at home or in a café somewhere.'

'And why is that?'

Rose hesitated. 'Well, the day I did have lunch here the meat was tough in the casserole – and when I've asked for a ham salad on two occasions, Mrs Davies said she can't supply extras without notice . . . so I stopped bothering.'

'Then that seems to be your explanation,' he said. 'The trouble lies with the kitchen staff.' He hesitated, then, 'I was wondering if I could take you out one evening, Rose? I saw you with Nick at the party . . . but unless you have a relationship I thought perhaps . . . dinner at the weekend?'

'I'm on nights all this week,' Rose said and felt a little awkward suddenly. 'But lunch one Sunday would be lovely . . . except that it can't be this week because I'm going on a picnic with some of the kids and their teacher and his own children . . .'

'That sounds rather pleasant. I wouldn't mind tagging along – do you think I'd be welcome if I contributed to the picnic?'

'I should think you would be more than welcome. The lads are going to have some driving lessons on the private airfield. If you bring your car they could have more turns – if you were willing?

'Yes, why not? It should be a lot of fun. I'd like that very much. Give me a time and I'll pick you up here – or at your home?'

'Here, and we're leaving at eight in the morning,' Rose said and reached for her notepad. 'I'll look forward to it – and I'll give Sister your message about the doubts you have concerning the children's eating habits . . .'

'Oh, and I wanted to talk to you about Andy and Beth . . . are they getting on better now?' He looked at her and she told him quickly about how their step-father had threatened the boy.

'I'll call in and have a word with Sergeant Sallis again,' he said, smiled at her again and left.

CHAPTER 17

Nancy was on duty that Sunday, alone except for Sister Beatrice, who was standing in for Sister Rose, the cook and Elsa. They didn't do much cleaning on Sundays, but the smaller children needed help with dressing and washing and Nancy usually saw to the drinks mid-morning, as well as giving Mrs Davies a hand with the clearing up after lunch. On Sunday afternoons most of the children went out to play with friends or attended Sunday classes, fun things arranged for them by the energetic young curate attached to their local church.

Once she'd taken a tray of drinks to the sick ward, Nancy was free until teatime. She sometimes occupied herself by baking and if Jinny had been at work she would probably have spent the time quite happily talking to her in the kitchen. Elsa was a sulky girl and seemed in a less than friendly mood that morning. She half-wished she'd been invited on the trip to the country with Rose and the others, but it would have been wrong to desert Sister Beatrice and leave her holding the fort alone. Yet it hurt a little that no one had thought of asking her. Wendy and Rose usually made a point of inviting her when they went on group outings to the pub for a meal or a church social, but she'd refused to go to the party when Rob asked and since then it seemed no one had asked her anywhere.

Nancy worked many more hours than could ever have been expected of her. She enjoyed her job, which always seemed a pleasure to her, and thought herself lucky to have been given her job and a home, because St Saviour's *was* her home. She could have found herself somewhere else to live years ago; her wage was sufficient to support her in a small flat if she so chose, but she'd never considered it. The children were her family, and Sister Beatrice, Wendy, Kelly and Rose were her friends.

Nancy missed the woman who'd been the head carer here when she first came. Nan had been almost like a mother to her – the mother she'd lost after that terrible bombing raid which had taken so many of her family. Nancy's mother had never recovered from that tragic night and slipped into apathy and drunkenness, taking little interest in her children.

Feeling tears prick her eyes, Nancy decided to go out for a walk. There weren't many parks in Spitalfields, only Itchy Park, which wasn't much of a place, just gardens round the church, not like the lovely parks in the West End, but she would walk for a while anyway, just to blow the cobwebs away.

Nancy didn't often allow the past to haunt her, but now and then she recalled all the trauma of her parents' deaths – and the effect that all the preceding events had had on her brother Terry. She supposed it was Terry's condition that had brought on this mood. Nancy had recently received a letter asking her not to go to visit her brother this month as he was in one of his black times.

We feel that a visit might make him violent and it is possible that he might attack you for no reason. There have been three outbursts recently and a female nurse was attacked. Your brother is becoming aware of feelings that he doesn't understand as he leaves childhood behind and for his own sake, as well as that of others, we have decided to keep him away from the female staff . . .

The idea that her brother might attack her if she visited him made Nancy sad. For years she'd gone regularly every month, though quite often he hardly knew her. She'd seen him as a child, never growing beyond the age he'd been when he'd been a victim of his father's brutality – and yet she knew that he was a man now and strong. If he were to become violent anything could happen.

Leaving St Saviour's, Nancy walked along the dusty street. There was a faint tang in the air, though she didn't know whether it was the drains that sometimes smelled bad in the warmer weather or if it wafted in from the river. Despite the warmth, the sky was overcast and the atmosphere heavy as if pressing down on the city, trapping the smells and the rising heat beneath a bank of cloud. Earlier the sun had been bright for this late in the summer, but it had become muggy and close, almost airless here in this old street with its ancient buildings and gutters choked with debris.

Nancy was lost in thoughts and didn't see the man running towards her until he knocked straight into her, sending her to her knees and going on past without even a backward glance. She gasped, because he'd hurt her and for a moment she was winded, her right knee stinging where she'd hit the pavement and landed on something sharp. As she struggled to rise, a small vehicle stopped abruptly at the kerb just behind her and a man jumped out. His hand was gentle as he raised her and she found herself looking into the face of the young decorator, a flush rising in her cheeks as he looked at her in concern.

'That lout could've hurt you badly,' Rob Thompson said angrily. 'He has hurt you – you're bleeding . . .' His hand moved towards her skirt but stopped as she flinched. 'Please may I see?'

Nancy nodded, too shocked to refuse. She could feel the pain and knew that it wasn't just a graze, and as Rob delicately lifted the skirt of her dress above her knee they both saw the shard of broken glass that had become embedded in her flesh.

'Oh . . . I knew it was sharp,' Nancy said. 'It's bleeding quite a lot . . .'

'Can you walk?' Rob asked anxiously. 'If you can hobble to the van I'll take you to the hospital. This needs attention straight away.'

'Yes . . . I suppose Sister Beatrice . . .' she said tentatively but he shook his head. 'No, perhaps not . . .'

'It needs to be removed and stitched,' Rob said, 'but they will probably X-ray it as well to make sure there isn't a splinter of glass left in.' He took hold of the piece of glass and tried to gently ease it free, but Nancy cried out and he apologised. 'Yes, it's too deep to take out by hand. I'm sorry. I think there's nothing for it but the hospital.'

'I was only going for a walk . . .'

'It was that lout's fault,' Rob said. 'I'd like to give him a good hiding for running into you and then just going off like that . . . Give me your arm, now put it round my shoulder like that and I'll make it easy for you.'

Nancy allowed him to help her. He was kind and gentle, concerned for her and she felt a little ashamed of herself for the way she'd behaved the first day they'd met. His smile was warm and caring and for the first time in years she found herself relying on a man to help her.

'This is so good of you,' she said shyly as he reversed into a side street and headed off back the way she had come, but avoiding the turning for St Saviour's and carrying straight on until the hospital came into sight. He parked safely, jumped out and opened the door, helping her out. Nancy took two steps forward and felt her leg go. Before she hit the ground, Rob had caught her and was holding her in his strong hands. 'So foolish . . . I feel a little strange . . .'

'I'm not surprised,' Rob said. 'Don't worry, you're safe now, Nancy. I've got you and I'll look after you. I promise I shan't leave you . . .'

'Sister Beatrice . . . things to do . . .' Nancy sighed weakly, her head swooning as she shut her eyes and leaned into the warmth of his body. It was so strange, because mostly she couldn't bear to be touched by any man, even a doctor, but she did feel safe in this man's arms . . . safe, and warm and protected and it was a good feeling . . .

'I'll let them know,' Rob promised as she felt her

senses leaving her but somehow knew he had her in his arms and was carrying her. 'Jinny will come in. There's nothing to worry about . . .'

When Nancy came back to herself she was lying on a bed with grey curtains round it and someone was sitting by the foot of the bed. It took a moment for her eyes to focus and then it all started to return: the fall, the blood and the pain and Rob carrying her into the hospital. She half remembered a nurse coming to look at her and giving her something to make her feel easier and then a doctor saying he was going to remove the glass and clean up the wound. Becoming aware of soreness in her right knee, Nancy gave a little moan and lifted a hand towards the man sitting patiently beside her.

'You must have other things to do,' she said, her throat tight. She didn't know why she wanted to cry. It wasn't because of the pain, because she'd cope with that, but something more emotional than physical. 'I'll be all right now . . .'

'I'll wait and take you home when they let you go,' Rob told her. 'They think they got it all, but you might have to come in again to have an X-ray and make sure. The doctor said he wouldn't keep you in so they'll check to make sure your blood pressure is all right and then they'll let us go . . .'

'If you want to go I could catch a bus . . .'

'I don't,' he said. 'Just relax and trust me, Nancy. I want to help – and I shan't expect any favours. I'd like to be your friend but I know I started off badly . . . embarrassing you the way I did . . .'

'No . . .' she smiled at him weakly. 'I was silly. I can't explain but one day I will . . . if we're still friends?'

His smile was radiant and Nancy felt something move deep inside her. He hadn't hesitated to step in and help, just as when he'd saved her from falling down the stairs. She did like this pleasant and caring young man, and it was time she let go of the past and stopped thinking that all men were like her father. Rob had proved himself a friend and Nancy found that she wanted very much to know him better, to be his friend . . . if nothing else. She wasn't sure she would ever be able to be more than that to any man, but perhaps in time she might feel comfortable and happy in his company.

'I'll always be your friend if that's what you want, Nancy,' he told her softly. 'I promise you that I will never hurt you – never do anything that frightens or upsets you . . .'

As Nancy looked into his eyes, she knew that he understood as no other man ever had. Rob sensed that she'd been badly hurt . . . that she was like a wounded fawn, starting at a footfall lest it be a huntsman returning to hurt her again. He couldn't know her history and perhaps if he learned the truth she would see disgust in his eyes, the disgust she still felt herself at the memory of what her own father had done to her as a young girl . . . but perhaps one day he would listen and he would still smile at her the way he was smiling now.

Perhaps it was time at last for Nancy to take a chance . . .

'You must rest.' Sister Beatrice looked at her in concern as she hobbled into her office the next morning. 'It was a very unfortunate thing to happen, Nancy. I'm very grateful to Mr Thompson for looking after you. Had he not happened to see the incident we should have been worrying about you still . . .'

'I'm so sorry to have made things difficult for you yesterday,' Nancy said. 'I just wanted a little air and I never imagined something like that could happen – it was so sudden.'

'It is the way of accidents,' Sister Beatrice said. 'Mr Thompson told me the hospital wants you to put your foot up for a few days and you are not to think of working. I insist you have a few days off, my dear – besides, you're due a holiday. You haven't had more than a couple of days off now and then to visit your brother . . .' She frowned as she saw Nancy's gasp of pain. 'Does your leg hurt?'

'No – it is Terry. They've told me not to visit for a while, because he's . . . he's become violent towards females and they think he might attack me.'

'Oh, Nancy my dear, I am so very sorry. I know you think the world of him – and he is all you have left of your family . . .'

'Yes, but he isn't my Terry any more,' Nancy said sadly. 'I wish he was different but he was too badly damaged . . .'

'If there's anything I can do?'

Nancy shook her head. 'No, I'm all right – but there's nothing I really want to do at the moment, though I wouldn't mind a trip to the sea one day before autumn sets in . . . but I shall rest. I can sit in a comfortable chair and read to the little ones . . .'

'Very well, Nancy, you know your own mind – but

I am here for you whenever you need to talk. I hope you know that?'

'Yes, Sister, I know. You've always been kind,' Nancy said. 'I think I'll go and read to the children for a little while.'

'Just as long as you don't try to work or carry heavy trays . . .'

Once Nancy had gone, Beatrice went back to looking through her desk drawers. She was looking for a small black notebook, which she used to make notes on the children's welfare. It was just a little jottings book really, and Beatrice always wrote her reports out in fair copy before Sandra typed them up for her records, which were kept locked in the metal file in her office. She saw it at last in the bottom drawer, which was odd, since she was certain she'd left it in the top left-hand drawer.

How could it have been moved? Sandra never went to Beatrice's desk unless she asked her, and it would be very unlike her to remove the book and replace it in another place.

Beatrice frowned as she glanced through it. One of her recent notes to herself was to have a word with Tom about his argument with the girl from next door. She'd done so and he'd said it was the girl's fault because she was a bully and he'd been standing up for one of their girls – but who would want to see what she'd scribbled about it?

Oh well, it hardly mattered as nothing was missing – but she'd felt a little annoyed, particularly because of the thefts. Nothing like this had ever happened at St Saviour's and it was most unpleasant, because it seemed that nowhere was safe unless it was locked.

CHAPTER 18

Rose was smiling as she walked into the ward that Monday morning. It was cooler out and there was definitely a change on the way. Wendy was wiping down the trolley she'd been using with disinfectant in water and there was a strong smell of it with an underlying odour of sickness in the ward. Rose's eyes moved over the beds and she saw that they had three new patients, all of whom looked a little sorry for themselves.

'What happened?' she asked as Wendy returned from tipping the bowl of water down the toilet in the rest room between the sick ward and the isolation ward. 'It looks as if we have some very sick children?'

'I think it is a tummy bug or something they ate,' Wendy said. 'I've had a stream of them overnight complaining of stomach ache and sickness. Sister Beatrice thinks it's more likely to be something they ate yesterday rather than a bug but at least six have been ill, though only these three are still feeling sick.'

'Did they go out to eat somewhere – buy things from a stall in the park or something?'

'No, they were all here for the whole day. Sister

Beatrice was very upset and she went off to the kitchen to talk to Mrs Davies. I think she blames her for this latest outbreak of vomiting.'

'Oh dear,' Rose nodded. 'Doctor Henderson did say he thought the quality of their food might not be up to standard and Sandra told me she'd had a word with Mrs Davies and hoped things would improve . . .'

'Well, they will now, because I haven't seen Sister Beatrice look so angry for years . . .' Wendy pulled a wry face. 'I shouldn't like to be in the cook's shoes if it is caused by bad food.' She shook her head and then laughed. 'Well, how did you get on? Was it a good day in the country?'

'Lovely.' Rose smiled at the memory. 'I can't tell you how much I enjoyed myself, Wendy. Mr Barton and Doctor Henderson both gave the kids a turn at driving their cars. We were on private land so it was quite safe and there's no law against the kids driving under the age for a licence providing they're not on a public road. You should've seen Andy. He was so good and his teacher was very enthusiastic about giving him proper lessons when he's older. He encouraged him to think of a career in the motor trade. Of course Andy is completely fixated on being a racing driver now; it probably won't happen but I suppose there's no harm in him having his dream.'

'None at all,' Wendy agreed. 'It will give him something to think about and work for . . . Oh dear, Joshua is about to be sick again . . .' She dashed off with her bowl as the young boy starting retching.

Rose looked through the reports and then started on the routine chores. Wendy was already due to go off duty, but she often stayed for an extra hour or so if one of the children was very ill. Rose heard the sound of another young boy starting to be sick and dashed to the rescue with another bowl. She thought it might be as well to call the doctor now, because they couldn't allow this to go on much longer in case the children were really ill. Anger rose inside her at the thought that this might have been caused by the children being given food that was either on the turn or contaminated in some way. She thought again that she wouldn't want to be in the cook's shoes if Sister Beatrice was on the rampage . . .

Jinny was in the kitchen chopping carrots when Sister Beatrice entered. Her expression was thunderous and Elsa and Jinny looked at each other, both wondering what they'd done now. Had more money gone missing and were they going to be blamed for it?

'I hope she doesn't pick on me . . .' Elsa hissed and Jinny nodded, feeling apprehensive herself.

'What did you give my children yesterday?' Sister Beatrice demanded of the rather apprehensive-looking cook. 'Six of them have been sick overnight and I believe it to be the result of food that has either been under-cooked or not kept properly and on the turn.'

'They had a nice beef pie with mashed potatoes and greens or a piece of fish cooked in the pan with chips . . .' Mrs Davies said. 'I got that fresh from the fish-monger on Saturday and kept it cool. I don't think you can blame me for their sickness . . .'

'But I told you . . .' Elsa blurted out and then stopped as Mrs Davies glared at her.

Sister Beatrice looked from one to the other, her gaze settling on Elsa. 'What did you tell Mrs Davies, Elsa?'

'She'll kill me if I tell yer . . .'

'And I shall dismiss you if you do not. Tell me the truth and I promise you will not be harmed.'

'She's a liar . . .' Mrs Davies burst out but was silenced by a look from Sister.

'I told her that fish smelled off,' Elsa said. 'It made me feel sick just to touch it . . . slimy and green it were in one bit. I cut that bit off but it weren't fit . . .'

'That is ridiculous! It was perfectly fresh I tell you.' Mrs Davies took a menacing step towards the girl but Jinny stepped forward, taking her arm and leading Elsa through into the scullery.

'Let them get on with it . . .' she whispered but the older women had retired to Mrs Davies' office and they couldn't hear what happened next.

Sister Beatrice poked her head through the open door of the scullery a few minutes later. 'Mrs Davies says that you didn't tell her the fish was off, Elsa. Do you give me your word that it was and that you did inform her?'

'Yes, Sister,' Elsa said. 'I swear it on me mother's life.'

'It didn't look fresh to me when it was delivered on Saturday afternoon,' Jinny said. 'I told Mrs Davies when I put it in the pantry that it wouldn't last . . .'

'I see . . .' Sister Beatrice nodded at them. 'Very well, I shall accept your word, Elsa.'

Sister departed and there was silence. When they ventured back into the kitchen some minutes passed before the cook appeared wearing her coat and carrying her purse and basket.

'You . . .' she said, looking at Jinny. 'Have you been spying on me? Did you take a notebook from my office? If I find out it was either of you two I'll make your lives a misery . . .'

'I told you, Sandra took a book to Sister Beatrice . . .' Jinny said.

'This was another book . . . somewhere else. I know you've been spying on me. Did you sneak in there and take the book?' Mrs Davies' eyes narrowed. 'If you took it in the hope of getting me sacked you'll be sorry – now give it to me and I'll say no more about it . . .'

'I've not touched your book and nor has Elsa,' Jinny said hotly. 'We're not thieves and we shan't be accused of it.'

'Well, it's too late now,' Mrs Davies muttered. 'But I'll get back at you if I find out which one of you it was . . .'

She glared at them, her anger making her cheeks red. Neither of the girls answered her and she nodded, as if accepting that they would not speak.

'I'm going shopping,' she said. 'You've got the sausages and the lamb to make a casserole. I suppose you are capable of preparing a simple meal between you while I've gone . . .'

Elsa pulled a face behind her back as she went out with a flounce in her step. 'Old bitch! I'd rather do it all than 'ave 'er breathin' fire down me neck all the time . . . I'm leavin' as soon as I can find another job. I ain't staying 'ere to be accused of pinchin' things.'

'We didn't take her book but I did see one of the kids in her office the other day. He was kneeling down on the floor, looking at somethin' I couldn't see . . .'

'Who was it?' Elsa demanded. 'You didn't tell 'er – why?'

'I wouldn't get anyone into trouble when I don't know why he was there . . .'

'I'd like to get 'er in trouble . . . the miserable old cow.'

'So would I,' Jinny said. 'I reckon she ought to get the sack for feedin' those kids food like that – bad fish would make anyone ill and some of these kids are vulnerable. Usually she won't buy fish, says it's too expensive, but I bet she got that cheap because the fishmonger knew it was goin' off . . .'

'I'm glad I stuck to a paste sandwich,' Elsa said. 'The meat was tough an' all. I reckon someone ought to tell Sister Beatrice what she makes us serve up half the time ain't right . . .'

'I think some if it is just down to buying the wrong cuts of meat; you need to cook it slow if you buy the cheaper stuff, but she just turns the oven up high and it goes tough,' Jinny said. 'But you're right, someone should tell Sister Beatrice . . .'

Jinny frowned as she started to prepare the children's lunch. The boy she'd seen coming from Mrs Davies' office was the same one she'd seen coming from the staff room the day she'd seen the drawer with the cash box open. Could Tom be a thief? What had he been doing in the cook's office? But why would he take a notebook? Money for sweets was one thing . . . but why steal a notebook? What was he trying to find?

The following morning, Jinny searched the pantry shelves looking for something to give the children for their lunch. She frowned, because there was no meat of any kind, very few vegetables and they were short of almost everything they needed. She glanced at the clock on the kitchen wall. If Mrs Davies didn't show up with the shopping soon, she didn't know what she could give the children when they came in for their meal. The cook hadn't been back since the previous morning and that was strange. It looked as if Jinny would have to make omelettes with chips and tins of peas for want of anything better. Perhaps that wouldn't be too bad, she thought as she began to assemble what they had on the table. She had some tomatoes which she could slice on the plates and that would make it look nice, but making cheese and egg dishes was time-consuming – unless she did some flans as well. And it looked as if there was a tin of Spam which could either be sliced cold or made into fritters . . . .

'What is this?' a voice asked as Jinny began getting tins and cutlery out ready. 'What has Mrs Davies asked you to prepare for lunch today?'

'Sister!' Jinny nearly jumped out of her skin as she turned to look at her unexpected visitor. 'Mrs Davies isn't here. I haven't seen her today. She said she was going shoppin' yesterday morning after your visit and she hasn't been in since – and all I can find is eggs, cheese, tomatoes, potatoes – oh, and a tin of Spam.'

'Are you sure there is no fresh meat? I seem to recall we normally have chops for the children on a Thursday?'

'We haven't had chops for weeks now,' Jinny said, frowning as she thought back. 'We mostly have scrag end of lamb in a casserole with vegetables or offal made into soups and pies – we have casserole four or five days a week . . .'

‘That was not my understanding. I was told you used the best cuts of meat and fresh vegetables from the shops. Mrs Davies assured me that she always buys the freshest food she can . . .’

‘Elsa told me you used to have decent food, but for the past few weeks we’ve only had rubbish stuff to cook,’ Jinny said. ‘I told Mrs Davies she ought to change her supplier when the meat was all fat and gristle but she said she knew what she was doin’ and it was all the money would run to . . .’

‘I know the budget is tight but we’ve always given the children good food. I shall have to get to the bottom of this . . .’ Sister looked upset.

‘Mrs Davies won’t let me do the shoppin’. I’m sure I could get better . . .’ Jinny followed her towards the office. She opened the door, leaving it for Jinny to follow inside. The left-hand drawer of Mrs Davies’ desk was left open and a cash box stood on the leather top. Its lid was thrown back and it was empty. Every other drawer had been left open and most were empty. ‘Mrs Davies kept that box in a locked drawer . . .’ Jinny faltered as Sister turned to look at her. Sickness rose in her throat as she saw disbelief and anger in the older woman’s eyes, and her hand went to her mouth as she fought to control her horror. ‘I didn’t take it . . . I swear I didn’t . . .’

Sister frowned, seeming to become aware of her. ‘I am not accusing you – but it seems clear that something is amiss here. There should be the best part of a month’s kitchen allowance here, because I gave her the money for September only yesterday – and if there is no food in the pantry . . .’

'I can make lunch just about,' Jinny said, raising her head. She wasn't guilty and she wouldn't let anyone make her feel that way. 'But there isn't much for tea. If I had some money I could go to the market and buy enough for a day or so . . . just until Mrs Davies comes back and explains . . .'

'I shall hope that she may do so,' Sister Beatrice said sternly. 'There has been mismanagement here at the very least and perhaps much more . . . If you come to my office after you've finished here at lunchtime I shall give you some money to buy us food. I hope I can trust you to behave responsibly, Jinny?'

'I swear to you on my life I won't cheat you,' Jinny said dramatically and saw a smile flicker in Sister's eyes. 'I'd rather die than betray your trust, Sister.'

'Well, I don't think we need to imagine anything so terrible,' Sister said solemnly. 'You'd better produce as good a meal as you can for now – and I'll visit you later to discuss the food for the next day or so . . .'

Jinny watched her leave, and then called to Elsa to start peeling potatoes for their chips. She decided that she would do Spam fritters with the chips, and cheese flans with tomatoes, and then a few omelettes. It wasn't much choice for the kids, but it would be tasty and was better than the bread and scrape some kids had to make do with . . .

To Jinny's surprise, the kids lined up for seconds and in one case third helpings. She'd had time to make some treacle tarts with extra pastry left over from the flans, and a bit of custard, though no other sweets were on offer, but the kids loved the chips, tinned peas and Spam fritters. Some of them had looked doubtful over the egg and cheese flans, but then she'd seen the same kids coming back and asking for more.

'I ain't tasted pastry like that,' Tom said and grinned at her. 'I reckon you made that, Jinny. This is nice fer a change . . . much better than them 'orrible casseroles . . .'

'I'm glad you liked it,' she said and smiled as she saw the last piece of flan snatched from under her nose. 'We'll have to see what we can do another day . . .'

'Cor, that was lovely,' Elsa said when they were washing up. 'Much better than old Grizzle Guts' pies. I real enjoyed that, Jinny. You ought to be the cook 'ere, not 'er.'

'They would never give me the job,' Jinny said and laughed. ''Sides, that was easy. Nellie taught me how to make pastry, and chips are easy, though a lot of hard work for you. She'd be a lovely cook for us, but they wouldn't ask her – she doesn't have any certificates or any of that stuff. She's just a good plain cook.'

'That's the best sort,' Elsa said. 'Muriel never made anythin' fancy but it were all lovely – at least that's what Nancy said. She did some of the cooking before you came but she didn't get on with Mrs Davies very well . . .'

'Nancy taught me some of the things I know,' Jinny agreed. 'I expect she'll take over until Mrs Davies gets back.'

'Do you think Nancy can help? She hurt her knee the other day and it's all she can do to hobble downstairs,' Elsa said. 'I reckon Mrs Davies has scarpered with the kitchen cash . . .'

'You shouldn't say that,' Jinny said. 'She probably

took it to buy more food. She'll turn up soon and wonder what all the fuss was about . . .'

But they finished the clearing up and there was no sign of Mrs Davies. Jinny got ready and went up to Sister Beatrice's office, her stomach fluttering with nerves.

She knocked and waited and then Sandra came out, looking upset. She forced a smile for Jinny. 'Sister will see you now,' she said. 'Don't look so worried. No one thinks you did anything wrong. I think we know who to blame for all this . . .'

Sandra walked off without explaining and Jinny went into Sister's office. The last time she'd been here was the day she'd been taken on as kitchen helper. Sister was looking grave but she raised her head and her expression softened.

'I've heard the children enjoyed their meal today and with what you had you did very well, Jinny. Do you think you can buy us enough food to last the week with this?' She held up six pound notes. 'It is all I have available at the moment. Our budget is always tight and I'm going to have to ask the Board for more money to last us the month . . .'

'I'll do my very best, Sister,' Jinny said. 'Have you any instructions as to what I should buy?'

'I believe I must leave you to see what you can get – but do your best for the children. In all my years here we have never had anything like this . . .'

'Has . . . Mrs Davies gone for good, Sister?'

'I believe so,' Sister said. 'Sandra has just told me that Sergeant Sallis rang her a few minutes ago. It seems that Mrs Davies had a son who was in prison for violent robbery and murder – and he broke out of prison three weeks ago. They rang to tell us to be careful if he came here, because he is dangerous and can be violent. I suspect that she may have taken the money for him, though whether she was under threat or not I cannot say . . . and we must not assume that she did take it, though it would appear the most likely explanation.'

'Oh, Sister . . .' Jinny's throat felt tight. 'If her son made her take it . . . she must have been frightened.'

'Perhaps,' Sister nodded. 'We shall give her the benefit of the doubt until we know more. Very well, Jinny. For the moment you will be in charge of the kitchen. Nancy will help as much as she can, but she has a great deal to do, and her leg is still sore, as you are aware. Run along now and do your very best for us . . .'

'Yes, Sister . . .'

Jinny tucked the money into her jacket pocket. Remembering the loss she'd almost suffered in the market once before, she was determined to take good care of Sister's money. As she left St Saviour's and walked through the grimy streets, she was thinking how quickly things had changed in a few days. It looked as if Mrs Davies might have been the thief all along, although Sister was right, they couldn't be sure. Someone else could have gone to the office and taken it. Yet she seemed the likely culprit. Perhaps her son had demanded money from her and she'd done it because he'd made her – and yet Jinny suspected she'd been taking the home's money for some time in one way or another . . .

Jinny looked proudly at the produce that filled the long pine table and overflowed on to the floor. Boxes of fruit, some of it soft and only fit for jam and puddings, some of it just ready to eat; carrots and potatoes, greens and suedes, also a large uncooked ham, a side of bacon, eggs in two long cardboard boxes, a large slab of cheese, sausages, a big parcel of pork chops and three pounds of best stewing beef wrapped in white paper. There were three large fresh loaves, six pots of strawberry jam, three of marmalade and two of Marmite for adding to soups and making hot drinks; Jinny liked it spread on toast, but most kids hated it, though added to a casserole it would make it tasty and do them good. Bags of flour and dried fruit, two slabs of butter, margarine and lard for cooking, also two catering-sized tins of corned beef and one of Spam, milk, custard powder and a large blue bag of sugar occupied the rest of the surfaces.

Sister's six pounds had gone much further than she could ever have dreamed and that was because when Micky spread the word that someone had done the children's home down, the traders had come forward with gifts and cheap offers.

'You come to me every week, Jinny girl,' one of them told her with a grin. 'I'll always find yer some stuff for them kids – and them nurses. Angels they is and so I've always said. Angels them girls wot look after them kids. My cousin's lad went there durin' the war while he was away and he says they're wonderful. You take that lot fer nuthin' terday and next time I'll let yer 'ave whatever yer want at 'alf price . . .'

Jinny had felt overwhelmed. She had far more than she could carry home but Micky had borrowed a small van and brought her back, carrying it all into the kitchen.

'I can't thank you enough,' Jinny told him. 'I can feed

the children now until Sister Beatrice gets more money for us . . .'

'Damned shame, stealin' from orphan kids,' Micky said. 'No one does that round 'ere. The ol' bitch ought to be ashamed of 'erself.'

'Yes, but perhaps she couldn't help it,' Jinny defended the cook though she didn't know why. Mrs Davies had hit her and she'd never appreciated anything she or Elsa did, always grumbling or finding fault. 'We don't know for sure it was her, Micky.'

'Stands to reason,' he said. 'What did she clear orf for otherwise?

'Well, it looks that way – but Sister says we have to give her the benefit of the doubt until we know for certain.'

'Sister's a nun so she's bound to say it – but you take my word. It was that cook and it's best she's gone out of the way . . .'

'All right – oh, Micky, you'd better go, someone is coming . . .'

Micky nipped out the back door sharpish as Sister arrived. She looked round the kitchen, an expression of bewilderment on her face.

'You couldn't have got all that for what I gave you, Jinny . . .'

'I've got ten shillings left over,' Jinny told her and smiled proudly. 'My friends down the market rallied round. That soft fruit is only good for making jam and puddings but the rest of it is really fresh and nice. We'll manage until Monday now. We've got plenty to go round . . .'

Sister Beatrice shook her head. 'The children haven't

had all this fruit since Angela left. It will do them the world of good, however you present it.' She smiled and nodded as she looked into the fridge and saw the parcels of fresh meat. 'You've done very well, Jinny. Please keep the change for another day. If you can produce miracles like this perhaps you should be in charge of the kitchen budget in future.'

'Will we have a new cook?'

'It will take a while to replace Mrs Davies, because we cannot pay the high wages some cooks demand. Nancy is going to try and manage with your help at least for a while . . . Do you think you can manage, Jinny?'

'Yes, Sister. I've been promised more food next week, if you will let me do the shopping . . . and I like cooking, though I'll never be as good as Nellie. She cooked for a school before she got married . . . and she taught me.'

'She sounds very capable.' Sister hesitated, then, 'If your friend wishes for a job, perhaps just lunchtimes since she is married – ask her to come and see me please.'

'Yes, Sister. When can she come?'

'Any morning – but let me know as soon as possible to expect her . . .'

'Yes, I will,' Jinny said and glowed with pleasure. Surely Nellie would enjoy cooking for the children and it would be easier for her than scrubbing office floors as she did now. 'I'll go and see her this evening . . .'

CHAPTER 19

Jinny was busy storing her produce and cooking for the remainder of the afternoon. She prepared the soft fruit and then put it in a cool place ready for making into jam the next day, and then she made a rhubarb crumble with custard and a lovely jam tart. Finally, she prepared tomato sandwiches and fruit scones for supper.

When she'd finished washing up, she was dying to put her feet up and relax, but mindful of her promise to Sister Beatrice, she got herself ready and went out to catch her bus.

All thoughts of Jake had fled her mind, because she'd had too much to think about recently, and it was only when she got off the bus and walked to Nellie's house that she realised she was vulnerable. However, there was no sign of him as she walked quickly through the small courtyard to her friend's home.

Nellie was surprised to see her and told her to sit down while she made a pot of tea and got some cake and sausage rolls out. Jinny realised she'd hardly eaten all day herself, because she'd been so busy.

'This is lovely,' she said as she munched the savoury

roll. 'I love your cooking, Nellie. It's much better than Mum's used to be – and that's why I thought of you when our cook went off . . .' Nellie looked at her curiously and Jinny laughed as she started to explain. 'So Sister said would you come and help us out for a while until she gets a new cook . . . ?'

'Cook for St Saviour's?' Nellie was surprised and pleased, a smile spreading over her round face. 'Well, that's nice to be asked – but I've got my man's tea to get and the house to look after . . .'

'It's just lunchtimes,' Jinny said. 'Me and Elsa can manage the teas and suppers and breakfast is easy – but lunch is a lot more work . . .'

'Just for a couple of hours or so then?' Nellie was clearly interested. 'Did she say how much she pays? I'm not greedy, lass, but I'll want a bit, 'cos it means givin' up my cleanin' in the mornin's . . .'

'Sister will pay you a fair wage,' Jinny said. 'You can come and see her one morning, just tell me when and she'll tell you what she needs and what she pays.'

'I get two pound and five bob fer scrubbing five days a week,' Nellie said. 'I'll be happy wiv that . . .'

Jinny hugged her. 'It would be lovely having you there, Nellie. Mrs Davies wasn't very nice. She hit us sometimes and never stopped moanin' – and the food she cooked was awful sometimes.'

'Sounds as if you're well rid of 'er, whether she took the money or not,' Nellie said. 'You tell your Sister Beatrice that I'll be there the day after tomorrow to see 'er and I'll start straight off. I've got to tell 'em at the office I won't be goin' in no more . . .'

Jinny couldn't believe how well the day had turned

out. It had started off in turmoil, but now it was wonderful.

'Are yer goin' ter pop round and see yer ma?' Nellie asked suddenly.

'What about Jake?'

'No need to worry about 'im fer a while,' Nellie said and smiled wryly. 'It seems 'e 'ad a bit of an accident down the Docks a couple of days ago, love. They say somethin' fell on 'im and 'e were lucky to get away wiv 'is life . . .'

'Jake had an accident?' Jinny was shocked, because somehow she couldn't see Jake being careless in his work. 'How?'

'No one rightly knows,' Nellie said, but turned away to refill her kettle and push it back over the fire. 'Pop next door and see yer ma, love, and I'll make us some cocoa afore yer go home . . .'

Jinny was thoughtful as she travelled home that night. Her mother had been tearful over Jake's accident, complaining about how she was going to manage without Jake's money coming in.

'The man from the Docks said I'd get a few bob a week,' she told Jinny, 'but I don't know how they expect me to manage on that . . . if Jake's back is broken I shan't be able to pay the rent.'

'What about your job in the bar?'

'I got the push from that,' her mother sniffed. 'They said I was drunk and not fit to serve drinks . . . It was just that jealous old cow out the back, because Jake preferred me to 'er.'

'Nellie is giving up her job at the offices,' Jinny offered

helpfully. 'I'm sure she'd put in a good word for you, Mum. That should make you enough to pay the rent . . .'

All she got for her encouragement was a snarl and a glare. 'I can't go scrubbin' floors at my age. I couldn't stand it . . .'

'Nellie does,' Jinny said. 'Perhaps Jake will be out sooner than you think.'

Her mother shook her head sorrowfully. 'Someone tried to kill 'im. Jake swears it was no accident that the rope holdin' the crate broke. Says he'd tested it 'imself earlier and it was sound then . . .'

'No, surely not,' Jinny said, a shiver sliding down her spine. 'Who would do that?'

'I thought you might know.' Mrs Hollis looked angry. 'Jake told me that you wouldn't come 'ome when I was bad and that bloke of yours threatened 'im. If Jake dies the police will come after 'im.'

'Don't be silly,' Jinny said. Micky wouldn't do that! She knew he wouldn't. Micky was generous and kind – look at the way he'd rallied his friends to give food to the orphanage that afternoon. He wouldn't try to kill Jake, even if he had said he would make sure Jake couldn't hurt her again . . .

Jinny's mother had continued to grumble at her until she left, telling her she should give her money while Jake was away. Jinny had taken five shillings from her purse and put it on the table, but she knew her mother wasn't bothered about the rent being paid – it would go on drink as always, and Jinny wasn't going to give her all her hard-earned wages to fritter away on strong drink.

At the moment Jinny wasn't earning enough to pay

her mother's rent. If she could afford it, she would contact the landlord and pay him directly, but she just couldn't manage it all, and it would be useless to give her mother a few shillings each week, because it would only go the same way.

Jinny worried for a few minutes but then pushed the uneasy thoughts from her mind. Deep down, she knew that her mother would solve her problem the way she always had – by picking up men and getting money from them or at least getting them to buy her drinks. In her way she was still attractive and with Jake out of the way in the Infirmary, she would go back to her old ways. What Jake would have to say to it when he came out was another matter and one which Jinny didn't want to contemplate.

She'd escaped her home to work at St Saviour's and even her mother's grumbling would not draw her back. She would simply have to find work or do what she always did when she was down on her luck . . .

Getting off her bus outside St Saviour's, she saw Micky sitting on a shiny green motorbike. He grinned as he saw her and she went up to him.

'I didn't believe you'd really got a motorbike,' she said. 'What sort is it then?'

'A Norton Classic – and a real beauty,' Micky said. 'What about comin' for a ride, Jinny?'

'I'd love to come on Sunday afternoon,' Jinny said. 'I've got tea to get now – but pick me up at three on Sunday and I'll come . . .'

'All right, we'll go for a little trip out to Richmond Park,' he said. 'I'll treat you to a cream tea somewhere if yer like . . .'

'Thanks,' Jinny said. It crossed her mind to ask if he knew anything about Jake's accident at the Docks, but he was looking so pleased with himself that she couldn't. 'I've got to start work in ten minutes . . . but I'll look forward to our outing on Sunday . . .' She smiled as he nodded, kick-started the bike and roared off down the road . . .

Sandra carried a tray of tea up to Sister's office the next morning. She knocked and was invited to enter, and having set the tray on the desk began to pour the tea for them both.

'I didn't want to make trouble for Mrs Davies, but it's obvious what she has been doing, using substandard produce and pocketing the difference,' Sandra said. 'It's far worse than we thought at first, because she was risking the children's health by giving them poor food.'

'It cannot have been going on long. I hadn't noticed anything . . .'

'She would make sure your meals were proper,' Sandra said. 'Mavis and the other carers had noticed but didn't like to make a fuss, because she was always saying you didn't give her enough to manage on . . . but taking money from Kelly's bag and the staff's treat box was her undoing.'

'We cannot be certain that was her,' Sister said. 'I know it looks that way – but Sergeant Sallis told me circumstantial evidence would not be enough in court. Not that I have any intention of it going that far. I was bound to report it – but it is up to the Board to press charges if the police arrest her.'

'No, you are right,' Sandra agreed. 'It looks bad

because she did not return – but we don't know for certain that she took the money . . .'

'If she did I dare say it was because of her son,' Sister Beatrice said. 'It seems certain she had been cheating us for some time . . . perhaps only a few shillings here and there. It may be that she was in some kind of trouble . . .'

'I can feel sorry for her if her son was putting pressure on her for money, but giving bad fish to the children is unforgivable.'

'I imagine she thought it wouldn't harm them,' Sister Beatrice said, 'but she was lucky it didn't kill that child, and that the others have recovered – had it been otherwise she would be in prison now . . .'

'Perhaps she feared that – and so she took all the money she could get her hands on and fled.'

'Whatever the case, it's just as well she went,' Sister said. 'She was not to be trusted and at least this way she's out of our lives. Jinny is going to be in charge of the provisions for now and her friend Nellie is probably going to help cook the meals. I'm told she is a good cook so I look forward to some improvement . . .'

'Jinny did well yesterday,' Sandra said, 'but we can't expect her to do it all – at least not yet. She's young to be in charge of staff and Nancy has too much work without taking on the charge of the kitchen. I could put in another hour or so . . .'

'You have plenty to do as it is,' Sister Beatrice said. 'I'm aware we're often short of staff and I know you help make beds and clean the dorms sometimes, so don't offer to take on more. It is our old problem of never having quite enough funds – but I think we shall manage as we are for a while, if Nellie obliges us and no one leaves or goes off sick for weeks on end.'

'It's such a big responsibility for you,' Sandra said. 'I think you must get very tired sometimes . . .' She looked at the nun anxiously, because she was looking a little weary.

'Sometimes I feel my age,' Beatrice admitted with a wry nod. 'However, we have to think of the children. They are always my first priority and I am upset to think that I did not realise the standards in the kitchen had dropped so low. These children have had enough of being hungry and given bad food – I am furious that that woman took their money for herself. I eat very little myself and was given a sandwich or an omelette whenever I asked . . . but it was not the same for the children I'm afraid.'

'I imagine it was all for her son,' Sandra said and frowned. 'Sergeant Sallis told me that they think he had outside help to escape – help that would have needed money to organise . . . No wonder she took money that belonged to St Saviour's.'

'And to the staff. Kelly lost a pound from her bag, you know . . .'

'Rose lost ten shillings from her purse the other night. She told me she saw a boy leaving the sick room and when she discovered her loss she thought it might have been him – but it may have been Mrs Davies, grabbing whatever she could.'

'It is lucky that I keep very little money in the office,' Beatrice said. 'It is usually locked in my file, because it is wrong to tempt others – but had I left it in my desk as I once did . . .'

'You might have lost that too.'

'I never imagined she would turn out to be a thief as well as a cheat. I do not understand how she could steal from vulnerable children.'

'Well, I saw a market trader delivering a box of vegetables to the kitchen just now,' Sandra said. 'It seems that word has gone round St Saviour's is in a spot of bother and they can't do enough for us.'

'I think that was down to Jinny. I believe I've seen her in the market with one of her friends. We must be grateful, because the Board will not be happy when I ask for more money to last the month and I do not like to run into debt . . .'

'Ikey would let you have a few pounds if you need it . . .' Sandra offered but Sister shook her head. 'He was furious when I told him what that woman had done – but he says it is unlikely they will find her in time to recover your money.'

'No, I imagine not,' Sister sighed. 'It will teach us to be more observant in future . . .'

Sandra gathered up the used cups and carried the tray back to the kitchen. Sister had refused the offer of money, but she would certainly help out in whatever way she could, washing up, peeling veg and making jam, because Jinny had so much soft fruit she couldn't get round to preserving it and do all the cooking too. It would be a relief when Nellie started work the next day . . .

'I heard about what happened,' Rob said when he spoke to Nancy later that day in the nurses' rest room where he was putting the finishing touches to the skirting boards. 'Nick said he was willing to put a few bob in the kitty to help St Saviour's out, and I'll do the same. It's a rotten trick that woman played on those kids – as if they haven't had it rough enough already . . .'

Nancy smiled at him. 'Thank Nick for us, but we've already had so many gifts of food and offers of help. I wouldn't feel justified in taking your money, Rob. Jinny told her friends on the market and they've spread the word. She's had loads of fruit and vegetables brought in already.'

'Well, tell your Sister Beatrice that we've made a little collection amongst some of our colleagues in the building trade of nearly ten pounds – and we can't give it back so it's there for her to use on behalf of the orphans.' He handed her an envelope, which was bursting with coins. Nancy smiled and tucked it into her apron pocket.

'All right, thank you. I'll give it to her later . . .' She hesitated and then, 'Some of us are going to give the kids a day at the zoo one day soon – if you and Nick wanted to come along . . . It won't be for a week or two, because I couldn't until my leg is better . . .'

'I'd love to,' Rob said at once. 'I haven't been for years – not since I was at school.'

'Well, you should,' Nancy said and smiled shyly. 'It was nice of you and your brother to help us. Now, if you will excuse me, I'm going to see if there's anything I can do to help in the kitchen . . .'

'I thought Sister told you to rest?'

'She did, but I could sit and peel vegetables or something,' Nancy said. She smiled at him and left, hobbling a little as she went.

Rob watched her, feeling pleased. It was the first time Nancy had spoken to him so freely and he felt as if they were really getting somewhere at last. He didn't expect it to happen all at once, given her history, but he believed she was beginning to trust him – and perhaps to feel more than just liking . . .

'Nice kitchen,' Nellie said when she walked in the next morning. She was wearing a spotless white apron that covered her floral print dress and looked very professional, and she tucked her hair beneath a cap that covered her hair. 'We need to start the way we mean to go on, don't we, my dears?' she asked and smiled at Elsa who was hovering uncertainly in the background. 'Now the floor looks nice and clean, and the sink in here is fine, but the range needs a bit of a brush up – and that table wants another scrub, Jinny.' She rolled up her sleeves. 'I'll scrub the table how I like it – and then we'll start on the cookin'. Can I trust you to clean the range in the mornin', Elsa? And in future I want you to scrub the table first thing, Jinny.'

'Yeah, I'll do that stove fer yer termorrer . . .' Elsa grinned at her because she didn't mind working for someone who treated her all right. 'What would you like me to do now?'

'Well, from what I've seen in the pantry, this is our menu for today: we're makin' a steak and kidney puddin' with creamy mash, carrots and greens, and we'll do a nice quiche with some of those leeks and a bit of cheese – and we'll cook a rice puddin' and serve it with them dried apricots soaked in a little sugar syrup to make them sweet . . . and jam tart with custard. Jinny, you can make a start on the beef puddin' – and peel a couple of those onions just to give it a little extra flavour . . . and you can prepare the vegetables, Elsa. When you've done them all, we'll have a cup of tea together and take stock of what we've got in the pantry.'

'Yes, of course,' Jinny said and smiled to see her friend in her element. Nellie's manner and speech were professional and Jinny knew she was making an effort to look efficient on her first day in the new job, whilst being her normal friendly self. Elsa was actually singing as she worked in the scullery and Jinny felt happier than she had the whole time she'd worked in the kitchen.

Now that things had settled and Mrs Davies had gone it seemed as if the future really was bright for them all. Micky was taking her out that evening to a little dance, and they were going for a long ride out on Sunday – and she wanted to tell him how much she appreciated his spreading the word about St Saviour's needing help. It wasn't only the market traders who had come up trumps. A butcher had brought round a large chicken for them and told Jinny that he'd supplied St Saviour's for years but hadn't been willing to sell them substandard meat so his account had been closed.

'I'll be happy to supply you again, miss,' he told her. 'I shan't overcharge you and you won't get any dodgy stuff from me . . .'

Jinny thanked him. He'd refused payment for the chicken and so far she only had the few shillings left from the original six pounds. Sister Beatrice had promised more and she'd told Jinny she would be in charge of buying their food in future. She'd suggested that it should be Nellie but her friend shook her head.

'I've no head for sums, lovey. I'll leave that to you. We'll decide what we need for the week ahead and send the menus to your Sister Beatrice to approve – and then you can buy what we need.'

Jinny nodded happily. She liked dealing with the friendly market traders and bought her own clothes from them. Adding up wasn't a chore for her and she would rather enjoy being in charge of the food – and it had helped her to make up her mind that what she wanted to do with her life was to learn all she could and become a professional cook. She liked living and working here and it was all she wanted to do for the next few years. Micky was a good friend and she liked him, but she didn't want to get married for ages yet . . .

CHAPTER 20

Rose met Rob when she was leaving St Saviour's the following Monday evening. He had his van drawn up outside in the road and was loading it with ladders, tins of paints and all his other stuff. Stopping to chat in the mild evening sunshine, she was surprised, because although everything was looking good throughout the home, she hadn't realised that he'd finished his work.

'Are you leaving us now?' she asked.

'Yes, I finished the last door this afternoon. Sister Beatrice says she's pleased and will recommend us to others . . .'

'Well, it looks lovely, fresh and clean everywhere,' Rose said. 'We shall miss seeing you and Nick about . . .'

'Oh, I'll be back to visit,' Rob said. 'Nick has probably told you he's giving another little party. I'm going to ask Nancy this time – and I'm sure Nick will be in touch with you if he hasn't already. It's on Saturday next week . . .'

'No, Nick hasn't rung for a while.' Rose was thoughtful, because it must be nearly two weeks since she'd heard from him and she'd wondered why. 'That sounds nice, I'll look forward to it,' she said and then suddenly remembered. 'Oh, I forgot to tell Sister Beatrice something important. Please excuse me . . .'

She ran back up the stairs and saw Nancy hobbling painfully towards her down the landing. 'Is that knee still sore?' she asked, concerned. 'Why don't you let me look at it for you? It won't take a moment and I don't like to see you suffering. It may be inflamed . . .'

'Oh no, it's all right, just a bit sore and stiff,' Nancy said. 'Really, Rose, I'm all right. I just wanted to catch Rob before he left and I suppose I was trying to walk too fast . . .'

'Well, he's still loading stuff,' Rose said. 'He just invited me to a party at Nick's house – and he's going to ask you. I expect he'll ask several of us again like he did last time.' She hesitated, then, 'I must speak to Sister Beatrice about one of the kids. If that knee is painful come and see me tomorrow . . .' She hurried off without looking back and did not see the rather puzzled and hurt expression on Nancy's face. She had reached the top of the stairs but hesitated, shook her head and then went back the way she had come.

The telephone in the nurses' home rang at eight that evening. Rose answered it and Nick's voice came over the line. She smiled because it was nice to hear from him again.

'That is Rose, isn't it?' he inquired, his voice growing warmer as she acknowledged it. 'Oh, good, I'm glad I caught you. I rang on Sunday but Jinny told me she thought you'd gone to the country with some friends?'

'Yes, that's true,' Rose said. 'There were quite a few of us – and we took some of the kids. We had a picnic and the men gave the lads driving lessons and then we all played rounders. It was a lot of fun and Stephen was terrific with the kids. He's so professional when we call him out, but he was like a different person, full of life and fun . . .'

'Sounds like you had a good time?'

'Yes, I did,' she agreed. 'I think everyone did – it made such a change to get right away from London and the heat and the noise.'

'Yes, it has been hot recently – that's why I thought I'd have another party in the garden while the weather holds. It's almost September now and the summer will soon be gone . . .'

'I expect so. I've been too busy to think of it . . . Rob told me you were having another party . . .'

'Yes. I wondered if you would like to come.'

'Yes, very much,' Rose replied. 'I enjoyed the last one – and I always enjoy going out with you, Nick.'

'Good, I wasn't sure . . . I suppose I'm a bit old and set in my ways for you. Henderson is probably more your sort . . . being a doctor . . .'

Rose caught her breath. Was that a hint of jealousy in his voice? She wasn't sure how he felt about her, because he didn't always telephone when he said he would and she couldn't be sure she wasn't just one of a number of women he dated.

'We're just friends,' Rose said, though she knew that might not be quite true as far as the doctor was concerned, because Stephen had kissed her goodnight when they parted on Sunday night; not passionately, but with warmth and the promise of more to come. 'I like to see all my friends . . . as I'm sure you do . . .'

'Yes, of course.' Nick sounded hesitant. 'I'll look out for you at the party then . . .' He put down the receiver sharply, making Rose draw back and look at it in surprise. Had she upset Nick by dating another man? It hadn't been an intimate date like dining and dancing, just an outing with others. Surely Nick couldn't be jealous? He'd taken her out three times since his party, but since then she'd heard nothing and she'd wondered if she'd upset him or perhaps he'd discovered he wasn't that interested in dating her. She couldn't recall him saying or doing anything that would give her the right to think he was serious.

No, of course he wasn't! She must have imagined that note of chagrin in his voice when she'd told him she'd been out with Stephen.

Rose wasn't sure how she did feel about Nick; she liked him a lot and she'd enjoyed her time with him very much, but their friendship hadn't progressed, whereas her relationship with Stephen Henderson had changed overnight, from that of simply nurse and doctor to friends. She'd felt happy and carefree in his company that Sunday and it had been such a lovely day, almost like the happy times she'd known as a child with her sister, before all the pain and loneliness of her parents' deaths and the long years of hard work when she'd struggled to become a nurse and escape the slums of her childhood.

She'd thought Nick just saw her as an attractive woman to take out occasionally – after all, he was still grieving for his wife, wasn't he? How would she feel if Nick asked her to be more than just a friend?

Feeling rather mixed up, Rose decided to wash her hair and have an early night. After tomorrow she would be on nights for a while and would give the situation some serious thought. The last thing she wanted was to hurt anyone, especially a man like Nick who had suffered so much – but she just didn't know how she felt. In fact, she was torn between Nick and Stephen, liking them both but uncertain whether she felt more than liking for either of them . . .

'I was looking for Nancy,' Rob said when he met Rose just as she was leaving St Saviour's two days later after being on night duty. 'I rang the nurses' home twice but I was told she isn't there I thought I'd come over myself and see what has happened to her . . .'

'Oh, didn't she tell you?' Rose said. 'I gather it was a sudden decision the other evening – after you left. She spoke to Sister and asked for a week's leave. Her leg is still too stiff for her to do much here and she's decided to go down and visit her brother . . . even though they've asked her not to . . .'

'Her brother?' Rob looked at Rose oddly. 'I didn't realise she had one . . .'

'She hasn't told you?' Rose frowned. 'I'm surprised she didn't tell you she was going away for a few days. Her brother is what some people would call retarded and he lives in a secure home in Cambridgeshire. He was in a fire as a small child and his father used to beat him, I think . . . it was a very sad case. Mr Adderbury had to have him sectioned after he became violent.'

'I didn't know. No one has ever mentioned it . . .'

'Perhaps I shouldn't have,' Rose said. 'Nancy may have wanted to keep it private – but she was coming to speak to you the other evening, when you were packing up. Did you not see her?'

'No. She said earlier she would come down but she must have changed her mind. I looked for her but she wasn't in St Saviour's – she must have gone home instead . . .' He looked hurt and puzzled and Rose felt uneasy because Nancy had been hurrying to see him – had she said something to make her change her mind? 'I don't know if I upset her. I told her you'd invited me to Nick's party and were going to invite her and some of the others . . .'

Rob made a noise like a soft curse. 'If you remember I didn't invite you, Rose; I said that Nick would – and I didn't intend to ask anyone else, unless you wanted to come with us as Nancy's friend . . .'

'Oh . . .' Rose's cheeks burned and she felt awful. 'I'm sorry, Rob, I had no idea that Nancy was so special to you . . . if I've spoiled things . . . I'm so very sorry. I wouldn't hurt Nancy for the world. She's had too much to put up with in her life.'

'Perhaps there's more I should know?' He arched his brows but Rose shook her head.

'I've said too much already. I shouldn't have mentioned Nancy's brother – and as for the rest I'll leave it to her to tell you when she's ready . . .'

She walked away hurriedly, feeling dreadful because she must have upset Nancy without realising it, and she wasn't the sort of woman who did catty things deliberately to hurt others. As soon as Nancy returned she would apologise and explain that she'd been invited to the party by Nick and not Rob . . . she just hoped she hadn't put Nancy off him for good.

Nancy booked into the small hotel she'd stayed at before in Cambridge. She carried her suitcase upstairs and dumped it on the bed, wondering what had made her ask Sister for time off just like that. She'd refused it when it had first been offered, because she wasn't sure it would be a good idea to visit Terry at the moment; she'd been told not to come for a while – and yet it was the only thing she could think of, the only place she could run to, to escape her distress. St Saviour's had been her home for so many years, but now she felt alone and friendless, even though she knew it wasn't so . . . but she had no one special, no one she could go to when she was hurting and know they would comfort and love her.

Yet even as she began to hang the few clothes she'd brought with her in the wardrobe, she knew she'd brought her troubles with her. Why did it hurt so much to discover that she was only one of several girls Rob was planning to invite to his brother's party – and not even the first to receive the invitation?

All he'd done was look after her when she'd fallen and hurt her knee on that broken glass. Yes, he'd smiled at her, and yes, he'd been gentle and kind, very protective and strong as he'd carried her into the hospital and then insisted on seeing her home and into her room. Had she not insisted she was fine then he would probably have come inside and stayed with her until he was sure she was over the shock, but she'd asked him to go, promised she was all right, even though she'd wept after he'd left.

So why had she thought his smiles were special for her and why had she allowed herself to think that at long last she'd met someone she could trust? Now it seemed that he'd just been charming her and she was only one of many . . . that he was the same base creature that her father had been.

No, that wasn't fair! Nancy knew it and admitted it. Just because Rob had other friends it didn't mean he was a cruel beast and she was wrong to label him that way, very wrong. It was just that she'd started to think he cared for her and Rose's careless words had destroyed that tenuous trust just like that . . . and Rose wasn't the sort who would deliberately hurt anyone.

Had it been some of the other carers who had come and gone at St Saviour's she would have suspected mischief, but Rose would never try to hurt her – she'd been hurt herself.

Tears slid down Nancy's cheeks as she put on her jacket again and went out. She couldn't sit here brooding all night. She would go to one of the many cinemas in Cambridge and treat herself, and then tomorrow she would arrange to visit her brother . . .'

CHAPTER 21

Ruby looked at her superior across Miss Sampson's desk. She'd been called in to her office to make her report and was feeling uncomfortable. Was Ruth mortally offended because she'd sent one of her girls down to Halfpenny House without asking her and merely sent a memo to that effect? She'd been a little offhand with Ruby lately and she'd retaliated in kind.

'Ah, Ruby,' Miss Sampson said. 'Please sit down. I wanted to congratulate you . . .' She read through a small paragraph in Ruby's report and nodded. 'Yes, a definite improvement in the behaviour of your girls recently I'm glad to say . . .'

Ruby swallowed hard, because she felt a bit guilty about her methods of achieving the improvement. She'd bribed the girls with a sweet ration and eased a few of the strict rules, and the results had been good – and yet she knew that the girls had been sent to her to learn discipline and some people might think she'd gone soft. Perhaps she had, but they'd all been so keen to have tea with the orphans next door, and some of the girls had volunteered to help with reading to the little ones on a Saturday morning, and a couple of the older girls had volunteered to do some washing-up one morning, because the kitchen girls were rushed off their feet.

'Yes, I sorted out a few problems and the trouble-makers seem to have quietened down. I haven't had a visit from the police for some weeks now.'

'Well, we always get a few troublemakers and you can disperse them – send the worst to a remand home, as you did Betty Goodge . . .' Ruth Sampson frowned. 'That was an unfortunate case, of course, because she attempted suicide and they transferred her to a mental institution, where I understand she is undergoing intense therapy . . . so perhaps it will lead to a better life for her . . .'

'Oh, that sounds hopeful,' Ruby said and some of the shadows lifted. 'I felt that I'd let her down . . .'

'Yes, well, the fact that she attempted suicide almost immediately did put a black mark on your record, and I was reprimanded over that other business – but we all make mistakes.' She paused and then smiled. 'I wanted to make you aware of what is in the pipeline, Ruby. It seems certain that we shall be taking over St Saviour's at the end of the year . . .'

'Sister Beatrice won't like that . . .' Ruby said without thinking. 'We've allowed the girls to mix with the kids next door for limited periods, but I don't think she would agree to a permanent arrangement . . .'

'She will not be asked to,' Miss Sampson said and a smile of satisfaction settled over her face. 'This is still in the melting pot but I believe you will be in complete charge of the home next year. I have long felt that we have more need of those premises than Sister Beatrice's children. Most of them could be dealt with by the hospital, or if fit and referred to us by the police, we can send them on to whatever homes we choose – wherever there is a vacancy . . . They would be with us only for a few hours at most. Any of our reception centres could deal with that . . .'

'So we are actually closing the orphanage and taking the building for ourselves – is that what you're saying?'

'Yes, more or less . . . though we haven't told the Board of St Saviour's in so many words . . .' Miss Sampson smiled smugly. 'It is time that woman was retired. Her methods are outdated – besides, we need more space for our girls and probably boys. I've been told they want to send us boys as well in the future. They need a home like this as there is nothing similar for young male offenders. At the moment they are either sent to borstal or prison and some cases are borderline; they are too risky to send to an orphanage, because they disrupt the others, but prison or borstal is too harsh . . . I think you've shown that it is possible to make unruly girls behave – so I imagine you can do it with boys too. No doubt you'll be given a male member of staff to help in case of violence . . .'

'What about sick and homeless kids, like those Sister Beatrice takes in? I thought we were going to have a reception centre for them too?'

'It has been decided that they will go to a specialised reception centre, which is due to open in December. There they will be examined by a doctor; those needing medical treatment will go to hospital and the healthy ones will be sent off to an orphanage wherever we can find a space . . .'

Ruby felt an uneasy sense of sickness in her stomach. She'd always admired and liked Ruth Sampson, looked up to her and, for a short time, even thought she might love her – but the gloating expression in her face now made Ruby want to vomit. She contrasted it with the compassion she'd seen in Sister Beatrice's eyes when she'd asked for her help with Emmeline. Within days the girl had been transferred to the Essex home and Sister Beatrice had assured her several times that she was doing well and seemed very happy there.

'Do the Board of St Saviour's know what you plan?'

'I'm not sure, but they've been made a generous offer and it is to their benefit to agree . . .'

'And I shall have a free hand in running the home?'

'As much as you do now, under my direction, of course. As I said, I am pleased with the improvements in the behaviour of your girls . . .'

How much of that improvement was down to the visits next door? Sister Beatrice had gone out of her way to welcome the girls who were chosen to have tea there. Ruby wondered if the improvement in behaviour would long survive the knowledge that there was nothing to look forward to in future. She would probably be forced to impose even stricter rules once they had male inmates living next door. Ruby could foresee a problem with keeping the more adventurous girls from paying clandestine visits to the boys' dormitories . . . and that would lead to punishment rather than treats. It wasn't what she'd hoped would happen in the future at all . . .

Ruby caught her breath, feeling too stunned to answer immediately. 'I'm to take over at the end of the year?' she said at last, still not able to believe all she'd been told. This would devastate Sister Beatrice, because Ruby was sure she had no idea that her home would close in a few months.

'Once it is agreed and settled. The Board of St Saviour's haven't actually signed yet, but my side of things is all ready to move – well, what do you say?'

Ruby was overcome and shocked. 'What can I say but thank you?' she said, realising that her superior was waiting. 'I never expected this . . .'

'I believe you are ready for an important promotion.' Ruth smiled at her. 'I thought you might like to go out for a drink and celebrate . . . say this evening?'

Ruby stared at her, feeling uncertain because the look in her eyes seemed to be saying all the things she'd once longed for. However, Ruth had shown a side of her that Ruby hadn't noticed before – or perhaps it was Ruby who had changed. Perhaps her recent exchanges with Sister Beatrice had worked like water on a stone, gradually wearing away the hardened exterior she'd built up to protect herself.

Taking a grip, she drew a deep breath and lied. 'Perhaps we could go for that drink another time,' she said. 'I have an appointment for this evening.'

Annoyance flickered in Ruth Sampson's eyes. 'Very well, just remember that what I've told you is completely confidential.'

'Naturally – and thank you for telling me and for putting me forward for what is a huge promotion for me. If it happens I shall do my very best to make a success of this new venture . . .'

Walking a little later through grimy streets that were suddenly overcast, the sky a threatening dark grey as the first spots of rain began to fall, Ruby hurried past inviting cafés and coffee bars, needing to be alone so that she could think . . . try to make sense of her feelings.

Her sense of ambition, which had been her main driving force for years, seemed to have deserted her, because she knew Ruth Sampson had been annoyed that she'd turned down her invitation. Ruby had lived for her work for as long as she could remember. As soon as she'd been old enough to break away from her aunt's domination and her uncle's filthy habits, she'd wanted to be someone of importance – someone who was a force for good and made a difference.

And that was the trouble, Ruby realised with a little shock. When she'd encouraged Ruth Sampson to take June Miller into care and place her with foster parents she'd really thought it was for the better – and the shock of knowing that she'd been instrumental in causing the child harm had shaken her to her core. Ruby had gradually been coming round to see things more and more from Sister Beatrice's point of view. She'd thought her a bore and old-fashioned at the start, but when Ruby really thought about it, compassion and justice never went out of fashion.

It was because of the nun's influence that Ruby had introduced a softer regime at the probationary centre, she realised that now, and wondered at herself. Her reforms might be thought soft by some of her colleagues, but they'd worked in this instance. She was aware that in some cases the changes might be seen as weakness and some hardened types would seek to take advantage – and she wondered if she was really the right person to take charge of the new centre.

And if she did – what would happen to Sister Beatrice and her children?

Ruby frowned, because she'd given her assurance that she would say nothing and yet she knew that the secret would lodge in her throat like a stone whenever she saw the nun or one of her staff. It was unfair that Sister Beatrice should be in the dark about the future . . . but the decision was not hers and she could not break a confidence.

As she approached St Saviour's, she saw Sister Beatrice emerge and look up at the sky. Ruby turned away to glance into the window of a new sandwich and snacks shop that had recently opened a few doors away. She went inside, lingering over her choice of lunch deliberately to give the nun time to walk on, because she knew the guilt she was feeling would almost certainly show on her face.

Having made her choice, she went back out into the street. Sister Beatrice had made little progress. She'd been stopped by a woman with two small children clinging to her skirts, their dirty faces turned up to look at the nun with shining confidence and trust. Sister Beatrice bent to whisper something to them, and then took a slender purse from her pocket and gave what looked to Ruby to be a florin to the mother, who clasped her hands and thanked her before they parted and she was allowed to move on.

Such a simple little act of kindness and yet it brought a huge lump to Ruby's throat. What must it feel like to be loved like that? She'd been told the nun was worshipped almost like a saint in these shabby streets where poverty and dirt must once have been the biggest killers, but she hadn't understood. The look in those children's faces had told more than a thousand words, and Ruby actually felt humbled. Sister Beatrice could have little money and yet she'd spared a florin for the mother, no doubt to buy food for her children.

Ridden by guilt, she hurried inside and up to her office. There, she automatically boiled her kettle and sat to eat her meal of cheese and tomato sandwiches, and drink her coffee. Just as she'd finished there was a knock at the door and one of her staff members entered. Marla was one of the newer carers and a plump motherly type with mousey hair.

'You're back then,' she said. 'I just wanted to tell you . . . while you were out, we had another little visit from the police . . .'

'Who was the culprit this time?' Ruby sighed, putting the remains of her lunch in the waste bin. 'And what did she do?'

'Well, actually, it wasn't something bad,' Marla smiled at her. 'Doris helped an old lady who fell over in the street. Apparently, she and one of the other girls got her sitting up and then the other girl ran to ask for a doctor and Doris stayed with the old lady and looked after her until the ambulance came to take her to hospital. I thought you would like to hear good news for once.'

'Wonders will never cease,' Ruby said and smiled. 'Thanks, Marla – and you were quite right, I am delighted to hear good news.'

She pondered on the news after her assistant left the

office. She'd thought Doris was a confirmed hard case, but it just went to show that there might be hope for her and other girls who were on the borderline. Had she sent Doris to the remand home the girl would never have had the opportunity to help that elderly lady in need – so perhaps her new regime was working after all. It might even be that if she was given the overall command of the new centre she might be able to make a difference.

Ruby lifted her head proudly. It wouldn't be her fault if she failed, and she wouldn't forget what she'd learned from Sister Beatrice – that sternness needed to be tempered by compassion and kindness.

It didn't completely ease her feelings of guilt concerning Sister Beatrice but she was coming to terms with that, managing to put it aside – after all, she had no part in these decisions . . .

As she entered the foyer of her apartment building that evening, Ruby was feeling depressed and restless. Seeing the bright flame of a girl's hair as she emerged from the lift, her spirits suddenly lifted. Carla smiled as she saw her and for Ruby it was as if the gloom of the day had lightened.

'Oh, I'm glad I've caught you,' she said as Carla approached. 'I wondered if you felt like having a drink later this evening.'

Regret came swiftly to the other girl's face as she shook her head. 'I wish I could, Ruby,' she said. 'I've made arrangements for this evening with a girl from work. Well, she works in the offices next door actually, and we met at a café, and both of us want to see the latest *Frankenstein* film. I'm sorry . . . perhaps we could do it another night?'

'Oh . . . yes, of course,' Ruby said and nodded, but she felt as if Carla had thrown cold water over her as she hurriedly entered the lift. It had taken her a lot of soul-searching to decide to ask her and Carla was obviously already making lots of new friends, going out and having fun. Why would she be interested in Ruby? She was younger, prettier and full of joy. Ruby felt old, grey and dull beside her and the mood of depression settled over her as she let herself into her empty flat, which felt stuffy and airless.

She hadn't made any real friends since she'd come to work in London and sometimes she wondered if life was worthwhile, even though she was being promoted and praised at work. As she took a half-bottle of wine out of the fridge and poured a large glass she wondered what the girl looked like who was going to the pictures with Carla . . . and if they would hold hands in the darkness.

Sipping her wine she switched on the TV show, saw that the hit musical show, *Oh Boy!*, was playing and switched it off again. She didn't feel like listening to popular music alone, even though she liked Tommy Steele's records.

Picking up her bag, she took out some paperwork from her office and began to go over it again. Her department was due for an inspection soon and she wanted to make sure she didn't get a black mark. Anyway, what else was there for her but work? It seemed that she would never find happiness or love . . .

CHAPTER 22

Jinny felt sick inside as she approached her mother's home, noticing the way the frowsy lace curtains at the window hung limply, and the step was still stained where someone had been sick over it; it looked as if the mess had just been left for the rain to wash away. Nellie's curtains were pristine white; her step had been stoned and scrubbed early that morning and her front door was free of the prevalent dust that came back day after day, blowing off the grimy streets.

Jinny felt ashamed of her home. Why couldn't her mother have been more like Nellie? Her throat was tight with tears she was too proud to shed, because she felt sad that her mother's life had been so miserable. Why had she turned to drink? Was it to blot out her loneliness?

Nellie had insisted that she visit her mother again, even though the last visit had been less than successful. 'You're all she's got, love,' she'd told Jinny when they were serving up the delicious minced chicken pie with crumbly pastry and tasty gravy that the kids had eaten every scrap of at lunchtime. 'You'll be safe enough while Jake is in the 'ospital . . .'

Jinny opened the back door and stopped in dismay at the sight that met her eyes. The kitchen looked as if a bomb had hit it, dirty crockery piled in the sink and on all the surfaces, dirty clothes on the floor and strewn over the furniture, bits of stale and mouldy food left about – and a huge rat on the table eating what looked like the remains of a pie and chips. No wonder Jake had wanted her back home! At least when Jinny was living here she'd kept it clean and tidy.

'Ugh!' she cried and picked up a broom standing in the corner, chasing the rodent round and round the room until it shot out of the back door. 'Disgusting . . .'

Jinny started collecting the rubbish, putting it into the old tin can they'd always used for scraps in the yard, and sorting the washing into piles. It stunk of sweat and worse and must have been lying there for weeks, some of it Jake's. She dumped her mother's into the copper in the scullery, which was filled with soapy water that had clearly been used once. She would light a fire under it if there was any kindling. It would give the clothes a bit of a swill and they could be rinsed in the sink once the piles of dirty dishes had been dealt with, but before she could do that she would have to clear out the old range, carry the ashes into the yard and get it going.

She paused on her way back from the yard and called out to her mother, thinking that she must be upstairs. No answer came and she frowned, because it was unlikely that her mother would have gone to the pub this early. Surely she wasn't sleeping off a drunken stupor at this hour? Jinny wouldn't have thought she had enough money to be able to drink all day . . .

She got rid of the ashes and then went back into the

kitchen and started making a fire with paper and wood. She'd just set a match to it when she something made her look up. There was something on the ceiling . . . a big dark stain that she hadn't seen before. A shiver of apprehension went through her, and Jinny suddenly felt cold. Something was wrong here – something more than the mess and the stink of stale food.

'Mum . . . are you up there?' Jinny asked and put her foot on the bottom stair leading to the bedrooms. She was just about to go up when the kitchen door opened and Nellie's husband walked in. 'Bert . . . I'm glad you're here. I'm sure something is wrong – look at that mark on the ceiling. What does it look like to you?'

Bert stared up at the kitchen ceiling and frowned. 'Nellie sent me round to see if yer were all right . . .' He grabbed her arm, edging her out of the way. 'You stop 'ere, Jinny love. Let me take a look first . . .'

'You think it's blood too . . .' Jinny felt scared. 'Mum! She wouldn't do anything silly, would she?'

'Just wait 'ere fer me . . .' Bert said and started up the narrow staircase. Jinny hesitated and then followed a few steps behind, unwilling to face whatever it was alone and yet compelled to see. It couldn't be her mother – could it?'

Bert went into the bedroom and she heard a muffled cry. Darting forward, she saw the shape of a body lying on the floor and gave a scream of fear, but Bert's bulk blocked her from getting nearer or seeing it properly.

'Run to Nellie now, and tell my boy Brian to go for the police. He's home on leave from the Army and it's a good thing he is if there's murder afoot. Tell 'im to get Sergeant Sallis if he can . . .'

'Is it Mum?' Jinny asked fearfully. 'Is she dead?'

'It ain't yer ma, Jinny; it's a bloke,' Bert said, looking sick himself. 'He's dead and it ain't pretty. There's been a fight 'ere and the police need to see this for themselves. Yer ain't touched anythin'?'

'In the kitchen . . . I put some clothes in the copper and cleared out the stove, that's all.'

'As long as you ain't touched anythin' important . . . no bloodstained clothes or anythin'?'

'I didn't see anything like that . . .'

'Right, get off to my missus and stay there. I'm comin' down with yer and I'll wait fer the police ter come . . .'

'All right.' Jinny obeyed, feeling numbed. She'd thought it might be her mother who lay there in a pool of sticky blood but it wasn't. Bert hadn't told her but she'd spotted a knife lying on the floor and she thought perhaps whoever was dead had been fatally stabbed . . . but was it Jake or a man her mother had picked up at the pub?

What had happened in her mother's bedroom and if she wasn't lying there dead, where was she?

Hours later Micky took Jinny back to St Saviour's in a car he'd borrowed from a mate. It was black and sleek and posh and at any other time she would have been curious, but she just felt numbed, shocked by the information that the body lying in her mother's bedroom was Jake's and his throat had been cut.

'There was a terrific fight,' Bert told them when he came back after the police had taken over the house. They were in charge now and they wanted Bert out of the way before they began their exhaustive search of the house, but Sergeant Sallis had told him that Jake's murderer must have been a man.

'It couldn't possibly have been Mrs Hollis,' he said. 'Whoever killed Jake was very strong, because he put up one hell of a struggle before he died. He must have had twenty stab wounds as well as the slash that cut his throat. We think that quite possibly his killer was also wounded in the fight but was obviously able to make his escape . . .'

'What about Mum?' Jinny asked, feeling sick and close to hysteria. 'She isn't there, is she? Where has she gone?'

'I wish we knew,' Sergeant Sallis said and looked at her sadly. 'I think she must have been in bed with someone when Jake came in – and clearly he went mad and the fight ensued. We don't know who attacked who . . . but perhaps Mrs Hollis took the chance to escape while they were fighting . . .'

Jinny swallowed hard. 'Why didn't she come to you and tell you what had happened?'

Sergeant Sallis looked down at his shoes. He cleared his throat uncomfortably, then, 'We arrested your mother three days ago for soliciting, Jinny. She was drunk and making a nuisance of herself in the pub and they asked us to do something about her . . .'

Jinny's cheeks burned with shame. She understood perfectly why her mother had not gone to the police for help. Fear had made her run from the vicious men fighting over who had the right to her home and her body, and it had held her back from entering a police station, because she feared they might put her in the cells again.

'Do you think she was injured too?'

'We found a man's bloodstained shirt, which probably isn't Jake's,' Sergeant Sallis said. 'But none of the female clothing had more than incidental splashing that would've happened during the fight . . .'

'When – when did it happen?' Jinny asked.

'Some hours ago – perhaps the early hours of this morning . . .' Sergeant Sallis looked at with concern. 'No blame attaches to you, Jinny. We know you cleared up a few things in the kitchen, but you couldn't have known what was upstairs.'

'I'd just seen the ceiling when Bert arrived,' Jinny said, swallowing hard. 'I thought it might be Mum . . .'

'I do not imagine you regret Jake's passing,' the police constable said, busily writing down everyone's answers.

'That is irrelevant, Cotter,' Sergeant Sallis barked. 'Jinny isn't implicated in any way. What she may or may not feel about the victim has no bearing.'

'Sorry Sarge . . .' The young officer looked abashed and crossed through something on his pad.

'Well, we'll leave it to you,' Sergeant Sallis said. 'One of my officers will stay here to guard the property until we've finished our inquiries. I dare say he would appreciate a mug of tea now and then, but knock the door and ask first, Nellie.'

'Yes, if yer say so,' she said, looking at Jinny anxiously. 'I just wish I 'adn't told yer ter come round and see yer ma . . .'

'Perhaps if I'd come more – if I'd given her money – it wouldn't have happened . . .'

'Don't yer go blaming yerself,' Bert said. 'Yer ma were alus in trouble, Jinny. Whatever yer gave 'er she'd 'ave spent it on drink . . .'

Jinny knew it was true but she still felt partially responsible for her mother's behaviour. She'd wanted more money and when her daughter wouldn't give it to her, Mabel Hollis had gone out picking up men off the street. Jake must have come back from hospital and found her with one of them lying in the bed he considered his and . . . after that it was impossible to know, and she could only guess, just as the police had. They would have to make inquiries, discover who Jinny's mother had taken back to her home and where she'd got to . . .

It was going to be a long drawn-out affair and Jinny was anxious, both for her mother's safety, and because, if the murder got into the papers, it might reflect on her. Would Sister Beatrice want her at St Saviour's if it all came out about her mother's arrest for soliciting and her being in bed with a man when Jake came back from the hospital . . . ?

'You're very quiet,' Micky said as he opened the car door for her and helped her out. 'Are yer worryin' about yer ma?'

'I'm worried that she might be hurt,' Jinny said, 'but if it all comes out . . . I might be asked to leave St Saviour's . . .'

'They'd never do that to yer,' he said gruffly. 'But, if it becomes too uncomfortable for yer, Jinny love, I'll look after yer . . .'

'No, you can't . . .'

Jinny shook her head but he put his arms about her and held her close. 'Don't worry, love. I'll be around to look after yer.'

'It was horrible, Micky – thinkin' it might be Mum

lying up there – and it's partly my fault she'd got a man with her . . .'

'Don't be daft, Jinny. She were always the same,' Micky echoed Bert's words earlier. 'Jake was bad through and through. He was either goin' ter kill someone or be killed himself. I reckon it's a good thing he's dead and out of the way. Jake was a devil, and would've come after yer again and again until someone stopped him . . .'

'Micky . . . you didn't . . . ?' Jinny stared at him, her eyes opening in distress at the thought.

'I'm not a bloomin' murderer,' Micky said and glared at her. 'I might 'ave put 'im in the 'ospital if I'd had the chance, though there were others only too eager to do it for me, but I don't like knives and I don't kill people . . . what the bleedin' 'ell do yer think I am?'

'You arranged that accident at the Docks?' Jinny stared at him aghast. 'Oh, Micky, you promised me it wasn't you . . .'

'It weren't exactly,' he said, looking angry. 'I knew these blokes 'ad a grudge against Jake because he's been double-crossing them and stealin' what they think of as theirs – and they were lookin' for 'im. I told them where to find 'im, that's all . . . Besides, Jake deserved all he got . . .'

'He didn't deserve to be murdered,' Jinny said. She felt like weeping because it was all so horrible. 'I hated him but I didn't ask you to do this – or tell someone else to . . . and now my mother's gone missing . . .'

Bursting into sobs of distress, Jinny used her key to release the garden gate; she went through and shut it after her so that he couldn't follow. He pushed against it in frustration as it locked itself.

'Let me through, Jinny,' he begged, staring at her through the bars. 'I don't want to leave yer like this. I know it was terrible for yer and I'm sorry you had to be there . . . but I can't say I'm sorry he's dead. I care about yer more than anyone and if killing Jake was what it took to make sure yer were safe, I might have done it – but I didn't. Please don't look at me like that, Jinny. You said you wished yer could break every bone in his body and he owed those men money . . . It wasn't even anythin' to do with Nellie.'

Jinny stared at him through tear-blinded eyes. Micky was right and she wanted to tell him that she knew he was her friend and she didn't blame him for any of this, but she couldn't find the words. All the pain and doubt of her unhappy childhood had come back to haunt her and she'd hit out at him in her pain.

'I'm sorry,' she whispered and fled through the night to the sanctuary of the nurses' home and her room where she could sob and rage until this anger and hurt was washed away in her storm of emotion . . .

Upstairs in her room, Jinny flung herself on the bed and gave way to her storm of grief. She couldn't bear all the pain and guilt that pressed down on her and because she'd been so worried about her mother, she'd lashed out at her best friend, because Micky had been her guardian angel since that day she'd run from Jake. She wished she could take it back, but she'd seen the anger and resentment in his face and knew he wouldn't easily forgive her. She'd been so happy and proud of her new role in the kitchen, Nellie's comforting presence making it all seem so much like fun rather than work, and now it had all gone wrong . . .

CHAPTER 23

'It never rains but it pours,' Kelly said when she stopped for her break mid-morning and found Rose in the staff room making coffee. 'That's what my ma used to say and she's right. Poor little Jinny, I don't like to see her lookin' so pale and anxious . . .'

'She's worried about her mother,' Rose said and passed her a cup of coffee. 'The police haven't found any trace of her yet; she seems to have disappeared. Nellie told me that Sergeant Sallis asked her where Jinny's mother drank and they've looked for her but she hasn't been near . . .'

'I suppose she's frightened – if not of the man who killed Jake, then the police. They say she couldn't have killed him, but she witnessed a murder and ought to have reported it. I expect she thinks she's in trouble . . .'

'Yes, perhaps, but the police wouldn't prosecute her. They know she fled in fear of her life, but this uncertainty is awful for Jinny. She was there in the house when the body was found – and if Nellie hadn't sent her husband round to make sure she was all right, she might have been there alone. She's only a kid and this is all too much for her . . .'

'I think it's more than just her mother,' Kelly said thoughtfully. 'I was in the kitchen when someone asked for her in the hall. She was disappointed when she heard it was someone from the council about the house. The rent hasn't been paid in a while and they want it back – I think she thought it was that boyfriend of hers . . .'

'You mean Micky. She brought him to Nick's party . . .' Rose's voice trailed away as the door of the staff room opened and Nancy walked in wearing her uniform. 'Nancy, I didn't think you were back until tomorrow?'

'I came back early,' Nancy said and Rose noticed that she too was looking pale and unhappy. 'My brother wasn't well enough to see me. I tried twice and in the end they told me he was being kept in restraint . . . He almost killed one of the female attendants and they refused to let me see him in case it disturbed him.' Nancy sat down with a bump in the nearest chair and burst into tears. Rose went to kneel by her side and hold her hands. Kelly watched for a moment and then mumbled an excuse before leaving them alone together.

'Oh, Nancy, I'm so sorry,' Rose said. 'You've suffered so much because of your brother and this must be painful for you.'

'I lost the brother I loved years ago when he attacked Sister Beatrice,' Nancy said and brushed the tears from her cheeks. 'I thought he might be getting better, but they told me he's been worse lately and so they've had to drug him. It was that or lock him in a padded cell and they didn't want to do that yet . . .'

'Perhaps it's for the best. At least he doesn't know . . .'

Nancy stared at her and for a moment rebellion flared in her eyes, and then the resistance went out of her and she nodded once. 'The doctor told me it would be better if I just let him go. They seem to think he may not have long left to him, because he has some kind of physical damage to his lungs now . . . He broke out of the home and stayed out for several days in the winter and that brought on his illness. He may just die in his sleep . . .'

'Would that be worse than the life he has now?' Rose asked gently.

'No – it's just that I hoped he would get better. For a while he did seem to improve, but they told me his mental state was always going to get worse and I must accept that he was gone from me in all practical terms . . .' Nancy stared at her miserably. 'He's my brother. I feel so alone . . .'

'You've got us,' Rose said, putting an arm about her to comfort her. 'We all care for you, Nancy – and I think Rob loves you. He's been here every day looking for you, asking if I knew when you would be back . . .'

'Has he?' Nancy swiped her face with the back of her hand. 'I wasn't sure.'

'If I hurt you by what I said about the party – it was Nick who invited me. I just assumed that others would be invited, because last time Rob was told to ask as many young women as he could . . .'

'Oh . . .' Nancy stared at her uncertainly. 'I just thought it would be daft to let myself like him too much . . .'

'It isn't my business,' Rose said and stood up. 'But if I were you, I would give him a chance, Nancy. I know you've been hurt badly in the past, but don't you think you should try to put it behind you and look to the future?'

'If I can,' Nancy said a little tremulously. 'I'm not sure I'm capable of physical love. My father did that to me . . .'

'I suspected there was something,' Rose said and smiled comfortingly. 'Sister would probably tell you to consult Mr Adderbury and I know he did give you some counselling when you were first here – but if I were you I'd trust Rob. He's a decent man and if you could bear to tell him everything you might find that it doesn't seem so terrible after all these years – at least, it is worth trying, isn't it?'

'Thank you, Rose,' Nancy said and took the hankie she was offered, blowing her nose and slipping it in her pocket. 'I'll give it back clean . . .'

'I've got Rob's phone number on his works card – would you like it?'

Nancy hesitated and then inclined her head. 'Yes please. I'll telephone him this evening – and now I'd better get on with my job . . .'

Andy glanced over his shoulder. He had an uneasy feeling that he was being followed and had been ever since he'd left the school grounds that afternoon. He'd been helping Mr Barton prepare their equipment for the start of next term, and when he left he'd felt this sensation of being followed, though he wasn't sure because he hadn't seen any sign of his step-father.

Andy hoped the Beast wouldn't turn up and spoil things, because Sister Beatrice had promised that he and

Beth would be going on holiday before the new school term started.

'How would the pair of you like a little holiday at the sea before you return to school?' she'd asked them and Beth's face had lit up like a star in the night sky. 'Well, if you're happy with the idea I'm going to telephone Angela Adderbury. She will fit you in and we'll probably send Keith and Tom with you for ten days. I shall take you down to Halfpenny House myself on the train and Angela will be with you when you go to Hunstanton . . . or rather Old Hunstanton, because that's where the cottage is, near the sea. You can just run across a quiet road and you're on the beach . . .'

Beth had been so excited that she'd got hold of Sister Beatrice's hand and kissed it, thanking her over and over again. The usually stern nun had bent and kissed the top of Beth's head and then stroked her hair.

'You both deserve a treat,' she told them. 'I'll talk to Angela today – she's lovely and you will like her. It's nice down there and I think you'll enjoy it . . .'

Andy had never seen his sister so thrilled and smiled to himself at the memory as he reached St Saviour's. It would be lovely to be away from the grimy streets of the East End for several days and he wouldn't have to keep thinking about his step-father. At least he was back safe because he'd reached the front door of his new home.

'Got yer, yer little runt . . .' Andy heard the voice he hated and feared as a hand descended on his shoulder, the fingers gripping hard. He kicked out and jerked away; struggling free he ran into the hall of St Saviour's but the Beast followed him, an evil grin on his face.

'Thought yer were clever, didn't yer, thought I couldn't find out where yer were hidin' . . . but I've got yer now and I'm takin' yer and that sister of yourn back where you belong, wiv me . . .'

'Let me go, you rotten devil!' Andy yelled. 'You ain't takin' me back there and if yer touch Beth the police will lock yer up and throw away the key – that's what Staff Nurse Wendy says . . .'

The Beast's fist connected with Andy's ear, making him scream out and another heavy blow sent him reeling. He staggered back into someone and heard a woman cry out in pain. Craning round he saw that Nancy had come up behind him and he'd knocked into her, stepping on her foot, but she wasn't looking at him; her gaze was fixed on his step-father and he thought he'd never seen her look so angry. Nancy was always quiet and gentle, always looking after the little ones.

'Who are you – and why did you hit Andy?' she asked in a cold hard voice that he didn't recognise as hers, but knew was one of authority. 'This child is in our care and what you just did is physical abuse.' She pushed Andy behind her as a couple of children came in the front door followed by a man Andy recognised as the one who'd painted their dorms.

'Never you mind, you whore,' his step-father muttered. 'That boy is mine and so is his sister. I've found 'em now and I'm takin' 'em wiv me.'

'You will never be allowed to take Andy or Beth,' Nancy said bravely facing up to him, though he was a big, heavily built man and towered over her. 'I don't know your name, but I suspect you're the man they ran away from . . . their step-father, and as such you should've taken care of them instead of beating and starving them.'

'Is that what the little runt told yer? 'E's lyin' through 'is teeth. I just asked 'em to 'elp me keep the 'ouse right . . . It's my duty ter teach 'em how ter behave proper . . .'

'I do not believe you. I've seen the bruises on their flesh and I know what you did to them. You're a bully and a brute and you should be in prison for what you've done. Scum like you are not fit to live, let alone have the care of an innocent child . . . .' Nancy said in a voice that carried to everyone in the hall. 'You will not take these children from us nor will you touch them again. You're a brute and a bully and I'm going to report you to the police . . .'

'You watch yer mouth. Yer just like all the rest of the bleedin' women – always naggin' a man. Well, see if you like this . . .' He moved towards Nancy with his hammer fist outstretched, his intention to hit her in the face. Nancy continued to face him fearlessly, refusing to let him get past her to Andy, but there was a sudden roar of rage from behind Andy and suddenly a man in white paint-spattered overalls rushed past him and launched himself at the Beast.

Arthur Phillips didn't know what hit him. Rob landed a punch to his chin and then a flurry of them to his arms, chest and stomach, felling him and sending him crashing to the floor groaning before he'd even had time to land one blow.

He lay there groaning, looking up at them through bloodshot eyes, clearly stunned by the ferocity and power of the blows. 'Who the bleedin' 'ell are yer?' he muttered. 'Bloody Sugar Ray Robinson . . .'

'No, but I was the school amateur boxing champion for a while,' Rob said, grinning down at him. 'Have you finished insulting my girl, mate – or do you want another taste? I don't think I've forgotten much . . .'

They eyed each other warily just as someone came down the stairs. Andy saw Sister Beatrice surveying the scene with what he thought looked like satisfaction.

'I think you should leave immediately,' Sister Beatrice said with an imperious stare at the man now struggling to his feet. 'I have telephoned for my friend Sergeant Sallis. He has been looking for you, Mr Phillips, and I think you will be sleeping in a prison cell for the foreseeable future . . .'

The Beast sent an angry look at Andy, got to his feet and ran off, pushing through a crowd of children coming in from school and scattering them. Andy looked at Nancy who seemed to be trembling now, as if she'd just realised what she'd risked for his sake.

'Is she all right, sir?' he asked of Rob, who moved forward swiftly and held Nancy in his arms as she swayed, her face turning very pale. 'You were so brave, miss. The way you stood up to him . . .'

Nancy wasn't looking at him. She was staring up at Rob and seemed to be on the verge of tears.

'Mr Thompson, why don't you take Nancy to the rest room, and help yourselves to a cup of coffee?' Sister asked. She turned to Andy as the couple walked away, Rob's arm still about Nancy's waist. They ignored the giggles of the children who had come in later and hadn't heard or seen what had happened. 'Go and have your tea, Andy – and don't forget to wash your hands first,' Sister said. 'Perhaps you will come to my office afterwards so that we can have a little talk please.'

'Yes, Sister.' Andy quailed inside, wondering if she was angry because Arthur had followed him in and whether she would cancel their trip to the sea. He joined the other children crowding the cloakrooms and then filing in to a gorgeous tea of fresh crusty bread, scones, jam, and butter and a coffee sponge filled with flavoured butter cream. There was jelly with fresh strawberries and apple pie and custard too and the kids were soon loading their plates, a hush falling as they started to eat, hardly believing their luck. Where had all this delicious food come from?

Andy was anxious but he didn't let his worry over Sister Beatrice's anger spoil his tea, because he had an idea that she might be angrier with others than with him . . .

Neither Rob nor Nancy touched the kettle but the staff room was empty so they just stood and looked at each other in silence until she noticed that his knuckles were red and cut.

'You hurt yourself,' she said, taking out a hankie to press against them. 'You're bleeding . . .'

'I hurt him more,' Rob said and smiled oddly. 'I'd have tried to sort him out sooner but you were doing such a good job of it yourself that I left it to you – but when he tried to hit you . . . well, I couldn't control myself. I'm sorry for showing you up, Nancy, but I can't abide men who hit women . . .'

'Oh Rob,' she said softly and her eyes filled with tears. 'You didn't show me up – you were wonderful. You did what we all wanted to do to that beast. He hurt those kids so much . . . and the police didn't seem to do anything about him . . .'

'Well, they will now because there are witnesses to his abuse of the boy.'

'We have a doctor's testimony but it was only Andy and Beth's word that he caused their injuries and the police interviewed him but then let him go . . . but I saw what he did and I think Sister Beatrice may have as well.'

'Well, I saw what he did too,' Rob smiled at her. 'You and I will stand up in court and tell them that he hurt Andy and was trying to intimidate him.'

'You might be in trouble for hitting him . . .'

'If I am they can lock me up for a few months.' Rob shrugged his broad shoulders. 'Besides, I doubt any court in the land would find against me once we presented all the evidence . . . No decent man is going to stand by and let a bully hurt someone like you.'

'I don't want you to get into trouble for my sake.'

'I'd do anything to protect you from harm, Nancy,' Rob said, a throb of passion in his voice. 'Don't you know that you mean the world to me? I love you – and I have from the first moment I saw you . . . It just hit me out of nowhere and I felt so bad because you seemed to dislike me.'

'It wasn't you, Rob,' Nancy said and her eyes were clear and untroubled as she looked at him. 'I was abused as a child by my father. He did unspeakable things to me and he beat my brother senseless when he tried to help me. I've always blamed myself because it might have been that beating that put Terry over the edge. Pa and Ma died in a fire and I've always suspected that Terry started it. For years I wasn't sure if he meant to but one day, when he was in the mental home, he said something that made me think he knew just what he was doing. He's violent, Rob, and he'll never come out – but I think it was what Pa did to him that made him that way . . . and I carry the scars too, in my mind . . .'

'He hurt you too but that didn't make you violent or cruel,' Rob told her in his steady calm voice. 'You can't know what turned your brother's mind, Nancy, and you never will. I know you did all you could for him and you've nothing to blame yourself for.'

'No, I realise that,' Nancy agreed, looking up at him. 'When I stood up to that bully just now I suddenly understood that there will always be men like him who cause untold damage with their selfish evil ways, but we can stop them if we try – and all men are not the same. If Ma had stood up to my father he might have stopped abusing us, but she let him get away with what he did to me and bullying Terry – but I'm never going to let anyone hurt me or anyone I care for again . . .'

'I would never harm you, Nancy – or anyone else, unless they threatened those I loved.'

'Yes, I know that too,' she said and smiled in a way that made him catch his breath. 'I wasn't sure if I could love you as you deserve to be loved, Rob – but I shall. You will have to be patient sometimes, because it won't all go away just like that, but I do know I love you – and I want to be with you, properly, as a woman with the man she loves . . .'

'Will you be my girl, Nancy?' Rob asked, looking down at her with what she could only describe as adoration. 'I promise I'll be patient. I won't ask for more than you can give.'

'I'd like us to be more than friends,' she told him and reached up to kiss his lips. 'But I need you to be patient and understanding . . .'

Rob drew her against him, holding her so gently that the slightest resistance would have broken them apart, but she didn't pull away and he bent his head to kiss her very softly on the lips.

Nancy had thought she would tense up if he kissed her properly, but she didn't, because his lips were warm, sweet and soft; they seemed to give and caress rather than demand and take, and she felt as if she wanted to kiss him back, to entwine herself about him and never let go, like a vine clinging to an oak tree. Yet in the same moment she also knew that she was strong enough to stand alone if she had to. Facing up to the man who had threatened Andy had made her aware of her own power and resilience. As a child she'd been used and defiled, but somehow she'd lived with that and perhaps grown stronger because of it.

Mr Adderbury had once told her that he believed she would be able to come to terms with what had happened to her and transcend it.

'You're a brave girl, Nancy. The way you've cared for your brother and taken everything on your shoulders shows how strong you are. I know you feel defiled and dirty because of what your father did, but he was the one in the wrong, not you. You do not bear the blame for any of it – what happened to your parents or your brother. All you ever did was to try to protect your brother. When you stop blaming yourself you will be able to move forward.'

Nancy thought that perhaps at last she'd managed to stop blaming herself.

She smiled up at Rob as he let her go. 'I do love you,' she said, 'and I shall marry you, one day, because I trust you, but not quite yet. I'd like to be courted for a while . . .' Her eyes sparkled with mischief. 'Shall we go out this evening and celebrate?'

'Would you like to go to a dance or for dinner?' Rob looked down at her as if the heavens had just opened and Nancy's heart caught with love for him.

'I'd like to try dancing,' she said. 'I've only ever danced with the children at the Christmas party . . . and I want to do all the things I've only watched other people do . . . I've felt so alone and now I want to learn to live and be happy, Rob.'

'And so you shall, my darling,' Rob said and touched her cheek lightly with his fingertips. 'I'll make sure you're never alone again . . .'

Rob drew her into his arms just as the door of the staff room opened, preventing him from kissing her.

'Whoops!' Kelly said, grinned and backed out. 'I'll leave you to it . . .'

'No, it's all right,' Nancy called her back and looked at Rob, her eyes sparkling. 'We're going dancing this evening . . .'

'And what else?' Kelly teased. 'When am I going to be matron-of-honour?'

'One day,' Nancy said because the happiness was bubbling out of her and she felt as if she had suddenly come to life after a long dark sleep. She lifted her brows to Rob and he grinned, looking as happy as she felt. 'But perhaps we'll get engaged and have a party here – with my friends . . .'

'We shall all look forward to that – and especially

the kids. I don't think you realise how much they love you, Nancy.'

'Let's have the party in September – when the school holidays are over,' Rob suggested. 'Perhaps the wedding in the spring or summer next year. Whatever makes you happy . . .'

Nancy smiled as Kelly went off to spread the news. They were all her friends, the children, carers, nurses and particularly Sister Beatrice. She would have an afternoon party on a Saturday and they would all have a special tea to celebrate here at St Saviour's, because even if she had children of her own, and she certainly wanted that, she would always have time for the people here . . .

Beatrice finished her call to Sergeant Sallis with a little smile on her lips. Arthur Phillips had made a mistake by trying to snatch Andy from under their noses and by beating the boy and threatening a member of her staff. She'd been assured that he would be arrested on sight and held in custody awaiting a trial.

She sat down suddenly as she felt a little dizzy and her heart raced. It had been quite a shock to witness that fracas in the hall and she needed a moment to catch her breath. It was so foolish to let the incident upset her, because Andy was not badly hurt. Nancy had acted promptly and bravely, though she too might have suffered at that brute's hand had not Mr Thompson acted so heroically. She did hope that he would not be accused of assault, but she'd given a full account to Sergeant Sallis and he'd said he would ask her for a written statement the next morning, but believed that

Mr Thompson had acted as a responsible citizen in defending a woman. Beatrice was only too willing to give him her statement. She disliked brutal men who beat children . . . for a moment a memory flashed into her mind, but she pushed it away. Such things were not worth remembering when it hurt so much . . .

Her heart had stopped its frantic beating. She opened her desk drawer to take out the report she'd been drafting for Sandra to type and stared because, instead of being in a neat pile, the pages were scattered, as if someone had been shuffling through them.

It was very strange, because this was not the first time it had happened recently. There was nothing of any value in her desk – the few pounds she kept in the cash box for emergencies was locked in the file – but someone had searched her desk and the shelves more than once recently. Why? What did they hope to find? And did it mean that Mrs Davies wasn't the thief after all? Had they wronged the woman in that regard? Sandra had suggested that perhaps she'd bolted because of the rotten food she'd been giving the children – which would leave them still with the problem of a thief at St Saviour's.

Nothing was missing this time, but nothing had been taken the last time things had been disturbed in her desk. Perhaps someone was searching for something rather than looking to steal? She took out her report and began to put the pages into order.

Who had entered her office and read her report? Who could possibly want this kind of information?

CHAPTER 24

A few of St Saviour's children were taking part in holiday work over the next few days, before starting the new school term. Several of the older ones had worked for some weeks in the summer; that work entailed helping with the harvest in the fields and various cleaning up projects for charity. It was good experience of what it would be like when they eventually left the orphanage and they were all excited, talking about what they'd done or were going to do.

'I'm going to work in the fairground at Clacton-on-Sea for a few days,' Keith told Andy when they were eating their tea that day. 'My parents were travelling folk before Ma got ill and they settled in London. When she died, Pa left me with Sister Beatrice and went off, but he's got me a job working at the fair for the end of the season and he says I can go travelling with him when I leave school next year.'

'Were your parents gypsies?' Andy asked, a little in awe of him.

'Only Pa,' Keith grinned. 'Me ma was a vicar's daughter and she fell in love with 'im one summer day and just ran off with 'im. We used to travel all over until she got ill when they were in London, and she taught me to read and write but I didn't go to school. Then she started fallin' over and being ill and they just stopped 'ere until she died, because she couldn't go with 'im . . . but Pa said I needed a proper education and somewhere safe to live so I came 'ere and he went off in the vardo . . . but 'e's got a job on the fairground and 'e says they've let 'im have me to 'elp out . . .'

'I'm sorry about yer ma, but you've still got yer dad,' Andy said, half envious. 'And he's come back for yer . . .'

'Yeah, Pa's all right,' Keith grinned. ''E gives me one round the ear when he's in a mood, but he's not bad really – better than your step-father anyway . . .'

'Anyone would be better than Arthur Phillips,' Andy said and grimaced.

'Have the police picked him up yet?'

'Not that I've 'eard, but they don't often bother to tell kids what's goin' on, do they?'

'They'll get 'im, mate, don't yer worry,' Keith said and took a great bite of his paste and tomato sandwich, chewing heartily with his mouth open. 'Yer'll be off ter Hunstanton soon fer a holiday and by the time yer get back to school 'e'll be safely locked up.'

'I 'ope so,' Andy said. He looked at his friend wistfully. Keith was one of the scruffiest of all the kids in the home – his socks fell down, he got holes in the knees of his trousers and his shirts were always missing a button – but he was fun and Andy liked him. He would miss Keith if he went off travelling with his father. He had other friends at school, including Tom, but he wasn't as friendly as Keith. There was something hidden about Tom, something he didn't talk about. Everyone knew it, though nobody spoke about it, because if you were a St Saviour's kid you stuck together. 'I shall miss yer when you leave.'

'I'll be 'ere till next summer,' Keith said. 'Pa promised me ma that 'e'd make me go to school until I was fifteen and 'e won't change 'is mind – so we've got another year ter go. Besides, you'll maybe want to stay down at 'Alfpenny 'ouse. Sister Beatrice said I could go down there if I liked – but Pa knows where to find me 'ere so I said I'd rather stay.'

'I want ter stay too,' Andy said. 'Mr Barton is goin' to find me somewhere to start workin' as an apprentice mechanic soon – just on Saturday mornings, and he said there might be a little job goin' soon.'

'He's all right,' Keith agreed. 'We're lucky 'ere wot wiv Sister B and Mr Barton. Some kids ain't anywhere near as lucky . . . Did you 'ear about Tom?' He leaned forward to whisper in Andy's ear. ''E got caned this mornin' – 'e was caught in the headmaster's study looking through 'is desk and wouldn't tell them why, so they caned 'im. 'E ain't come down fer tea 'cos 'e can't sit down. I told 'im I'd take him a bit of somethin' up to the dorm when I go . . .'

'Why does Tom do things like that?' Andy asked. 'Does he pinch stuff?'

'Dunno, mate. I ain't asked, but 'e's never nicked anythin' orf me.'

'Nor me,' Andy admitted, 'but I know 'e's hidin' somethin'.'

Keith thought for a moment and nodded. 'Yeah, I

reckon yer right. I'll ask 'im why 'e did it when I take his tea up . . .'

Beatrice entered her office to discover a boy trying to open the top drawer of her office file, which was locked. He had a kitchen knife and was trying to pry it open, but when he saw her, he hung his head, shuffling his feet as if afraid of her vengeance. She stared at him in silence for a moment and then frowned.

'What are you doing, Tom?'

For a moment Tom stared at her in silence, a belligerent look in his eyes, and then his gaze dropped. 'I ain't doin' nuthin' wrong if that's what yer think. I ain't a thief.'

'I didn't imagine you were for one moment. There is nothing in my office that anyone would wish to steal – but won't you please tell me what you're looking for?'

Tom shook his head. 'Can't . . .'

'Why not – you must know what you want?' she asked patiently.

His face was red and he looked as if he wanted to cry. 'I only know I 'ad a mother and sister once and I don't know where they are. I want to know what happened to them . . .'

Beatrice's heart twisted as she saw the forlorn look in his eyes. His story was such a sad one and she'd known that one day he might ask questions, but she hadn't expected him to remember his mother and sister.

'Have you started to remember?' she asked gently. 'To remember things before you came here to us?'

Tom shook his head again, then, 'Just vague things. My mother taking us both on her lap . . . me and . . .'

He stared at her desperately. 'I know it was my sister but I can't remember 'er name . . .'

'Why haven't you asked me?'

'I was afraid you might say I made it all up . . .' His dark eyes struck a chord and she felt his pain like a shaft in her heart. 'They said I made things up at that other place . . . but I didn't. I know 'e did bad things to me . . . and 'e was supposed to be a priest . . .'

'Yes, it was very wrong of him and I believe he has been punished. You were very young when it happened, Tom, and a lot of years have passed,' Beatrice said in the same gentle voice. 'Do you want me to tell you about it? About your mother and sister . . .' She held out a hand to him. He moved a little closer, staring at her warily.

'Yes, please . . .' he said in desperation. 'I know there was a girl I liked called Jean but you took her away . . . she wasn't my sister?'

'No, Tom. I should've taken you with Jean if I'd known you were such good friends. Your sister's name was Mary Jane but you called her Janey. Your mother was widowed during the war, when you and Mary Jane were just babies. She was your twin, you see, and that is perhaps why she's still there inside you even though she isn't here any more . . .'

'Is she . . . are they both dead?' Tom's eyes widened with distress.

'Yes, they were both killed in the accident. You were on a train, all of you, returning to your home in London from a holiday by the sea and there was an accident – a train crash, caused by bomb damage on the line. It was terrible and in all the newspapers at the time. You were badly injured and your family was killed instantly.

They think you survived because your mother threw herself on you and Mary Jane, but unfortunately they both died. Extensive inquiries were made to find your extended family but no one was traced and when you were recovered enough you were sent to an orphanage. Not this one at first unfortunately . . .'

Tom's face was on fire but then he raised his gaze to hers. 'You know what they did to me at my last place?'

'Yes, I do, Tom, and it shames me that anyone could do that to a child in need. You were still suffering from the trauma of the accident, not truly aware of what was happening around you, so I'm told – and it was only after you were attacked by that person at the home that you seemed to come to yourself. As you said, no one believed you at first. They thought it was all mixed up in your head. So you ran away to London and lived under the railway bridge until the police found you and brought you here to us three years ago, and we've tried to look after you since then. I hope you've been happy here?'

Tom raised his head, tears in his eyes. 'Are you sendin' me away 'cos of what I just did?'

'No, I'm taking you to Halfpenny House. You'll go on holiday to the sea with the others and Jean has been included in the trip – she told me you protected her from bullies and were like a brother to her. I cannot give you back your family, Tom, but I can give you a friend who is lonely for you. Angela told me that she has asked repeatedly if you are going down there to live – so would you like to go?'

'Yes, please,' he said, hesitated, then, 'Why didn't you tell me about my mother and sister before?'

'I wanted you to recover properly from your ordeal,

Tom. Your mind couldn't take the truth at first. It was too much for anyone to accept – losing both your mother and your sister in a terrible accident and fighting back to life, only to be abused by someone who was there to protect you. You were still vulnerable and there is a reserve in you with others that sometimes sets you apart. I wasn't sure you could trust me enough to believe what I said . . .'

'Everyone trusts you, Sister,' Tom said. 'You never lie to us . . . all the kids respect you.'

'Thank you, Tom . . .' Beatrice's eyes pricked with tears but she would not let them fall. 'I want to give you all a better life . . .' She hesitated, then, 'I once had a son with the same name as you – but he died in a fire. His step-father got drunk and accidentally set the house on fire and my Tom couldn't get out . . .' Her voice shook with emotion as the memory struck at her heart.

'I'm sorry, Sister . . .' Tom came round the desk and suddenly clasped her about the waist, giving her a fierce brief hug. His voice was hoarse as he moved back and looked up at her. 'You must have cried a lot for 'im . . .'

'Yes,' Beatrice agreed, and a tear slid down her cheek. 'I did – but then I found God or perhaps He found me and I was given another chance in life. Looking after all my children here I have been blessed. Perhaps in the country with Jean as your friend and all the others you will discover a new life – a way to be happy again . . .'

'I wish you were coming too,' Tom said and then looked away. 'I'm goin' now. I'm sorry I looked in your desk. I've been lookin' everywhere – in the nurses' rooms and in the cook's office . . . I saw her hide a book once. I thought it might be about me so I went back and took it . . . but it was just full of figures so I put it back, but after she'd left. I didn't know she was goin' . . .'

'None of us did. Where was this book hidden?' Beatrice asked, frowning. 'Not in her desk?'

'No, she put it under a loose floorboard wiv some money – that's what made me think she was hiding it . . .'

'Ah, I see . . .'

'I know it was wrong of me to take it, but I put it back . . . and I didn't take any money ever . . .'

'Do you think you could get the book and bring it to me please? If I'm not here you could put it on my desk.'

'Yes, Sister.' He hesitated, then, 'You're not cross, are you?'

'It's all right, Tom. You shouldn't do things like that, but I do understand why . . .'

Beatrice sighed as he went out and closed the door politely behind him. Tom was just one of her damaged children; those the world had mistreated, abandoned or neglected who made their way here somehow, and she did what she could to restore what others had destroyed. One of the things that made her life so worthwhile was the trust that these children felt for her – and to hear a boy like Tom say those words healed the hurt inside her. She, like them, had known pain and loss and she often felt that they had helped to heal her every bit as much as she healed them with her love and care.

She'd lost the man she'd loved to the war, been forced to marry a man she disliked because she was carrying a bastard child, as her father had shouted at her when he bullied her into a marriage she should never have made. She'd endured cruelty and slights for four years for the sake of her son – and then she'd lost her Tom in a fire that had taken his life and that of his drunken step-father.

In her despair Beatrice had almost died, but something inside her was too strong. She was a fighter and then a voice from somewhere inside her had told her that there was a life for her helping others. She'd given her life to God and then she'd been chosen to come here and, Beatrice realised, that this was where she must stay until she was no longer needed and then she would join Angela in the country. Tom and children just like him needed her to be there when they were ready. She would tell Angela that she would accept the job she had so generously offered her when the time came. For now she had the welfare of St Saviour's and all her children to concern her.

A wry smile touched her mouth as her thoughts moved on and she realised that the book Tom had found in his searching was probably Mrs Davies' secret accounts. Sandra had suspected they existed but no one could find them. Had they found them at the time Beatrice would have confronted the woman with her guilt, but now she found it hardly mattered; it would do no one any good to hound the woman, and she could find it in her heart to understand why a mother might steal for her son. A mother's love was perhaps the strongest emotion of all . . .

Beatrice looked through the book Tom had left on her desk in disbelief, comparing it to the official record of kitchen expenditure. Now she was able to see quite clearly that Mrs Davies had been systematically robbing them, of a few shillings at the start, and then, suddenly, about two months before she left so hurriedly, the amounts had become pounds. It was hardly surprising that she'd been forced to give the children sub-standard food, because she'd stolen almost half of what she'd been given for food those last few weeks.

Knowing she had the evidence she needed to convict the woman of theft, whether or not she'd stolen from others, Beatrice stared down at the figures for a long time. She felt like weeping, because she'd taken the woman on trust and she'd betrayed her. Yet she suspected that she may have been pushed into it by her son. No doubt she'd stolen to provide him with funds for his escape, perhaps to another country – and wouldn't most mothers be capable of such a crime?

Beatrice couldn't forgive her for what she'd done to the children. Once, she would have had no hesitation in giving the information to the police and letting the law take over, but something held her back. The woman had fled, taking the contents of their cash box with her, but the kindness of the market traders had saved them from the consequences of her act and perhaps that was why Beatrice could not find it in her heart to crave revenge.

She rubbed at her chest absent-mindedly. She must be turning soft in her old age. A smile touched her lips as she locked the books away in her drawer. She couldn't be bothered with the woman; the police would probably never find her anyway, and there were far more important things on her mind . . . like taking those children down to Halfpenny House at the weekend . . .

Andy held tightly to Beth's hand as they boarded the train. She was a little nervous as it let off steam and someone blew the whistle, but she managed a smile for her brother and then Sister Beatrice got them all settled in their seats. There were five children, Andy, Beth, Tom, also a girl called Mary and her brother Jack. Those two had bought comics and giggled and talked to each other in their corner of the carriage, not communicating with anyone unless Sister spoke to them.

Tom sat next to Andy and grinned at him. 'I'm looking forward to this, ain't you?' he asked.

'Yeah, I am,' Andy agreed. He was relieved to get out of London for a while, because his step-father still hadn't been arrested. 'I've only been to Southend once, never to Hunstanton . . . wherever that is . . .'

'I can't remember if I ever went to the sea,' Tom said. 'I think I did with Mum and Janey, but I'm not sure – there was an accident and I 'urt my head so I don't remember much before . . . St Saviour's . . .'

'What happened to your family?'

'Dad was killed in the war and Mum and Janey died in an accident . . .' Tom leaned in so that only Andy could hear. 'A train accident . . . but they don't happen often. I asked Sister and she said it was rare, so don't worry about Beth . . .'

'She'll be safer out of London,' Andy said and nodded grimly. This was a different Tom, someone he could get on with. 'Our step-father kept threatenin' us. She hates him and so do I . . .'

'I'm not comin' back to St Saviour's,' Tom confided. 'Sister's had all my stuff sent down ahead of us. I'm stayin' down there to look after Jean – she's my special friend and I stopped the others bullying her at school. Sister didn't take me last time but she says she was wrong: Jean needs me to look out for her.'

'Just like Beth needs me,' Andy agreed, nodding in a conspiratorial manner. 'Girls can't look out for themselves like us, can they?'

'Nah,' Tom agreed and snorted with laughter as Mary suddenly looked at him from her corner. 'She's stuck up, that one – do yer think her folk were rich?' he asked in a whisper.

'I don't know,' Andy admitted. 'They ain't like us – and they ain't very friendly. I hope they don't go off alone when we get to the seaside . . . it's more fun if we play rounders on the beach and build things together – at least I think it will be . . .'

'Yeah, I reckon yer right,' Tom said and pulled out a bag of sherbet lemons that he offered to Andy, Beth, Keith and Sister Beatrice and then, after a pause to the brother and sister in the corner. They shook their heads so he raised his eyebrows at Andy and put them back in his pocket, whispering, 'More for us . . .'

Andy nodded and glanced at the two in the corner. No one knew them because they'd only arrived two days ago and were going straight down to Halfpenny House. They didn't speak like Londoners; in fact they spoke posh and their shoes were better than the other kids had, though they were wearing the regulation uniform. He wondered briefly why they'd come to the orphanage, because neither of them looked as if they were starving. Perhaps they'd just lost their parents, but they didn't seem to be grieving, just wrapped up in their own world.

Mary realised he was staring; she glared at him and then turned her head away. Andy flushed and inclined to Beth, whispering to her and asking her if she was all right.

'Yes.' She smiled at Tom. 'Thank you for the sweet, it's nice . . .'

'They're my favourites,' he told her. 'You can have another in a minute. I've got plenty left . . .'

'You may all eat your packed lunch whenever you wish,' Sister Beatrice said. 'It's too expensive to buy food on the train so make it last for as long as you can. We shall have tea when we get to Halfpenny House . . .'

'Yes, Sister,' the children chorused and most of them started to open the white cardboard boxes they'd been given before they left St Saviour's.

They each had cheese and tomato sandwiches, two sausage rolls, a rock bun and an apple, as well as a small bottle of orange squash. Sister opened hers and ate a sandwich, then drank a little tea from her flask, but the children ate theirs steadily until the box was empty, her good advice forgotten.

Sister ate another sandwich, then took out a little silver pocket knife and cut the sausage rolls into six pieces, ate one piece herself and offered the others round; she did the same with the apple and smiled as it disappeared into hungry mouths.

'If the trolley comes round you may use a little of your pocket money to buy sweets,' she said but the children all shook their heads and said they were full.

Sister nodded, closed her eyes and appeared to sleep. Tom looked at Andy and they giggled but Sister opened one eye and they subsided. Even with her eyes closed, Sister Beatrice knew just what they were thinking and saying . . .

CHAPTER 25

Nellie looked at Jinny's face and sighed. Her young friend was fretting and all over a good-for-nothing mother who should have been ashamed of herself for what she'd put the girl through in her short life.

'What's wrong, love? Wishin' you was off to the sea with the kids?'

'No . . . though it would be lovely on such a warm day,' Jinny said and smiled. 'You must be boiling, Nellie, standin' over that stove for hours like you do . . .'

'I'm used to it, love, and this is a nice airy kitchen. Some places stifle you, but this is cool compared to many . . .'

'It isn't too bad,' Jinny admitted. 'Beats workin' in a factory or scrubbin' floors, which was all I was offered, until I came here.'

'You landed on yer feet 'ere, love,' Nellie said. 'So why the glum face – is it yer mum? Are yer worryin' over 'er?'

'Yes . . . at least part of it,' Jinny admitted and issued a sighing breath. 'I quarrelled with Micky and I haven't seen him since. I went down the market last Saturday but I couldn't see him – and Dave said he hasn't seen him around for a while.'

'Ah, I see, gone to ground, 'as 'e?' Nellie frowned at her. 'I've wondered about young Micky and I'm sure a lot of others 'ave too – 'e 'as a lot of money to spend for an ordinary chap of his age.'

'I've asked him and he says he does what he feels like – but it's all legal. I'm worried, Nellie. I said things to him I shouldn't after he's been so kind to me. You don't think he would . . . he wouldn't harm himself?'

'Jump off Tower Bridge and drown 'isself?' Nellie crowed with laughter. 'No, I don't see Micky as a quitter, love. More like 'e's took 'imself off fer a 'oliday in all this 'ot weather . . .'

'He wouldn't go off and leave me to worry!' Jinny said indignantly, but Nellie could see the idea had lifted her spirits a little.

'Why not then? Yer told 'im yer didn't like 'im, didn't yer? Why should 'e bother what you think?'

'I was upset. I didn't mean to fall out with Micky. He's been so good to me, Nellie – and I miss him . . .'

'I know yer do, love,' Nellie said and then chuckled. 'One thing I know about Micky is that 'e'll turn up again. You can't keep 'is sort down fer long . . .'

'I do hope so,' Jinny said but she got on with making her Victoria sponge with a will. 'I wondered if he sent those strawberries for the kids the other day, but Dave said it was one of his mates off the market.'

'I know the kids enjoyed them wiv the jelly,' Nellie said, 'but they'll 'ave ter make do wiv plums in custard fer tea tonight. We ain't goin' ter get somethin' like that too often . . .' The younger children who hadn't been chosen for work or special summer projects were still at St Saviour's. Nancy and Kelly had promised them various treats, paid for by the money Nick, Rob and some others had collected. Most of them were going to see a matinee of Walt Disney's *The Lady and the Tramp* that afternoon, which had come round for a second or third time, because it was so popular, and a trip to Southend had been arranged for the weekend, which Jinny had been asked to go on.

'No, that was a real treat,' Jinny said and smiled. 'They're much too expensive in London – but some of the older children have gone strawberry-picking in the country. They get bed and board and as many strawberries as they can eat . . .'

'They shouldn't tell our kids that – they'll eat the lot,' Nellie chortled. 'Now, I think that's enough shortbread biscuits. Pop 'em in the oven for me, Elsa, and we'll 'ave a cup of tea . . .'

She glanced at the old newspaper in which she was about to wrap potato peelings. 'Those poor kids,' she said and showed the article to Jinny. 'Look what they had ter do ter get into their school in America . . . all those state troops out just so a handful of black children could go to school. It makes you realise how lucky our children are here – even though they're hungry and abused sometimes, at least they can all go ter school whatever their colour . . . even though some folk still don't like serving coloured folk in cafés but it's better 'ere than there I reckon . . .'

'The law says the segregation must end according to the paper, but some people want to stop them . . .' Jinny read on. 'Oh, it says here that Stirling Moss has a good chance of winning the Italian Grand Prix at Monza this weekend . . .'

'Who's 'e when 'e's at 'ome then?' Elsa asked and poured boiling water into the pot. 'Can I 'ave one of them coconut kisses, Nellie?'

'Yes, of course you can,' Nellie said and smiled. 'Stirling Moss is a racing driver – a real good one so my Bert says . . . Leave go of that paper, Jinny. I need it ter wrap these peelings . . .'

Micky looked at St Saviour's as he passed it on the bus. He'd just got back to London after hopping on a merchant ship and working his passage to France for a few days. His boss had wanted him to deliver some goods, but he didn't want them to go through the usual customs routine.

'I've got an arrangement with the ship's captain, see,' Big Sam told him. 'They take stuff out that the bloody government charges too much tax on – and bring stuff back fer me in exchange. No money changes 'and so it ain't exactly doin' 'em out of anythin' – but it ain't legal neivver . . .'

'Why do yer need me?' Micky asked, because it was the first time he'd been asked to do anything that was strictly illegal. He ran a few bets, helped out some nights in a gambling and strip club as a bouncer, and traded goods in his own right through various market stalls, but he'd stayed just the right side of the law so far. The strip club wasn't strictly according to the rules, of course, but Micky only guarded the door and warned them if there was a raid coming as well as getting rid of the rough element. You always got some men who made a grab at the naked girls when they'd had too much to drink, which happened most of the time, because the hostesses encouraged them to buy drinks all night.

Micky had enjoyed the brief break from the heat and dust of London's crowded streets. He'd investigated the goods he'd been required to accompany to their destination, and those he brought back. They'd taken good Scotch whisky that had never paid duty out and brought back a special French cognac without all the import taxes normally imposed. Had the transaction involved drugs Micky would have pulled back and refused to have anything to do with it, because he couldn't abide the misery heroin inflicted on the addicts you sometimes saw at the club or on the streets, but he didn't see anything wrong in exchanging one consignment of drinks for another – the only ones to lose out were the blooming tax collectors and no one cared about them either side of the Channel.

Some crimes were despicable and Micky knew where he drew the line, but cheating the taxmen – well, that was just good fun. Everyone in business did it, he reckoned, as much as they could, from the market lads with cash in their back pockets to the filthy rich businessmen who owned huge companies and paid fancy lawyers to get round the financial laws and avoid paying what they owed, and what was good for the rich was good enough for Micky. After all, he intended being one of them in the not too distant future.

He wondered if Jinny had missed him. He'd missed her, though he'd enjoyed his little adventure, which had all gone off without a hitch. His boss had been pleased, because the previous consignment had been a case short and he'd suspected he was being cheated.

'You're a good kid,' Big Sam had told him, squeezing his shoulder with his hammer fists. 'Stick wiv me, Micky, and you'll get on . . .'

Micky smiled and agreed, because for the moment he still needed Big Sam's wages. He wasn't making enough out of his own deals for what he planned, because his idea was to go into legitimate business for himself once he had enough money saved and the right opening presented itself. A decent living and a home of his own wasn't enough for Micky; he wanted real money, but there were limits to what he was prepared to do. He wanted nothing to do with drugs and if he'd been asked to smuggle them he'd have refused. He'd seen how many lives could be destroyed by such things and the ruthless men behind them . . . No, Micky wanted his own business, but he thought he might try importing stuff from France and India, even China perhaps, countries that had vibrant, interesting goods to sell. People were beginning to like more exotic tastes, spices and foods they hadn't seen before, and there had to be some money in that, but Micky needed money to set up his business . . .

An idea of what he wanted for the future was gradually forming in his brain. All he needed was a bit of cash behind him and then he could visualise the business empire that would make him rich – but it was getting enough together for a start that was the problem. Micky was prepared to work hard to get on and his little holiday had given him a few ideas.

Micky thought he would visit Jinny the next morning

and see if she'd got over her mood. She'd pricked his pride when she'd blamed him for something that wasn't his fault, but he still liked the plucky girl who'd stood up to her step-father and made a life for herself. In fact, he was pretty sure he was in love with her, even though they were both too young to get serious yet. She was part of his plans for the future but he had a lot he wanted to do before he settled down – and Jinny was too young. They both had to do some growing up and he had to get his foot on the ladder . . .

CHAPTER 26

'We're having the party here in two weeks,' Nancy said, holding out her left hand, 'but Rob got me this now, because he couldn't wait to give it to me . . .'

'That is gorgeous,' Jinny said as Nancy shyly showed off the small diamond cluster ring on the third finger of her left hand, which was slender and shapely, her nails very neat and clean. 'It suits your hand, Nancy, and I don't think I've ever seen you look so happy.'

'Thank you,' Nancy said and her cheeks were a pretty pink as she blushed, green eyes shining. She'd had her hair cut to a shoulder-length bob and it suited her so much better that way. Jinny thought how pretty she was now that she'd lost that thin, haunted look about her face, and decided she might have her own dark locks shorn. 'I haven't ever been this happy.'

'Congratulations on your engagement,' Rose said. 'I'm so very pleased for you, Nancy. Rob is a nice man and hard-working. He deserves you and you deserve him.'

They were all in the big comfortable kitchen, Jinny working while Nancy and Elsa helped themselves to just-cooked biscuits and tea from the large brown teapot.

'I feel so lucky,' Nancy said and her eyes met Rose's. 'I never thought I would ever get married and I can hardly believe it now. Rob was willing to wait if I wanted, but I said I'd like to have a party here now for our engagement so that all the kids can join in – and then we'll have a quiet wedding in the spring . . .'

'Wonderful!' Jinny said and looked up. 'I hope we're all invited?'

'Of course you are,' Nancy said. 'Rob is paying for the wedding but I wondered if you and Nellie would make the cake for us?'

'We'd love to,' Nellie said, speaking for the first time as she looked up from her pastry making. 'It can be our wedding present to yer, Nancy, and it will be a pleasure to make it fer yer . . . If we make it soon it will mature lovely by the spring when we ice it.'

'Yes, I'll do whatever I can to make it special,' Jinny said. 'I like Rob. He always says hello and asks how you are and that shows he's got a good heart – just about good enough for you, Nancy.'

'Oh . . .' Nancy blushed. 'I'm not that special . . .'

'Yes, you are,' Rose chipped in and everyone made murmurs of agreement. 'I hope you won't leave us immediately you get married?'

'We've agreed that I should stay on until I have a baby . . .' Nancy was really blushing now and Jinny giggled.

'You will make a wonderful mum,' she told Nancy. 'The kids all love you – and Sister Beatrice thinks the world of you.'

'Sister Beatrice has been wonderful to me,' Nancy said. 'If we hadn't been brought here I don't know what would have happened to us . . .' A little shiver went through her and for a moment her smile dimmed.

'Yes, you're a Halfpenny Street girl,' Jinny said. 'You belong here . . . and I think that makes you lucky. I sometimes feel that I don't belong anywhere. The council told me I've got to get the house cleared because my mother hasn't paid the rent for months and they're taking it back. They say she doesn't qualify for a house now that I don't live there – and they're going to pull them all down soon.'

'We got our letter this mornin',' Nellie said and grimaced. 'Bert says they'll put him out afore 'e moves, but I've started to ask round. We shall have to go in the end whatever we say or do . . .'

'Oh, Nellie, I'm so sorry,' Jinny said. 'I thought they were just sayin' it to make me have the house cleared. I'm not sure what to do with Mum's stuff . . . Most of it is worthless, but she might need her clothes and personal things . . .'

'You still haven't heard from her?' Rose asked. She hesitated, then, 'Sister might let you have a spare room in the nurses' home to store your mother's things – just until you know . . .'

The words hung in the air, casting a shadow over Nancy's happy news. Jinny swallowed hard and then smiled at Rose and thanked her. 'I'll ask Sister when she comes back from Essex and then I can get someone to do the clearing. I'm sure Dave from the market will know someone who can clear the house and bring what I need over. I'll go there myself now the police have finished and start throwing all the rubbish out . . .'

'I'll help you to do that,' Nancy said, smiling at her.

'And I know Rob will put as much as he can in his van and bring it round. I'm sure Sister will say yes to your borrowing another room, which means we could go there this evening and make a start on the packing.'

'That's so kind of you to offer,' Jinny said, surprised but pleased that Nancy should offer her help like that.

'We Halfpenny Street girls should stick together,' Nancy said and her happy smile was back in place. 'You're not alone, Jinny. Once you become one of us we look after you . . .'

'Yes, that's right,' Rose said. 'I'll come and give you a hand too. I've got a couple of days off so I don't have to go straight home and get to bed for a change . . .'

Jinny blinked, feeling happy to have friends. She felt as if she belonged here now – and that was a good feeling. Nellie had always been her friend but Nellie would soon be homeless herself. She and Bert were being turned out of the house that they'd lived in all their married lives and that was bad news. Nellie would normally have offered to help, but she was going to be busy, searching for a place to live and packing up her home . . .

'I don't suppose there's much to sort out really,' Jinny said, feeling ashamed to have brought her friends to the shambles the police had left. It had looked bad enough before they turned everything upside down, but now it was a real mess. 'I don't know what the police were looking for, but they've had everything out of the cupboards and drawers . . .'

'I don't think that was the police,' Rob said and looked grim. 'I'm sorry, Jinny, but it looks as if you've had burglars in. I think you'll find any valuables have gone.'

'I'm not sure there was anything worth having left,' Jinny admitted ruefully. 'We used to have a few things – a nice clock, a writing box and fountain pen that belonged to my dad – and Mum's engagement ring – but she sold all those. Her silver teapot she had as a wedding gift from the house where she used to clean . . . it all went on drink years ago. It's just her clothes and shoes, perhaps some sheets and towels if there are any decent . . .'

They'd come armed with cardboard boxes but when Jinny started to search her mother's room she found only a few shabby dresses, all her better things that she'd used for work had gone. They weren't expensive but they were what her mother liked, and they were missing. She found a few books that had been her own, which she packed, one decent set of sheets and a blanket; all the others were either covered in blood or torn. The furniture itself was old and Jinny didn't think any of it worth saving. She found one leather handbag and two pairs of shoes and packed them, but everything else was being shoved into sacks to take to the rubbish tip.

'Do you want to try selling any of this at the second-hand clothes market?' Nancy asked, picking up an armful of assorted and rather dingy clothing and dumping it into a box.

'I don't think they would buy them. No, I'll take them to the rag-and-bone yard . . .'

'I'll take all this stuff there for you,' Rob said. 'You'd be surprised. Some of this old furniture will fetch a few bob. You couldn't store it for long, Jinny, and your mother will only be able to find one room, and that may be furnished. Just take what you want yourself and I'll clear all this stuff out for you, get the place cleaned and give the key back to the council.'

'All I want is in those two boxes. I can store those easily in my room.'

'That's it then,' Rob said. 'If you're sure there is nothing else, I can finish off here for you tomorrow.'

Jinny felt tears sting her eyes as she saw the look that passed between Nancy and Rob. They were being so kind and so tactful, because there was only rubbish here and none of it was fit for anything but the tip.

'Well, if you're sure. Why don't we all go and have a coffee? I'll pay . . .'

'Lovely,' Nancy and Rose said together. 'You lock up and give Rob the key, Jinny, and he'll see to it all for you,' Nancy smiled and nodded encouragingly.

Jinny followed them to the van and they all squeezed in, she and Rose in the back amongst the few boxes they'd already loaded. It caused some giggles and Jinny's mood lightened. If her mother came home, Nellie would tell her where to find her daughter. She'd got a few of her mother's clothes, enough to tide her over until she was able to start work again and buy some more – and if she didn't come back . . . Jinny shook her head and blocked the ready tears.

She'd been told by the council that she must clear the house and she was doing the best she could. If Jinny's mother blamed her it wouldn't be the first time, and she would give her a little money she'd saved and help her find a comfortable room until she was settled.

Rob had arrived at a lively café where they could hear loud jazz music from a jukebox belting into the night air as they piled out and trooped inside. If Jinny had tried clearing the house alone she would still be struggling with it, and crying over what her home had become . . .

She lifted her head, determined to put it all behind her and enjoy the rest of the evening with her friends before she went home to Halfpenny Street . . .

Jinny was busy at the scullery sink the next afternoon when someone entered behind her and encircled her waist with his arms. She jumped and turned round in surprise, half-knowing who it must be but still unsure.

'Micky!' she cried as she looked into his handsome face and felt a curl of pleasure mixed with annoyance. 'Where have you been all this time?'

'I had some business to see to,' he said lifting his brows. ''Sides, I wasn't sure you wanted to see me?'

''Course I do,' Jinny said crossly. 'I was upset over my mother. I'm sorry I said those things to you. I didn't mean them . . .'

'I know you didn't,' he said and grinned at her. 'I was hurt fer a start but then I knew you was just upset. I would've come afore this but I've been askin' around, tryin' ter find out if anyone knows where yer ma is . . .'

Jinny felt tense as she looked into his eyes. 'Have you discovered anythin'?'

'Well, yes and no,' he hedged. 'If I 'ave it ain't good news, Jinny love. I've been to the morgue but she ain't there – so I think it might be 'er in the Infirmary. They told me there's been a woman brought in in a bad way. At first they thought she was drunk but now they're sayin' she's lost 'er mind and she's on her way out, Jinny.' He put out his hands to steady her as she gave a little gasp and collapsed against him. 'I'm sorry. It may not be yer ma, Jinny, but it sounds like 'er . . .'

Jinny nodded and her face was pale. 'I knew something bad had happened to her, Micky. After all this time and the police had heard nothing even though they've searched . . .'

Micky made a snort of disgust. 'They couldn't find a dog with two legs unless it jumped out and bit them! Do you want to go and see 'er? Only the Infirmary say she might not last the night . . .'

'I'm not sure if I can be spared . . .'

'It's all right,' Nancy said, coming into the scullery. 'Your friend told me you would need some time off. I'll take over here, Jinny – and I'm so very sorry . . .'

'Thank you,' Jinny said in a muffled voice. She was hurting so much that it was like a physical pain in her chest. Everything seemed to be shrouded in mist and her mind had gone numb. Even though she'd been prepared for the worst this was a shock and she couldn't stop the tears dripping down her cheeks.

'She ain't worth it,' Micky said, putting a protective arm about her shoulders. 'Remember how she treated you, Jinny. It ain't your fault, love. I know it feels rotten now, but you've still got me . . .'

'Have I?' Jinny asked, but even though he gave her a hug she wasn't reassured. He'd gone off for weeks without contacting her, and even though it was Micky who had brought her the news she needed, she wasn't sure that she was really important to him . . . .

Alone in her room late that night, Jinny couldn't hold back the salty tears. They dripped down her cheeks and her nose, into her mouth. Her mother was dead. Jinny had been there as she breathed her last, but although she'd held her hands and for a moment her eyelids fluttered, Jinny couldn't be sure she knew – and perhaps it didn't matter. They hadn't been close for years and Jinny had been hurt so many times; she hadn't thought she could cry for her mother any more and yet the tears wouldn't stop.

She sat on the edge of the bed until the storm of grief was over and she felt numbed. Nothing had really changed, because she'd lost her mother long ago when she turned to drink and picking up men out of her loneliness or desperation.

Getting up to wash her cheeks, Jinny realised that she couldn't go back and change the past, but she could look to the future. Nellie was teaching her different things to cook, plain simple tasty food, but Nancy had mentioned a course at night school where she could learn to make fancier food.

'I think the classes are quite cheap,' she'd said. 'You could go one night a week, Jinny, and then you'd have the qualifications to be a cook in your own right – you could probably work in a good hotel or do private catering one day in the future.'

'I'd like to be better than I am and able to make lots of wonderful food, but I don't want to leave here yet . . .'

'We should be sorry to lose you,' Nancy had told her warmly. 'I know Sister is very pleased with you, Jinny. Your place here is safe for the time being but things change and move on – and one day you might want to work somewhere else . . .'

Jinny knew she was right. She was very young yet, far too young to think of proper courtship or marriage.

Micky was her friend, a special friend who had helped her a lot, but she had other friends. While Micky was away, she'd had a coffee with Dave in the café near the market and he'd asked her to the flicks one night. Jinny had thanked him and told him she would let him know when she was free, but if she went to night school on her free evening, she wouldn't have time for dating, and perhaps that was a good thing. She'd lost her home and her mother and it wasn't the right time to get involved in relationships. The way Dave looked at her, Jinny thought he would have a ring on her finger the second she was sixteen, and she'd be a mother before she could blink, because Dave came from a big family and he'd told her he was looking to have one himself.

One part of Jinny longed to be a member of a large family, loved and safe and never alone, but the other half of her wanted to learn all she could about being a cook. She'd seen wonderful creations in the second-hand cookery books she'd started to browse on the market. One had been filled with pictures of wonderful wedding cakes, and the steps to achieve pure smooth white icing and then to decorate it were set out step by step.

Jinny sat up in bed with the light on beside her and started to read the book she'd recently purchased; the pages were a bit creased and spotted, but the instructions were clear and good.

She would create a lovely cake for Nancy, because she was kind and generous and she'd made Jinny feel that she belonged here at St Saviour's. Jinny was a Halfpenny Street girl and instead of crying foolish tears for a mother she'd lost long ago, she was going to learn how to make the best wedding cake ever for her friend.

CHAPTER 27

'This is great, ain't it?' Tom looked at Andy who was riding one of the donkeys on the sands at Hunstanton. He took a great lick of his ice cream and glanced at Jean who was playing happily with Beth, building sand-castles further up the beach and decorating it with the big white pebbles that were everywhere on the beach. 'I ain't never 'ad so much fun . . .'

It was September now and their holiday was in its last few days, but they would never forget it. A light wind was blowing off the sea and the waves were crested with white horses as they raced towards the shore. Summer was almost over, and it was time for school again, but they'd been given a few days' grace before they returned.

Andy got off the donkey, gave it a pat and grinned at the man who'd given him the ride for nothing. 'Thanks mate,' he said. He'd rather have gone on the dodgems at the fairground but the owner there wasn't a soft touch like the man who looked after the donkeys. He'd given all the St Saviour's kids a ride if they wanted it and none of them had used a penny of their pocket money. Andy thought the donkey rides couldn't be making much of a profit if the man kept giving free rides, but just then some kids came with their father and he bought them all a turn. Andy walked along the beach until he reached the girls and Tom who had joined them.

Five other kids were staying at the Halfpenny House cottage. Angela Adderbury had brought them all; her husband had come down with them, but he'd gone back to London, because he had important appointments. So they were here with Angela and two other carers from Halfpenny House. One of them was the art teacher, Miss Jill Savage, and the other was a carer named Hester Miles.

Miss Savage was a lot of fun to be at the sea with, Andy thought. She took them searching for starfish, crabs and other tiny sea creatures to be discovered in little rock pools on the beach at Old Hunstanton. When they found something of interest, they put it in a pail of water so that they could study it and make drawings on the sketchpads she gave them.

'We always let our living creatures return to their pools, children,' Miss Savage told them. 'You can keep any unusual stones you find, of course, but treat living creatures with respect please.'

Andy knew that his drawing was crude, as was Jean's. Beth and Tom had a feel for it, though, and theirs were really good. He was happy to see his sister bonding with Jean and Tom. Jean had been following Tom like a little shadow, clearly delighted to have him back. Beth was happier than Andy had ever seen her. She loved it here at the seaside; her laughter rang out time and time again as they raced along the shore and splashed each other at the water's edge. As a treat, Angela took all the children to the funfair. The boys went on all the maddest rides, but Jean and Beth stuck to the horses that went up and down and preferred to throw hoops over prizes. Jean shone at that and managed to win small fairings for both her and Beth.

The wind was whipping the sea into waves crested with yellowish-white foam and the sky was grey. They'd had good weather up to now, but it looked as if it might break soon, and it was getting a bit cool. None of the kids minded, keeping warm by racing up and down, but Miss Savage looked a bit cold.

Watching Beth eat candyfloss and ice creams as they sat or played on the beach, Andy knew his sister was content, away from the threat of her step-father and no longer afraid. When she told Andy that she wished she could stay there forever, he knew he had to think through things very carefully.

Sister Beatrice would be pleased if they chose to stay here, because St Saviour's was only supposed to be temporary and they were expected to move on after a few weeks, and his special friends were here; Keith had sent a postcard and told him he'd be leaving St Saviour's soon after Christmas, to travel with his father. Andy wanted to stay in London, because Mr Barton had promised to find him a Saturday job in a garage and he was learning to drive – but perhaps he should stay here for Beth's sake.

'Would you like to stay at Halfpenny House instead of goin' back ter London?' he asked her when they were sitting quietly reading after supper. 'You wouldn't come here to the sea often, no more than we could if we're in London – but they're nice people and the Beast wouldn't find us here.'

'Would you stay with me?' Beth looked eagerly at him. 'I'd love to be here with Jean and Tom; they're special friends, Andy – the best we've ever had – but I don't want to stay if you're goin' back ter London.'

'If it's what you want, Beth, I'll stay too,' Andy said and received a hug for his pains. 'I'll tell Miss Angela tomorrow . . .'

Andy swallowed his disappointment as Beth hugged him and told him he was the best brother ever. When he was old enough he could apply for a job training to be a mechanic and one day he might learn to drive properly and become a racing driver. Beth needed him with her and he'd liked what he'd seen of Halfpenny House. It was more modern and bright and there were lots of things for the kids to do after school. In Halfpenny Street the most they could do unless they were taken on a trip was kick a football in the road or chalk a hopscotch board on the pavement. In the Essex home there were playing fields and a lot of countryside to explore, as well a gym so they could play pirates on the equipment, as they had the night before they came down to the sea – and there was a small TV set in the hall so they could all watch it.

It would be a new life for them both and Andy would never have to worry about his step-father again . . .

'We brought the children back to Halfpenny House last night,' Angela said to Sister Beatrice on the telephone at the end of the holiday. 'Andy, Tom and Beth all want to stay here with us so there will be no need for anyone to fetch them back. I've inquired about school places and we should have them fixed in by next week . . .'

'Ah, I'm so pleased,' Sister Beatrice replied. 'Though I'm a little surprised. I thought Andy had his future mapped out in London. He has plans to become a mechanic and work for a racing car team – and ultimately to drive one . . . Please tell him that Stirling Moss won at Monza. I think he would like to know that . . .'

'How clever of you to know, and original of Andy to have such ambition,' Angela said. 'I'm glad you told me. He seemed quite sure of his decision and I imagine that it is for his sister's sake. So I shall speak to Mark. He knows so many people and we may be able to sort out a little Saturday job in a garage for Andy – and perhaps an apprenticeship once he leaves school. Naturally, I can't guarantee his Saturday job is with racing cars, but I shall do the best I can for him.'

'You always do,' Sister Beatrice said. 'You will let me know as soon as you're definite about the closure?'

'Yes, of course. I've been busy trying to find extra space for the children that will need to be admitted here when St Saviour's closes. The Board have plans for a new wing, but that can't be put into action for some months – so it will be a matter of squeezing as many beds as we can into the rooms we have.'

'Well, that is what we've always done at St Saviour's. Some of our older children are leaving after Christmas. They have jobs already and are ready to move into hostels. However, I shall continue to take in children in need until the last . . .'

'Of course, you must . . .'

'So Tom is quite happy to stay on with you? I've been a little anxious about him, I must admit.'

'You should have watched him building the biggest sandcastle you've ever seen – and charming the donkey man into giving them all free rides. I think there is no doubt that he will achieve what he wants, Sister, whatever that may be. All we have to do is give him a little help . . .'

'He'll be all right with you,' Sister Beatrice said and Angela could hear the smile in her voice. 'Well, that is a relief concerning Beth and Andy, because the police still have not caught their step-father. I spoke to Sergeant Sallis again this morning and he was angry that the man had eluded them yet again. However, he can have no idea where the children are so they should be quite safe with you and the sergeant assures me they will get him in the end.'

'Yes, I am certain of that,' Angela replied. 'Now, what about you, Sister? Mark wondered if you were quite well last time he saw you . . .'

'I think I have a touch of arthritis, or so the doctor tells me. He has given me a liniment to use and says an Aspro may help – but I shall not take them unless it becomes necessary.'

'It sounds unpleasant for you,' Angela said, 'let's hope the liniment helps.'

'It is nothing I cannot manage.'

'No, I'm sure. Well, it was lovely to talk to you. I shall keep in touch and let you know how the newcomers are settling in . . .'

Angela replaced the phone after farewells were

exchanged. She was sure that Sister Beatrice was suffering more than she had let on and felt pleased that she would most likely be working with her again soon and able to keep a friendly eye on her. In the meantime, she was making preparations to take over once Mrs Mellors left Halfpenny House.

Angela and Mark had discussed the twins' education and talked to them, earlier that year, about the boarding school they'd chosen.

'Hildersham Manor caters for children with special talents,' Mark told his sons after extensive research. 'You're good at all sports, Simon; they have a wonderful cricket team, and the boys can choose between football and rugby – and there's an Olympic-sized pool in the town nearby. You would have your choice and may find that you want to make some form of sport your career . . .' His gaze moved to Edward, the quieter, more thoughtful of his sons. 'They also have an excellent music teacher, Eddie, and I've spoken to the Latin master. He takes Greek with boys who wish to learn and I know you hope to study antiquities at university and perhaps carry it on to later life.' He smiled at them both. 'The choice is yours, lads. You can go to the local grammar school for a perfectly good education when you're old enough but you're eight next birthday so that is some years yet and I think a public school education would suit you better . . .'

'Boarding school please, Dad.' The twins spoke together, of one mind as they always were. 'As long as we stay together,' Simon continued. 'Eddie got bullied at our last one, but I soon sorted them out . . .'

Mark smiled, because both he and Angela often

puzzled over how alike the boys were in some ways and how different in others. Simon was taller and broader than his twin and much more active, joining every sport going and haring round on his bike when there was nothing more interesting to do – while Eddie preferred to sit in a shady spot on the lawn in summer or by the fire in winter and read.

Angela knew that once the twins were settled at boarding school she would find her days long and so she'd agreed to take on the post of Superintendent until such time as Sister Beatrice could join her, but she had made it clear that she needed an assistant she could trust to take over in an emergency. Her family must come first and if the twins had not wanted to go away to school, she would have waited to return to work until they were old enough not to need her.

Sighing, Angela turned away from the phone and went upstairs to start packing their trunks. Mark always sent their luggage on ahead so that they could travel light with just overnight bags. Hearing the sound of happy laughter coming from the twins' room, she smiled. At least her two were fine and looking forward to their new school . . .

CHAPTER 28

Ruby read the newspaper report with a sense of excitement. It concerned the Wolfenden Report, which was going before Parliament and recommended that homosexual practices performed in private between consenting adults should no longer be a criminal offence.

If the suggestion was taken up and passed by Parliament it would make so much difference. Someone like Ruby would be free to offer love where she chose without fear of shame or loss of position; even though being a lesbian wasn't a criminal offence, this would change people's views entirely. She took a pen from her bag and drew a circle round the small paragraph. It was such a tiny piece of information and yet it could make so much difference to her and to others like her – to Carla perhaps.

The thought of Carla kept running through her mind as she walked home. Did she dare to take the newspaper upstairs and show it to Carla? Perhaps they could have coffee together – and talk about things . . .

Ruby had wanted to visit the friendly girl's flat before this, but she was afraid that she might be tempted to go too far and that Carla would be disgusted. If she showed her the report it would be a natural thing to discuss what it meant and how Carla felt about it.

Ruby's tummy was tumbling with nerves as she got into the lift and went up to the top floor. She paused outside the door, her finger poised over the bell, and then her courage deserted her. Supposing she'd misread that look in Carla's face – supposing she saw disgust and derision in the other girl's eyes? No, she couldn't just arrive on Carla's doorstep out of the blue and expect the invitation to coffee still stood; she would wait until they met again and then ask Carla to come to her place.

Taking the newspaper from her shoulder bag, she tucked it under the door. It wouldn't go all the way, but Carla would discover it when she opened her door. If she felt as Ruby did, she would understand and perhaps she'd come down and ask her up for coffee again . . .

She turned and ran back to the lift, afraid now of being caught. Why did she have to be different? Why did she have feelings for another woman rather than the desire to be a wife and mother, as society thought right? What was wrong with wanting a career – and a love affair with someone of the same sex?

Wishing she'd had more courage, Ruby pressed the button that took her down a floor to her own apartment. Why had God made her this way if it was a sin? The question had haunted her for so long and she was no nearer to discovering a satisfactory answer . . .

Rose picked up the telephone in the nurses' home and smiled as she heard Nick's voice. She knew he'd been working in South London on a new housing estate and was extremely busy. He'd told her after his last party that he wouldn't be around to take her out for a week or two. It was mid-September now and Rose was getting ready to leave for a holiday in Yarmouth with Mary Ellen and her husband Billy Baggins. Rose's sister had just received her final exam results and they'd decided on a caravan holiday to celebrate her passing with flying colours. Billy had invited Rose to go with them, telling her that they wanted to say thank you for everything she'd done for her sister, which had made Rose shed a few tears.

'Nick, you just caught me,' she said, looking at her battered suitcase on the bed. 'I'm about to leave for a week's holiday in Yarmouth with my sister and her husband Billy . . . It's the first time they've ever been away to the sea for a proper holiday. It's a bit late in the summer, but if we're lucky it could be nice – and it was cheaper than in August . . .'

'Sounds nice,' he said wistfully. 'I wish I could come with you.'

'Why don't you come down on Sunday for the day? We could take a picnic on the beach – or go out for a nice lunch . . .'

'All right, I will,' he said, surprising her. 'I'll drive down on Saturday afternoon, stay at a bed and breakfast for one night and meet you in the morning – where and when?'

'Ten o'clock by the Britannia Pier,' Rose said and smiled. 'I shall enjoy that, Nick. I'm glad you rang me. Another few minutes and I'd have left . . .'

'So am I,' he said and something in his voice made her tingle. 'I've missed you, Rose . . .'

She held the phone for a moment longer as he replaced

the receiver his end and stared at it for several seconds Rose had never been sure where she stood with Nick. Sometimes she thought he really cared about her, at other times she thought he was just lonely and still grieving for his wife. Because she didn't know how to place him in her world, she'd tried to block thoughts of more than friendship from her mind.

It was different with Stephen Henderson. Rose had felt comfortable in his company from the start, and she knew he liked her a lot. They'd kissed a few times, warm sweet kisses that she enjoyed but didn't set her heart racing. Of the two men she thought she probably liked Nick the most – but there was something he was holding back from her and because of it Rose wouldn't let herself like him too much.

Picking up her suitcase, Rose ran across the garden and out into Halfpenny Street. She needed to catch a bus to take her on her way to the mainline station, where she was meeting Mary Ellen and Billy. For the next few days she was on holiday and determined to forget everything that bothered her and have fun.

'Is it today that you meet your friend Nick?' Mary Ellen asked when they walked over to the shower block at the end of their row. They were both yawning after a late night out at a show and then a long walk on the beach after they left the pier. Billy had bought them shandies at one of the pubs on the long promenade.

'Yes, I'm meeting him later and we'll have the day together – so you and Billy can have some time on your own . . .'

'We're all right,' Mary Ellen said and laughed. 'Billy

is as chuffed as can be because he could afford to give us both this holiday, Rose. He's worked like a Trojan to keep me through college but now I should be able to get a proper job and he has a little money to spare – and he was the one that suggested you should come with us as a treat . . .'

'I don't know why your Billy is so nice to me,' Rose said and looked at her sister awkwardly. 'I wasn't nice to him for a lot of years . . . and I put you in St Saviour's when you didn't want to go . . .'

'You couldn't have done anything else,' Mary Ellen said and gave her waist a squeeze. 'If you'd just stayed where you were in a dead-end job neither of us would've got anywhere. Besides, I was happy at St Saviour's . . . Billy and me had all that time together as kids and that's why we're so happy now.'

'Yes . . .' Rose frowned. 'I've heard a whisper it may be closing soon. I don't know what Sister Beatrice will do then . . .'

'Surely they wouldn't do that,' Mary Ellen said. 'Do you think she knows?'

'She hasn't said anything to me yet – but she did tell me that if I wanted to specialise in paediatrics she would give me a good reference . . .'

'I hope it doesn't happen . . . what will the kids do if St Saviour's isn't there?'

'I suppose the social will find a place for them, but it can't be the same – it isn't the same as it was when you were there, Mary Ellen.'

'No, I don't suppose so . . .' Mary Ellen sighed. 'Well, we can't worry about it now, because you have to get dressed and go and meet your boyfriend.'

'Nick isn't my boyfriend . . .' Rose said and her sister raised mocking eyebrows. 'Well, I do like him but . . .' She laughed and ran ahead of her sister into the shower block. 'Beat you to it . . .'

Rose left the caravan park just after nine and strolled along the seafront towards the Britannia Pier. The wind was a little cool, but the sun was still warm if you found a sheltered spot. The pier was the furthest one from their caravan park and opposite a rather impressive hotel, which she knew did special lunches. Rose would have been happy to buy a meal at any of the little cafés along the front, because a simple meal of tomatoes on toast would have suited her, but she had a feeling that Nick might prefer the hotel.

As she got to the pier with its theatres, shops and amusements, she saw Nick waiting for her. He was standing with his back to her looking out to sea and she saw a small biplane flying close to the water trailing some kind of message behind it . . . a message from someone on holiday to his girlfriend by the look of it. Rose was laughing as Nick turned and then, as she saw the way he looked at her, her heart caught.

'Rose!' He came towards her, smiling, his eyes alight with pleasure as he took her hands and leaned in to kiss her softly on the lips. She felt a thrill of pleasure as she looked into his eyes. 'It's nice here on such a lovely day. I'm glad I came down . . .'

'So am I,' Rose said and meant it. She smiled up at him, feeling warmed and happy; the day was so much brighter now that he was here. 'How are you – have you been working too hard? You look tired . . .'

'We've been very busy so perhaps I am tired. I could do with a break . . .' He looked about him and took a deep breath of the salty air. 'What shall we do – find somewhere to sit and have a drink? It's too cold to swim with this wind . . .'

'Yes, let's go on the pier,' she said. 'We'll walk to the end and then find a sheltered place to sit and have a drink.'

'Good idea,' he agreed. 'It's still too good a day to be inside despite the breeze. It will be autumn soon enough. My wife hated the winter and I promised her a winter holiday in the sun when we could afford it . . . but I rather like the English coast, even though it can be cold.'

'Do you still miss her very much?' Rose asked the question that had nagged at her for a long time.

'No, not really,' Nick said and looked straight at her. 'What we had was over long before she died. I feel guilty about it, because when she was so ill I wanted to love her, but it just wasn't there any more . . .'

'I'm sorry, Nick,' Rose said softly. 'I shouldn't have asked a question like that . . .'

'Why not?' he said. 'You have every right to ask – because we need to get these things out in the open. I care about you, Rose. I think I'm in love with you and I don't still love Helen.'

'Oh . . .' she said and her breath caught because he was clearly waiting. 'I feel more than friendship for you, Nick, but I was afraid . . .'

'Afraid of getting hurt?' he asked and nodded. 'It's the way I felt at first, Rose. I wanted to tell you almost from the first but I wasn't sure . . . you do have other friends . . . male friends, I know.'

'Stephen has kissed me a couple of times and I like him a lot but . . .' She saw the pain in his face and touched his hand quickly. 'I don't love Stephen. I wasn't sure at first how I felt about you, Nick. I was hurt once pretty badly and I didn't want to make a mistake again. We went out a few times, but then you didn't phone for ages . . .'

'I told you I was busy. I had a huge job on and was pretty whacked out when I got home at night . . . But to be honest I wasn't sure whether you wanted to go out with me on a regular basis. I didn't want to get too fond of you in case you didn't feel the same.'

'Yes, I did – I do . . .' Rose smiled and then felt herself blushing – and she hadn't done that since she was a teenager.

'Do you think you could love me enough to be my wife?' Nick asked and she heard the apprehension in his voice. 'I'd rather you tell me if you just want to be friends . . . we can go on just as . . .'

Rose moved towards him and softly kissed him, right there in front of all the people walking by. Some smiled, some whistled and one or two looked disapproving of a public display of affection, but this was a holiday town and Rose didn't care what other people thought as Nick's arms closed about her. She could feel his tensed-up emotion and see the anxiety in his eyes and laughed.

'I don't think you choose to love people, Nick. You either do or you don't . . .' she whispered, 'and I do . . . I wasn't sure but now I am . . .'

'Rose darling . . .' It was as if the sunshine burst out of him and his smile lit up the day. 'I'm so glad. I've wanted to tell you for weeks but the time never seemed right . . .'

Rose reached for his hand and they stood with hands clasped, staring out to sea watching a small boat crammed with trippers chugging along the coastline. Overhead, the gulls wheeled and dived, their shrill cries loud in the sky. She smiled, feeling the sun on her face and happiness start to spread through her. She heard music from someone's transistor radio; it was playing Tab Hunter's hit, 'Young Love' . . .

'We'll have that drink now to celebrate,' she said. 'They do a nice milkshake in that bar – or we can go for a stronger drink later . . .'

'Let's have a milkshake for now,' Nick said and grinned like a small boy. 'I haven't had anything like that for years – a knickerbocker glory – that's what I fancy . . .'

Rose giggled, catching his enthusiasm. She was just so happy. They had lots to talk about, plans to make for the future, but just for today she felt like being free and doing all the things she'd enjoyed as a child. Not that treats like this had been hers very often. East End kids didn't get trips to the sea often, and that was what Rose loved about St Saviour's – the way Sister Beatrice and Angela Adderbury had fought to give the Halfpenny Street kids all the things most of them had never known.

They spent most of the day wandering about, visiting the funfair and the rock shop where the sticky sweet was boiled and rolled out while still hot until it got thinner and thinner. They had decided against eating in a hotel and bought fish and chips to eat on the beach with beer and lemonade shandy, and huge soft ice creams afterwards.

They paddled at the edge of the sea, Rose carrying her sandals as she allowed the water to wash over her toes. Afterwards, she washed her feet under a tap near the promenade and Nick wiped them for her with his handkerchief. He bought her a kiss-me-quick hat and stole a kiss, and then he bought her a pair of pretty earrings from the stall at the end of the pier.

'Just to remember this day . . .' he said and Rose laughed and bought him a leather belt from the same vendor.

Joining hands they walked further along the promenade. Neither of them wanted to visit the shows or waste time eating in restaurants; they were eager just to laugh and tease and learn to know one another, to enjoy a stolen day from busy lives and relish the knowledge that they were in love.

Nick drew her to him and kissed her as the sun went down. 'I had so much to say to you,' he told her. 'We'll talk another day – when you come back to London. I want to marry you, Rose, but there are things you should know – and I must tell you . . .'

'Can't you tell me now?'

'No, my darling. It's been a wonderful day but I want you to meet my children, and I need to have you in the right surroundings so that I can explain things . . . All you need to know for now is that I love you . . .'

He kissed her again, sweetly, deeply, and Rose swayed into his body, wanting so much more. She was a woman now, not a girl, and ready for love. She needed to make love with him so that she felt a part of Nick, a part of his life.

'I shall tell you everything,' he whispered as they stood at the entrance to the caravan park, 'and I hope you will still love me and want to marry me. Keep well, my darling.'

He was smiling as he got into his car and drove away and yet Rose sensed that whatever he had to tell her was serious. She worried at it for a moment and then pushed it from her mind. Rose knew what she wanted now and that meant she had to tell Stephen that she could only be his friend. She suspected that it would hurt and shock him, and she dreaded it, but it had to be done. She would telephone him at his surgery tomorrow, arrange to meet for a drink when she was back in London, and then she would tell him that she was going steady with someone else.

Pushing all else from her mind, she entered the caravan to see Mary Ellen and Billy tucking into fish and chips.

'They look good.' She smiled as her sister nodded and offered her a chip.

'Did you have a lovely day?'

'Yes, thank you,' Rose said and accepted the cup of tea Billy offered. 'It was lovely on the beach last thing when everyone else is in the pub or at the theatre.'

'Yes, me and Billy had a walk up the other end earlier on,' Mary Ellen said, 'but I want to see that show on the pier we talked about before we go home and I'd like a boat trip too . . .'

'You can get Rose to go with you,' Billy said and grinned. 'I'll be content with a paddle at the water's edge . . .'

Rose smiled at their banter, because she knew Billy would do whatever Mary Ellen wanted; he always did. Two more days of fun with them and then she would be back at work – and Nick was going to give her dinner at his home so that they could talk. He'd said they would have something simple and prepare it together and it sounded intimate and lovely. Rose couldn't wait . . .

CHAPTER 29

Jinny started to feel better once her mother's funeral was over. On Nellie's advice she gave all her mother's clothes and bits to a charity.

'They'll help some poor soul and yer ma don't need 'em now,' Nellie said. 'I've sorted some of my kids' things out and took 'em down the charity stall. I reckon I've found a place as will do us, but my old man still says 'e'll make 'em put 'im out afore 'e leaves – but 'e'll be sittin' on the floor, 'cos once I've got me 'ouse I'm orf with all me bits . . .'

Jinny laughed and shook her head. She knew that Nellie had given up her own dreams of a lovely new council flat for Bert's sake. He could never have settled away from the streets he knew and loved and so Nellie had searched for a house that she could afford to rent in the same area. She'd found a slightly better one than she'd lived in for years, but the rent was higher and so she'd offered to do a few more hours at St Saviour's, which Sister Beatrice had been pleased to accept.

'I'm afraid you and Jinny will be on your own for a time,' she'd told Nellie. 'Elsa is leaving us at the end of the month and I shall have to find a replacement for her.'

Elsa had already told them in the kitchen that she was leaving. She was over the moon because she'd been lucky enough to get a job in a branch of Boots on the perfume counters.

'I'll go to sea and be a sailor!' Nellie exclaimed to Jinny afterwards. 'If she can get a job like that you should be able to get anything you want, love.'

'I don't want to be anywhere but here,' Jinny told her with a smile. She was going to miss her friend Elsa, but she had lots of other friends at St Saviour's and she'd joined a cookery course at evening class.

'Come on then,' Nellie challenged. 'Show me how they taught you to make Queen of Puddings at evening class, and then I'll show you my way – and we'll see how the kids like it best.'

Jinny smiled, because Nellie was always setting her little challenges, rallying her whenever she let herself feel down. 'I bet they'll like yours best,' she said, 'but it will be fun seeing which one they choose.'

In the end both puddings were cleared and no one grumbled; everyone seemed happy and content and Jinny was beginning to feel that way herself as she settled into the life at St Saviour's. Now and then she would feel grief because she'd lost both parents and had no one special of her own, but she was so busy working, learning and going out with friends that she hardly had time to feel sorry for what might have been . . .

Micky came round once in a while and took her to the flicks on her Saturdays off. They'd been to see *Bridge on the River Kwai*, *The Barretts of Wimpole Street*, and *The Curse of Frankenstein*, which had come round again. Micky liked *The Curse* of *Frankenstein* and the war film and thought the other was soppy, but Jinny enjoyed it. She just enjoyed going out with him and the pain of losing her mum had begun to lessen as the autumn took hold and the temperatures dropped.

Everyone had a good time at Nancy's engagement party, and it ended up being more like a kids' treat than the kind of party most people wanted for their engagement, but Nancy was happy and Rob didn't care one way or the other as long as his Nancy smiled at him.

So then it was October and the papers were filled with the news that the Russians had put a man-made satellite into space; it was called Sputnik 1 and was orbiting five hundred miles above the Earth and sending back signals – which hadn't pleased the Americans who had wanted to be the first in space.

In the kitchens at St Saviour's the launch was a ten-minute wonder and then the talk returned to local matters. The nights had started to pull in and it was getting colder at night when Micky said he wouldn't be around for a while.

'I'll be back in a few days,' he told Jinny and kissed her as he left her outside the nurses' home that night. 'I shan't be able to take you out this Saturday though. Be good – and remember you're my girl . . .'

'Where are you goin'?' Jinny asked but he shook his head and grinned at her.

'What yer don't know won't hurt yer,' he said and tapped the side of his nose. 'It's just somethin' I have to do, love, 'cos I don't want to be stuck in a stinkin' little hovel for the rest of me life like me ma. I'll see you soon, Jinny . . .'

She watched him go doubtfully. It worried her that Micky wouldn't tell her what he was doing, who he worked for or where he went when he disappeared like this. Jinny felt that he was doing something he shouldn't and that made her uneasy. She liked Micky and she was grateful to him, sometimes she thought her feelings went deeper – but she didn't want to become too involved with him if he was going to end up in prison. Jinny had had enough of men who drank and went off and left their families . . . She decided that next time he just turned up and asked her out she might say no . . .

Rose had enjoyed herself working in Nick's kitchen all that Saturday afternoon. He'd been out in the garden much of the time, weeding and cutting the lawn. He'd offered to take her out for a meal instead, but she'd wanted to cook a nice meal for him, and now she had it all ready as he came downstairs smelling of shower gel and aftershave.

'Something smells delicious,' Nick said and walked over to kiss her. 'Is there anything you want me to do, Rose?'

'You can open the wine so that it breathes a little . . . isn't that what a decent red needs? To be at room temperature and allowed to breathe . . .'

'So they say.' Nick looked at her choice of burgundy and smiled. 'We had this once before . . . let me guess, we've got roast beef . . .'

'It's one of the things I can cook,' Rose said a little uncertainly. 'Roast beef and Yorkshire. Mum always made hers lovely and light and crispy. I hope you like it that way?'

'I'm sure I shall,' Nick said. 'I don't know how you found the time to learn to cook. You must have studied for years to become a Sister at the London hospital . . .'

'Yes, a long time and it wasn't easy,' Rose said. 'We mostly had cheap filling stuff at the canteen so whenever we could a few of us got together and cooked a proper lunch. One of the girls had her own small flat so I learned in a tiny kitchen, not a lovely spacious one like this . . .'

'Helen wanted a big kitchen so I planned it for her, but she never got to use it much. I always regretted that for her . . .' He handed Rose a glass of rich red wine. 'Would you be happy in this house, Rose – or would you prefer I sell it and buy something else . . . something that was just ours?'

'Oh, it would be a shame to sell a lovely house like this,' Rose said and looked about her. 'Do you think your children will accept me . . . if we marry?'

'In time, though it may take a while. You'll have to meet them next time they come home from boarding school, let them get used to you gradually,' Nick said with a sigh. 'That's just one of the problems of a second marriage, isn't it? I don't want Helen to be a ghost at the feast . . . if you feel that this is her house and still belongs to her I'd much rather find us something else.'

'No, I haven't felt that,' Rose said, sipped her drink and then put it down as she moved towards him, looking up into his face. 'I do know that you're worried about something, Nick. If it isn't grief then what is it? You said I must know everything so why not tell me now we're alone? It seems to me that you keep putting it off . . .'

'Yes, I know . . .' He sighed. 'You wouldn't rather eat first . . . I don't want your lovely dinner to ruin.'

'All right, we'll eat first,' Rose said and bent down to remove a perfectly cooked joint from the oven. 'But then I want you to promise you'll tell me what's worrying you. I've known there was something for weeks and you said you'd tell me, but you haven't . . .'

'I promise I'll do it after dinner,' he said and something in his voice sent a little chill down her spine.

Everything had been eaten and enjoyed, the dishes packed into Nick's miraculous new washing-up machine. Rose had thought of the piles of dirty plates at St Saviour's and thought how much Jinny would appreciate something like it there, but she wasn't likely to get something that expensive. Nick certainly wasn't short of money. He'd been a successful builder before his wife died, though his business had declined afterwards, but since joining forces with his brother he was climbing the ladder once more.

They took the tray of coffee into the sitting room where an electric fire had been turned on to warm it up. Nick didn't like coal fires, because he said it created smog in towns and that caused too many problems, so he was about to install oil-fired central heating and there was a pile of radiators in the hallway waiting until he and Rob had time to put them up. Rose curled up in an armchair near the fire and let Nick pour the coffee; he'd insisted on making it with fresh ground beans and it smelled delicious. She looked at him expectantly as he sat on the carpet at her feet.

'There's no way to say this any differently, Rose . . . I was responsible for my wife's death . . .'

Rose gasped and recoiled, because it was the last thing she'd expected him to say. 'What do you mean? You caused her accident or . . . ?'

'No, the accident was her own fault, because she drove too fast on an icy road, but I helped her to die. I knew what she was doing and I stood by and let her take her own life . . .' Rose stared at him in shock. 'She begged me so many times to leave the bottle of the pain killing pills with her, and she was always asking for more; even though I never gave her the bottle, I guessed she was hoarding them. She hated being the way she was, crippled and in terrible pain; the doctor told me that if she took too many it could kill her . . . and still I allowed her to go on adding to her hoard. I didn't try to stop her. When she asked me to leave the whisky bottle that night I knew what she wanted and yet I couldn't deny her. I placed it on the cabinet beside the bed and walked out of the room and the house . . .'

'Oh, Nick,' Rose said and drew a sobbing breath. 'You didn't cause her death – you just didn't stop her.'

'The police didn't seem to think I was blameless. They lectured me for letting her hoard pills, and for leaving the whisky there. I should've been aware and taken them from her, according to them . . . If I'd told them I guessed what she was going to do that night, they would've arrested me for conspiracy to take life. I could have been charged with murder or at least manslaughter and I would probably have gone to prison.' His eyes were bleak as he looked at her. 'Instead, I lied and said I must have left the whisky bottle by accident when I went out . . . I was too cowardly to own up to what I'd done . . .'

Rose got up and knelt by his side on the carpet. She looked into his eyes and then she leaned forward to kiss him on the lips.

'I don't think you're a coward. What good would it have done if you'd gone to prison for an act of mercy? Your children need their father to be here for them, not locked up in a cell for years.'

'You don't think I'm a coward – or worse?' he asked. 'It's been hanging over me all this time – nearly driven me mad at times. I left her to die alone, Rose. I knew it was wrong. I should have made her go on living despite the agony she was in . . . but she begged me to leave that whisky bottle . . . and then I walked out, because I couldn't be there when she did it.'

'It was what she wanted. There are times when desperately sick people just do not want to live . . .'

'Does that make what I did any better?' he asked, looking wretched. 'I've sometimes felt that I shouldn't be alive and enjoying life because she can't.'

'You didn't force her to drive recklessly and you didn't hold her down and force the pills into her,' Rose said. 'As a nurse there have been times when I've wished I had the courage to end a patient's life when they were suffering too badly . . .' She paused, then, 'Did you know that Stephen Henderson was accused of giving one of his terminally ill patients an overdose that killed him?'

'Yes . . . he was cleared in the end, because there was no proof that he'd administered the fatal dose knowing that his patient had already been given his morphine dose for that night. He told me himself; the blame actually lay with the nurse who had forgotten to write it up in the dangerous medicines book.' Nick looked at Rose. 'I let Helen die because I couldn't stand her suffering any longer . . . and I'd been advised to send her to a special hospital where she could receive constant care, but she told me she would rather die than go there so . . .'

'So you allowed her to die as she wished. I don't think you're a bad man, Nick – but you are a brave one.'

Rose moved closer and put her arms about him, her face close to his. Their foreheads touched and for a moment neither of them spoke and then he gave a great shudder and drew her close, his arms tight around her.

'You're a nurse and you save life. I thought you might hate me when you knew – and I thought if you did it was my punishment . . . that I didn't deserve to be happy . . . It's the reason I stayed away from you for a while, because I was sure you wouldn't accept what I'd done.'

'Sometimes we can save lives, sometimes there's nothing we can do but ease a patient's pain and make them comfortable . . . and sometimes the medicine we give people gradually kills them. Some doctors are tempted to give more – a fatal dose to put patients out of their misery, but their oath doesn't allow it and nor does the law. I think one day there may be a law that lets terminally ill patients decide for themselves – and that after all is what Helen did. She decided for herself, Nick . . .'

'Yes,' he said and she saw tears of relief run down

his cheeks. 'So do you think you could marry a man like me, Rose?'

'Oh yes,' she said with a smile as she sat back on her heels. 'I think I might and I don't see why we should wait for ages either . . .' She stood up and Nick scrambled up after her. Rose held her hand out to him. 'Let's go to bed – and then when you make me breakfast, we can decide when it should be . . .'

'Rose, I love you so much,' he said and took her hands, looking deep into her eyes. 'I thought my life was over, as far as personal happiness was concerned . . . that it was what I deserved, but you've given me a reason to be happy again.'

Rose looked up into his eyes, eyes that were suddenly clear of doubt and self-torture, and knew that she'd made the right decision. For a time she'd been unsure whether it was Nick she wanted or Stephen, but Nick needed her and Stephen would easily find another woman to take out. He'd been disappointed when she'd told him she couldn't go out with him again, but she'd known he didn't really mind. She suspected he'd wanted an affair, whereas Nick really loved her – and that was something Rose hadn't expected to find. She'd given a lot of years to her training so that she could provide a home for herself and Mary Ellen, but her sister was happily married and well on the way to achieving her heart's desire of becoming a teacher, and although Rose had no intention of giving up her work as a nurse just yet, she hoped that one day in the future she would have both a husband and children.

CHAPTER 30

Ruby didn't know why the poets spoke of autumn as a season of mellow mists and fruitfulness with such awe when in reality it was dank and often chilly in the evenings, especially if you lived in a cheerless flat hardly big enough to throw a cat. Not that she wanted to swing anything particularly, but that evening she'd had a trying day; one of her staff had stayed off sick without letting her know; she'd caught another care assistant slapping one of the girls and, when she asked for an explanation, she'd been told the girl had been cheeky. Afterwards, she'd reprimanded the assistant in her office and been reminded the girls were minor offenders sent there as a punishment.

'It's getting like a bloody rest home 'ere,' Belinda had complained. 'You used to give them a good slap if you felt like it – how do you expect us to keep discipline if you go soft on the girls?'

Ruby was tempted to dismiss her instantly, but reminded herself that there was some truth in what she said. The trouble was that Ruby was developing a conscience, perhaps more than she could afford to have in her job – and yet she'd seen for herself the way girls responded to a slight relaxation of the rules. Now that having tea with Sister Beatrice's children was a regular thing they all looked forward to it, and she knew they needed something to work for, a reward of some kind if they were to try to do better . . . to become the decent citizens that society demanded.

Sighing, Ruby reached for the bottle of wine she'd taken to bringing home at least twice a week. She was finding life lonely and half-wished that she'd taken Miss Sampson up on her offer of a drink that night; it had never been repeated, and yet the gloating in her eyes as she'd spoken of taking over St Saviour's and summarily dismissing Sister Beatrice had turned Ruby's stomach. Until that moment she'd been blindly admiring of her superior, but in a flash she'd seen the true cut of the woman and she hadn't liked what she'd seen.

What was really disturbing her, Ruby realised, was that she felt guilty because she was party to a secret that concerned Sister Beatrice and it left a nasty taste in her mouth. Her early dismissal of the nun as a fool and a dinosaur had completely reversed, and she'd come to realise what a wonderful job Sister Beatrice really did and now . . . Ruby's thoughts were interrupted as her doorbell rang and she went to answer it, grumbling under her breath. Who the hell was that just when she was ready to settle down to an evening by her electric fire with a glass of wine?

The young woman who stood outside had frizzy red hair that stuck out at all angles but looked fantastic. She was wearing a full red pleated skirt, red shoes and a white jumper with spangles that accentuated her pointed bra beneath, and her eyes were green. Ruby's breath caught in her throat as looked at Carla, the girl from upstairs . . . the girl she'd heard singing to loud music in the mornings: the girl who had so often been in her thoughts since they'd met in the lobby a few times, and she'd helped Carla move in. Although Ruby had passed on her evening paper a few times, and Carla had stopped her when she was on her way to work and thanked her, their friendship hadn't gone past a greeting and a little chat when they met – and Ruby had shied away from her since she'd refused to go out for a drink because she was already going out with a friend.

'Hi,' the girl said nervously and Ruby saw that she was clutching a bottle of Ruby's favourite wine. 'You're going to think this is the most awful cheek . . . but you've never taken up my offer of coming in for coffee and I thought why don't I go down there and bring this . . .' Her smile was like a flickering beacon, ready to be extinguished by Ruby's displeasure, and Ruby knew instantly why she was here. 'I'm feeling lonely and fed up and I wondered if you felt like company?' Her pale skin flushed bright red as she hovered, fear of rejection in her eyes.

'Come in, Carla,' Ruby said and smiled, opening her door wide so that this marvellous girl could enter and thinking how pretty she was. 'I've been meaning to come and see you – and I popped the paper in your door a couple of times, but you weren't there . . . and I suppose I wasn't sure if you really meant it when you asked me up . . .' What Ruby truly meant was she'd seen an invitation in Carla's eyes but had been afraid that she was misreading it. Her heart quickened as she saw that look again and knew that she hadn't been wrong. Carla wanted more than friendship – she wanted the kind of relationship Ruby had only dreamed of until now.

'I did, I really did,' the vibrant redhead said, speaking more confidently now, as if she knew that she'd been right. They were the same and already Ruby could feel the mutual attraction. Carla wasn't afraid to let her see now and she moved into the room and sat down on a cushion in front of the fire, making herself instantly at home. The cheerless room seemed suddenly warmer and brighter, as if Carla had brought the sunshine with her. 'At least it's cosy and warm. I'm out of money and I don't have enough coins to feed the meter . . .'

It was on the tip of Ruby's tongue to ask why she'd bought the wine rather than put money in her electric meter, but she knew it was just an excuse to come down and park in her living room. Carla was sure of her convictions; even on the few occasions they'd met, she'd read Ruby's thoughts – and she had more courage than Ruby.

Ruby brought glasses and a corkscrew and sat on another cushion in front of the fire. 'How did you know this was my favourite?' she asked, taking the bottle and coping with the cork with expert ease.

'I've been watching you. Twice when we met in the lobby it wasn't by accident; I know when you get home and I came down so that we could talk – and I saw the wine in your bag,' Carla said and the look in her eyes was a mixture of invitation and a spaniel dog pleading. Was she like Ruby, desperate for love and physical affection, but afraid of the social repercussions it would cause? 'I wanted to please you – have I?'

There was something in Carla's manner that suggested openness and a warm heart, both of which were a refreshing change from everything Ruby came into contact with at work. Suddenly, she knew that sometimes you had to put your personal feelings first and take a chance. Unless she was willing to risk rejection she might never find the warm loving relationship she craved.

'Yes, you have,' Ruby said and reached forward to kiss her gently on the lips. Carla's eyes sparkled and she giggled. 'I think we shall be good friends, Carla.' She moved back but her eyes never left the other girl's.

'It's better having a friend than being alone in a place like this,' Carla said and leaned in, kissing her back with what could only be passion. Ruby felt warmed right through as she poured wine into their glasses and passed one to her new friend. 'Women like us need to stick together, Ruby – don't you think so? I know it's difficult – especially for you, because of your job . . . but don't you think it might be worth it? Don't you think the attitude to women like us is stupid?'

'Oh yes,' Ruby said, suddenly free of her inhibitions, because she knew she didn't have to hide with this girl. 'You were just what I needed, Carla: a ray of sunshine on a grey day. What do you do for work?'

'I'm a secretary in a boring office filled with men,' Carla said and grimaced. 'They chat me up all the time and pat me on the bottom; I just smile and pretend – but I hate it. Still, I couldn't go on living in the country; it was stifling me. I've got a few women friends here, but they aren't like us. All they talk about is men. You know what I need . . . don't you?' Their eyes met in shared understanding.

'Oh yes, I do,' Ruby smiled and sipped her wine. 'Because I want it too . . . almost since the first time I saw you . . .'

She felt so much better all of a sudden. She had a new friend, someone to have fun with – and perhaps even a lover. This wouldn't be her first affair with another woman; that had happened in college with a tutor, who had initiated her into the pleasures of same-sex love, but since then she hadn't dared to approach anyone. And she'd spent some months imagining herself in love with a woman she no longer liked. Carla was like a breath of fresh air blowing the staleness from her life. It was odd how clear everything had just become. She'd been brooding over what she ought to do – but tomorrow she would go and talk to Sister Beatrice . . .

'I hope I'm not intruding?' Ruby asked as she knocked and entered at the command to do so.

Sister Beatrice looked at her over the top of her reading glasses and then took them off. 'Why don't you sit down, Ruby?' she invited.

Ruby sat; she swallowed nervously, because when she'd been sitting by the fire with Carla it had been simple to think she could just breeze in and tell Sister Beatrice what had been told to her in confidence, but it wasn't easy. If all hell broke loose over this, Ruby could lose her job, and yet she couldn't live with herself if she didn't – and somehow her job was no longer all important. Ruby couldn't have said honestly that she was in love yet but she was certainly enchanted with her new lover, because a few drinks later that was what Carla had become.

'This is difficult . . .' she began as Sister Beatrice removed her glasses and looked at her expectantly. 'If you'd been told something was going on that you didn't agree with . . . something that would hurt others . . . would you tell even if it was breaking a confidence?'

'Ah . . .' Sister Beatrice nodded and then smiled. 'I believe you are about to tell me something that I've just this minute been told by someone else . . . a good friend. It seems that the Board of St Saviour's has finally agreed to the council's Children's Department taking over the orphanage for its own purposes . . . and the handover will go ahead on the thirty-first of December . . .'

Ruby expelled a long breath, feeling as if her balloon had been pricked. 'I should've told you before, but I was torn two ways.'

'I'm pleased you decided to do the right thing,' Sister Beatrice said and nodded. 'My friend told me as soon as she heard from her husband, who is on the Board of the charity, and naturally she rang me to let me know. I have been offered the position of Superintendent there . . .'

'So will you be moving there?' Ruby asked, surprised, as Sister Beatrice got up and went over to her file, unlocking it with keys she kept on a chain and attached to a hidden pocket in her habit. She took out a bottle of sherry and two small glasses, brought them back to the desk and poured a little of the rich wine into each. Ruby thanked her, sipped hers and discovered it was good, not sickly sweet like some brands but a nice flavour.

'Yes, I believe so,' Sister Beatrice said and lifted her glass in salute. 'Good health to you, Ruby, and thank you for coming to warn me. I appreciate the gesture.'

'It gave the person who told me far too much pleasure . . .' Ruby confessed and to her dismay she found herself blushing under the nun's penetrating gaze. She felt as if she could see right into her heart and see the tiny seed of new life growing there. 'I'm so glad you won't be out of a job or . . . whatever nuns do . . .' Ruby wasn't into religion and the thought of living in a convent gave her the horrors, but she'd overcome her dislike of nuns in their dull habits, because of her admiration for Sister Beatrice.

'I could always return to the convent, but I want to continue my work for as long as God grants me the strength,' Sister Beatrice replied. 'We were given to understand that a part of the building would be kept for receiving children in need, but they would of necessity be passed on within hours if not days – and that is the main difference . . .'

'No, that is not their intention,' Ruby said, shocked that the St Saviour's Board had been lied to. 'I've recently been told that we would be taking young male offenders as well as the girls in future but the street children would go to another centre that will open by the end of the year.'

'Are you certain of this?' Sister Beatrice frowned as Ruby nodded. 'In that case I shall have to let my friends know. I imagine it is too late to change anything now, but I know that some of the Board at least will be extremely angry that they were not given the whole truth.'

'I wish I'd told you sooner but . . .'

'You had been told in confidence and you have your own future to consider.'

'I am to be in charge of the home, but, as you know, I've tried to make things easier for my girls – and that is how I'd hoped to continue, but if a stricter regime were imposed I might have to consider leaving. I think I might be happier working with the kind of children you have cared for all these years, Sister. And I should like your advice on the matter . . .'

'I am a little surprised, Ruby . . .'

Ruby could have laughed out loud at the look of sheer amazement on Sister Beatrice's face, but she kept her expression serious, though inside the joy of life would not be suppressed. Ruby had never felt so alive, never felt as happy as she did now, and it was because at last she'd found a way to live as she'd always longed to, even if it had to be kept private. One day perhaps women like her would be able to shout their happiness to the world, but for the moment it must be kept hidden . . . except that today it would not stay inside.

'I believe your methods of teaching youngsters to behave are better than mine were at the start, and I would be grateful for any advice you thought you could pass on. I wish you were not going so far away.'

'There is always the telephone, Ruby.' Sister Beatrice's eyes sparkled with some secret amusement. 'I am not sure that my giving you advice would please Miss Sampson . . . but I am always available to you and I shall make certain you have both my address and my phone number . . . And now I'm sure we both have work to do.'

Ruby felt herself dismissed, but for some reason she didn't mind. The resentment she'd felt for Sister Beatrice had gone, together with the doubts and shadows that had haunted her for such a long time. Of course she would never forget the mental or physical abuse that had destroyed her childhood, but she could move on from it at last.

'Please keep me informed of any news you may have.' She resumed her normal efficiency. 'I must not keep you from your work any longer . . .'

'One thing . . . shall you keep my staff on here when you take over?' Sister Beatrice asked.

'Much will depend on my remit, but I have often wished we had the kitchen facilities you have – ours is much smaller, the food we give our girls very basic, because they have school lunch – and also the nurses. I feel we would need them, so my answer is yes, if they wished to stay.'

Ruby returned to her side of the building. Her confidence was high and she felt able to cope whatever happened. She would make a start by inviting Belinda to her office and asking her whether she wished to continue to work for her. She would make it quite clear that any punishments in future would be given out by Ruby and no one else . . . there was still a case for punishment, but only when it was right and fair.

Wonders would never cease! Beatrice marvelled at the change she'd witnessed in Ruby Saunders. It was as if the raw, inexperienced girl who had been so sure of herself when she first came here had matured into someone much deeper and infinitely more caring. Some of the bitterness and deep sadness had lifted from her eyes, and she actually looked younger, more attractive.

Beatrice could not help wondering what had happened

in the young woman's life to bring about such a change, but never considered for one moment that she had in any way contributed to the catharsis. For herself, she felt invigorated, ready for the changes to her life.

She rang Angela and told her what she'd been given to understand about the closure of the reception centre.

'So they lied to us and they have no intention of continuing our work.'

'I dare say they decided it wouldn't work to combine the two, and perhaps it makes sense. It will be the end of St Saviour's as we know it, Angela – but it does mean that we must bring all our children with us.'

'I think you should start sending us a few each week,' Angela said. 'Mark will be furious about this. We thought we had time but now we must work faster. I am determined that our orphans will be kept together.'

'Perhaps we can find a temporary building nearby?'

'Mark spoke of putting up a prefab in the grounds until we can get the new wing built – and I think he's already made inquiries. Once I tell him what you've told me, he'll move on it immediately.'

'Good. I can see that you have everything in hand your end, Angela. I shall begin by gathering the staff together and informing them of the move. Any member of my staff that wishes to move can speak to you about an interview with the Board, if that's necessary. Ruby told me that she would like to keep the kitchen open and would keep our present staff if they wished to continue here . . .'

'Is it true that Ruby Saunders has been offered the job running the whole place? After what happened with those foster parents . . .'

'I think that Ruby has learned her lesson,' Beatrice said. 'I didn't believe I'd ever see the day but she does have compassion. She might do better than you imagine . . . better than Miss Sampson herself, I'm certain.'

'It will need someone who can stand up to Miss Sampson, otherwise she will interfere every step of the way . . .'

'Well, perhaps Ruby Saunders will surprise us . . .'

'Yes, well, I'm relieved it is settled. Now we can all concentrate on the future – and I do look forward to working with you again immensely.'

'I shall consider it a pleasure . . .'

Beatrice mused over that telephone call. Ruby had surprised her a great deal this morning. She didn't know what had happened, but something had definitely changed her for the better. She rather thought it had started happening some months back – perhaps when she discovered what a huge mistake she'd made over June Miller's foster parents – but it was far more noticeable now. Ruby had risked her job to inform her of what was planned for the future and it must have taken courage to do what she'd done – and perhaps that was what was needed to take on the kind of job that was being offered her. Beatrice wasn't sure she would feel up to it herself . . .

CHAPTER 31

'Well, that was a surprise,' Nellie said after Sister Beatrice had announced that St Saviour's was closing at the end of December, and that all the children would be transferred during the next few weeks. 'You could've knocked me down wiv a feather when she said all them kids was off to Essex . . .'

'I will speak to my staff individually about the future, because you all have a choice to make about where you wish to work and live when St Saviour's closes,' Sister Beatrice had announced. 'The children are all being taken to Halfpenny House, where I shall continue to care for their welfare. Since there is a great deal to be done we shall have a quieter but happy Christmas here, with one party that those of us that remain can enjoy together . . . But in the meantime everything will continue as usual, and anyone with any doubts or concerns is free to come and talk to me about the move or anything else that worries them . . .'

'I wonder what will happen to the staff,' Jinny said. 'Kelly and Wendy and Sister Rose . . . and us . . .'

'You could get a job as a trainee cook anywhere,'

Nellie said. 'Sister will give you a reference and I'll help you all I can . . .'

'What about you? You enjoy working here, don't you?'

'I'll see what's on offer,' Nellie said. 'I did see an advertisement fer a cook's job at a primary school. It was in the paper they wrapped me spuds in down the market. It's fer the new term next year – so I might apply for it . . .'

'I'd like to cook, but I couldn't take a cook's job alone yet. I'm not qualified.'

'Why don't you talk to Sister about it?' Nellie suggested. 'She might 'ave some ideas. She 'elps her kids find work and I'm sure she'll do the same fer you if you ask her.'

'Yes, I think I shall. I'll go up when we've finished lunch and ask if I can talk to her.'

'You do that,' Nellie smiled. 'If I was offered the job at the school I'd take you on as my assistant – if they'd let me . . .'

'I know . . .' Jinny sighed. 'I've loved working here with you, Nellie.'

'Well, it ain't over yet, love – we've still got Christmas to come. You heard what Sister said, it's going to be a quieter one this year but we shall still have a party . . .'

'I spoke to Ruby Saunders,' Beatrice said when Rose came to talk to her in her office. 'She says she's hoping to employ a couple of nurses when she takes over – but she may not have a free hand in choosing her staff. Besides, you might not wish to continue working here . . .'

'I think I shall look for a part-time job, perhaps just a few hours in the mornings at a doctor's surgery,' Rose said and smiled. 'Nick and I are planning to marry soon.

We're going down to see his boys at boarding school this weekend, and if they're all right with the idea, they'll be coming home to live. That means I shan't be able to do much more than a few hours a week . . .'

'I needn't worry about you then,' Beatrice nodded. 'Wendy has told me she's going back to hospital nursing and she intends to specialise in paediatrics; she was going to give me a month's notice at Christmas, so she'll stay on until then and go straight to her refresher course afterwards . . .'

'What about Kelly and the other carers?'

'Some of them will wait and see if they get offered work with the Children's Department, but Mavis told me she has been offered a job in Peacocks and was going to leave next month anyway . . .'

'You'll be short-handed if the others follow suit . . .'

'No, because we're taking as many children down as Angela can cope with each week from now on. Nancy and Kelly are taking a party of ten this weekend. I thought the younger ones should go first, as they are more nervous and I want them settled before Christmas. At least six of the older boys are due to leave school soon and they won't want to move to the country. I am going to see if I can find them accommodation in a youth hostel when we close. Normally, I'd give them longer to make the transition, but this time I have no choice . . .'

'This will make such a lot of work for you,' Rose said. 'If there is anything I can do, you must tell me.'

'Sandra is taking as much of the load as she can, dealing with all the paperwork. We have to release the children to Halfpenny House and a full report must accompany each child that we send down – but much of that is straightforward.'

'What about you?' Rose asked and frowned. 'Where will you live – have you had time to discuss that yet?'

'Angela says there is a small cottage that was used by Mrs Mellors. It's furnished so I shall merely have my own few bits and pieces to take down . . .'

'Well, if you need a hand with the packing, I'm sure Billy and Mary Ellen will be delighted to help. I know she is coming to see you at the weekend, because she was upset when she heard the home was closing.'

'I dare say it was a shock . . . as it has been for all of us. I think many local people will be upset by the closure, but there really is nothing to be done this time.'

'Yes . . .' Rose sighed. 'The time has flown since I first brought my young sister here. She hated me for making her come, but once she settled down she was happy . . . the kids are going to miss you, Sister.'

'I shall be at Halfpenny House for some years I hope.'

'I meant the kids of London . . . the hungry, desperate kids that come here from the streets. Oh, I know the Children's Department will deal with them. They will be fed and cared for after a fashion – but it won't be the same.'

'St Saviour's was unique,' Beatrice said, a wistful smile playing about her mouth. 'It was the sum of the people that worked here and the people who made a home for those in need in the first place . . . Everything is different in this bold new world, Rose, and perhaps it is best that we move on – but I think we shall be missed . . .'

'*You* certainly will,' Rose said. 'Everyone I meet is in shock. Some of the local women wanted to protest and force the authorities to think again, but I told them it was too late.'

'Much too late.' Beatrice smiled. 'Progress marches on, Rose, and we must all march with it or be swept aside by the tide.'

'I want it to be a good Christmas for all of us, though most of the children will be in Essex by then,' Sister had told Nellie and Jinny in the kitchen some days later. 'I've spoken to some people I know, Jinny, but as yet the only hope I have for you is to take a professional culinary course. You would live in at Mrs Jenkins' cookery school and attend her classes, as well as helping her run her catering business in the evenings and at weekends, and when you leave at the end of a year you will have certificates that prove you are a qualified cook with practical experience. After that I think it will be much easier for you to find work than if you continued at evening class, which would take much longer to complete.'

'Do you think Mrs Jenkins will take me, Sister?' Jinny asked anxiously. 'Is the course very expensive?'

'Normally, I think it costs about twenty pounds,' Sister Beatrice said. 'However, I once helped Mrs Jenkins recover from an illness and she is prepared to waive the fee – providing you pass the interview, and in return for your agreeing to work in the catering business when not in class. Of course you will get some time to yourself. One evening a week and Sundays I believe . . .'

'Oh, that is so kind of her – and you,' Jinny said. 'Do you think I shall pass the interview, Sister?'

'I've given you a good reference and I'm sure Sandra would put in a word for you too – and then it's up to you, but I have every hope you will make me proud of you . . .'

'Oh, thank you,' Jinny said. 'When is the interview?'

'A letter will come to inform you,' Sister said. 'So, now you are both certain of my wishes for Christmas Eve? We shall have a party and the girls from next door will be invited to join us with Miss Saunders and those members of her staff she cares to bring. On Christmas Day we shall have a simple meal and watch Her Majesty broadcast to the nation on the television Billy Baggins was kind enough to give us . . . Did you know that the speech was to be on television instead of the radio this year? I didn't until Billy told me.'

'He gave the television to you, Sister,' Jinny said. 'It's his present to you to thank you for all you did for him and Mary Ellen . . .'

'And very generous it was too,' Sister Beatrice said. 'I shall take it with me when I leave, but until then we may all enjoy it. Billy is going to drive me down to Halfpenny House. He and Mary Ellen will take my bits and pieces in a car he is borrowing and I'll ride with them. I said I would go on the train but he insisted that they would take me. Angela is coming up to fetch the last of the children herself the day after Boxing Day . . . and I shall then finish up here and hand over the keys . . .' A little sigh escaped her, but she raised her head, determined not to show any sign of distress that so many years of her life were ending, but Jinny guessed how she must feel.

Jinny was grateful to Sister Beatrice for helping her to find a position after the home closed. She and Nellie had made Nancy's wedding cake and given it to her, and received the promise of an invitation to the wedding. After that they'd turned their attention to making Christmas puddings and cakes and preparing mincemeat. Although most of the orphans would have left for Essex by Christmas, it was important to make the party a good one for the girls from the probationary centre and the staff, since it was to mark the end of an era.

November had fled after Sister Beatrice announced that St Saviour's would be closing at the end of the year. Thanks to the second-hand television Billy Baggins had given to Sister Beatrice, everyone saw the Russians send their dog Laika into space; they heard that the House of Lords was to admit women peers; and that Christian Dior, the king of French fashion, had died. A new British singing sensation called Tommy Steele and the Cavemen were storming the stage and TV screens; in Paris the heads of all the countries in NATO had met and agreed to allow USA missiles to be based in Europe, because of what was perceived as the Russian threat; and Elvis Presley had been drafted into the American military.

At St Saviour's life was changing fast too. The carers had been busier than ever; as well as the trips to Halfpenny House, they had packing to oversee, sorting out dark cupboards and discovering stuff left behind by children who had gone on to other lives. Most of it had been taken to the charity stall on the market, and Jinny had carried paper bags stuffed full of old clothes, discarded puzzles and games, and a cricket bat to the charity stalls.

When her duties were over in the kitchen each day, she'd helped Kelly to clean out the cupboards and pack the children's things. Every week at least six children had departed for the orphanage in Essex, some of them looking apprehensive, others excited, all of them clutching parcels wrapped in brown paper and tied with string.

By the second week of December only a handful of orphans remained, all of them aged thirteen or older, the senior boys having left to take up their apprenticeships and find a new home in a youth hostel. Five others were due to leave for Essex on Boxing Day and the other three were girls of fifteen and sixteen, who had volunteered to stay and help Sister Beatrice until they left to take up the jobs she had secured for them and their accommodation in a hostel for young women.

Micky came to visit Jinny at the beginning of December. He told her that he might not see her for a couple of weeks, but would definitely be back by Christmas.

'What are you doing?' Jinny wanted to know. 'You're always coming and going. The last time we went out was at the end of October. Since then I've only seen you twice for a few minutes, just for a coffee and you never have time to talk. I never know when I'm going to see you . . .'

'I've been busy,' Micky said and his eyes didn't quite meet hers. 'I'll tell you about it soon, I promise . . .'

'Why should I care?' she said huffily. She'd hoped he might take her dancing before Christmas and ask her out for Boxing Day, which was when her duties officially finished at St Saviour's and she was due to leave for her cookery course.

'Because you're my girl,' Micky said and grinned at her, pulling her into his arms and giving her a quick kiss. 'You know it's true, Jinny. I've been busy that's all – and when this is over I'll make it up to you, I promise.'

Jinny shrugged again and he went off looking a bit down, but she didn't like him being secretive and was afraid he might be doing something that would get him into trouble with the law. Micky set his own rules and she knew that some of his schemes were a little dodgy. She just hoped he wouldn't do anything that got him locked up in prison.

It was as busy as ever in the kitchen, because although the orphans were leaving for Essex each week, the girls from the probationary centre came to lunch and tea every day now. Ruby Saunders visited the kitchen and talked to Jinny and Nellie. She seemed disappointed that neither of them was staying on after the orphanage closed, but asked them to apply to her if they needed a job in the future. She and Sister Beatrice were often to be seen walking about the building and having long discussions, Ruby making notes on a clipboard she carried with her.

'You'd think that Miss Saunders had taken over already,' Kelly said with a disapproving sniff. 'She asked me if I'd stay on for a while, but I told her I couldn't . . .' Her eyes sparkled with pleasure. 'I didn't tell her why, Jinny, but I'll tell you – I'm having a baby . . .'

'You must be delighted,' Jinny said and gave her a quick hug. 'I'm so pleased for you, Kelly – and I'd love to come and see the baby when it's born.'

'You'll always be welcome, you and Nellie – and Nancy. All of you really . . .' Kelly smiled and touched her stomach. 'My husband is over the moon.'

'I'll just bet he is,' Jinny said. 'Come on, sit down and I'll make you a cup of tea.'

CHAPTER 32

It was so quiet now that most of the children had gone. The nurses' home was empty apart from Sister Beatrice, Rose and Jinny. Only three dorms were now occupied at St Saviour's and they had closed down the isolation ward after Wendy left, because it was no longer necessary. Ruby had told her that after long discussions with Miss Sampson it had been decided that they would keep only one nurse on after the orphanage closed. She would deal with day-to-day problems like sore throats and accidents. Any inmate taken seriously ill would be sent to the hospital.

'Miss Sampson says it is an unnecessary luxury,' Ruby had told her during one of their long chats in her office. 'As you know, I would've preferred to keep the nurses and the wards, as you have, but I've been told we cannot afford to waste money.'

'I dare say Miss Sampson has her point,' Beatrice had soothed. 'After all, that's what the hospitals are for. When we opened St Saviour's we were dealing with very sick children often brought in in terrible condition and the hospitals were filled with wounded soldiers.

There was nowhere else for the kids in those days. Your girls are healthy and full of life – and it is expensive to keep the wards open. It has been a struggle to find the funds all these years . . .'

'You sound tired,' Ruby said and looked concerned. 'Are you quite well, Sister?'

'Perfectly,' Beatrice said more sharply than the inquiry deserved. 'You understand the arrangements for Christmas Eve? We shall have the present giving in the hall and then tea in the dining room. I'm sorry there is no tree this year, but with the younger children gone I considered my limited funds would be best spent on small gifts and a good meal.'

'It's good of you to do it at all,' Ruby said. 'I've always given the girls a decent meal on Christmas Day but I'm afraid they've had no gifts – though I should like to make a donation to the fund this year . . .'

'That will not be necessary, Ruby. I've agreed a fund with Angela, who has been generous as always. The gifts are small but everyone will receive one – and I shall play carols on the radiogram Angela presented to us last year. Have you decided which of your girls you will permit to attend the church service with Nancy and Rose and our children?'

'Yes, I'll give you a list. There are ten who wish to attend and they're all quite sensible.'

'Good, then we shall be pleased to include them. The service is on Christmas Eve and they will come back for the party.'

'I've been told some of my boys will be arriving on the first of January. I need to have a few adjustments made – some locks on downstairs windows in particular.

Do you think those builders who did the renovations would come in? I know it's short notice . . .'

'I'll speak to Rose. She is getting married to the builder after we close you know. I'm sure she can arrange it for you. Nick is very obliging . . .'

'Good.' Ruby stood up. 'I think that's all . . .'

'Yes, I believe we've covered everything,' Sister Beatrice nodded. 'Have you heard what will happen to the nurses' home yet?'

'No, I haven't been told. I think they may sell it off . . . Again, Miss Sampson considers that it is unnecessary to provide accommodation for our employees in this day and age and too expensive . . .'

'She may well be right,' Beatrice said. 'Well, good evening, Ruby. I shall see you on Christmas Eve if not before.' She sighed as the door closed behind her visitor. All these plans and talks were more tiring than she could ever have imagined, and she would be glad when it was all over and she could join Angela in the country . . .

As she left St Saviour's to retire to her own room for the night, Beatrice could not remember a time when the place had seemed so empty. She felt a wave of loneliness and uncertainty and then, quite suddenly, there was a burst of laughter from one of the boys' dorms. The feeling of despair left her as swiftly as it had come. It was the end of an era but soon she would be taking up a new position amongst friends and with the children she loved . . . there was still so much to look forward to . . .

*

Jinny felt that she'd made real friends at St Saviour's. Wendy had already left to take up a training course at a hospital, although Rose was still here and Nancy and Sandra, but most of the carers had gone. It was a much reduced family at St Saviour's now, but as Jinny left that afternoon in mid-December to do her Christmas shopping, she felt that her life had never been better. She was going to buy presents for all the staff and she might get Micky a little gift too, though he didn't deserve one, because she'd heard nothing from him all week.

Thanks to Sister Beatrice, there would be small gifts for all the children on Christmas Eve, including the girls from next door. This year there was no tree and the gifts would be given out by Sister Beatrice herself. They would not have a carol service at the home, but Rose and Nancy were taking some of the children to a service at the church on Christmas Eve.

Jinny wished that her mother was alive so she could have given her something nice, but in her heart she knew the only present her mother would have wanted was booze, and there was no way she would have spent her savings on that.

'What yer doin', Jinny luv,' Dave asked as she approached his stall. 'Lookin' fer a new dress fer Christmas?'

'No, I'm spending my money on presents for my friends,' Jinny said and smiled at him.

'What yer lookin' fer then, luv?'

'Oh, scarves or gloves, perhaps some perfume . . . not sure yet . . .' Jinny said and lingered. There was a beautiful red dress with a full skirt and a sweetheart neckline that looked as if it was her size but she resolutely ignored it. 'Have you got anything that costs about five bob and looks as if it cost more?'

Dave grinned at her. 'The girl wants a bargain . . . well, look, 'ere then – I've got a box of silk scarves special for the Christmas trade and you can 'ave first pick . . .'

Jinny immediately fell in love with the beautiful scarves. They looked worth four times as much as Dave was offering them for and she asked him again if he was sure they were only five shillings each.

'How many do you want then?' Dave asked and Jinny fingered them reverently. She would have liked a pretty red one for herself, but her money would only stretch so far and she wanted to contribute two pounds to the fund Sister Rose had set up to buy gifts for the children.

'I'd like these five please,' Jinny said and selected five of the prettiest ones she could find.

'Right, that's a quid to you, love,' Dave said and pushed them into a paper bag for her. 'If you change yer mind about a dress you can pay me after Christmas . . .'

'I'm not goin' anywhere special,' Jinny said. 'I'll probably pop to the pub with some friends one evening, and I'll be workin' over Christmas Day – I've nowhere else to go and Nellie wants the day off to be with her family. She thinks Colin and his family may be home for a little holiday then.'

'Not going anywhere for Christmas?' Dave raised his brows. 'What about comin' to a special dance with me this evenin' then? '

Jinny hesitated, but she hadn't been anywhere for ages other than to the flicks with Nancy and some of the children on a Saturday afternoon. They'd taken the kids to see *The Lady and the Tramp,* which was showing again at the local cinema for the umpteenth time, so it was more work than an outing for her and Nancy, but the kids had loved it, and if she told the truth so had Jinny. There had never been money for things like that when she was a kid so she supposed she was sort of making up for lost treats.

'I'm clean and decent and I don't bite,' Dave said with a grin and Jinny giggled, feeling happy and excited all at once. 'I like you, Jinny, and I'd never hurt you. I know you're Micky's girl and . . .'

'No, I'm not,' Jinny said, making up her mind. 'And I'd love to come to the dance this evening.'

'Great! Where shall I pick you up then?' Dave looked really pleased with himself and Jinny smiled.

'Outside St Saviour's, please. I'm a Halfpenny girl,' she said. 'I want to be a really good cook, Dave, and that's what I'm going to do – one day maybe I'll get married and have kids, but I want to be someone first.'

'You're someone right now as far as I'm concerned,' Dave said, 'but I know you just want to be friends for now and that's all right with me . . .'

Jinny paid him for her scarves and went on her way. She had a few more gifts to buy and then she had better get back and finish her work so that she would have time to wash her hair ready for the evening . . .

Jinny thought Dave looked really smart in his pale grey suit and white shirt with a darker grey tie, his black winkle-picker shoes polished to within an inch of their lives. He'd slicked his hair back with Brylcreem and he smelled of a light aftershave. Wearing her best dress and with her dark hair freshly washed and curled with kirby grips so that it fluffed out about her face and curled over her ears, Jinny felt smart and proud to be with Dave.

The dance was held in a small hall with soft lighting that changed colours as a ball spun from a pendant in the ceiling, and the band was on a stage at one end of the room, at the other a bar selling soft drinks only. The floor was highly polished, which made it easy to dance, and though Jinny wasn't sure of all the steps for some of the dances, Dave seemed to know them all. He surprised her by being a really good dancer, and he was patient, telling her to follow him and helping her to pick up the various moves. By the time they'd danced the first six dances she was ready for a long cool orange juice. Dave drank the same and seemed to enjoy it.

'I never saw you as being one for dances like this,' she said, feeling happy. 'I thought you would prefer goin' down the pub with your mates.'

'Yer live and learn,' Dave said and grinned. 'Amateur ballroom champ 1955 and '56 . . .'

'Really – you're not kidding me?' Now Jinny was shocked, because Dave's cockney cheek and patter had led her to believe he was one of the lads and this was a new revelation.

'I enjoy a few pints wiv me mates now and then,' he said with a grin, 'but if I've got a chance of a good partner I'd take a dance any time . . .'

'I'm not much good as a partner for you,' Jinny said mournfully and noticed that a young blonde woman was looking at them a little resentfully across the room.

'You could be if we came regularly,' Dave said. 'We

could even go to classes on a Tuesday night if you were free?'

'I don't get much time off,' Jinny said regretfully. 'I'm going to catering college when St Saviour's closes . . . but I'd like to come to a dance sometimes . . .' She caught her breath as the striking blonde walked up to them.

'I've been waiting for you to ask me to dance, Dave,' the girl said, ignoring Jinny. 'It's a tango next – and you know we need to practise that if we're going to win the championships this year . . .'

'Oh, sorry, Lou,' he apologised. 'I'll ring you – this is Jinny. I'm with her this evening.'

The attractive blonde turned hard blue eyes on Jinny. 'I'm sure Jinny would spare you for one dance – wouldn't you, luv?'

Jinny felt prickles down her spine. If looks could kill she would even now be lying dead at Lou's feet. 'If Dave wants to practise with you that's all right with me. I'll just sit here and watch . . .'

Dave looked uncomfortable, but the music had started and Lou had grabbed his arm. He threw Jinny an apologetic look and allowed himself to be dragged on to the dance floor. Jinny watched, because she'd never seen a dancing display like it, all the dramatic moves and head twists were fascinating – and she wasn't the only one. Most of the other dancers had drawn back, giving them room to glide across the floor in a miraculous series of twists and turns that Jinny found thrilling. If she'd been Dave's girl she might have felt jealous, but they were just friends and she enjoyed the performance, clapping at the end as did many others.

Dave returned to her alone, looking slightly rueful.

'I'm sorry about that, Jinny, but Lou was right – we do need to practise if we're going to enter the competition, let alone win this year.'

'It must be lovely to be able to dance like that,' Jinny sighed. 'I loved watching it. You were wonderful, Dave – and so was she. You looked as if you fitted together . . .'

'You're not annoyed with me for dancing with her?'

'No, why should I be?' Jinny asked. 'I don't own you and I wouldn't dream of spoiling your chances. You must tell me when the competition is, because I'd love to come and watch you and Lou.'

'You're a great girl,' Dave said but seemed a bit disappointed. 'It would've been nice if you'd been a bit jealous . . .'

Jinny laughed and took his hand. 'Why? We're friends, Dave. If I'm ever your girlfriend I might feel differently – but tonight I just want you to show me how to dance some more, because I'd like to learn. All I've ever done is a bit of jiving or Rock 'n' Roll . . .'

Dave's face lit up instantly. 'I'll teach you,' he promised, 'and then, when you're good enough, you can be my partner in the competitions.'

Jinny shook her head. 'I think I've got a long, long way to go,' she said but she didn't mind. She was enjoying herself despite the interruption by his dancing partner, and she intended to make the most of her evening out.

'Did you have a lovely time?' Nancy asked the next day when she gave Jinny a hand with the baking. Nellie was having her day off and the two of them were alone in the kitchen. 'Rob took me to a dance up West last night. It was a surprise for my birthday and it was wonderful. We had dinner and then danced all night. I could hardly wake up this morning . . .'

'Our dance wasn't so posh, but it was lovely. I didn't know it could be so much fun. Dave is a wonderful dancer. If you saw him on the market you'd never think it, but he gave me a really nice evening – and we won a bottle of wine in the draw. There was a turkey and lots of chocolates, but Dave thought the wine was best and he gave it to me . . . but I said he should take it, because he bought the tickets and I'd never open a bottle of wine just for me.'

Nancy nodded and looked thoughtful. 'When you live in the nurses' home like we do there's nowhere to invite your friends for a drink . . . I never wanted to for years, but you will as you get older and then you may need a place of your own.'

'Not for years,' Jinny said. 'Dave is a good friend, Nancy, but I want to learn to be a proper cook and find a good job.'

'You're sure to get one when you finish that course.'

'Yes, I hope so,' Jinny agreed. 'What will you do when we close, Nancy?'

'Rob's aunty has said I can live with her until the wedding,' Nancy said with a happy smile. 'I shall find a job somewhere, but Ruby asked me to stay on and help her with setting things up here – so I might, just for a few weeks. I feel a bit sorry for some of the girls next door. Rob and me have decided on April for the wedding – and I'd like you to be my bridesmaid. I don't have any family so would you come and stay overnight and help me on the day?'

'I'd love to,' Jinny said and they hugged. 'You're my family, Nancy. I don't have anyone but Nellie – and everyone here . . .'

'We'll be sisters and friends,' Nancy said. 'Shall we have a cup of tea before we start getting things ready?'

'I'll put the kettle on,' Jinny said and was in the act of filling it when someone entered the kitchen.

'Nellie . . . we didn't expect you today,' Nancy said. 'What are you doing here?'

'I need to talk to Jinny,' Nellie said and looked upset. 'If yer 'avin' a cuppa I could do wiv one – I feel proper upset . . .'

'Is something the matter with Bert?'

'No, 'e's as fit as a fiddle,' Nellie said. 'I've got 'im paintin' the new 'ouse – no lass, it's for your sake I'm upset. I don't rightly know 'ow to tell yer . . .'

'Sit down, Nellie. You look pale.' Nancy drew a chair for her, but Nellie ignored her, looking at Jinny.

'It's Micky,' she said. ''E's in the 'ospital, Jinny – 'ad a nasty accident yesterday so Bert says . . . and you'd best go and see the lad, because they're sayin' 'e might not come round . . .'

'Micky's hurt bad?' Jinny's stomach clenched with fright. 'How did it happen? Did someone hurt him . . . was he attacked?'

'No, I don't think so. Bert said 'e'd 'ad a fall and was in a bad way, that's all I know, love. I think you ought to get on up the 'ospital now . . .'

'I've got to help get the tea for the kids . . .'

'No, go now,' Nancy said. 'I can manage tea on my own . . .'

'No need fer that,' Nellie said. 'I'll stop and give yer a 'and – unless you want me to come wiv yer, love?'

'No, I'm all right, thanks for comin' to tell me,' Jinny said. 'I'll be back when I can, Nancy . . .' she said, taking off her apron. She went to fetch her coat and purse and then hurried out into the bitter cold of a mid-December afternoon.

She was on thorns as she waited for a bus, her stomach clenching with nerves. What kind of a fall had Micky had and how bad were his injuries? Tears stung her eyes, because she'd been offhand with him the last time she'd seen him, annoyed because he wouldn't be around to take her to some of the Christmas dances. And she'd gone out with Dave and enjoyed herself and perhaps Micky had already been hurt and asking for her . . .

CHAPTER 33

'Where shall we go for Christmas dinner?' Carla asked and handed Ruby a glass of her favourite wine. 'You're not working on the day, are you?'

'No, I made sure I got the day off this year. We've got a party on at St Saviour's Christmas Eve. You can come if you like and then we'll go somewhere afterwards. I thought we'd have a few drinks and then I'll cook us a lovely chicken dinner here on the day . . . unless you really want to go out?'

'I don't care what we do as long as we're together,' Carla said and reached forward to kiss her, her lips tasting of wine. Ruby ran her tongue round her lips, enjoying the combination of Carla and wine. 'I've got you lots of presents . . .'

'You shouldn't spend so much on me,' Ruby said and touched her frizzy hair, a shaft of pure happiness piercing her heart. 'You're always buying me something.'

'Only little things,' Carla said and laughed. 'If I was rich I'd cover you with diamonds and pearls . . . I love you, Ruby. I've never known anyone like you and you've made me happy.'

'You've done more for me than you'll ever know,' Ruby said and put her arms about her, kissing her on the lips. 'You taste wonderful. I've got presents for you too – but I was thinking . . . wouldn't the best present be if we looked for a flat that was big enough to share?'

'Could we?' Carla asked, a little doubtful. 'I know we could afford it if we shared the expenses . . . but do we dare? Won't people talk? You've got to be careful in your job, Ruby . . .'

'No one will think anything of it. We're just friends sharing a flat to make it easier to afford,' Ruby said. 'We'll have our own rooms in case you want to sulk . . .' She laughed and avoided the punch Carla aimed at her ear. 'Besides, I want to live with you, my dearest one. I want to wake up beside you – and the hell with what anyone else thinks.'

'Oh Ruby, I'd love it,' Carla said and put her arms about her neck, bringing her head down to hers. She traced Ruby's mouth with her tongue and then slipped it inside, deepening the kiss until they had to come up for air. 'You're wonderful and so brave. I was miserable for ages, not daring to speak to you because I was sure you would be disgusted if I tried to kiss you . . .'

'Why do you think I didn't come for coffee? I thought I might not be able to stop myself touching you – and I was afraid of your rejection . . .'

'Daft! I fell head over heels the first time you offered to help me with all my stuff,' Carla said. She danced off around the room, her red skirt flying. 'I'm so happy . . . Happy Christmas, Ruby!'

'It's not Christmas just yet . . .'

'It is for us,' Carla said. 'And it will be for the rest of our lives . . .'

'Yes,' Ruby said and smiled as her friend danced to the Rock 'n' Roll music blaring out from the TV as the popular music show *Six-Five Special* started. 'Come on, let's watch this and see what's new this week . . .'

'I'm glad we decided to delay the wedding till the second week in January,' Rose told the little gathering in the kitchen. 'It was too much of a rush to have it before Christmas with all the preparations for the closure – and Nick didn't want to wait for the spring so we thought we would have a winter wedding and go to Austria for our honeymoon . . . and we're taking the boys with us . . .'

'Austria – in the mountains, skiing?' Kelly said. 'That sounds absolutely wonderful, Rose. I've never been abroad though we've talked about it . . .'

'You're taking his sons with you – on your honeymoon?' Nancy asked.

'Why not? They're really good lads and it will be fun for all of us. I think it's the best way to get used to each other,' Rose said happily, and turning to Nancy. 'When are you getting married?'

'We thought May at first, but now we've brought it forward to April,' Nancy said, looking shy but very happy. 'Rob says our house will be ready by then. He's been doing it up for ages, long before we met. We're going down to Devon for a few days for our honeymoon – but I'm looking forward to having a home of my own.'

She broke off and everyone went quiet as Jinny walked

in looking pale and tired. Nancy stood up and went to put her arms around her, giving her a warm hug.

'How are you, love? Nellie told us Micky had come round from his operation OK but she seems to think he'll be ill for some time . . .'

'Yes, he broke his leg in two places and he's in a lot of pain – but it was the head injuries that had the doctors worried. They thought he might have done a lot of damage but he was lucky . . . the silly idiot. He could've killed himself! He should never have been up there in the first place . . .' Jinny blinked as the tears stung her eyes. 'I had no idea he was working on a building site . . .'

'He asked Nick for a job weeks ago,' Rose said. 'I feel guilty for not telling you, but he wanted to keep it a secret. He told Nick he was fed up with running errands for bookies and buying dodgy stuff and wanted to get into a proper trade. I think he wants to put some money aside for some business he's after . . .' She sighed. 'It was Micky's own fault, Jinny. He wasn't supposed to be up on that scaffolding in the first place. He doesn't have the experience but Nick says he wants to run before he can walk . . .'

'Yes, I know, he's always been like that,' Jinny said and smiled at her. 'Bert was in on the secret. He said Micky wanted to impress me. He'd been away on various jobs for his old boss, clearing houses and various things, made some good money – and now he wants to do what Rob has done, buy an old house and make it nice . . . then he's going to sell it and open a business importing spices and food, and he'll probably buy another house and do that one up for us . . . He wants to be rich . . .' Jinny sighed and shook her head.

'He's doing it for you,' Rose told her. 'Apparently, he realised that his old line of work would never please you and he wanted to make you happy so he got some money together and then asked Nick if he'd take him on, teach him the trade. He's bought a wreck of a house, but they're going to rebuild it and sell it together. Nick advised him to tell you, but he said he was waiting until he'd got something to show you.'

'Well, I know now,' Jinny said. 'Oh well, at least he's alive, though in a lot of pain. What do you want me to do, Nancy?'

'Can you make a seed cake for a start?' Nancy said. 'Nellie will be here soon I hope and then we can start on the lunches – but I want to get ahead with the party food if I can.'

'Yes, and we'd better get out of your way,' Rose said. 'Kelly, can you help me make a list of all the bed linen? Miss Saunders asked Sister for it . . . honestly, if she couldn't have thought of that before this . . .'

Busy making a seed cake, Jinny listened and smiled in all the right places to the happy chatter about her friends' weddings and their plans. Her eyes felt tired because she'd hardly slept since she'd visited Micky in hospital and she wanted to cry. The last thing she wanted to do was watch everyone getting in the mood for the Christmas party, which was taking place that afternoon and evening.

This year only a few of the children had been to a pantomime and a screening of one of Disney's films. They would all get a small gift that afternoon, and then listen to some carols on the TV and have a special meal. Jelly, blancmange, tinned fruit as well as the usual cakes and sandwiches were planned – and the girls from next door were coming to have their tea and listen to the carols.

Sister Beatrice seemed to think it was a good thing to bring the girls from next door for the Christmas treat, though Jinny knew some of their staff didn't think much of it, but of course it would all be in Miss Saunders' hands once the last of the orphans had gone. Jinny knew that a cloud was hanging over all the St Saviour's people, despite the decorations and festive talk. They were all trying to be cheerful, but everyone would be sad when the doors finally closed.

For days now local people had been calling at St Saviour's leaving cards and small gifts of food, sweets and fruit, many of the tokens for Sister Beatrice herself. Some of the women had been in tears, calling it a crying shame that she was being forced to leave them.

'The bloody Welfare lot ought ter be ashamed of themselves,' several people had said. 'I remember what it was like in the war – nowhere for them poor kids to go until she come 'ere. Took 'em all in she did – ain't no one like our Sister Beatrice and it won't be the same wivout 'er . . .'

Jinny felt sad at the thought that her friends would be dispersed after Christmas. She was looking forward to her new job, and to spending more time with Micky when he was on his feet again, but she would miss working with Nancy and the others. So far Micky had been too groggy to do more than clasp her hand and tell her over and over how sorry he was for spoiling her Christmas. He'd got her a present and had planned on taking her out that night, but now she'd have to wait until he was out of hospital to have their celebration.

'Don't be so daft,' she'd told him. 'Just get better and then I might forgive you for scaring me half to death.'

He'd managed a weak chuckle then and Jinny smiled at the memory. Even a broken leg and a sore head couldn't change her Micky – and he *was* her Micky. She'd known it for a while but wouldn't acknowledge it, but now she knew that she didn't want to lose him from her life. She had lots of friends, including Dave, but Micky was special. Jinny was too young to get married, but she wouldn't say no to going steady when he was up and about again . . . but no more going off for weeks at a time without telling her what he was doing!

She greeted Nellie as her friend arrived, rolled up her sleeves and started to peel the vegetables for lunch.

'You carry on, Jinny love,' Nellie said. 'I can manage this. We've got shepherd's pie fer lunch and some nice stewed fruit and rice pudding afterwards – all nice and easy so we can concentrate on the party . . .'

'All right. I'll make a start on the sausage rolls and mince pies,' Jinny said. 'Nancy's made the trifle and fruit jellies . . .' Jinny went to the pantry to fetch what she needed and returned to see that Nellie was talking to someone.

'It looks as if you've got a visitor . . .' Nellie said and glanced towards her. 'Why don't you take five minutes to talk to 'im?'

Jinny saw Dave grinning at her. His errand was clear,

because he was carrying a prettily wrapped parcel which he placed on the kitchen table.

'I brought yer present in . . .' he said and his neck was red. 'I hope yer like it, Jinny love.'

'Oh, Dave, you shouldn't,' she said, a little embarrassed. 'I didn't buy you anything . . .'

'It's for the lad to buy the presents,' Dave said proudly. 'Look, I know you'll be orf up the 'ospital after work to see Micky – but I'll give yer a lift in me van if yer like?'

'It's very kind of you,' Jinny thanked him. Dave was a friend, nothing more even though he might like to be. 'You could see him for a few minutes yourself.'

'Yeah, perhaps . . . I'll see yer later . . .'

Dave beamed at her and produced a sprig of mistletoe. He kissed Nellie first on the cheek and then Jinny briefly on the lips, and as he turned to leave and Sandra entered, he kissed her too on the cheek. He went off whistling and Nellie nodded her approval.

'Now that's a nice lad,' she said, 'but you ought ter be straight wiv 'im, Jinny love. If it's Micky yer want . . .'

'Yes, it is, Nellie. Micky knows I'm not ready to get married, but we know where we are now – and we'll see how things go . . .'

'Micky really cares about you,' Nellie said. ''E's been a bit of a lad but 'e's always looked out fer you – and 'e'll settle now, you'll see . . .'

'Yes, I know,' Jinny said and smiled at her. 'He's had a shock and so have I. You've always been my friend, Nellie. I don't know what I'd have done without you – and I'm going to miss you when we leave here . . .'

'My 'ome will always have room for you,' Nellie said

and nodded at her. 'My boys are comin' back fer Christmas and we'll be 'avin' a party. Come when you've finished 'ere, love. I don't like to think of yer alone on Christmas Day.'

'I shall pop in to see Micky and then I'll come,' Jinny said. 'But I shall miss working with you, Nellie.'

'You know where I live and you'll get time orf,' Nellie said. 'It will be new and exciting for you, love. You'll make new friends – and then Micky will be out and things will be better. Now cheer up, we're goin' ter 'ave a lovely party this evenin'. I'm looking forward to the carols on the TV. Maybe we'll get a second-hand one for ourselves this next year now I've got that job at the school . . . in the meantime we're goin' ter 'ave a bit of fun.'

'Yes, we must make the most of it,' Jinny said. 'I'd never seen a TV until Billy brought in that one for Sister. It was nice of her to share it with the rest of us . . .'

'She's a good woman,' Nellie said. 'There will be a few tears shed around 'ere when we close, that's fer sure . . .'

CHAPTER 34

Another Christmas party come and gone, Beatrice thought as she sat at her desk later that evening and contemplated her own future. She would attend midnight mass at her local church and after the festivities were over she would find time to visit the convent and talk to Mother Superior. She wanted to talk to her friend of many years before she left London for good, because she did not think she would return in the future.

It had been a good day this last Christmas Eve at St Saviour's and there had been lots of happy faces amongst the staff and the children that remained. She'd made time to speak with all of them and talk of their futures. All the children were happy about what was happening, those that were going down to Halfpenny House and the girls who were going on to new jobs and new lives.

Ruby's probationers had behaved themselves beautifully. Beatrice had watched their faces, seeing the excitement and the pleasure such simple treats as one of Jinny's rock buns, some strawberry blancmange and tinned peaches brought to these girls, who were in her opinion more sinned against than sinners.

A couple of them had been a bit cheeky to Jinny and Kelly, but Beatrice hadn't seen any malice behind it. She felt admiration for the way Ruby had stepped in when a quarrel started over the prize from a Christmas cracker between two of her girls.

'It ain't fair, miss,' one of the girls said. 'She pulls harder than me and she got both prizes.'

'Well, that's the way it works, Bettina,' Ruby said. 'You can pull mine with me and see what happens then . . .' Of course she'd made sure that the girl got the larger end of the cracker and, as luck would have it, it contained a small, brightly coloured bead bracelet which Bettina swooped on with joy, stretching the elastic over her hand. 'It was my cracker,' Ruby told her, 'but you won so the prize is yours. Next time you pull a cracker with someone make sure you hold it with both hands close up as I showed you and you may win again . . .'

Beatrice was quietly pleased with the change in Ruby Saunders. She wasn't sure how much was down to her own influence and how much to other factors, but the girl was certainly much happier. Her action over the cracker was much what Angela would have done in the circumstances. To have taken one of the gifts from the other girl would have gone against the spirit of the game. If you get the prize it's yours and children had to learn that they couldn't have what they hadn't earned. Beatrice approved of Ruby's justice, which wasn't quite the way she would have handled it, but was fair enough. She suspected that, not too long ago, Ruby would simply have confiscated both prizes. Indeed, she would probably have refused to let her girls have them at all.

This Christmas visit had been a good idea; it had given Beatrice the chance to witness Ruby in control and she was feeling much better about the future of St Saviour's after the charity had relinquished it to the council. Angela had telephoned just after lunch that day.

'I wish I could be with you,' she'd apologised. 'I've got a party to organise here and I just couldn't manage to pop up even for a quick visit . . .'

'You sent me money for gifts and that was very welcome,' Beatrice said. 'You mustn't feel as if you have to apologise, Angela.'

'No, but I should've liked to be there at the last party – but soon you'll be with us. It's not the end is it, but the beginning of something new.'

'Yes, of course. A long and happy relationship I hope. I wish you and your family a very happy Christmas, and I'll be down on the thirty-first of December . . . after I've handed the keys to Ruby . . .'

'That's right,' Angela said. 'I shall get up before then to take the children down and we'll have everything ready here for you so that you can move straight in. I can't tell you how much we're all looking forward to having you with us.'

Beatrice murmured her thanks and replaced the receiver. Someone knocked and she invited them to enter. Billy Baggins and Mary Ellen walked in bearing a gift, which they placed on the table.

'More presents?' Beatrice frowned. 'Really, you should not . . . I do not need material things, my dears. We give up all such vanity when we enter the convent.'

'This isn't just from us,' Billy said. 'Some of the local people wanted you to have a special gift . . . and they asked Mary Ellen to buy it and us to give it to you this evening.'

'Everyone here loves you, Sister,' Mary Ellen said. 'All of us contributed as well as the local people and we hope you'll like what I've chosen. It's to remind you of your time here . . .'

'I thank you all for the thought, though I must say I've never been so spoiled in my life.'

'You've done so much for all of us . . .' Billy said. 'We'll be here early on the thirty-first, Sister, and we'll take you down to Halfpenny House . . .'

'Everyone is so kind . . .' Beatrice felt tears sting her eyes but refused to allow them to fall. 'Thank you, Billy – I think myself well repaid for anything I may have done for you.'

'You don't know how much you did,' he said and then leaned forward to kiss her cheek. 'Happy Christmas, Sister!'

'Happy Christmas to you both,' Beatrice replied. 'Goodnight . . .'

She sat back in her chair as the door closed behind them, then reached out and drew the parcel to her, untying the pretty ribbon. Inside the flat parcel was a leather case for notepaper, envelopes and a pen. It was a thoughtful gift and something she would find useful, she thought, blinking as she saw the message inside. It had been signed by so many people . . . some of them children who had long ago left the home and others she'd helped over the years.

Sighing, she leaned back against her chair, her eyes closing. It had been such a busy day and she was very tired. The memories of her years here, and the years she'd spent in the convent, came flooding into her mind – happy times and times so unbearably sad that they caused a pain in her chest.

She saw again the face of the man she'd loved so desperately. Wearing his uniform he looked tall and handsome and a little afraid, as he should because he was going to war. A war from which he never returned.

The pain in her chest was getting worse and her breath rasped as the memories followed on sharply. Her father's fury when she'd confessed that she was pregnant, the beating he'd given her to make her marry a man she'd never liked – and then the misery of years of unhappiness, broken only by the sweetness of bearing her beloved son Tom.

'Tom . . . Tom . . .' she whispered as the pain grew and shuddered through her in waves. 'I couldn't save you, my darling . . . I couldn't save either of you . . .'

Tears were misting her eyes, trickling down her cheeks, but then through the mist she saw them, walking towards her. The tall handsome man in his uniform and the small child, hand in hand, walking through a sunlit day as the mist cleared and suddenly there was no more pain.

'My darlings . . .' she whispered as she went to meet them, into the sunlight and a place where there was no pain and no memories, just love. 'You've come for me . . . God sent you for me . . . together . . .'

'Rose found her when she went to say goodnight,' Angela said and her voice was choked with tears as she turned to Mark. 'She was just sitting there in her chair and Rose says she looked happy – at peace, as though she'd found something precious . . .'

'Well, perhaps she had,' Mark said. 'Sister Beatrice was a religious woman. We must hope she is at rest now – and that heaven is all she'd hoped it would be . . .'

'If there is a heaven she will be there,' Angela said and the tears were falling fast. 'I shall miss her, Mark. I know we were not always friends, but we became so – and I was looking forward to having her here, perhaps taking care of her when she was older.'

'Yes, I know, my darling,' he said and crossed the room to put his arms about her. 'But life goes on and it is all the richer for having known Sister Beatrice. She must have been ill for a while, but she wouldn't give in until she was sure all the children and her staff were settled.'

'I shall go up and arrange whatever needs to be done,' Angela said. 'And I'll close up the home and bring the children back just as I promised her . . .'

'Yes, of course. I'll ring her convent and ask where she should be buried. I doubt she made a will but they may know what she wanted. If not she may have told Nan . . . they were friends for years.'

'Yes . . .' Angela wiped her tears. 'I'm not sure but I think she had a son that died.'

'Then she will want to be buried close by, I dare say,' Mark nodded. 'We'll consult the convent as to what they think right and then we'll arrange it, my darling. We'll do it together . . .'

The quiet churchyard was filled with mourners. So many that it was hardly possible to see where they ended. The church had been filled to capacity and several people had stood outside, even though it was bitterly cold. They had come to say farewell to a woman many had loved but few had known.

Angela looked round at the faces of people who had worked at St Saviour's, others who had lived there under the nun's sometimes stern but always compassionate regime, and smiled. Jinny was standing with Nellie and a young man on crutches; Nancy, Mary Ellen, Billy and Rose were together, all four of them crying as the coffin was lowered into its resting place, as were so many others. Nan was there with her husband, clutching a small posy of flowers; Kelly and Hannah and the local butcher, also Sergeant Sallis; Wendy had got time off from work to attend, also Sally Rush, Michelle, Alice, Bob and their children. Father Joe, her old friend, had taken the service; some nuns in their black habits stood quietly to one side, but mostly it was the local people and the children, so many that Angela didn't even know half of them. It was a sad occasion and everyone looked upset, sniffing and wiping their eyes.

Then, as if to lift their spirits, the sun suddenly decided to come out from behind the clouds and everywhere was warmed by its healing touch; it lingered for a few minutes, impossibly warm for the time of year, touching them all, as if it had been sent to cheer them.

'She's saying goodbye to us,' Angela said and held tightly to her husband's hand as she blinked away her tears. 'Trying to comfort us, to remind us of all the good in life . . .'

'Yes,' Mark said and smiled at her, ruffling his sons' hair fondly. 'I do believe she is . . .'

A Q&A WITH CATHY SHARP

You've had a long career as a writer, how did it start?

As a child, I was always making up stories in my head about a princess in a castle being rescued by a prince who would carry her off and look after her. A bit of a loner, I wanted the enchantment of being truly loved so I made up my own stories. When I was older and started to put down some of the stories in my head, my first attempts were awful. It took years of trying, rewriting and learning from my mistakes before I had something published, and even then it was romance rather than the stronger fiction I write now. So I would say writing comes through experience.

What stories inspired you when you were starting out?

I used to read Ethel M Dell and several others of her era, and then I read Mills & Boon Historical stories, and it was these Historical books that made me want to write and brought my first success. I had more than seventy books published with Harlequin Mills & Boon before my sagas really caught fire.

Where did you get the idea for *The Orphans of Halfpenny Street* series?

I had it in mind to write a series about children in trouble and my agent put me in touch with a wonderful editor who has lots of good ideas bubbling about in her head. She was looking for a series about an orphanage, and she had some ideas that sparked my imagination and so we put our heads together and I wrote a synopsis and three chapters in two days. The editor loved it and that was the seed of a beautiful flower that blossomed into the Halfpenny series. We met and talked a couple of times and I rewrote and rewrote until it all came together.

Have you done a lot of research and if so, what is the most surprising thing you have discovered?

I research only what I need to for any particular book, because, if I do masses of it, when I write the book it all comes out like a history lesson and I can lecture my readers for pages. That isn't what fiction is about. The story and passion behind the idea makes it appeal to readers, and, in my opinion, the research should be woven into the book so lightly that you hardly realise it is there. It's always best if it comes over as news or a conversation, or a thought, as when Sister Beatrice thinks about abuse in children's homes. I don't enjoy books when someone tries to teach me something or moralises at me so I don't expect my readers to stand for that either.

I think the thing that surprises me most about researching the past is the terrible suffering of people before our modern age. Today, we complain about poverty and sickness, but, at least in Britain, we really don't suffer in the way they did a century or more ago, when so many people went hungry day after day and died of things that the doctors can cure today. Living standards were appalling in the majority of workers' homes. Often they didn't live to be much more than forty, and in some earlier centuries twenty-nine was a good age, and so many children died in their early years. Our standards are much higher and we don't expect a child to suffer hunger these days, though there are unfortunately still cases where they suffer both hunger and abuse, and we all condemn and hate it when we hear of it.

What does your typical writing day look like?

I get up, have breakfast and have my bath, and then I just sit down in my study in an armchair and write on the laptop until lunchtime. I seldom do much writing in the afternoon, except to read through a few pages. I used to write all day but that is too much for me these days. I work straight on to the computer and I always revise a few pages of the previous day's writing before I start new work. It reminds me of what I was thinking when I left off, always reluctantly – but we have to eat!

Where do you find inspiration for your characters? Are any of them based on real people?

None of my characters is a real person, but little bits of them are. I will notice habits that amuse me and put them into a character, and I remember things people have said that impress me and I use a form of their opinions when making a character come to life. I find that characters mature and grow as I write the book, and I always go back to the start and change the first chapters as my people evolve and I understand that they just would not have said or done something I made them do before I knew them – and in the case of the hero – fell in love with him.

What hobbies do you have in your spare time?

What spare time? :) I read a little in bed and I watch TV in the evenings, but I find there is almost always too much to do in a day.

When on holiday in Spain I enjoy walking on the sea front, swimming and just lying in the sun. I love eating out there – and here – when I find somewhere nice, but apart from holidays there isn't time for many hobbies.

What would be your 'Desert Island' book?

Can I have my kindle instead please? I could take so many more books with me. Of course it would need to be powered by the sun, but surely they can invent one of those? I've just read all ten of the *Last Kingdom* books by Bernard Cornwell in one go – couldn't put them down: hoping there's another in the pipeline. I've read so many lovely books how could I choose one? I suppose, if a gun was put to my head, it would have to be *Gone With the Wind*. It would take me ages to read and I do love it, but then I rather like *War and Peace* and . . . No good, I refuse to be marooned without my kindle – powered by the sun!

If you weren't a writer, what would you be?

I think I might have been a teacher. My mother was and I considered it but things didn't go to plan, as they say. I left school early to work for my father as a hairdresser. It was a mistake but I reached where I wanted to be eventually.

What are you writing about next?

At the moment I'm busily weaving another series about orphans – but this time it is a much earlier period, when they were usually sent to the workhouse if their parents could not feed them. And what a terrible experience that was for parents and children. I'm enjoying all the terrible situations I can put my poor little children through, but don't worry, I shan't let them die or starve unless the plot demands it, and I use my books to punish the evil ones. Just wish I could do it in real life too!